ALSO BY K[

Blade of Traesha Trilogy

Daughter of War

Weapon of Rulers

THE MAKER

SUPERNATURALS OF NEW BRECKEN
BOOK 1

KELLY COLE

KCB

Copyright © 2022 by Kelly Cole

All rights reserved.

No part of this book may be reproduced in any form or by any electronic or mechanical means, including information storage and retrieval systems, without written permission from the author, except for the use of brief quotations in a book review.

ISBN 979-8-9853212-5-8

I wrote this one for Anna

This work of fiction contains subjects that may be difficult for some readers. Please visit www.kellycolebooks.com for a list of content warnings.

CHAPTER 1

Nora shuffled her feet, bumping into the person behind her in line. She threw an apology over her shoulder. They were only three people away from the bouncer now.

"Will you just relax?" Annaliese hissed. "It's going to be fine."

Nora nodded and wiped her sweaty palms on her jeans, fingers catching in the purposeful holes near the right pocket. They were next. Nora tried to mimic Annaliese's casual posture and realized her best friend already had her ID out and ready. Nora hastily pulled Adriana's driver's license from her pocket and clutched it. The plastic edge bit into the fold of her hand.

Adriana was twenty-four. Five years older than Nora. Her hair was dark brown, not black. Her eyes were closer together. She was Nora's only cousin who also had freckles, yet her skin was darker. Nora's thoughts spiraled through these differences as she waited for Annaliese's excellent fake ID to get her friend waved inside the Maker. Annaliese winked over her shoulder as she sauntered through the door.

Nora stepped up to the bouncer and let him take Adriana's ID from her hand. He barely glanced at the picture before waving Nora through. Nora let out the breath she'd been holding and allowed a thin smile to creep up her lips. She got in. Easy.

The smile died when faced with the reality of the dark, humid, packed club. Where would she even start?

Annaliese's thoughts had gone in the same direction. "How are we supposed to find one here?" she asked.

Over the pounding base, Nora could barely even hear her friend. Lacking an answer, she pretended she couldn't at all.

"Nor, can you smell them or something?" Irritation had Annaliese grinding out the words. She knew very well that Nora had heard her. Nora was supposed to take point tonight, but all she wanted in this overwhelming setting was for Annaliese to lead the way like she always did in their friendship.

Sweat gathered under Nora's hair. She wished for a hair tie. Neither of them had been prepared for the stifling heat of the club after the brisk wind outside. She pushed up the sleeves of her blue cardigan, but it made little difference.

"Let's start with drinks," Nora decided, pointing to their left.

Elbows up, they twisted their way to the bar running along the wall. The charcoal gray backdrop, shiny black bar top, and blue lights overhead made an ominous feeling settle in Nora's stomach. It was too dark and loud and she'd never been inside a bar before, let alone a packed club on Fourth Street.

Several bartenders were serving with practiced efficiency. How they even heard the drink orders over the music was a mystery.

Annaliese was too short to see over shoulders like Nora, but when she caught sight of the bartenders, her lips pulled down in a begrudgingly impressed frown. Nora widened her eyes to show her agreement. The bartenders were stunning. The white girl furthest from them wore a dress so dark red that at first glance, it looked black. She served in a showy fashion Nora thought people only used on TV, flipping bottles and pouring multiple drinks from the same hand. At the other end of the bar, a Black bartender served drinks to a bachelorette party, pouring out a row of neon shots so long it nearly stretched his third of the bar. The girls were screaming and obnoxious, but he handled them all with a patient, contagious, if not slightly strained, smile.

Somehow Nora and Annaliese found two empty stools in the middle of the bar. Annaliese immediately angled herself away from the couple making out behind her and pulled a face. Nora shot her a sympathetic cringe and turned to wave down the nearest bartender.

Annaliese sat straighter in her seat as he turned from the wall of bottles and neared. This bartender was tall. And not in an awkward, lanky, unsure way. His eyes were a crisp blue that flashed in the lights of the club. He wasn't even sweating as he took drink orders and made his way closer. He didn't look happy to be there, but his scowl alone was probably what caught Annaliese's eye. Like calls to like and all that.

He stopped in front of them. Nora took a breath to order and he slid a cool gaze over her.

"Not twenty-one," he said. Then, just like that, he turned to the next waving credit card. Nora let out her breath, deflating completely.

"Hey!" Annaliese wasn't so easily brushed off, but the bartender was now four people down and loudly shaking ice between the metal cup and pint glass. "That's bullshit!"

How had he known they weren't twenty-one? Nora looked at herself and Annaliese in the grimy bar mirror backing the shelves of bottles. They didn't look that young.

Nora caught sight of something in the reflection and whipped around. A girl was leading an older man dressed in a sports jacket onto the dance floor. Something burning in the girl's expression made Nora track their progress. She narrowed her eyes as she watched, ears straining to hear what the girl said to make him laugh. He kept looking back at his friends, raising his eyebrows in triumph. Yet the look on the girl's face made it clear she was the one in control of the situation. She kept smiling at him, almost pitying.

The girl wasn't tall, but her presence overshadowed everyone around her. She had her brown hair wrapped up in a careless bun. Loose curls framed her face artfully. Her clothing was black, sparse, and covered in holes. Her cheeks were flushed, teeth white and flashing in a wide smile. She was thin and lithe, moving through the crowd with ease. Heads turned to watch her pass. Nora craned her neck, but the girl and man were soon swallowed by the mass of bodies.

Nora turned to Annaliese. "You good here for a minute?"

Startled, Annaliese nodded. It appeared to be more a nod of habit than agreement, but Nora had to follow this lead. Her gut told her this was important. This might be it.

"I'll be right back." Nora jumped from her stool, pushing to get closer to the couple. The girl's hands were on the man's shoulders when Nora spotted them again. He leaned closer to listen to the girl and nodded eagerly.

Nora stumbled to a halt when the girl's eyes locked on her own over the man's shoulder. She smiled, red lips pulling back. Nora blinked. The girl's canines were too thin. As Nora stood transfixed, the teeth slipped further from the girl's gums.

"No!" Nora tried to push closer in earnest now, but by the time she reached the couple, the vampire had clamped down on the man's neck and swallowed hard once. The vampire pushed him out of her way as Nora drew to a stop in front of her. The vampire was still smiling, blood clinging to the base of her teeth and slicking her gums.

Nora momentarily lost her nerve. She stared, speechless. As often as Nora had heard about vampire feedings, she'd never seen it. She'd expected more violence. More greed. More shame when it was over. None of that was present on the vampire's face.

Nora swallowed. The vampire tilted her head, bun flopping to the side. Her smile turned crooked, cruel in its beauty and failing to reach her appraising eyes. Their electric blue looked familiar. The vampire raised a hand, palm to the ceiling, and beckoned Nora closer with a finger.

Nora clenched her fists and threw back her shoulders, shaking off her initial shock. This was exactly why she had come to this club. To find a vampire. To set her plan to lure said vampire to the Den. Then, during the full moon a little over three weeks from now, she would kill the vampire so she could make the change. She would officially join the pack. She wouldn't be left out of meetings or full moon runs or the power that clung to her family anymore.

Nora forced herself to grin back at the vampire, close-lipped, nothing like the vampire's varied smiles. Since her father died, it took Nora too much effort and thought to arrange her face into a real smile. So she did her best. She knew the effect wasn't nearly as striking. She hoped it conveyed confidence, at least.

The vampire quickly closed the distance between them to speak in Nora's ear. Not quite touching, but close enough that the warmth of body heat was noticeably absent. Even more disconcerting, the vampire didn't have a scent.

They were the same height.

Nora heard the vampire inhale deeply. Smelling her. Nora's blood turned cold. Did vampires feed on her people? Was she in danger?

Why couldn't she move?

"What's your name?" the vampire asked, her voice matched everything about her. Sharp, full, vibrant.

A bead of sweat gathered and slipped down Nora's neck. "Nora."

The vampire's smile shifted again. Nora was fascinated by her lips. The vampire could arrange them in so many ways.

5

"Nora," the vampire breathed. The shape of Nora's name fit perfectly within her growing grin. "Dance with me, Nora."

Without waiting for a response, the vampire grabbed Nora's wrists and settled Nora's hands on her waist. She was so skinny she fit perfectly in the curve between Nora's thumbs and fingers.

Nora knew she should be plotting. She knew this girl was the enemy. But Nora started to dance with her. Too many nights moving by moonlight had trained her to love the feel of her body swayed by music.

The vampire let out a delighted laugh and spun between Nora's hands. She backed up against Nora, her body fluid and confident. She dropped with the bass and twisted as she came back up, hands traveling Nora's sides and to the flaps of the cardigan. Her knuckles brushed the skin above Nora's tank top. The vampire's fingers were so cold in the oppressive heat of the club.

Using her grip on the cardigan, the vampire drew Nora closer still. One cool hand went to Nora's shoulder and pulled so they were cheek to cheek, their bodies perfectly aligned.

"What are you doing here, Nora?"

The vampire drew her hand upward, skimming Nora's neck. She peeled a strand of sweaty hair off the skin under Nora's ear. Embarrassment clutched at Nora, but it melted as the vampire wrapped the wet strand around her finger between their faces. Her nail was long and painted red, contrasting with the dark shade of Nora's hair, made darker with sweat. Every nerve in Nora's body came alive as she watched the vampire twist her hair.

She realized she had forgotten the question. "What?"

The girl smiled and gently pulled her finger free, Nora's hair unspooling. The girl stuck the sweat-dampened finger in her mouth, her wicked smile curling up around it.

Nora's brain bottomed out.

The girl slowly pulled the finger out of her mouth,

directing all of Nora's attention to her bottom lip. She licked it once her finger was clear. "Why are you here, Nora?"

"Just… girl's night," Nora said, gesturing vaguely to the bar and remembering Annaliese. She started to turn her head to check on her friend, but the girl caught her chin.

"If you want to succeed in this little game of yours, you're going to have to practice lying. That was terrible."

"W…what?"

"You look warm, honey." The girl took hold of Nora's cardigan again. She pulled off the knitted layer and Nora let her. The girl's smile finally faltered, lips pressing thin. Nora blinked.

"You picked the wrong club, pup."

Nora followed the girl's gaze, looking down at the exposed tattoo encircling her bicep. Multiple moons in different phases. The tattoo of her pack. Nora suddenly remembered why she was here. Why she came up to the girl in the first place. The vampire.

With vampire charm.

Nora hadn't believed it existed.

"You're coming with me," Nora said, amazed by the strength of her voice. She went to grab the vampire's wrist and the girl danced away with another laugh, Nora's cardigan in her hands. The vampire snaked her arms through the sleeves and lifted it to her nose. Her eyes twinkled above the knitted blue.

She winked, then snapped her head up.

"Wolf! Wolf!" the vampire cried.

The crowd of humans came to attention at her shouting. She pointed at Nora. A man grabbed Nora's arm; a woman took the other. They started to pull her away.

"No! No! She's a vampire! You have to stop her!" Nora tried to fight off the humans but was reluctant to hurt them, unsure of her body's new strength.

The vampire laughed as she was joined by the scowling

bartender, eyes matching sets of blue crystal. He watched Nora struggle with disinterest. The vampire girl shot Nora another smile and grabbed his arm. They turned and were quickly engulfed by the crowd.

Nora hated how her stomach dropped when she realized the vampire wasn't even going to look back.

Nora was escorted from the club by the same bouncer that let her in. Once outside, she yanked out of his cold grip. He crossed his arms and Nora noticed a skull tattoo on his forearm. The skull had a cigarette between its teeth, a trail of smoke snaking up toward his elbow.

Nora shook her head and glared up at him. "You have no idea what you're doing! She's—"

"A loyal customer. Don't come back if you know what's good for you. Tell Gabriel to stay out of our business."

Nora froze hearing her alpha's name. The bouncer eyed her own tattoo with disgust.

Nora knew most people were aware of supernaturals now. New Brecken was the first city to accept their presence officially. In the last few years, they were even granted citizenship. The city went so far as to legalize vampire feeding within reason. All these changes were prompted by a desperation to bring in income. A new distribution plant three cities down had left New Brecken's warehouses empty. The rise in gangs deterred people from moving in and spurred many to move away. Names like Hunter and Umbras and Browning ruled. As New Brecken fell further, its leaders turned desperate. A group of three vampires stepped out of hiding. They offered a solution. Those in charge listened. The vote was cast.

Supernaturals gained their rights.

No one could deny the clubs rumored to be run by vampires along Fourth Street and the tourism they brought in boosted the city's economy substantially. Some believed the city did all this just to get attention, not because vampires were real.

They came just to see if the stories were true. One night spent at the clubs on Fourth Street was enough to convince anyone.

Yet Nora couldn't wrap her head around this. The rumors were all true. She knew supernaturals were real, but she'd been skeptical that vampires would so blatantly flaunt their perversions. And Nora seemed to be the only one surprised. How could the humans accept the vampires so easily? How could they protect vampires over the pack that worked the last twenty years to keep the bloodsucking monsters at bay?

The bouncer clanged the door shut behind him, jarring Nora from her thoughts. She sank down on the curb and texted Annaliese. Her friend showed up five minutes later, shining with sweat and pissed. Nora winced. The club scene was basically Annaliese's worst nightmare and Nora had abandoned her to it. She didn't even get the vampire. She had no plan. Was no closer to her goal. A complete waste of time.

Annaliese didn't speak or wait to see if Nora was following her, just turned for the parking lot. Nora jumped up, stumbled on the curb, righted herself with a blush when laughter came from the line of people waiting to get in, and hurried to Annaliese's side.

"Listen, I'm sorry—"

"Five minutes. Shut up for five minutes."

Nora did. They reached the car in silence. Annaliese rolled the windows down immediately and turned off the radio station she'd let Nora play on the way over. Her hands clenched on the steering wheel. Nora watched them closely while Annaliese drove. Once Annaliese relaxed her grip, Nora figured the five minutes of quiet had passed.

"I really am sorry."

Annaliese sighed. She wasn't a fan of apologies. "Did you at least find one?"

"Yes. Kind of. Not really. She got away before I could figure out anything about her. I think she charmed me." Nora missed her cardigan as chilly air buffeted her through the window.

"Charmed you?"

"Yeah. Vampire charm. How they lure in victims."

"Oh."

Annaliese finally took pity on her and rolled up the windows. Nora gave her a slight, grateful grin. Annaliese wasn't ready to return it, but she relaxed against her seat, dropping one of her hands into her lap after merging into traffic.

"It was so strange," Nora continued, "The humans knew what she was. They defended her when she told them I was a werewolf. I don't even think they were charmed."

"Huh."

"And the bouncer knew who Gabriel was."

"Really? Did Matt say that place was vampire owned?"

"No. Just that they go there sometimes. He thought there would be less of them at the Maker for me to deal with than the clubs further down Fourth."

"But the humans got in the way," Annaliese said slowly. She was as mystified as Nora. "How often do you think they feed on them?"

Nora remembered how easily the vampire had gotten the man to bare his neck for her. How she'd only taken a single drink and her cheeks had already been flushed. Was it possible the humans there knew what was happening? Did they go willingly or were they all under charm? Humans were curious about vampires, yes. But there was no way they actually wanted to be fed on.

"I think the vampire left with that rude bartender," Nora suddenly remembered.

Annaliese scoffed. "Asshole. No one else even came up to me after he brushed us off. I could have used a drink too."

Nora fell quiet, her chest heavy as her failure settled. Minutes later, Annaliese pulled the car to a stop in front of the Den.

"We'll find one, Nora. There's still a month until the full moon. This was only our first try," Annaliese said.

It bothered Nora that her human friend was so ready to put herself at risk by joining this hunt, but she was too grateful for Annaliese's steadying presence to dissuade her.

"What if we don't? What if I can't kill one?"

Annaliese shrugged. "You apply for UNB next fall and we find an apartment and learn to enjoy clubs like normal college-age kids."

Nora's throat went tight, straining her voice. "I can't leave my pack."

"Then you'll kill one." Annaliese spoke with such confidence Nora was gripped with the urge to hug her. Instead, she nodded and left the car, bracing herself to face her pack as she walked up the path.

When her father first established the Den in New Brecken, supernatural territories were smaller, the lines more rigid, and secrets still protected. In an effort to avoid unnecessary conflict, her father bought an old Victorian-style home in an old neighborhood south of the river, far from Fourth Street and the warehouses on the other side of the city. In the last twenty years, the homes on this street had grown rundown, the upkeep too expensive. The houses surrounding the Den looked more like sets of horror films, but Gabriel loved to work on their home in his downtime. The robin egg blue siding was a splash of color on the eerie street. The white shutters and trimming were repainted just last summer. The cold had killed off Heather's garden, but the memory of it was enough to make Nora sniff the air fondly. The Den smelled like wolves and popcorn.

Nora missed the days when the pack wasn't so busy trying to make ends meet and the Den had smelled like home-cooked meals. Like her mother's favorite recipes.

The screen door squealed and slammed as Nora walked inside, drawing the attention of her pack clustered in the main room. This used to be Nora's favorite room in the Den. Members of the pack often gathered here, piled on top of one another and loudly watching TV or arguing pointlessly. She'd spent her childhood pestering the adult wolves who came and went. Many were her cousins, aunts, and uncles, but the pack grew more diverse when her father settled in New Brecken.

Nora, half white from her mother's side, used to feel she belonged in every conversation, Spanish or English. Now the pack was smaller, its members tenser. The memory of her parents crowded the room whenever Nora walked inside, hushing conversations and triggering the pack members' instincts to protect. The Morales line had grown too short.

Nora's eyes found Gabriel quickly, sitting across the room at his desk. She dropped her gaze, not wanting to invite questions about her night. Nora picked her way across the room, which involved stepping over sprawled bodies, wolf form and human, cuddling, snacking, and sleeping. Luis lifted a leg off the ground in a playful attempt to trip her. Nora should have been able to recover her step, but her legs didn't want to cooperate and she fell into the couch. Face burning under the laughter, Nora let Tío Marcus help her back up.

"Don't worry, Nora Mora, it happens to all of us before el cambio," he said.

Nora ducked her head and nodded.

"Nor!" Matt noticed her entrance and called to her from one of the recliners. He held a controller and was playing against Lupe at some shooting game on the second TV. "Nor!" he repeated, shouting overly loud because of the headphones he wore. "How'd it go?"

"Yes, Nora, I know we're all wondering," Adriana said. Nora sighed, pulled out her cousin's ID, and tossed it to her.

"I found one." There was no point in lying. "But no dice this time. I'll go back."

"Where are you looking again?" Adriana asked.

Nora saw Matt shake his head quickly from the corner of her eye. She scrambled for a lie.

"This dive bar on Fifth Street. We heard a rumor one was hanging out there."

Adriana let out a barking laugh. "Fifth Street! You're lucky you made it back alive. Anything under Six is swarming with vampires. Anything north of the river at this point, really." Adriana shook her head. "At least you didn't try Fourth."

A few wolves chuckled. Heather let out a huff, the warm breath of her snout brushing Nora's ankle.

"I wouldn't recommend going back there, Nor," Gabriel said from the desk. The intensity of their alpha's mix-matched gaze was like nothing else. He'd told her once an incident with a fork in elementary school led to an eye replacement, explaining why one was blue and the other brown. But the colors weren't what captured Nora's attention. It was the power brimming there, raw and compelling.

"I'm tired. I'm going to head to bed." Nora was surprised when they let her slink from the room without another word. Less surprised when Matt scrambled up to follow her, Lupe protesting about their ruined round.

Nora climbed the four flights of groaning stairs to her attic bedroom. She crossed to her window, opened it, and maneuvered onto the roof, refusing to think how much clumsier she was now. She'd been doing this for years. She wouldn't fall.

Nora was the only wolf living at the Den besides Gabriel with her own room. Even so, the sharp hearing of her housemates and lack of personal boundaries meant little was private. She'd grown accustomed to going to the roof for quiet. Her eyes found the moon quickly, a waning orb in the sky. She settled onto her back.

"Did you know it was a vampire club?" she asked when Matt's red hair appeared. He pulled himself up effortlessly to join her.

"What? No! Of course not! I swear DJ said the place was

safe. Why? What happened?" He reclined beside her, propping himself on an elbow to watch her face.

"The humans there are in on it. When the vampire called me a wolf, they kicked me out."

Matt's eyes widened. "But... DJ said—"

"How long has it been since DJ's been there?"

"I guess awhile. He called it by its old name."

Nora flopped her head to the side to look Matt full on. "And we didn't think with a new name like the Maker it wouldn't belong to vampires now?"

Matt snorted. "I guess we should have thought that one through. I thought it was just to draw in tourists. I swear, I'll find a better spot. There have to be places they hang out without their makers. Gabriel mentioned more unclaimed lowers showing up in the warehouse districts. We found a dead one a couple days ago north of the river."

Nora shuddered. "Where do they keep coming from? They aren't allowed to turn humans. We would know and catch them, right?"

"No idea. Gabriel is convinced the vampire leaders know more than they're letting on, but all the registered makers have an alibi each time the lowers show up. They think they're coming in from other cities, but they seem too fresh. What was the scene like at the club?"

"Mostly humans. I think. There was a vampire girl there. Maybe a guy, too, but I couldn't tell for sure. I only saw her drink. Right in the middle of everyone."

"But she didn't try to fight you herself? Maybe she is a good target then."

Nora considered. She hated how much her memory was laced with the girl's charm. How it made her heart beat faster and her stomach pool with heat just thinking about the way the vampire danced against her. How she twirled Nora's hair around her finger. Put it between her lips and—

Nora swallowed and forced the memory away. "Yeah. Maybe. I'll have to go back."

"I'll go with you," Matt said, taking Nora's hand.

"No, I have to do this myself. Just like you did. Just like everyone else did."

"But I smell Annaliese on you." He was on the verge of whining, the tone reminding Nora of the boy he'd been.

"I needed a ride. I was just scouting the club. I knew she'd be safe. I won't take her with me again."

Matt snorted. "Good luck with that."

Nora sighed. "I know. She can be so stubborn. She wants to be part of it, even though it's risky." And she and Nora both knew how much Nora needed her there.

"Annaliese can take care of herself. She always has. Even when you were going through the first stages of the change."

Annaliese hadn't blinked when Nora's senses began sharpening. When she'd first started lifting her nose in the air and cocking her head at every distant sound. Even worse had been her building strength and clumsiness. It had taken her a while to stop breaking things.

Okay. She still broke things. But less often.

"I know. This is different," Nora said.

"It's not. Not to her. You have to be firm if you don't want her involved."

Nora knew he was right, but the thought of leaving Annaliese out of any part of her life left her hollow. "She's my best friend."

Matt clutched his chest and gasped. "I've known you way longer."

Nora laughed and pushed his shoulder, rolling him onto his back.

"Ouch," he said, "You're not even going to try taking it back."

"Nope." Nora smiled a bit, but things had been strange between her and Matt lately. When he started rubbing his thumb along her knuckles, she sat up and went to the edge of the roof.

"I need to shower off the club."

"Yeah. You stink."

Nora pulled a face and carefully lowered herself down to her window. She could still feel the heat of Matt's hand on her skin. Frowning, she resisted the urge to rub it off.

CHAPTER 2

Poppy stirred three times counterclockwise and once straight down the middle. It was an old trick of her mother's, a family secret, and she nodded in satisfaction when the scent of vanilla wafted up in the steam. She turned from the stove to let the mixture boil and leaned over the chemistry notes she was studying. Poppy rubbed her temples after reading the same sentence three times. It was hopeless. She frowned over at her brew, daring it not to be strong enough.

She straightened when her roommates barged into the apartment. Her heart dropped. Topher had the early shift, but still, Poppy should have been in bed hours ago. She hadn't realized it was so late.

Topher shot her a tired smile as he dumped his tips into the jar on the island. It was full to bursting again. Poppy made a mental note to deposit it soon. Colbie leaned against the front door with a sigh and lifted the sleeve of the cardigan she was wearing to her nose, inhaling deeply. Poppy was nearly certain Colbie hadn't left wearing a cardigan.

Poppy turned the knob on the stove and snapped off the burner. She moved her concoction to the side to cool.

"So? Did we have fun tonight?" she asked her roommates.

Topher flashed another small grin and settled into the armchair. He let his head fall back against the cushion, his eyes sliding shut. Exhaustion pulled at his pale features and concern pulled at Poppy's gut. Colbie flopped onto the couch with a sigh, expression mirroring how Poppy felt.

"You have to drink, Topher."

He waved her words away. "I'll get a drink."

"Not Julia's old stuff. You know it's not working like you wanted. You need fresh. Life energy, like Poppy says."

Topher shrugged, the motion sending him deeper into the cushions. "What are you making, Pop Rocks?" he asked.

Poppy felt her cheeks warm as she admitted it was a love potion. Topher still had his eyes closed, but he raised an eyebrow.

"Smells delicious." Colbie's voice was muffled by the cardigan, her nose still buried in the knitted yarn. Poppy wasn't sure if she meant the cardigan or the brew.

"I thought we strove to avoid the clichés in this household." Topher pointed at the ceiling as he mocked the words Poppy said often.

"Yeah, yeah. But I need it. To pass my class."

"No judgment, but are you trying to sleep with your professor, Popsicle?" Colbie asked. She now had the wide hood of the cardigan pulled up over her face, only her chin still visible. Even Topher cracked an eye open at the sound of his sister sniffing like a dog.

When she quieted with a sigh, Poppy responded, but it was getting harder to ignore Colbie's strange behavior. "It's not for the professor. Molly said if I helped her with her boy troubles, she'd give me her notes and quizzes to study. She took this class last semester."

"Molly doesn't know you're a witch, does she?" Colbie peeked out from under the hood to ask.

"No, just that he's in another class of mine. I told her I'd bring her up when I saw him."

"It's all making sense now," Topher said. He shifted, slinging his legs up over the arm of the chair and laying sideways. He was too long to fit comfortably, but he still looked ready to pass out. Colbie pulled a face at him and stood, throwing back the hood. She stomped into his bedroom. Poppy heard the door of his mini fridge and Colbie returned with a packet of blood. She threw it at her brother.

"You only have two left."

Topher sighed and popped a hole in the plastic with his nail. He swallowed the contents in three gulps, grimacing at the taste. He didn't look all that much better.

"See?" Colbie said, "You need fresh stuff."

"Julia will murder me," Topher muttered. A weak excuse and everyone in the room knew it. Poppy suspected it had been weeks since Topher last cared what his long-distance girlfriend did or didn't do. Poppy's suspicions only solidified when his phone pinged and he made no move to answer it.

"You need to feed, Topher," Colbie put enough concern in her tone to let him know she was serious but let the subject drop. She'd had her say, but she wasn't one to force her will on anyone.

Colbie settled back onto the couch, lifting the cardigan sleeve to her nose once again.

Poppy's curiosity finally got the better of her. "What's with the sweater?"

"She pulled it off a pup," Topher said.

"What? A werewolf came to the club?"

"Just a pup," Topher repeated. Poppy figured he must mean a werewolf who hadn't made the change yet.

"One of Gabriel's?"

Colbie nodded. Poppy had some idea what a pup had to do to become a full member of his pack and frowned. Gabriel's pack usually refrained from coming to the clubs when the vampires stayed in line. As far as she knew, the vampires had been behaving.

"Should we be worried?" Poppy asked.

Topher shrugged. "Probably not. As long as Zayn or I am there."

Poppy crossed the room and sat on the couch. Colbie settled down, resting her head in Poppy's lap. She pulled at the cardigan, wrapping it more securely around herself. The girl was always moving. Topher got like that too, when he wasn't starving. Now he was statue still, eyes staring blankly at the ceiling.

Colbie heaved a sigh. "I swear to god, I'm in love."

Even Topher was shocked by her words. He sat up so quickly Poppy missed the motion. Poppy stared down at Colbie, speechless. The vampire just closed her eyes and lifted the cardigan sleeve to her nose again, taking a delicate sniff.

Topher slid off the armchair to sit in front of his sister. He pulled her arm down and looked into her face for a long moment. Poppy didn't have to know Colbie as well as Topher did to see the sincerity in the girl's face. Topher blew out a breath and let his forehead fall against the cushion.

"What are we going to do with you?" he asked.

Colbie laughed. "Just stop me from following her into the Den. I don't know if I'll be able to help myself."

Poppy woke to her alarm with no memory of falling asleep on the couch. One of her roommates had covered her with a blanket. Their doors were closed now, sunlight a gentle brush against the curtains. Someone had poured her potion into vials, stoppering each one. Poppy was willing to bet it had been Topher. She smiled at the neat row of glass bottles as she brewed coffee.

Poppy changed into a fresh t-shirt and leggings. She twisted her auburn hair into two braids and pulled on her favorite ballcap to hide the fact she hadn't washed it in three days.

Poppy took a strange pleasure in these small lazy acts since leaving home and her mother's comments on her appearance were no longer a concern.

Chugging a final cup of coffee, Poppy gathered her bag and left the apartment, love potion in hand. She made it to campus early enough to find a parking spot and went to meet Molly at the library. They had plans to study calculus before Poppy's first class.

Molly was always easy to find. Her hair was a frizzy blond, artfully managed mess and she was one of the few who took advantage of the rolling stand-up whiteboards the university library kept scattered along the floor. Today, Poppy found Molly sitting with a familiar-looking girl wearing bulky Ray-Bans glasses. They already had their laptops open, calculators out, and notes spread across the table.

Poppy offered a smile as she neared and the girl nodded and reached for her coffee. Molly perked up upon spotting her.

"I'm hoping you're here because you've made progress with Alex. Not that I wouldn't help you either way, obviously," she said by way of greeting.

"You would?" Poppy asked.

"Of course! But tell me you have good news."

"Too soon to know, but I have English with him today and I have a good feeling." Poppy barely stopped herself from checking the potion in the side pocket of her bag as she took a seat.

"This is Annaliese. We went to high school together and she's in Perry's afternoon class. I'm naming this study group Locals Only." With the legalization of supernaturals, an influx of students had applied to NBU in the last couple of years. Rumors of vampires really drew the college-age crowd. Molly turned to Annaliese. "Poppy was homeschooled, but she's good at math. Between the three of us, we might get through this."

Poppy snorted and pulled her textbook out.

"I think we have chemistry together, actually," Annaliese said.

Poppy nodded, finally placing the girl's face. "Yeah, you sit in the back, right? How do you feel about the exam?"

Annaliese shook her head. "Why do you think I'm hanging out with Molly? She keeps all her notes and tests."

"Hey!" Molly protested.

Poppy laughed. From her first glance at Annaliese's scowl, she hadn't expected the girl to have a sense of humor. Maybe it was just the calculus putting that look on Annaliese's face.

"Where were we?" Molly asked. Annaliese gave a curt answer and they all got to work. Poppy took the first chance that presented itself to pluck one of Molly's curly hairs from her sweatshirt and slip it into the potion under the table. It hissed faintly, but neither of her study partners noticed.

They hit a lull when Molly filled up the whiteboard and took a moment to wipe it clean. She addressed Annaliese over her shoulder. "Why are you so tired today?"

Annaliese sighed and rubbed her eyes under her glasses. "I went out last night."

"You? On a Sunday? Where?"

Annaliese shrugged like it shouldn't be surprising. "Some club. Nora wanted to go."

"How'd you get in? And you're still friends with Nora? What's she up to?"

"A fake and why wouldn't I be? She's been working in the family business."

Molly nodded. Family business could mean anything in New Brecken. Most locals knew not to ask. "You know this means you have to go out with me sometime. I have to see what drunk Annaliese is like."

Annaliese shrugged again. Molly frowned at the noncommittal response.

"Let's go over number ten again," Annaliese said.

They turned back to their notes, only to be interrupted

when someone walking by hit the back of Poppy's head with their backpack.

"Oh, I'm so sorry!"

Poppy recognized the voice and turned with a ready eye roll, unable to make it convincing when she grinned.

"Hey, Oliver."

He looked wired, a giant sweating frappuccino in hand and his sandy blond hair sticking out in nearly every direction. It always made Poppy smile to see him on campus. He usually looked immaculate, but here, schoolwork was his only concern.

"I hear Colbie's got a new crush," he said, shrugging his bag back on.

"Word travels fast."

"Well, she called me this morning." They couldn't say much more in front of Molly and Annaliese, but Oliver's eyebrow wiggle promised a conversation later.

"Who's this, Poppy?" Molly asked, leaning forward over her notes.

Oliver was adorable and sweet in a way quite a few girls loved, but his boyfriend loved more. He juggled his books and drink, nearly dropping it, and stuck out a hand.

"I'm Oliver."

"Molly." She flashed him a cheeky grin. Poppy thought she heard Annaliese snort into her coffee cup. She set it down to shake the hand Oliver extended to her next.

"Annaliese."

"Nice to meet you both. Well, Popcorn, I need to hit the books, but I'll catch you later? We need all the details."

"Sure thing."

Oliver waved and vanished between the stacks, heading toward his favorite study room.

"Damn, Poppy, you were holding out! Forget Alex; put in a good word for me there!"

"Sorry, Molly, he's taken."

"Can we get back to the problem?" Annaliese asked. Molly made a big show of reluctantly picking up her marker.

Poppy got home from her lab at six. Molly sent her a text right as she walked through the door. It was a screenshot of a message from Alex asking her out.

Poppy smirked. "I still got it."

An obnoxiously upbeat pop song was playing from the bathroom, accompanied by Colbie's terrible singing. Topher came out of his room, hair disheveled from sleep. He cast a bewildered look from the bathroom to Poppy. Poppy shrugged and forced a smile. He looked so pale it caught her off guard.

"This isn't good," he said and yawned.

"Does she get like this often?"

Topher shrugged and shook his head simultaneously, too tired to come up with a better answer.

The bathroom door burst open and Colbie came out with a towel wrapped around her body and another one twisted up in her hair. Her small speaker blared in her hand. She shouted to be heard over it. "Oh, good! Poppy's back. And you're awake! I haven't seen you up this early in ages."

Topher shot his sister a glare and pushed past her for his turn in the bathroom. She hiked up her towel when he jostled her and stuck her tongue out at him.

"I don't think waking up this early was his choice," Poppy yelled over the music, giving the speaker a pointed look.

Colbie smiled and turned the sound down. "You should come out with us tonight, Pop Tart." Colbie lowered her voice and looked back at the bathroom door. "Between the two of us, I think we could convince him to drink. He's practically starved."

"I have a test Friday, Colbie. I have to study tonight."

Colbie's face dropped into her perfect, practiced pout. It

was the face Topher never said no to. The face Poppy now associated with trouble. "It's Monday! You have all week to study."

"No, Colbie. I have to sleep sometime!"

"Just sleep in! You don't have class until eleven tomorrow."

"How do you even know that? You sleep all day."

Colbie didn't answer but reached for Poppy's hand, catching her towel under her biceps when it slipped again. Something about Colbie's face, the wild energy in her movements, and the way her eyes darted to the cardigan hanging by the door gave Poppy pause.

"Please, Poppyseed. Popsicle. Pop Rocks. Corn Pops. I need a wing woman. I need one so bad."

"You really think she'll come back to the Maker?" Poppy shook her head, remembering what was important here. "She wants to kill you, Colbie! Are you crazy?"

Colbie's blue eyes lit up. "Exciting, isn't it?"

Poppy shook her head, but Colbie's smile said she knew she'd won. At this point, Poppy didn't trust Colbie enough to be careful and Topher was too thirsty to be any real help.

Colbie dragged Poppy toward her room and slammed the door behind them.

"So, which one? Casual? Dress? My red skirt?" Colbie asked, gesturing to the clothes laid out on the bed. At least four outfits had already been cast aside and crumpled on the floor. Poppy pushed a romper aside and sat down. After a moment's thought, she snapped her fingers and summoned a dress hidden in the side of Colbie's closet. Her friend always forgot she owned it and looked stunning in it. Colbie caught it as it flew toward her in the air.

"Popcorn, you're a genius."

The black dress fell nearly to Colbie's knees, the main reason she hardly ever wore it. But it had diamond-shaped cutouts along the base of her ribs and crisscrossed straps for a back that showed off plenty of skin. Colbie dropped her towel and stepped directly into it, forgoing any sort of underwear. She bent and let the other towel untwist and fall off her head before knotting her hair in its customary bun and snapping a hair tie in place. Usually, this was the extent of the effort Colbie put into her appearance. But, tonight, she frowned at her reflection in her vanity.

"Think you'll dress up?" she asked Poppy.

"Probably. I need to wash my hair and do my makeup."

Colbie nodded. She sat down at her cluttered vanity and made eye contact with Poppy through the mirror.

"Make me tempting enough for a werewolf."

CHAPTER 3

Topher's head was pounding. He nearly kissed Poppy when he heard she had agreed to come. Until he drank, he wouldn't be able to match Colbie's energy by a long shot.

Poppy drove them to the club, Colbie practically bouncing in the passenger's seat the entire way. She rolled her window down and stuck her head out to howl. Topher rolled his eyes but couldn't fight a smile. He reclined across the backseat so no one would see and rubbed his forehead. His hair brushed his fingers and he thought again about how he needed a haircut. It had gotten harder to find a trustworthy barber since the whole vampire thing. Few were open at night and he didn't trust Colbie anywhere near him with scissors. He learned that lesson early in life.

Colbie howled again, making a group of people waiting at the crosswalk laugh. The smell of them drifted into the car. Topher's stomach rumbled. His mouth watered and familiar disgust rose in his throat. Colbie was so excited that he hoped the wolf girl would be there tonight. Yet that only made it so much more important that he gave in and drank. Colbie would need him fresh if anything went wrong.

Colbie pulled her head inside when Topher's phone started to ring.

"You should answer. How long has it been since you talked to her? I don't know why you haven't just ended it. You've never had a problem with breakups before."

It was true. Topher hadn't. But Julia was more complicated. Julia knew him before. Back when he was human. And she hadn't run after he was turned. She'd been there for it all, first as the friend he needed and slowly, they fell back into old habits. She'd seen his reluctance to feed from the beginning and volunteered her blood.

Julia cried so hard when she left for school that she made herself sick.

Topher was desperately afraid she was addicted to him.

The ringing stopped and Colbie sighed. When it started again, Topher held the side button until his phone powered off, never once looking at the picture on the screen. He waited for the guilt to come. To feel something for the girl he had dated off and on for three years. He hated himself even more when he just felt relief from the silence.

They pulled into the lot nearest to the Maker. Poppy took advantage of the employee parking, knowing Lana would recognize her car. Topher got out, "forgetting" his phone in the seat.

Colbie leaned to check her makeup in the side mirror one last time before turning to Topher. "How do I look?"

She rarely asked for assurance. Rarely suffered from nerves. She hardly even thought twice about her appearance now that she could use charm to get or get rid of attention.

Topher stepped forward and put his hands on her shoulders. He bent so their matching blue eyes were level. "You look stunning. If anyone could turn a wolf into a vampire lover, it's you. I pity the girl because she's about to lose her heart."

Colbie's nerves vanished behind a happy smile. Whatever this girl said to his sister, whatever she'd done, Topher prayed to every force in the universe Colbie wouldn't end up hurt. He needed his sister whole. He depended on Colbie to keep him from breaking into pieces.

Topher straightened and Colbie linked arms with him and Poppy as they turned for the Maker.

"First thing, we need to get you a snack," Colbie said, tugging him close.

Topher groaned.

The line for the club wasn't long yet at a quarter until eight. They skipped it anyway. Jaeger nodded at them as she let them pass. Her heavy eyeliner and half-shaved head would have been enough to intimidate the line into compliance even without her being a vampire.

Once inside, Colbie squeezed Topher's arm and slipped into the crowd, nose in the air, sniffing out her prey. Topher smiled, watching her go. Poppy stayed at his side. She quirked an eyebrow at him expectantly when he looked down.

"Want a drink?" he asked.

"If you get one."

Topher snorted and took her hand to lead the way through the crowd. As usual, it parted for him. People stopped to watch him pass, pupils dilated. For the millionth time, Topher wished he was just a bit shorter. Not quite so noticeable. That his charm didn't ebb out and affect the human's around him so strongly.

He nodded at Zayn behind the bar and his friend was quick to pour Poppy her favorite drink. She flashed him a smile over the tequila sunrise in thanks. "No Oliver tonight?"

"Not tonight. He's studying."

"Lucky guy." Poppy shot a glare at the crowd, no doubt intended for Colbie.

She took a sip and made a shooing motion at Topher. "Go find someone, Topher. You can't keep putting it off. You're wasting away before my eyes."

Zayn nodded his agreement and Topher sighed. No use denying it. His jaw ached from the smell of blood around him. Not even the bitterness of alcohol could dilute it. Just acknowledging his hunger made his fangs slide out.

Topher turned, leaning against the bar on his elbows, he considered his options. As always, his biggest problem would be finding someone sober. He avoided alcohol-tainted blood whenever possible. He'd suffered one too many secondary hangovers and the taste brought back too many memories.

Topher spotted someone familiar. After a moment's hesitation, his hunger urged him to push off the bar and cross the room, letting the path clear for him again. For once, he let loose what control he had over his charm. He was tired. Let them watch him. Let them want him.

It pleased him to see that even when purposefully released, his charm was a feeble beast compared to normal. Hunger had weakened it.

Topher nearly lost his resolve to feed.

Relief washed over Rebecca when their eyes met. She stopped biting at the hangnail on her thumb and smiled. Topher inclined his head and she followed him to the hallway containing the bathrooms and stairs to the upper floors. It was darker there and those passing by knew better than to comment or watch. Topher nodded to Tamera as she left the hallway, cheeks flushed and a dazed man close on her heels. She winked. It had taken the two of them hooking up after a horrible shift to warm to each other, but only in an ideal world did one choose their maker.

"How you been?" Topher asked Rebecca when they drew to a stop. He could tell she was just itching for this, but still, he put it off.

"Good. For the most part. I got close today. Stressed about the new job. And I might be getting my kids back."

"Rebecca! That's amazing!"

She tried a smile, but it wobbled. "I mean it, Chris. I was close. I almost ruined it all."

Topher sighed. "Here." He took up her hand and flipped it to expose the inside of her wrist. Steeling himself, he licked the skin there. Rebecca instantly relaxed, the lines on her forehead vanishing. Topher hated putting people at his mercy like this but helping people like Rebecca hold on to their sobriety made it easier. He could drink, thinking maybe, just maybe, he was doing more good than harm.

Those who came to him knew they couldn't count on him for a hit. Knew Topher wouldn't give it to them if he smelled drugs in their system. But when they got the chance to let him feed on them, they all took it. Rebecca once said it was the best high of her life. The track marks inside Topher's arms ensured he never forgot how those words could ruin someone.

Lana said vampire saliva wasn't a drug. She said it wasn't even similar. Topher tried to let her reassure him, but he suspected his affected people differently. It was more potent than other vampires'. Like his charm.

Still, his saliva was better than heroin or other drugs. Not even he could deny that. There were no physical side effects. In fact, vampire saliva had healing properties. And it gave some people the desire to eat healthier, their bodies responding to being fed on with cravings for the foods that would make them taste better. Topher knew he helped Rebecca stay sober. Because of that, she had a job. She was getting her children back. He could give her this.

But god, he hated it.

Topher used his index fingernail to slice a thin line into her skin. Biting gave victims more of a high, but Topher rarely sank his fangs into people. He put Rebecca's bleeding wrist to his lips and tried to ignore her moan of pleasure as he drank.

Topher only took a few swallows, but by the time he looked up, three more recovering addicts were hanging out by the bathrooms. Word already spread he was feeding tonight. With a final lick, he closed the gash on Rebecca's wrist and sent her stumbling on her way, ignoring her thanks. Topher beckoned Johnny closer. When Topher smelled the older man was still clean, he repeated the process.

By the time Topher left the hall, he felt better than he had in days. Since Julia's blood had gotten too stale to quench his cravings. Colbie was right about fresh blood being better. Riding waves of energy, his charm close and vibrant, Topher agreed with her. The crowd stopped to stare as he walked by, heads listing to the side without their owners knowing why. Topher did his best to ignore their exposed throats, the pulses that beckoned him.

He knew himself well enough to understand he'd feel horrible about this when he woke up tomorrow.

"That's much better," Poppy said when she saw him. She was still at the bar, sitting with one of the girls he remembered refusing to serve last night. Everything was brighter, his mood a hundred times improved. He was even happy to see the girl was glaring fiercely at him. It was so refreshing when his charm didn't immediately infect the humans around him, making them disgustingly eager to please.

He couldn't show his pleasure, though, or his charm would come out. He matched her expression and worked to dampen his good mood.

"Colbie having any luck?" he asked Poppy.

She shrugged. "Haven't seen her. This is Annaliese," she said, gesturing to the girl. "She's in my chemistry class and we keep running into each other."

Topher fought the instinct to offer his hand and gave the girl a cool nod instead. "They say it's a small city." He pointed to Poppy's empty glass. "Want another?"

"Yes. Annaliese looks like she needs one too, but Zayn's been busy."

"What will it be?" Topher asked Annaliese, turning to her

without thinking. She blinked at him. His heart fell as her expression went slack.

"What will it be?" she repeated, numb.

With some regret, Topher pulled in his good mood the rest of the way, cutting off his charm as completely as he could. He closed off his features, arranging his face into a stony mask. He worked so hard to rein it in that his entire body tensed with the effort.

Annaliese shook her head like she'd suddenly come out of a trance.

"What do you want to drink?" he snapped, directing the annoyance he felt toward himself at Annaliese for good measure. She narrowed her eyes again, a wrinkle appearing between her brows. Much better.

"I don't need a drink from you. Not after you were such a dick about it last night." She crossed her arms, pulling into herself.

"I try to avoid serving minors."

"How thoughtful. Why don't you avoid me now?"

Poppy heaved a sigh, sympathy in her green eyes when she looked at Topher. For the millionth time, he was grateful witches had ways to block vampiric charm.

"More tequila," Poppy said. Topher nodded and moved down the bar, ducking under the nearest hatch.

Zayn smiled when Topher entered his space and accepted the twenty Topher slipped him to cover the tip for dealing with Poppy drunk. They never had to pay for the actual drinks. Topher stopped in front of Poppy and Annaliese, ignoring the humans straining to get his attention.

He made quick work of pouring two shots and grabbed the lime wedges and salt.

"Cheers!" Poppy waited for the girl to tap shot glasses. Annaliese copied Poppy's movements as she licked the salt at the base of her thumb, threw back the tequila, and stuck the lime wedge between her teeth.

"Another!" Poppy cried around the lime clamped between her teeth, slamming her shot glass down. Topher poured her another liberal shot and arched an eyebrow at Annaliese in question. At her curt nod, he poured her one too.

Poppy was about to ask for a third round when Topher glanced down the bar and saw Lana. His maker had recently dyed her hair an ashy blond and he didn't recognize her at first. When their eyes met, she gave him a wink and turned away. He breathed a sigh of relief, realizing she wasn't there for him. Not tonight, at least.

"I want to dance," Poppy said. Topher checked himself before he grinned at the slight slur in her words. For being so reluctant to join them, she was going for it now. "Come with me!" she bid them.

Annaliese was quick to shake her head. "I have to wait for my friend. She'll be back soon."

Poppy shrugged and slipped off her stool. Topher waited, hesitant to leave Annaliese. She'd looked so miserable and tense sitting alone last night.

He refilled a drunk girl's water and let her engage him in conversation as he watched Poppy make her way into the crowd. Her face quickly filled with rapture as she spun and twisted within the mass of dancing bodies. Topher stifled his jealousy. If only he could draw upon the energy of human life so non-invasively.

The drunk girl's boyfriend came to collect her, glaring at Topher until he charmed him enough to let go of his suspicion. They left soon after. He turned to find Annaliese watching him closely.

"What?"

She bristled. "Why don't you just go dance?"

Topher rolled his eyes. Fury lit the girl's expression. It had been a long time since he'd mastered his charm enough to make a human this frustrated with him.

"I don't need babysat," she insisted.

Topher poured her another shot. "No one said they were babysitting you."

"Go away." Topher didn't move. Annaliese pushed the shot back to him. "Seriously. Leave me alone."

Noting the real edge in her voice, Topher nodded. He pushed back from the bar, half wishing he'd been on the schedule that night for an excuse to stay nearby.

He grabbed Zayn's arm as he passed. "Hey, keep an eye on my friend Annaliese will you?"

"Sure, man. You going to talk to Lana?"

Topher snorted and ducked out from under the bar. He went to find Poppy. Not a minute too soon either. She had started glowing.

CHAPTER 4

This was stupid. It was against Gabriel's orders. There were other places to find a vampire. Matt had offered to help. It was reckless, but Nora wanted to do this alone despite everything. Annaliese waiting at the bar didn't count as backup. Gabriel and Matt both captured their vampires on their own. Her father had expected it. And Nora would be an idiot if she didn't pursue this vampire girl who made no move to fight her. Who let her close enough to dance. There were ways to get used to charm. To ignore it. Nora just had to stay focused.

Nora wiped her palms on her jeans and followed the vampire girl. She was easy enough to spot. The vampire prowled the outskirts of the dancing mob and occasionally sniffed the air. Searching for her next victim. Nora halted each time the vampire was stopped by humans. Anger pulled her gut watching them flirt with her. How willingly they pulled the girl closer. To their necks. How they smiled when she clamped down.

Nora shuddered. She resisted the urge to pounce on the vampire each time. Instead, Nora took a steadying breath and stayed out of sight as she followed. Suddenly, the vampire straightened. She turned on her heel and slipped into a dim hall. Nora hurried after her.

The vampire paused to nod in satisfaction at a boy bent over a woman's hand. With a jolt, Nora realized it was the bartender from the night before. And he was drinking from the woman's wrist. The act took his total concentration and the vampire girl slipped by without him noticing. Nora was quick to follow, swallowing hard while her stomach turned.

Nora felt hot with nerves and hatred as they continued up several flights of stairs. With a clang, the vampire threw open the door to the roof and spun out into the open night. Nora crouched in the dark entrance, but when the vampire stopped, she looked directly at Nora with a smile that made her stomach plummet. She'd known Nora was following her.

"Better up here, right?" the vampire asked.

Nora frowned and cautiously stepped out onto the roof. She sniffed the air in vain, searching for a trap. She couldn't even smell the vampire. There was nothing but the humid city scent hanging in the air.

"I like your braid," the vampire continued.

Nora stumbled, bewildered by the creature before her. The vampire turned and walked to the edge of the roof, leaning so far over the low wall that her feet lifted off the ground for a moment and made Nora's breath catch. She cleared her throat and walked to the vampire's side.

The girl turned, still leaning over her crossed arms, her bun flopped above the city street below. She squinted up at Nora, scrunching her upturned nose.

"You're not going to kill me," she said.

Nora was suddenly furious. She thought how easy it would be to push the girl over, but a fall like that still probably wasn't enough to kill a vampire. "How would you know?"

The vampire closed her eyes. "Call it intuition."

"I'll call it stupid."

"Then why haven't you whisked me away? I've always

wanted to see inside a den. *The* Den, I suppose. Gabriel's is the only one left in the city, right?"

"Screw you."

The vampire's eyes snapped open. She straightened suddenly, standing toe to toe with Nora. "What happened to the others?"

"You can't be serious."

"Can I be curious?"

Nora glared and pressed her lips together.

The girl laughed into the night sky, turning to the wall again. "I like you, Nora. And you came back. You like me too."

"I don't."

"So kill me. Take me away. I'll tell the humans to leave you alone. But you won't. Because you like me."

Nora rolled her eyes. "Your charm won't save you, no matter how much you use it to distract me. I have to kill a vampire to complete the change. You shouldn't be so sure I won't hurt you."

"Hmmm."

They fell silent, Nora staring at the vampire and the vampire watching the people in line and smoking along the street below. She had one of the most interesting faces Nora had ever seen. For every soft and rounded feature, the next was sharp and pointed. It nearly wasn't pretty, yet it was. Very. Nora's face grew warm as she looked her fill.

The vampire eventually let out a sigh. "You like me," she said again, turning to give Nora her full attention and catching her staring.

"I don't even know your name."

"Colbie West." The girl held up a hand and Nora shook it without thinking. Again, she was struck by the lack of body heat coming off the girl. Unnatural.

Colbie didn't let go of Nora's hand as she shifted closer. The vampire reached for Nora's braid with her other hand, running her fingers lightly over the twists. Nora watched the girl's pale, slim fingers. Her nails were painted black tonight.

With a start, Nora stepped back. "Stop it."

"What?" Colbie's blue eyes were all mock innocence. She angled her head, lips bunching into a practiced pout.

"I *don't* like you. Maybe I can't kill you, but... just stop. Nothing is happening here."

"Because I'm a vampire?"

"And because you're a girl."

Nora felt another spark of irritation when Colbie only lifted her eyebrows, unconvinced. But she did take a step back.

"I see," Colbie said dryly.

"Who should I take if not you? That boy in the hall—"

"Touch my brother and I will leave your body a bloody mess on the steps of your den," Colbie said, voice completely unaffected. She could have been complimenting Nora's braid again. Nora felt the nip of cold in the night air.

"I didn't know vampires had siblings."

"I won't tell you who to take. I stay out of gang business. Become a killer if that's what you want, but I'm not playing any part."

Nora snorted. "Every vampire has a maker and all the makers are in a gang. So which of the Big Three do you belong to?"

Colbie crossed her eyes at Nora before turning back to the night. Colbie didn't speak for so long Nora shifted on her feet, the awkward moment clawing at her throat. She couldn't think of anything else to say. Not that Nora should be trying to make small talk. She should be leaving. Spending time with Annaliese. Finding her next target if she really couldn't go through with this.

"If nothing is happening, why are you still here?" Colbie voiced the very question Nora was wondering herself.

"I...."

Colbie smiled when Nora faltered. She held out her hand. "Give me your phone?"

Damn her vampire charm. Without thinking, Nora pressed her phone into the other girl's palm. With a quick motion, Colbie grabbed Nora's hand before she could pull away and pressed her thumb onto the home button to unlock it. Nora bit her lip as she watched Colbie's nails tap over the screen. She jumped when the sound of a phone ringing interrupted the night. Colbie smiled with satisfaction, bringing out her own phone and ending the call.

She handed Nora back her phone. The lit screen showed a new contact, *Vampire Colbie*. Nora snorted.

"Just so you don't forget," Colbie said. She was smiling still. All confidence. "Feel free to call when you hit a wall with this vampire murdering thing. Or if you change your mind about girls."

Nora glared at her. "I won't be calling." She turned to leave the rooftop.

"That's fine," Colbie said to her back. She waited until Nora was at the door before saying, "Oh, and Nora?"

Nora turned back. "What?" she snapped, crossing her arms. Then dropping them when that didn't feel right. Colbie didn't respond for a beat, watching Nora close instead. Nora shuffled her feet.

Finally, Colbie spoke, "I don't know what Gabriel's teaching you, but charm doesn't work on werewolves." She watched the effect of her words with a wide smile and turned back to the rail. "I look forward to hearing from you."

Face burning, Nora had to try twice to get the door open. She hurried down the steps to find Annaliese, the vampire's words replaying in her head.

Annaliese was at the bar where Nora had left her. And she was drunk.

"Nor! We can get drinks tonight! I got drinks tonight." The words came out thick and slurred.

Very drunk.

With effort, Annaliese focused on Nora's face, eyebrows drawing together. "No vampire?"

Nora shook her head. "We need to leave."

Annaliese wasn't happy about it, but she allowed Nora to grab her arm and help her from her seat. Nora was reminded painfully how small her human friend was, how delicate her bones were. She weighed practically nothing leaning against Nora and letting herself be led from the bar. Nora should never have brought her along. Having her for support wasn't worth the risk.

Nora swore again when Annaliese was bumped by a dancer and nearly fell to her knees. She looked up when Nora got her righted. "I don't feel so good," she muttered.

"How much did you drink?"

"I dunno. Shots. Zayn kept giving them to me."

"Who the hell is Zayn?"

"The not asshole bartender."

"I beg to differ," Nora said. She pulled Annaliese out of the way of a passionately kissing couple.

They finally cleared the dance floor and made it to the door, only to look up and see Colbie, already grinning as they stumbled outside. She stood with another girl and the bartender she'd said was her brother. He flicked out his cigarette as he turned to see what caught Colbie's eyes.

"*That's* asshole bartender," Annaliese reminded Nora unnecessarily. His face darkened. Once again, Nora was knifed with guilt, realizing how stupid it had been to leave her friend behind surrounded by vampires and drinking.

"Yes, it is!" Colbie said, delighted. She squeezed her brother's arm. "And that's the wolf girl, Nora!" The girl with her widened her eyes, a vivid green, but neither spoke. Colbie plowed on. "Nora, this is Poppy and Topher."

"Topher? Like a gopher?" Annaliese lifted her head to ask incredulously.

"Like Christopher," Colbie explained. The boy in question only took another drag from his cigarette, face still hard.

Colbie waited expectantly. Nora nodded. How did this girl keep pulling her into conversations? "We're just leaving."

"Stop touching me," Annaliese muttered, pushing out of Nora's grip. She steadied herself on the brick wall of the club. Nora closed her eyes. So they were at that point in the night. Nora knew all too well what came next.

The other girl, Poppy, looked at her friends. "Do something."

Colbie just laughed.

Topher shook his head. "No chance."

Poppy rolled her eyes and turned back to Nora. "Do you two need help getting to your car?"

Nora hesitated, watching Annaliese close. Sure enough, her face went ashen and she turned to the wall. Nora sighed and stepped back as Annaliese began to vomit.

"We'll probably just wait this out. She won't forgive me if I let her puke in her car."

"I'll get you a garbage bag," Topher said. He dropped his cigarette and ground it under his foot before slipping back inside the club. Colbie glared at his back as she picked it up and took it to the nearest trash.

They went quiet, the line of club goers a buzz of background noise and Annaliese's gagging filling the space between them. Colbie still looked amused, but Poppy winced every time Annaliese started up again.

"I feel like this is my fault," Poppy said. "I shouldn't have left her."

Colbie laughed. "You weren't the friend she came here with, Pop Tart."

Nora sent her a glare but couldn't argue. Annaliese seemed to have gotten over the worst of it. She turned and slid down the wall to sit next to her mess. Groaning, she dropped her head into her hands, her tightly curled hair flopping forward to hide her face.

Poppy stepped closer and crouched next to her. "You know about the supernatural?" she asked.

Annaliese nodded into her hands.

"I've found vampire saliva to be the best hangover cure."

Nora lunged for Poppy, who fell back with a startled shout. Colbie, moving as quickly as Nora could ever hope to, jumped forward and grabbed Nora's hands, locking them behind her back.

"Don't touch her!" Nora shouted at Poppy, frantic for her helpless friend and mindless of the quiet that fell over the line. Her rage was complete and foreign. The animal inside her broke through.

Poppy straightened and brushed herself off. Nora seethed but stopped struggling when Poppy didn't make another move toward her friend. Colbie pushed her away. The anger on her face looked completely out of place.

"She's not even a vampire. Chill out."

Topher returned at that moment, a water bottle in one hand and a black garbage bag in the other. He handed them both to Nora, making no move to approach Annaliese and the mess she'd made on the pavement.

"You should go. We don't get called in a lot, but she might attract cops. No one wants to deal with that."

"We were just leaving." Nora tucked the garbage bag under her arm and went to help Annaliese again, swallowing a growl of frustration when her friend jerked out of her grip. Her insides chilled when she stopped to take in Annaliese's appearance fully. "Annaliese, where is your jacket?"

"Dunno."

"The keys are in your jacket."

"Bar stool?"

Topher rolled his eyes and cut the line to get back inside,

saying something to the bouncer that made her laugh. Nora felt her cheeks heat. She hadn't wanted to see Colbie again and now they were stranded in front of the club with her.

Poppy and Colbie started to talk with the ease of close friends, naming people they had seen inside and tidbits of gossip. Nora tried not to listen in, but it was inevitable. The vampire was connected to way too many people at the Maker. Her insides chilled when Colbie mentioned Lana, a minor maker Gabriel despised. Was that who had turned her?

Conversation shifted to how Poppy knew Annaliese and the class they shared. It would seem Nora had no control over the supernatural in her friend's life. How was she supposed to fulfill her duty as a wolf and protect the humans if she couldn't even shelter her best friend?

Nora was relieved when Topher finally came back, only to groan when he shrugged and showed his empty hands.

"Damn. That sucks. We can give you a ride home if you want," Colbie offered way too cheerfully.

"No. We'll just call an Uber."

"Honey, no Uber's going to pick this one up," Colbie said, gesturing to Annaliese right as she leaned over and began to puke again.

Poppy pursed her lips. "Yeah, that's not happening."

"I'll go get the car." Topher slipped away yet again.

Annaliese groaned Nora's name before she could protest further. She untwisted the water bottle cap and knelt by her friend, hating every aspect of this situation. Gabriel would murder her if he knew she was accepting help from vampires. Colbie looked way too pleased. Topher looked so unhappy that even unsuspecting humans walking by gave them a wide berth.

Why had Nora insisted on coming back to the Maker? This was so beyond stupid.

CHAPTER 5

Topher didn't love the thrilled smile on Colbie's face as he pulled up to the curb. His sister was practically vibrating with excitement. She neatly jumped over the stagnant water gathered in the gutter and climbed into the car. Poppy shook her head, amused, as she got into the passenger seat.

Topher rolled his window down when Annaliese's scent filled the car. Poppy shot Colbie a look and she repositioned the garbage bag around Annaliese, who was moaning again. Topher swallowed his guilt. He should have realized how Zayn would take his words. His friend and coworker had been turned so young he didn't know the true pain of a hangover. Zayn rarely cut people off when he should, a habit that earned him a lot of tips but led to more than one customer being carried out of the club. That or Lana sent one of them after the human to sober them up.

When the car's occupants were settled, Topher pulled out swiftly into traffic.

"Where am I headed?" he asked.

"Food," Annaliese grunted into her bag. Topher fought a smile. He hadn't expected that.

"Beautiful idea," Poppy said, pointing to the next right turn. Topher nodded and drove them in the direction of her favorite diner, Patty's. Annaliese seemed to perk up by the time they turned into the potholed lot. At least her head had come out of the bag and she was sipping her water.

"No one's going to bite me, right?" she whispered too loudly to Nora.

The smile edging Topher's lips died.

"No promises," Colbie whispered back with a wink before throwing open her door.

"Don't mind her," Poppy said.

Annaliese didn't seem to be listening anymore. Colbie's open door brought in the smell of greasy hamburgers and Annaliese scrambled for her seat buckle. She nearly passed for sober as she hurried inside, Nora on her heels.

"I like them," Poppy said, smiling at Topher. He grinned back but rolled his eyes to the roof of the car. This entire situation could only mean trouble.

"Aren't you going to get anything?" Annaliese asked. "It's on me."

"Your wallet was with your keys," Nora reminded her.

Annaliese's eyebrows bunched and she checked for her jacket, but she didn't say anything. She reached for one of the cups on the table and grabbed Topher's water. He quickly snatched it from her, careful not to spill any.

"Hey!"

"Thought you were opposed to the idea of vampire saliva," Topher said before taking a sip. Annaliese's eyes widened, fear temporarily breaking through the drunk haze, but it was forgotten when the waitress arrived with her, Poppy, and Nora's burgers. Poppy was addicted to the veggie patties here.

Even as she ate, Topher felt the werewolf watching him and Colbie closely. Colbie kept meeting his eyes and smiling, utterly content with the wary attention she received.

He was getting dizzy from shaking his head at her.

"You look better," Colbie said when their companions fell silent to eat. Topher looked down at his hands and noticed his nail still had blood under it. Usually, he kept cleaner than that. He popped it in his mouth and narrowed his eyes at his sister.

"Did you see Rebecca?" she pressed.

Topher nodded. "She's got a new job. Hoping to get her kids back soon."

Colbie's eyes warmed. "Good."

Topher knew she was trying to ease his conscience. He appreciated her effort, even if it made him want to squirm. "Guess what Tamera was wearing tonight."

"Bitch," Colbie muttered. It was practically a knee-jerk reaction at this point. Poppy snorted into her glass.

"You have to let it go," she said.

"But they're my favorite strappy red heels! She said she just wanted to borrow them," Colbie protested.

"Is the clothes stealing a vampire thing?" Nora asked pointedly. Topher had been thinking she might be too quiet for his sister, but after that comment, he liked her a bit more. Colbie's smile was dazzling. The werewolf dropped her eyes back to her plate.

Topher wasn't sure how he ended up next to the human girl with Nora on her other side and Poppy and Colbie across the table. He wasn't happy about it, especially when the girl fumbled her ketchup and shot a stream onto his hoodie sleeve.

"Sorry," she mumbled around a fry. She used another fry to clean some of the glob up and popped it into her mouth. A smile tugged at Topher's lips. He watched in dismay as the girl's expression went slack. She pressed closer to him on the booth, head tilting.

47

Topher's stomach turned. "You know what? I'll meet up with ya'll at the apartment." He stood and put his water in front of Colbie and out of Annaliese's reach.

"What? No!" Colbie began working herself into a pout. Topher put a hand up to stop her and shot a pointed look at the human still ogling him. Understanding cleared his sister's face.

"Fine. Call your girlfriend back while you're walking." Colbie brought out his phone. She must have grabbed it from the backseat and turned it on. "She's only called you eleven times."

"What, in the last two minutes?" he asked, tone as dry as he could get it. Colbie snorted.

"Just call her, Topher," Poppy said.

Topher shrugged and turned from the table. He pushed out the diner's doors and was hit by Lana's scent. Spiced like ground cinnamon with nothing to sweeten it. He tensed but continued walking. Maybe he'd been wrong to think she wasn't at the club to see him.

Lana leaned against the next building over. She wore a black, sleeveless turtleneck and red pants. Colbie once joked Lana didn't wear other colors because she was afraid of bloodstains. Topher hadn't laughed.

"Christopher," Lana said by way of greeting. She pushed off the wall and fell into step beside him.

"Lana."

"You friends with Gabriel's puppies now?"

"Not really. Colbie does her own thing. As you know." He let an edge of warning enter his tone.

Lana ignored it. "I have a job for you tonight."

Topher hated those words. Lana stepped up to a low sleet gray car parked on the curb and got in, leaving the door open for him to follow. Brady was already sitting passenger and turned with a greeting. A blissed-out human sat behind the

48

wheel. Topher could already feel himself pulling away from the situation. Letting himself disappear into the recesses of his mind. The place with memories of sunshine and Colbie's unmatched smile and monotonous school days. A time before needles and pills and blood and moonlight.

The drive to the job wasn't long, but it dragged. Topher came out of his imaginings long enough to note they were deep in vampire territory on Fourth street, outside Blue Blood. They parked in the back and were let inside by the burly bouncers. The pulsing music of the club was muffled. Every human lingering in the halls looked blissed. Some of their necks were bumped and mangled from too many years of careless fangs. Topher shut himself away from the sight and followed Lana up the stairs. He wished he were back at the diner, Colbie spouting ridiculous nonsense and Poppy grinning around her fries.

Lana burst through the black metal double doors at the top of the steps. A man was sitting on a chair in the middle of the VIP room in front of them. Connor Grace and Sarah Patter stood next to him, faces dark. The room was ripe with the smell of vampire recently turned; blood gone bad. Maddening thirst twisted the seated man's face.

"I saw a *demon*. It attacked me," the man gasped.

"Stop your lies. Who turned you?" Grace demanded.

The man shook his head. "It was the demon."

Lana sighed and turned to Topher. "Work your magic. We need answers."

Topher stalled long enough to bunch up his sleeves, heart twisting at the sight of the fresh ketchup stain. He met the man's terrified eyes and noted the swirl of shadows tattooed on the side of his neck. One of Umbras's men. At least he didn't recognize him. Topher braced himself and approached.

This would not be pleasant.

"Where are we taking you?" Poppy asked Nora as they left the diner.

Colbie paused and sniffed the air, her eyes narrowing. She got into the driver's seat without commenting but pulled out her phone to text someone.

"What's up?" Poppy asked.

"Nothing," Colbie muttered, watching her screen. She drummed her fingers on the steering wheel with her free hand. It was the first time all night her friend seemed to forget about Nora's presence.

"Um," Nora hesitated, glancing at Annaliese. The human girl looked ready to drop. "I can't bring her back to the Den like this."

"Her house?"

"Well…"

"Keys were in my jacket. Parents are out of town," Annaliese mumbled as she lay down in the backseat. Nora glared and shoved her friend to make room.

"Excellent," Colbie whispered. Her excitement sounded slightly forced as her head snapped up from her phone and she started the car.

Was it Topher? Poppy didn't want to press, but she worried about him. The bleak expression on his face when he'd charmed Annaliese wouldn't leave her mind. But they couldn't talk about it in front of a wolf.

"Our place then?" Poppy asked.

Nora didn't look particularly happy, but she didn't disagree. She rested her head against the window and huffed out a breath.

They drove home in silence.

"Topher isn't back yet," Colbie said as she exited the car in the lot in front of their apartment.

Poppy frowned. She didn't like the tense set of Colbie's shoulders one bit. What or who had she smelled outside the diner?

"Good. He's horrible," Annaliese muttered.

Poppy suspected between the food and her short nap on the way here, she was speaking less through drunkenness and more with genuine sentiment.

Colbie punched in their building code and straightened. Her smile was too sweet. "Hey, listen. You're going to have to cool it with the shit-talking my brother."

Annaliese's eyes narrowed. She drew herself up to her full height, which didn't help her much. The girl couldn't have been over five-three.

"Hey, listen," she said, drunken slur almost, but not quite gone. "He acts like an asshole. I'm going to call him one. He's free to call me whatever he wants in return."

Colbie pursed her lips, but her expression eased after a moment of thought. She opened the dirty glass door and started up the stairs to their apartment. "Fair enough. Just as long as it won't be a problem. And you understand if it does become one, I won't hesitate to charm you into playing nice."

Annaliese snorted. "Yeah, fine. Tell him to play nice too."

"This isn't necessary," Nora cut in. "We won't be seeing him or any of you enough for this to be a problem."

"I have a feeling otherwise." Colbie beckoned them all inside the apartment and shut the door. "Right, Popcorn?"

When the room's attention turned to her, Poppy shrugged and picked up the teacup she'd left on the counter. She looked at the still soggy dregs on the bottom. "Yeah. You two will be back. And another wolf. Our paths are linked."

"Another one of my pack?"

Poppy squinted into the cup. Reading leaves always gave her a headache. "I don't think so. All I can tell is the third presence is just as harmful as you two. Or equally not as harmful. Just linked. It's really not all that clear." She dumped the contents into the trash and rinsed out the cup.

"Since when do vampires read tea leaves?" Annaliese asked. She let out a yawn and walked up next to Poppy, drinking right from the kitchen sink faucet before Poppy could think to offer her a cup.

"I'm sure one of us has," Colbie said, coming out of Topher's room with two of his shirts. She threw one to each of their guests. Nora snatched hers out of the air. Annaliese just watched hers fall to the ground and left it there.

"I'm not a vampire," Poppy said.

It took Nora a beat to put it together. She gasped. "You're a witch?"

Annaliese's eyes widened, but when Poppy didn't elaborate, she shrugged. "Are you going to be up much later? I have class in the morning."

"You can use Topher's bed." Colbie gestured to the door she left open. Her tone darkened. "He won't be home for a while."

Why?

"And I can give you a ride to campus in the morning," Poppy said, shaking her anxious thoughts.

Annaliese shrugged in an accepting manner and moved toward Topher's room. She paused in the doorway. "Holy pillows and blankets."

"Oh yeah. He's a burrower." Colbie smiled fondly.

There was the sound of bedsprings as Annaliese got herself comfortable. Poppy felt a spark of jealousy. There had been a few nights where she couldn't sleep and crashed in Topher's room instead. His bed was legendary. His appreciation for comfort exceeded anyone else Poppy knew and his blankets always smelled like dryer sheets. Poppy suspected he had a smidge of OCD where laundry was concerned.

"You sure she's okay in there?" Nora asked.

Colbie dropped down on the couch, patting the cushion next to her for Nora. Poppy took the armchair.

"Yes. I don't know where he went, but he doesn't usually go to bed until eight or so." Poppy suspected Colbie was omitting something. She pulled out her own phone and texted Topher. *You good?*

"You really can't go out in the sun?"

Poppy studied Colbie's face as she talked to Nora. Colbie wasn't as prone to bouts of sadness as her brother and yet Poppy had never seen her so animated. Despite her missing brother, her smile was effortless and bright. Poor Nora was helpless under its glow.

"We can. Just like we can eat. It's just both experiences aren't nearly as pleasant as they once were. Topher fought the sleep schedule for a bit, but it's too hard to go against the instincts once they form." Colbie shrugged. "Want to watch something?"

Nora blinked at the change in subject. "Sure."

Colbie turned on an adult cartoon with aliens and a drunk grandpa. Poppy settled into the cushions, knowing she'd regret staying up so late but still not trusting the werewolf alone with her friend. She'd have to spike her coffee with a reviving potion in the morning.

Nora stayed on the opposite end of the couch from Colbie. Eventually, the werewolf couldn't keep her head up and drooped into the high arm of the sofa. It was then Poppy noticed the girl looked exhausted. That her expression had been pinched all night, only now evening out in sleep.

From that point, Colbie didn't even pretend to watch the show. She stared at Nora until Poppy felt like she was intruding and slipped into the bathroom to get ready for bed. When she came back out, Nora was covered with a blanket and Colbie had taken the armchair, still watching. Poppy ruffled her friend's bun on her way to her bedroom and Colbie glanced away just long enough to shoot her a smile.

"Topher okay?" Poppy whispered.

Colbie shrugged. "He's with Lana. Not much we can do."

"Did he text you?"

53

"No, but Brady did when I asked the group chat." They shared a helpless look. There wasn't anything to do but hate the situation. "Goodnight, Pop."

Poppy nodded and took herself to bed, thinking about Topher for too long before sleep claimed her.

CHAPTER 6

Nora woke from a hazy forest dream with a stiff neck and dry mouth. She sat up, hand going to her frizzy braid. A glance out the window confirmed it was still mostly dark out.

"Morning, gorgeous."

Nora jumped and found Colbie's shadowed form on the recliner. In the dim glow from the streetlight outside, Nora could see she'd changed into a cut-off sweatshirt and black biker shorts. Her bun was still in place, but now her face was scrubbed clean of makeup. A book slid off her lap as Colbie stretched and Nora noted how well vampires must be able to see in the dark. Would she have vision like that after her change?

"What are you doing up?" Nora asked. She felt like an idiot the instant the words slipped out.

"Well, my time it's only about seven pm."

"That was a stupid question."

Colbie smiled not unkindly. "How'd you sleep?"

"This couch is admittedly very nice."

"Isn't it? Topher picked it out."

Nora looked down and shifted the blanket. She couldn't

keep eye contact with Colbie long before her thoughts grew too confusing.

"Hungry?"

Always. "A bit."

"I'll see what Poppy has by way of breakfast food."

Colbie sprang up. Her movements were always so fluid. Nora caught herself staring as Colbie's cropped sweatshirt revealed the muscles and dips of her lower back multiple times as the vampire reached to open cabinets. Nora's hands twitched at the sight of soft-looking skin. She pulled out her phone to distract herself.

Three missed calls from Gabriel. A dozen messages from Matt.

She opened those first.

Where the hell are you?

Nor!

Nora Mora! Gabriel's been asking about you since 11. I'm covering for you, but he is not happy. I repeat, not happy.

Hey, so how are you going to make this up for me?

Nooooooooooooooooor!

I'm this close to going full hound dog and tracking you down.

Nora sent a quick message saying she was with Annaliese and accidentally fell asleep. She put her phone away. She wasn't ready to face her pack again yet. A vampire was making her breakfast.

Nora was such a failure.

"Bacon? Eggs? Toast? Cereal? Damn, Poppy buys herself a lot of food." Colbie's voice echoed a bit in the cupboard her face was in.

"Cereal is fine." The thought of watching Colbie cooking for her did strange things to Nora's chest. "Do you miss eating?" Again, Nora regretted her question instantly.

Colbie came back to the couch, juggling three boxes of cereal, milk, a bowl, and a spoon. She laid it all out on the coffee table and settled back into the cushions next to Nora, pulling her large hood up over her hair and stealing some of the blanket.

"So warm." She sighed. "And no. Not really," she cut a look at Nora as she weighed her next words. "Just... blood tastes better than food ever used to."

Nora's hand jerked as she poured her cereal.

"And it's nice not to worry about my weight. Liquid diet and all that," Colbie finished, patting her flat stomach. Her voice lowered, face as conflicted as Nora had seen it yet. "It's probably not healthy to be happy about that, but my weight used to consume my thoughts. That was worse."

Nora studiously poured her milk. "Doesn't it bother you?" she asked. "They're people. Not a diet."

Colbie picked at the fraying sleeve of her hoodie. It was a soccer sweatshirt with the state championship logo faded down the middle.

"Not as much as it does Topher. He's got a real complex about it. I stopped feeling bad about it when humans started asking me to drink from them. When the first man smiled and walked away like nothing happened, it was hard to regret. I made him happy. I got two drinks and felt warm for about three seconds. I pulled in the next person; I didn't even have to flex my charm. She thanked me. So, I guess the choice was think of myself as a monster or accept freely given energy and enjoy it. And I don't think I'm a monster."

"You don't?"

Colbie shook her head, a sad smile lingering on her lips. "Do you really think I am?"

"I don't know you."

"Do you want to?"

"No."

A pause. Colbie tugged on her hood strings, scrunching it around her face. Nora focused on her cereal so she wouldn't smile.

"Because I'm a girl."

Nora took a bite and didn't bother to respond.

"You know, you can talk to me. I make a good friend. We can be friends."

"No."

"Because I'm a vampire?"

Nora shrugged. Colbie sighed, loosened her hood, and drew up her feet. Nora barely concealed a flinch when the vampire stuck her cold toes under her thigh.

"Just talk to me," Colbie's voice was low and pleading. And something else.

"Are you trying to use your charm?" Nora could feel it pressing on her desires, but it was easy enough to brush aside.

"Told you it didn't work on your kind. I gave you that. Now you tell me something."

"Fine." Nora took another bite. Colbie's serene expression didn't falter, even when milk slipped out of Nora's mouth and she quickly wiped it off her chin. She swallowed. "Fine. My dad used to be alpha of the pack here. When he started, it was him, my mom, my aunts and uncles, and a few friends he'd made. By the time I was ten, there were forty of us. He gained power by aligning with the human gangs north of the river. As much as the humans were willing to hurt each other, they all agreed what the vampires did was unacceptable. Especially then, when drainings were more common." Colbie's toes wiggled, but she stayed quiet. Nora pressed on, suddenly needing this girl to understand.

"But he died two years ago. And my mom left. The pack was there for me. They're my family. I went to human high school and met Annaliese and even that friendship has gotten me into trouble a couple of times with them. They question my alliance if I spend too much time away from the Den. Packs have a structure. We have traditions. Our way of life doesn't work unless we follow pack law. Mates are for life unless hierarchy gets disrupted. And we need more members. Werewolves are a dying breed. My alpha has already hinted that I need a mate."

"He wants to *breed* you?"

"No, no. *No.* It's not like that." Colbie looked skeptical. Nora ignored it and pushed on, trying to make her understand. "The pack is everything to me. I won't mess it up."

"There's a reason those societal structures are greatly out of fashion."

Nora rolled her eyes. Her cereal was getting soggy. "We're wolves. We have the instincts of wolves. Once I make the change, I won't have any doubts. My animal brain will take precedence. It won't matter if humans are more progressive."

Colbie worried her bottom lip and Nora couldn't hold her gaze. She finished her cereal. She stilled when Colbie leaned forward and picked up her braid, trailing her fingers down the woven strands and taking out the hair tie. She undid the braid and began combing out the knots with her nails. Quick, sure movements. Nora's stomach swooped every time Colbie's fingers brushed against her scalp.

Colbie redid the braid much too soon. No, *not* too soon. Colbie shouldn't even be playing with Nora's hair. Once the hair tie was back in place, Nora leaned away.

"I'm sorry about your parents," Colbie said. And Nora recognized the braiding for what it was, an attempt at comfort. She picked up the neat plait and looked at it for a long moment.

"It doesn't matter. Not to you. My dad was killed by vampires."

"It shouldn't matter, maybe. But it does."

"Colbie," Nora started but paused when Colbie's eyes slid shut at the sound of her name. "Colbie, you have to—"

The apartment door burst open. Colbie didn't react, but Nora had been so engrossed in the conversation she hadn't heard Topher out in the hall. The spoon in her cereal bowl clattered against the rim when she startled.

"What are they still doing here?" Topher demanded, sounding almost strangled.

At this, Colbie's expression shifted, worry pinching her face. She untucked her toes and got off the couch. "Where have you been? You look like hell."

"Is that blood?" Nora demanded.

Topher paled further as he looked down at himself. He did indeed look terrible. Hair disheveled, eyes rimmed in red and bright with something like panic. He dropped what he'd been holding and grabbed at the fabric of his hoodie.

"No, it's ketchup," Colbie said, approaching her brother slowly and grabbing his arm. Colbie was reassuring him more than her, Nora realized. "Just ketchup, remember, Toph?"

Topher's throat bobbed with the force of his swallow. They were loud enough that Poppy woke up and came out of her room. Topher pulled away from Colbie and went to the bathroom. From his frenzied movements, Nora braced herself for the door to slam, but he clicked it shut gently.

"Alright, time for you to leave," Poppy declared, moving toward Topher's room to get Annaliese. Nora sprang over the back of the couch and barely caught herself when she stumbled on the blanket.

"No. I'll wake her up."

In Topher's room, Nora sat down heavily on the edge of his bed. She could just make out Annaliese's nose and mouth under the mound of pillows and blankets. When jostling the bed didn't wake her, Nora called her name until Annaliese sat up in a rush, hair wild around her face from being under the blankets all night.

Annaliese groaned and dropped her forehead into her hands. Her sweat stank like tequila.

"What time is it?"

Nora checked her phone, ignoring the new messages filling the lower portion of the screen. "It's 7:30."

"Head hurts like hell."

"I'm not surprised."

"Do you think Poppy was serious about vampire saliva being a hangover cure?"

"Don't even joke about that. Come on, we need to go."

"I have class," Annaliese said, pulling off layers of blankets and struggling out of the bed. She was still fully clothed; only her shoes kicked off in the middle of the floor.

"Poppy said she'd take you."

"How are you getting home?"

"Are you kidding? I can't go home smelling like this place." Nora didn't know if her packmates could smell vampires or not, but she wasn't willing to risk it.

Nora opened the bedroom door and Annaliese winced from the light as they entered the main room of the apartment.

"Hungry?" Poppy asked from the stove.

Annaliese pulled a face. "My mouth tastes like beef and onions."

"Interesting," Colbie muttered. She was still by the door and bent to pick up what Topher had dropped when he came in.

"My jacket!" Annaliese came fully awake and ran across the room to clutch it to her chest.

"Was that where he went off to? Why didn't he just say?" Poppy asked, glancing toward the bathroom. The shower was running on the other side of the door.

"I don't think so… Well, maybe at one point, but that's not why he looks so awful," Colbie answered. She tugged her hood lower and wrapped her arms around her stomach. Nora resisted the urge to put her own arms around Colbie to comfort her.

What the hell was happening?

"I'll take some eggs," Annaliese said. She put on her jacket and sat on one of the stools at the kitchen island. She fished out her keys and tossed them to Nora. "Go shower at my place if you can get to my car. Just pick me up at campus later, deal?"

"Deal." Keys in hand, Nora paused. "You sure you're okay here, Annaliese?"

"Yeah. Poppy's cool."

"Very cool," Colbie said. She still stood by the door. They held eyes as Nora reached for the handle. Colbie didn't move, just watched Nora leave, for once unsmiling.

Nora ran down the stairs and stepped into the parking lot as her phone started buzzing with another call from Gabriel. The sun was just beginning to rise.

She stopped short on the concrete steps. Annaliese's car was parked in the apartment lot. Apparently, Topher had made use of the keys in the jacket he found. Nora squinted up over her shoulder at the windows above. Who were these people?

When a still hungover Annaliese dropped Nora off at the Den after a lazy day of watching TV in Annaliese's basement while her friend studied, Nora was relieved to make it to her room with minimal pack interaction. Gabriel and Matt weren't mad about the missed calls and she was able to blame Annaliese's drunkenness for her absence. Unable to calm her thoughts, Nora soon found herself on her roof.

She watched the sunset for a bit, willing her mind to quiet at the sight. She didn't want to worry about killing vampires or what phase the moon was in. How close and yet how far away her change felt. She pulled out her phone and stared at the screen before opening her contacts. Vampire Colbie. Taking a deep breath and holding it in her chest, she pushed the phone icon.

Nora put the phone to her ear. Each ring was jarring, but the click of it being answered nearly prompted Nora to drop her phone into the bushes below.

"Well, this is a pleasant way to wake up," the vampire said. Her voice was soft and smoothed by sleep. Nora swallowed.

"Hi."

Colbie chuckled. "Hey, yourself." The vampire let out a moan across the line that raised the hair on Nora's arms.

"What are you doing?" The question came out sharp with panic. Nora cringed.

Colbie laughed. "Stretching. Relax. That is unless you want to—"

"Stop. No."

Colbie laughed again. Nora pressed her free hand to her cheek when she felt it lifting in a smile of her own. The expression felt foreign. Everyone in the pack told her they missed her smile.

"Do phone calls mean you changed your mind? Am I going to see you again?"

Nora swallowed. If she was honest with herself, she hadn't stopped thinking about Colbie all day. Colbie's lips. Colbie's concern for her brother. Colbie believing being a vampire didn't make her a monster. Colbie's toes under her thigh and fingers in her hair. Colbie. Colbie. Colbie.

Nora had never felt like this before.

"We shouldn't."

"Why not? We already established you weren't going to kill me."

"You decided that. And I haven't changed my mind."

"So why call?"

Nora picked at the hole in her jeans, pulling forth the excuse she'd come up with. Hoping with equal measure that it would fail or succeed. "We should tell Poppy and Annaliese it won't happen. They shouldn't be friends."

"Tell them what won't happen?"

"They hung out on campus today. They think we're all friends now."

It had felt easy at Colbie's apartment. At least, until Topher came back. Nora thought with a pang about Colbie and Poppy's familiarity. Their generosity with their space. The comfort they felt together, openly discussing their different species. No hatred. No us vs. them. No painful memories. It was how Nora felt when she escaped to Annaliese's house. Nora frowned at the roof beneath her.

"Well, I like that. Poppy needs more daytime friends. Although I think you already know, friends wasn't exactly what I had in mind for *us*. I'll take it. It's a start, at least."

Nora caught herself wanting to smile again. The fluttering in her stomach wasn't entirely unpleasant, even if it was unfamiliar. She yanked at a thread in her sweater, snapping it.

"Nora?" Colbie's voice went low. Nora pulled her knees up and hugged them to her chest.

"Yeah?" she copied Colbie's tone.

"I think we both know something's here. Please try. Don't be scared of me."

Nora drew in a shaky breath.

"I notice you aren't disagreeing with anything I'm saying." She could *hear* Colbie smiling.

Nora yanked the phone away from her ear and ended the call. She dropped her forehead onto her knees and squeezed her eyes shut, trying to expel the image of Colbie's smile.

Her phone vibrated.

Vampire Colbie: You still aren't disagreeing. Have a goodnight, Nora. I'll be thinking about you too. Call anytime you like

CHAPTER 7

Nora lasted two days in her resolve to stay away from Colbie.

She was determined to throw herself into her hunt and spend time with her pack. That was what was important right now. She'd waited her whole life for this, for the moment she changed and ran under the moon as a member of her pack.

So why couldn't she get the vampire out of her mind? Why was her stomach in constant knots, making eating difficult?

Gabriel quickly became insufferable, demanding to know her plans for capturing a vampire and shooting down her ideas. She'd thought to hit a different club as they were the only places vampires were guaranteed to show.

"No, no, no," he shook his head so fast his shoulder-length hair fanned out. "Clubs are too risky. The vampires swarm them and there are too many humans in the way. You won't make it out alive. You shouldn't even be in their territory. They'll smell you a mile away."

"They won't. That's why clubs are better! So many other smells mask my scent."

"No."

"Then what's your idea?"

"Find one on the street. Follow it. Learn its habits. Break into its home the day before the full moon and bring it here. You have weeks to come across one and start hunting, Nor. Take your time with this. You're too impulsive. Don't let that lead you to mistakes. Vampires are too clever for that."

Matt stepped in at this point, wrapping Nora's hand in his.

"I'll help you find one. We can walk neutral streets and parks. Sometimes the weaker vampires feed in those areas."

"Better yet," Gabriel continued, "take out one of the new unregistered, unclaimed vampires we've seen a rise of. We've been doing our best to take care of them and the makers insist it isn't them," Gabriel rolled his eyes, clearly not believing their claims, "If you can find one of those monsters, you'll be saving human lives."

Nora thought of the night Gabriel killed his vampire. One of Sara Patter's more notorious seconds who drained a human the week before. He'd managed to pull the vampire from his car in the middle of Fourth Street. Right in front of her club, Blue Blood.

Nora didn't want to join the pack because she'd found a vampire too weak to be accepted by its own people. She wanted to look strong and sure like Gabriel had when he brought the minor maker before her father. She wanted Gabriel to look at her the same way her father looked at him. Well, she wanted her father to give her that look. She had to settle for Gabriel.

She was tired of being treated like a child no matter how many hours she spent training with Gabriel, Matt, Lupe, and Patrick. Every minute she lifted, ran, and sparred came undone the moment her new body stumbled or knocked something over. She didn't want to be a source of amusement anymore.

Worse, she knew it wasn't her clumsiness that made the pack treat her like they did. They saw her as fragile. The memory of her breaking after her father's death was always foremost in their minds.

She stood from the couch, the air getting too heavy to breathe in the Den.

"I need to walk," she said. Matt moved to go out with her, his hand still holding her own. "By myself."

She jerked out of his grip more forcefully than she intended. The closer they got to the next full moon, the stronger she became. Thinking about how strong she'd be after the change made her heart pound. She was restless with anticipation. She would show them she was a true Morales. Hurting still, but no longer broken.

Rush hour traffic hoping to avoid the stalemate settled on the main roads blew through the neighborhood as Nora set off walking. She didn't have a car. The pack had one and Gabriel held the key, but everyone else was on their own. Most members had odd jobs. Others were paid well for their protective services. With no skills in the real world, Nora had resigned herself to living off pack funds until she changed and got hired as a wolf like the rest of her pack.

For now, she had Annaliese. She pulled up their messages.

What are you up to?

Home. Asleep. Zzzzzzz

Come get me.

What part of zzzzz don't you get? I need naps. I have a test in a couple days. My head hurts from all the studying.

I need out of here. Gabriel and Matt are driving me crazy

They can't help how much they love you

Nora cringed reading that. *Please, A. I'll owe you one.*

You already owe me a million. A pause and another message. *More like a billion. Where are you?*

Nora smiled and detoured to the nearest park, picking out a bench to wait for her friend. She watched the humans milling around. A man with a tiny dog on a leash had to stop every ten feet while someone exclaimed over it. The dog growled at her as he passed. Nora swallowed the urge to snarl back. That was a first.

67

By the central fountain, a couple was kissing passionately. Nora's eyes caught on them when their heads turned and she realized it was two women. Her cheeks warmed, watching how their bodies seemed melded together, the ease of their smiles between kisses. Nora was flooded with a strange sense of inadequacy and dropped her gaze.

A man and woman walked by, hand in hand. She felt nothing watching them together. That wasn't new. But the lingering desire to examine, to study, the two women kissing was.

She put her fingers to her lips. Wolves weren't ashamed of physical desire. She'd been raised surrounded by it, understanding it. Naked bodies before and after changes had been a part of life. Open affection in wolf and human form a near-daily occurrence. She'd kissed Gabriel before he was alpha. She'd kissed Matt once before his change when they got drunk on the roof under a full moon while the pack was out running. She'd slept with soft human boys she met through Annaliese and school, drunk off the idea of a life in their world. She wasn't a stranger to kisses and more. But the intensity hadn't been there. There hadn't been *need*.

And it definitely hadn't left her stomach knotted two days later.

Nora jumped when a car honked behind her. She ripped her eyes away from the kissing couple to find Annaliese parked behind her. She ran to the car, feeling intrusive and ashamed.

She almost groaned when Annaliese glanced from the women at the fountain and back to her. She'd noticed her staring. Face burning, Nora waited for the teasing. Or a sarcastic remark. Or just a bored eyebrow raise.

"You know," Annaliese started as she shifted into gear. "It's okay."

That was so unexpected that Nora sat quietly for a moment. Her throat felt tight. She looked down at her interlocked fingers and cleared it.

"It's not okay." When the words came out, they sounded miserable.

In a rare moment of affection, Annaliese set her hand on Nora's arm. "I know your pack is pretty stuck in the past and you've been ingrained with the values of pack structure and all that. But with me, with nearly all of New Brecken, it's safe. It's okay. It's more than okay. You know what I mean, right?"

Nora nodded, her twisting stomach relaxing under the assurance in her friend's steady gaze, the pressure of her hand squeezing Nora's forearm. Annaliese had never shied from Nora's wolf half. She hadn't blinked when Nora came to her, destroyed from night terrors and plagued by memories of her father's death. Numb from her mother's abandonment. Annaliese had been constant and reliable. Her human friend rarely spoke about her history, but she was right. No matter how dark Nora's world felt, Annaliese was safe. She was the reminder Nora needed that most of the world was safe for her.

Nora sighed and settled back in her seat.

"Where are we going?" Annaliese asked.

"I don't care. I just had to get away from the pack."

"You don't want to go to the Maker?"

Nora considered. She did want to go. The very thought breathed life back into the butterflies in her stomach. Or they could go to Annaliese's house. Hide out in the large basement that was her friend's bedroom. Watch TV, eat junk food, and shut off her brain while Annaliese studied and got a good night's sleep before her upcoming test. She knew which option Annaliese would prefer. Nora's chest warmed because Annaliese had offered to go to the club anyway.

"Let's just hang out at your place."

"Cool." Annaliese took the next left and Nora turned to look out the window. Her mind drifted back to the kissing couple. She thought about Colbie smiling at her under the lights of the club, teeth white, gums slicked with blood. The way Colbie danced against her. The strip of skin showing across her taunt stomach.

Nora caught her train of thought and turned to Annaliese. "How have classes been going?"

Annaliese started at Nora's abrupt and too loud question. She took her eyes off the road just long enough to raise an eyebrow at Nora before answering. This second semester was proving harder than her first, but she'd made a couple of friends through studying with Molly Hendricks and Poppy at least.

Nora paid attention like she'd be tested later on Annaliese's response. She needed the distraction.

An hour and two empty pints of ice cream later, Nora's phone buzzed with a text message. She was tempted to ignore it. It was probably Matt again, but Annaliese looked up from her notes, curious.

Nora opened the message and her cheeks warmed. The picture showed the TV in Colbie's apartment. Poppy's back took up the foreground, notes spread across the coffee table in front of her. On the screen was a grainy, old horror movie. The man in the picture sported hideous tufts of hair and foaming fake canine teeth. His arms hung awkward and elongated at his sides. His clothes were a shaggy mess of a costume and he appeared to be howling at the oversized moon.

Another staccato buzz. *You*, Colbie wrote.

Annaliese snorted, reading over Nora's shoulder. "Have her ask what Poppy got on number twenty-three. I don't think I'm doing it right."

Nora complied. "She said Poppy isn't there yet." Another buzz and Nora's heart swooped. "She said we should come over to study. Poppy needs help."

"Sick." Annaliese jumped off the bed and stuffed her notes and books into her backpack.

Nora hesitated just long enough for Annaliese to make an

impatient sound. Heart racing, she texted Colbie back. *We're coming.*

Colbie's response was lightning fast. *I love chemistry.*

Nora smiled at her phone.

Topher glanced at Zayn when the smell hit him. Zayn's stormy expression confirmed he wasn't imagining things. Topher served another round of shots and sniffed the air again, looking to his left where the scent originated. Sammy was serving down the bar, but she was even less gifted with her senses than Colbie. She hadn't noticed anything unusual yet.

Zayn made his way closer, pouring generously in his haste.

"What are they doing here?" he hissed.

Topher shrugged, frowning. Some of the humans' enthusiasm to get his attention died out when he made that face.

"Does Lana know?"

Topher sniffed again, filtering out the scents until he found their maker's. "She's with them."

"Does she need us?"

Topher hoped not. "Someone will get us if she does. She has Brady with her now and Jaeger is close by. There are only two wolves."

Zayn pursed his lips and turned back to the crowd of humans shouting over the music. More than anything, Topher wished these people, most here because they already suspected the club was run by vampires, realized they didn't have to shout for him to hear them. Thursday nights were half off rum and Cokes and the bar had been bustling since seven-thirty. His ears had been ringing since eight.

Topher continued serving drinks, sharing looks with Zayn and keeping an eye on the back entrance to the stairs. In the rooms above, Lana was meeting with members of Nora's pack. He had no idea what such a meeting meant, but it couldn't be good. Had Nora told them about Colbie? The thought was chilling.

Amira came up to the bar with a significant look. Topher smelled weed on her, but she was otherwise clean. Topher didn't want to be slowed and muddled tonight, though. He shook his head. She sighed and went in search of someone else.

Zayn perked up when Lana, Brady, and the two wolves came down the stairs and passed in front of the bar. Topher made eye contact with the larger wolf. He had shoulder length, dark hair and mismatched eyes, blue and brown. Topher kept his face arranged in a glare, letting the other man break eye contact first and tracking their progress out of the bar.

"I said rum and Coke!" the customer across the bar roared. Topher turned his glare on the human, who stumbled back a step. Indignation was quickly replaced by terror.

Lana said goodbye to her guests and approached Topher's section. Her presence made humans cringe away, clearing her a stool without a word. Topher barely spared her a nod when she sat and served another customer first. A brief show of disrespect he would assuredly suffer for later, but it felt too good at the moment.

"Christopher," she said. Breezy, unbothered. He prepared himself.

"Lana."

"I need a drink."

Topher pointed at the woman on Lana's left. "Vodka." The man on her right. "Jack."

Lana sniffed and turned to the woman, who went still—immediately taken by Lana's powerful charm. Topher looked away as Lana drank deeply. When the woman sagged, Brady appeared out of the crowd and helped her away, keeping the woman from protesting with his charm. He would take the blissed human upstairs to recover from the blood loss and Lana's potent saliva high.

Lana's eyes went glossy as the alcohol in the human's blood hit her system. She sighed. "The wolves have agreed to attend the meeting. Things are falling into place."

Topher didn't respond, but Lana had his full attention. Just like she wanted. But *what* meeting? She wagged a finger at him. "Watch your back, Christopher. After your showing on Monday, we've gotten attention from the Big Three."

Topher tried to keep his face mild, but Lana smiled when she saw how much her words bothered him.

"This is what it takes for our answers, darling. Don't say I didn't warn you."

Lana stood and went back to the stairs. Topher gripped the edge of the bar, knowing if he picked up a bottle right now, he'd probably shatter it.

He turned to Zayn. "I'm going to take my break now."

He found a boy his age stumbling around, the smell of tequila heavy and intoxicating in his blood. In seconds he was enthralled in Topher's charm, waiting and expectant. Head tilted and smile edging his lips. Tequila had been Topher's drink of choice when he was human. The smell of it reminded him of escape. Of empty bottles on the pavement. Of worse and worse decisions. Needles and pills. A time when it was cold. A time spent lost. Without Colbie. Yet, a time with— Topher couldn't think about that now.

He clenched his fists and stumbled out into the night, leaving the boy disappointed behind him. He got into one of the taxis idling on the curb.

"Give me your wrist." The man didn't hesitate and let out a sigh as Topher cut the delicate skin and drank, letting the nicotine from the cigarette still in the man's hand flood his veins.

He grabbed the pack and the man's lighter before he left the cab, commanding the man not to pick up a passenger for at least an hour. The man nodded and settled his head back, blissed and content to sit and ride the high. Topher lit a cigarette, smoking it down to the filter and pretending he was getting a slight buzz from the stick and not the blood he just drank. The habit itself was relaxing. Familiar. Human.

Topher smoked two more before returning to the club. Zayn wrinkled his nose at the smell but didn't comment. Tamera came in soon after and Zayn started counting out his till. Topher turned back to the bar. Just three more hours and he was off. He could survive three more hours. He'd survived much worse.

CHAPTER 8

Colbie insisted they wait in the parking lot. Poppy hung back and shook her head at her friend's antics, especially when Colbie pretended to throw herself in front of Annaliese's car just before she braked.

Laughing, Colbie ran around to Annaliese's window. "Poppy said she's hungry. Want to get food before we start this study session?"

"Sure?"

Colbie waved Poppy over and they climbed into the backseat.

"Where to?" Annaliese asked.

"Patty's?" Poppy suggested.

"That diner from the other night?"

When Poppy confirmed, Annaliese started driving that way.

"Popsicle, you eat so many hamburgers you're going to give yourself a heart attack."

Poppy crossed her arms. "I don't think the rules are the same with veggie patties."

"Same grease. It can't be good for you." Colbie jiggled the button to roll her window.

Poppy snorted. "Stop fidgeting. God, you need to eat."

"What? And get more energy?" Colbie stuck her tongue out and leaned between the front seats. "Annaliese! Unlock me!"

Annaliese jumped when Colbie shouted in her ear. "Sorry. My little sister is always playing with her window. She's climbed out before."

"Same." Colbie continued pushing the button until Annaliese found the right switch on her door to unlock them. Colbie rolled her window down and stuck her head out immediately. Poppy watched Annaliese and Nora exchange a look. It was tangible in the air how much Colbie's liveliness upset the established balance of their friendship. Poppy could understand. Colbie took a minute to get accustomed to.

Annaliese drove them toward the diner and Poppy called ahead to place their order to go. They were nearly there when Poppy realized Colbie had pulled her outside in such a rush that she'd forgotten her bag.

"Shit. Do you have money, Colbie?" she asked.

"No...."

"I can cover you," Annaliese said.

"No need, just swing by the Maker. It's close and Toph will spot us," Colbie said.

Annaliese and Nora shared another look, but Annaliese passed the diner and went on to Fourth. Colbie directed Annaliese around to Lana's private lot. Annaliese slid into a spot, shoulders tense as she shifted into park.

Poppy looked over at Colbie, who smiled back and made no move to leave the car, though she was closest to the entrance and it was her idea.

Poppy sighed. "I'll be right back."

The line was nearly wrapping the building, but the bouncer gave Poppy a nod. He stopped her before she could get inside.

"Tell Topher we got two bachelorette parties coming in. He's the only guy behind the bar tonight."

"No Zayn?"

"He just got off."

Poppy ducked inside and elbowed her way to the bar. She could see the vibrant life energy hanging in the air, casting the club in a blue glow that begged her to draw it in. It filled Poppy's lungs and pulsed through her veins. She drank it up but was careful not to absorb too much. She didn't want to start glowing again. Topher had given her enough of an earful last time.

Topher nodded when she reached the bar, his face the stiff mask he wore around humans. He worked his way closer, hands moving a little too quickly to pass as human as he mixed and poured drinks. Tamera came in from the back carrying a keg, making it look too easy for her small frame. How anyone didn't immediately know they were vampires was beyond Poppy. In a practiced dance, Topher skirted out of Tamera's way and planted himself in front of Poppy. He looked tense, eyes skipping down the bar. Topher's gaze rested briefly on the boy next to her. He had startlingly dark brown eyes for his blond hair. Probably dyed, but it worked. Poppy eyed him, checking for the threat Topher might be seeing.

Topher was still looking at him when he asked, "What's up, Jalapeño Popper?"

Poppy laughed. "That one might be a stretch."

"It's better than Blow Pop." Topher shrugged, finally giving her his full attention. He pressed his lips together to keep from smiling, but his eyes twinkled. The boy went quiet and leaned toward Topher.

"I need some cash," Poppy said quickly, hoping Topher wouldn't notice his slipping charm. She hated the way his face shuttered when it happened.

Of course he noticed. The smile left his eyes, but his voice was still teasing. "Colbie's been a bad influence on you."

"She rushed me out the door. We're going to go pick up

food at Patty's and this was closer than going back home. We just forgot."

Topher shook his head at her but turned toward the tip jar kept on the back wall between the registers. He said something to make Sammy laugh as he counted and turned back with a handful of bills.

Poppy shoved them in her pocket.

"Be careful, okay? Watch Colbie. We had some wolves in here just a bit ago. She outside still?"

"Um, yes. In the car." Topher nodded and Poppy debated telling him who his sister was in the car with. It didn't seem fair to worry him further. "Muscles says two bachelorette parties are incoming."

Topher checked the dance floor. "Where's Zayn when you need him?"

Tamera was scooping ice and heard him. "I think Oliver came to meet him. Good luck getting him back behind the bar now. It's all you, babe."

Poppy felt her smile falter. She'd never noticed before how comfortable Topher was with Lana's other vampires. Poppy always thought of Topher, herself, and Colbie as a unit. It was disconcerting to realize Topher belonged to other people. A group of friends he did all he could to keep separate from Poppy and Colbie. Only Zayn was allowed to overlap.

Just then, Poppy was swarmed by the bridal party. Topher managed to wave Poppy goodbye before she ducked out of their way, the burst of excited energy from the women making her head spin.

Poppy kept holding in her laugh, especially when Annaliese made eye contact with her over their mess of chemistry notes. They both glanced at the couple on the couch and back to their papers, lips pressed together and eyes shining with mirth.

Colbie was relaxed as could be on the couch behind them, but Nora sat so stiff and awkward that Poppy felt sorry for her. Even though it was hilarious. And adorable.

Colbie had her toes tucked under Nora's leg and was painting her fingernails, going over the black with a coat of shimmering silver. The TV provided background noise, but Colbie wasn't even pretending to watch and Nora looked too distracted to be taking much of anything in.

"I thought this wasn't going to keep happening," Colbie said in a low voice, breaking the silence that had lasted on the couch for half an hour. Annaliese and Poppy's pencils froze as they strained their ears.

"It won't. Annaliese needed to study," Nora answered. In tandem, Poppy and Annaliese realized how obviously they were listening and picked back up with their writing.

"You couldn't stop thinking about me either," Colbie stated. Poppy wished once again she possessed even half the confidence Colbie did. It was genuinely staggering sometimes.

Nora crossed her arms but didn't respond. Annaliese was fighting another smile.

Poppy took pity on the werewolf. "I'm confused on this one," she said, shifting her paper so Annaliese could see.

Annaliese walked her through the steps and Nora and Colbie fell silent. They finished the problem and Poppy was surprised to see it was the last in the review packet. She yawned and stretched her arms up.

"Anyone up for something sweet?"

"I'll have whatever you have simmering on the stove. It smells fantastic," Nora said.

Poppy cut a glance toward her sleeping drought. "That's not for you."

Colbie snorted. "Don't they teach you anything in the pack?" she asked, exasperated. "You can't just go around drinking potions."

Nora scowled. "I didn't know it was a potion."

Poppy remembered the day the wolves moved in down the street from her childhood home. Her mother watched them close, refreshed her wards, told her daughters to stay away, but eventually deemed the pack was not a threat. And the wolves really were clueless. They were so obsessed with vampires that they didn't notice the coven of witches right under their noses. Considering that they'd taken it upon themselves to police the vampires, Poppy was shocked Nora seemed to know as little about Colbie and Topher as she did Poppy. Nora had thought Colbie charmed her when they first met. Poppy found it sweet but also pitied Nora for how much she had to figure out.

"Unless you want to sleep like the dead, I suggest you don't drink that one. Or any of the vials Poppy keeps in her room. Off-limits."

Poppy smiled, noting the protective edge in Colbie's voice as she instructed Nora. Poppy went to the kitchen area and opened the cabinet, digging around for something to soothe her sweet tooth.

"How does it work then? Your magic? Do all witches use potions?" Nora asked.

"No." Poppy tried to put enough firmness into the word not to invite further questions.

"Which coven are you from? Why don't you live with them?" Nora tried. There were two known in the city, where werewolves, vampires, and even humans took their business. Poppy wasn't from one of the known ones. Tension between the covens was at an all-time high, forcing those who didn't want to get involved into hiding.

And now Mother Kallow was running for mayor. Her platform didn't mention her magical prowess, but it was common knowledge. The other covens were angry and fearful about what this exposure could mean. It was all made worse by the fact that she had Solas's backing, one of the three most powerful vampires in the city.

Poppy had no desire to get into the politics.

She ignored Nora's question and grabbed a pack of store-bought cookies before going to sit on the couch. Colbie dropped her feet to the floor and scooted over to make room, edging closer to Nora. Nora's back straightened impossibly further.

Annaliese reached back and grabbed a handful of cookies before getting up and sitting in the armchair. "I'm guessing this means you're done with studying?"

"Yeah, I think we've got it." They settled in to watch TV, passing the cookies back and forth until two rows were empty. Nora might have finished off an entire one by herself.

Poppy let out another yawn and glanced at the clock. "I'm going to get some sleep," she announced. Annaliese woke with a start. Poppy hadn't even noticed the girl had drifted off.

"I'm half tempted to pass out in Topher's bed again. It might have been the best sleep of my life," Annaliese said.

Colbie laughed. "Go for it. He doesn't mind."

"Really? He doesn't strike me as the kind who likes his space invaded."

"He doesn't care," Colbie insisted, raising an eyebrow at Annaliese for questioning her knowledge of her brother or possibly for the concern in her voice.

"Who cares if he cares?" Annaliese proclaimed, catching on and going toward the bedroom. She stopped at the door to wink at Nora, who looked absolutely betrayed.

"I'll give you a ride to class in the morning," Poppy called. Annaliese shot her a thumbs up and went inside. Once again, Poppy swallowed her jealousy.

Poppy took a quick shower, deciding she could go another day without washing her hair and keeping it away from the spray. She readied for bed and left the bathroom in her favorite robe. Colbie had retucked her toes by the time Poppy went to the kitchen to pour her potion into multiple vials, leaving one out for Topher and carrying the rest with her. After an exchange of goodnights, she shut herself in her room.

Poppy loved her room. She loved her life in this apartment. She still couldn't believe her luck at finding the ad the West siblings put up on Facebook: *Vampires looking for roomie. We only bite sometimes.*

Now she knew Colbie would have made the post, Topher likely laughing and shaking his head as he let her get away with whatever she wanted. Poppy was the only person who had responded to their ad. She'd been desperate by that point.

Topher and Colbie had taken one look at the car full of plants Poppy showed up with and started planning how to make it work. She remembered standing there in stunned silence as they both took a pot and helped her unload, bouncing ideas the whole time. Her room was now lined with two layers of shelves, the top one draped and cramped with what Topher called her personal jungle. Glowing blue vials strung from the ceiling held a complex brew to keep the indoor plants alive. Underneath the plant shelf were rows and rows of potions, liquid, and powder, most concocted from the plants thriving above them. Poppy possessed a green thumb and a way with brewing that surpassed all her sisters, even if she did worse with all other forms of magic.

She balanced the new vials in an empty section and made quick work of watering her herbs, flowers, and vines, whispering magic words of growth as she worked her way around the room. In the far corner was the stash of chemicals she'd stolen from the labs at school, the elements and substances for an experiment she had begun playing with. She'd yet to test any of her chemically mixed potions, but by using magnesium in her sunlight brew, she was half sure she could make it flash even brighter when exposed to air.

With everything in order, she curled up in bed. Mouse, the black cat Topher had gotten her after she first complained about avoiding cliches, jumped up to join her. He made himself comfortable on her stomach. The cat hated company and could almost always be found sleeping in Poppy's laundry hamper. She loved him.

"I was right, Mouse. Margot would be proud of me. I'm rarely right when I try to read tea leaves, but I think those two will be around for a while."

But who was the third person in the leaves? The other wolf who would enter their lives? And would they be a change for better or worse? Poppy nestled Mouse closer and tried to think of wards and other forms of protection she might use to keep Colbie, Topher, and herself safe. She would guard this new life of hers at all costs.

CHAPTER 9

Colbie wiggled her toes for attention once they were alone. "How have you been?" she asked.

"Fine," Nora barely stopped herself from biting the word out. Nerves left her irritable.

"Are you still pretending we aren't friends?"

"We aren't friends."

Colbie wiggled her eyebrows. Nora fought a smile. How did she go so quickly from forgetting how to smile to working to keep one off her face?

"Because I'm a vampire?"

"Stop asking me that."

"I'm just trying to understand. Or maybe get you to understand. You called me. Now you're here. You don't hate me."

Nora sighed and dropped her head back on the couch. "That's the problem. I should hate you."

"Because I'm a vampire."

"Yes!"

"It's not like I chose this."

"Sure. You didn't choose to join the most powerful group of people in the city."

"I didn't." Nora looked at her, but for once, Colbie's eyes

were down. She pretended to check if her nails were dry. "I was attacked."

"Who attacked you?"

"Secret." Colbie still wasn't looking at her. "So, what do you like to do in your free time?"

Nora sighed. "We can't be friends."

"We won't know unless we try."

"I don't want to be your friend," Nora said, wincing when her voice wavered.

Colbie slowly looked up and searched Nora's face. She lifted a hand, giving Nora time to back away before she brushed her knuckles down Nora's cheek. Her fingers were so cold, but Nora couldn't lie to herself any longer. That wasn't the reason she shivered.

"Nora—"

"Don't," Nora jerked out of Colbie's reach and drew in a sharp breath. She was suddenly very sure she was about to cry. Since her father's death, tears were always so close to the surface. Nora hated it. She blinked hard and squeezed her hands together.

Colbie studied her for a long moment. Nora struggled to hide her embarrassment. The vampire moved slowly again, untucking a foot and sliding it behind Nora's back. She grabbed Nora's shoulders and gently pulled Nora into her chest, lowering them to lie on the couch. Nora's thought went to her weight, the hours of training behind her dense, muscular build. The way she'd been eating non-stop for weeks as her body prepared for the physical toll of the change. She didn't want to crush Colbie. She tried to balance on the elbow between Colbie and the couch, but the other girl's arms tightened, squeezing Nora to her chest, solid and sure.

"It's okay, Nora. I got you. I want to have you."

"This can't happen," Nora whispered.

"Then leave."

Nora told herself to get up. To forget about this strange

vampire girl who looked at the world and challenged it with all the confidence Nora had been missing since everything rocked so violently two years ago. Who looked at Nora like she was something to be reckoned with. Something intense and special. Not like something fractured and ready to shatter.

She should go.

"I can't." Nora's voice choked off. She relaxed into Colbie's chest and let herself cry in frustration and painful hope. Colbie waited, stroking her hair and picking through the knots. Occasionally she lifted her head closer and Nora suspected she was getting smelled but didn't comment.

The tears eventually stopped, but Nora didn't move. She liked how it felt in Colbie's arms. Liked it more than she would ever have expected. She would probably be kicked out of the pack for this. Would even Matt forgive her? She didn't know. At that moment, she didn't care.

"Better?" Colbie asked.

Nora shook her head and shifted, putting them chest to chest as she snuggled closer. Colbie pressed a firm kiss into Nora's hair and she let out a shaky sigh. She relaxed completely when Colbie's short nails scratched gentle, lazy strokes down her back.

They lay in silence for a long time. Nora's thoughts shifted to the time they had spent parked in front of the Maker, waiting for Poppy to come back with cash. She'd been replaying the scene all night.

She had kept looking at Colbie's reflection in the side mirror. While they waited, Colbie rested her head half out the window on her crossed arms. The hungry look in her eyes as she watched humans make their way through the line had been unsettling. The wind shifted the loose curls coming out of her bun.

"I smell wolf," she'd said.

"Me?" Nora asked.

"No, not as good as you smell. But similar. Your pack, I'd guess."

"Maybe they just walked by?" Nora inhaled deeply but couldn't pick up the scent herself.

"Maybe." But Colbie hadn't sounded convinced.

Suddenly, Colbie perked up, shoving almost her entire torso out the window as a group came out of the club and huddled to vape and smoke. "OLIVER!"

Her shout drew the attention of one of the white guys huddled. He jumped away from the group and ran at the car with his arms wide. Colbie nearly fell out the window when he reached them. They exchanged a tight hug.

"Hey, babe!" He ruffled her bun as she slid back into her seat. He leaned down to look inside. In a stage whisper, he asked, "Is that wolf girl?" Then he met Annaliese's eyes and blinked. "Hi, Annaliese!"

"Uh, hi," Annaliese looked as startled as Nora felt.

"Oliver! How do you know Annaliese?"

By then, another boy from the huddle had made his way over. Nora recognized him as one of the bartenders. He met her eyes and pulled Oliver away from the car with a snarl, wrapping a protective arm around his waist.

"I'm good, Zayn. Colbie won't let anything happen." Even so, Oliver leaned into Zayn with a pleased expression.

"Maybe, but that's my job."

Oliver rolled his eyes, but his lips quirked into grin his boyfriend couldn't see.

Colbie looked at the club with new interest. "Are you both sticking around?"

"No, just came to pick Zayn up. Place looks popping, though."

"Have you eaten?" Colbie asked the bartender.

"Not for a bit," Zayn said. His arm tightened around Oliver. Nora noted the skull tattoo on his forearm, the black shaded in smooth lines into his dark skin. It looked familiar.

"I was going to wait," Colbie opened her door. "Want to hit the alley, though?"

Zayn nodded. His shoulders relaxed when they turned from the car and Nora. His laugh bounced back to them when Colbie jumped onto Oliver's back and the boy took off at full gallop, only to stumble when Colbie used her charm to make a human in line follow them.

Annaliese was stunned. "That was weird."

"You can say that again. How do you know him?"

"I think Oliver said hi to Poppy in the library the other day. I'm surprised he remembered my name."

As if conjured by her name, Poppy came back, looking around in a panic when she didn't see Colbie. "Where'd she go?"

"She ran off with Oliver and Zayn?"

Poppy's shoulders relaxed. "Oh, okay. They'll be back soon."

She got in and slid over to her seat. Nora twisted to look at her. "How does Colbie know humans? Are they from here?"

"They are, but they know Oliver through Zayn."

"How do they know Zayn?"

Poppy had given Nora a weird look. "He's another one of Lana's. Couldn't you tell?"

Nora stayed quiet, turning to face forward again. No, she hadn't been able to tell Zayn was a vampire. She didn't know who else was one of Lana's to make Zayn another one. At least Nora had heard of Lana, a powerful second to one of the Big Three. How was she supposed to find a vampire on the streets if she couldn't recognize one snarling at her from a couple of feet away?

"The smoking skull tattoo is Lana's?" Nora's memory jolted when she locked eyes with the bouncer watching over the line.

"Yeah."

"But Colbie doesn't have one."

"Colbie isn't Lana's."

Nora frowned, but there wasn't time to ask about this before Colbie returned. She gave Zayn and Oliver hugs and got back in the car. Zayn tugged gently on Oliver's hand, eyeing Nora, but the human still bent back into Colbie's window. His eyes were bright. Smile lazy and constant. Nora's stomach clenched at the obvious signs of feeding.

"Bye, Annaliese! Nice to meet you, Nora! Hello and see you later, Poppyseed!"

He straightened and pulled Zayn's arm over his shoulders, tucking himself in tight to the vampire's side. They walked off. Colbie whistled at them as Annaliese pulled away from the curb. Oliver flipped her off with a laugh and Zayn bent slightly to bury his face in Oliver's neck.

At the time, her head had swum, conflicted with the image of tender vampires and the monsters she'd been raised to hate. Nora took a steadying breath now, Colbie's gentle embrace giving more evidence to a new side of the creatures.

Nora started blinking slowly, her eyelashes brushing the sweep of Colbie's neck.

"Sleep," Colbie whispered, reaching and sweeping her hand over Nora's eyes. Nora smiled and let them shut. Colbie was perfectly still beneath her, her heart beating a steady rhythm, her breathing even and effortless despite Nora's weight on her chest. The confused panic of Nora's thoughts settled. Just a muffled buzz in the back of her mind.

"I should have killed you when I had the chance," Nora muttered.

"Honey, you never had a chance."

"Shut up."

"Hmmm."

Nora's heart skipped when Colbie's hand rested at the base of her ribs, where the dip of her waist was barely present. She was vibrantly aware of every inch of her body pressed against Colbie's. How her muscled stomach completely covered

Colbie's thin, flat one, even angled to the side as she was. The vampire girl was all bones and coiled strength. Her skin soft and cool to the touch. It was a strange and alien awareness. Not unpleasant. Thrilling and comforting. Warm against cold, mingling and balanced.

Lulled by Colbie's steady breaths, Nora let herself forget about the pack. She slept in a vampire's arms and didn't dream.

Nora woke in a rush and pulled her head out of the puddle of drool. Colbie set her book on the coffee table and looked at the wet circle on her chest.

"Disgusting," she said, the expression on her face almost convincing and her double chin making it even better. Nora let out a laugh and Colbie's blue eyes widened. She blinked slowly, lips curling in satisfaction. Nora's cheeks warmed under the intensity of her stare.

"Good morning," Nora said, attempting to move past the moment. She awkwardly pushed herself out from the comfortable crease of the couch.

"Morning." Colbie made no move to wipe the drool under her collarbone. Nora pulled down her sleeve and reached to do it for her. Colbie went still under her attention.

"Time?" Nora asked.

Colbie checked the inside of her wrist and the small silver watch Nora hadn't noticed before. "Nearly five. Topher will be home soon. You get enough sleep?"

Nora shrugged. "As I get closer to the change, I sleep less. More just scattered naps and not a full night."

"Closer to the change?"

Nora shrugged. "Probably next full moon will be my first shift."

Colbie nodded like this was completely normal information and stretched.

"When do you usually sleep?" Nora asked.

"Depends on the time of year. We typically just go out with the sunlight. We stay up much longer during winter, going to bed around eight and getting up at five in the evening. We try to see as much of the real world as we can. Summer is harder when the days are so long, but we try not to sleep our lives away. Topher sleeps more when he's avoiding drinking, though. He'll probably go to bed as soon as he can." Colbie gestured to the sleeping draught still waiting on the counter.

Nora frowned. "Avoiding drinking?"

Colbie chose her words with evident care. "Topher hasn't adjusted especially well to the whole vampire thing."

"Really?"

"Yeah. The feeding, the clubs, the politics. It all bothers him."

"You said you weren't involved in all that."

"I'm not. Never said he wasn't. He's Lana's favorite." Colbie's face went cloudy and sad. Nora knew this was valuable information. That Gabriel would tuck it away and ask for more details. But with Colbie's worried expression, Nora scrambled to change the topic instead. Before she could, the door opened and Topher himself came in.

It wasn't the same storm of frustration and swearing as last time, but the hard look he sent Nora made her feel distinctly unwelcome.

"What happened?" Colbie asked, sitting forward on the couch.

"I'll tell you later," he said. He walked to the island and pulled the cork from one of the vials, downing the contents in one swallow. He continued to the bathroom. The Maker's smell clung to his clothes.

"Should I get Annaliese out of his room?" Nora asked Colbie.

"No. If he wants to talk, he knows I'm here. If he's going to be grumpy, I'm not in the mood to coddle him. He can deal with it," Colbie said, sitting back again and turning on the TV.

With a few tugs, she convinced Nora to curl into her side again. "At least he fed tonight."

"That mean Annaliese is safe?"

"Topher barely eats. He won't eat your friend." Colbie's voice was tight again, so Nora gave her what she wanted, snuggling in close and turning off her mind once more.

CHAPTER 10

Topher took a near scalding shower, his mind already turning sluggish from the sleeping draught. He wrapped a towel around his waist and ignored his sister as he went to his room. He drew up short upon opening the door. The human girl was back in his bed. She woke from the inpouring of light and blinked at him. For once, his scowl was genuine.

"Should I go?" she asked. Her eyes widened as she took in his bare upper body. The scars and tattoos marking him. Her gaze lingered on his forearms. He wondered if she knew the significance behind the tattoos there.

Topher went to his dresser, pulled on a sweatshirt, and awkwardly slid into a pair of shorts under his towel.

"You can. Or you can scoot over. With the sleeping draught, I'm going to be unconscious in about two minutes, so it doesn't matter."

Her eyebrows pulled together, but she moved to the edge of the bed, pulling his blanket with her. He crawled up the other side and yanked it out of her grip to cover himself.

"My favorite," he said, dimly aware his words were slurring. Annaliese huffed but shifted around and jerked a different blanket from underneath him. It was a bit of a process, full of yanking and scowling and frustrated sighs as they repositioned the covers and pillows. Topher let himself sink into the mattress she'd left warm and smelling of life. He was under a blanket she was laying on, ensuring no skin-to-skin contact. He only hesitated a second before shoving his feet under her warm legs.

"*Jesus*," she hissed, moving away from the cold.

"My bed. My rules." Topher couldn't see her over the pillows she'd stacked between them.

There was a pause, a bit of grumbling, and Annaliese put her legs back where they were. Blissful warmth pressed into his feet.

Topher wasn't aware of anything else until he woke up the following evening. The memory of Annaliese's scent clung to the pillows on her side. He resisted the urge to press his face into them and discover if any warmth remained as well.

Colbie was awake and much too cheerful when he left his room, blinking and rubbing the remnants of the sleep potion out of his eyes.

"Good morning! Are you in a better mood now?" She pulled a cookie sheet out of the oven, a sight Topher hadn't seen in a year. He experienced a swoop of déjà vu.

"We need to talk."

"So you said."

"I'm serious. Where's Poppy?"

"Still at her lab."

Mouse ventured out of Poppy's room with a meow and began wrapping himself between Topher's legs. Colbie settled the cookie sheet on the stove, her special snickerdoodles steaming slightly. Topher's heart broke.

"Colbie…"

At his tone, Colbie finally stilled. She turned off the oven and turned to face him, shoulders tensed.

"What is it?"

"I know I didn't say anything before. That I encouraged you, but..." Topher walked around the island and stood before Colbie, needing to watch her face. Needing to see the hurt there and let it linger as the punishment he deserved. "I don't think you should see the werewolf anymore."

"Her name is Nora."

Topher winced. "Yeah. Nora."

Colbie crossed her arms. "Why the hell not?"

Topher took a deep breath. "Two members of her pack came into the club last night. They met with Lana. I think there's more going on than Nora is letting on."

Colbie's face drained. "What was the meeting about?"

"I don't know. Lana didn't say. I just don't trust the situation. If the pack aligns with the vampires, Colbie, I can't let you get caught up in that."

She flinched from his words. "You'll get caught up in it."

"I don't have a choice. I have to keep you safe." Swallowing his guilt, Topher grabbed Colbie's arms and leaned to hold eye contact. "I swear, I'll figure it out. If there isn't any danger to it, you can keep talking with her. I just need you to put it on pause until I'm sure it's safe."

Colbie considered. Finally, she shook her head and straightened her back. "No, Topher. Don't stick your nose into it. I don't want you putting yourself at risk. I've barely known her a week. I'll just call it off."

Topher pulled Colbie in for a long hug. Her voice was steady, but she couldn't quite meet his gaze as she spoke.

Colbie smelled like wolf, just as he was sure he smelled like human. How quickly those two had wrapped themselves in their lives.

"I'll call it off *if* you promise to eat regularly," Colbie said into his shirt.

Topher stiffened. "Fine. Fair."

Colbie relaxed in his arms. "And not Julia's gross stuff."

"Not Julia's gross stuff," Topher agreed.

Colbie stepped back and raised her hands, forearms crossed and pinkies up. Topher mimicked the stance and linked their pinkies. They shook on it twice in the manner they had made promises since childhood. Colbie's smile wobbled, but she nodded resolutely, grabbed the hot cookie sheet, and dumped the snickerdoodles into the garbage.

They stared down at them piled among the rest of the trash.

"Probably should have given them to Poppy," Colbie muttered.

"Yeah. Bit wasteful," Topher said, slinging an arm around his sister's shoulders. She relaxed her head against his chest and heaved another sigh.

"Damn."

Colbie joined Topher when he left for work later that night, likely to ensure he held up his end of the bargain. Her eyes occasionally slipped toward sadness, but she did her best to maintain a cheerful front. Oliver sat across from Zayn at the Maker's bar. He welcomed Colbie to the stool next to him with an enthusiastic hug while Topher left to find someone to feed off. Tori was there, three months sober and finally gaining weight. She thanked him twice before she left the hallway and he returned to the bar. Colbie noted his flushed cheeks and gave him a small, satisfied smile.

He joined Zayn behind the bar. Colbie's phone was sitting between them. Topher put his on the bar next to it. Three missed calls from Julia. Two unopened messages from Nora. Oliver shook his head at them.

"I know I usually tell you to stop moping and focus on the

positive, but this really does suck," Colbie said, watching their screens go black.

"Pick a different word." They jokingly avoided the word suck when Poppy told them it was a cliche for vampires to use.

"It blows."

"Better."

They shared a smile and Topher turned to help the couple who sat down a few stools over.

"They're starting early," he heard Colbie mutter to Zayn.

"Hey!" Oliver gestured to his empty pint glass and Topher's tight stomach loosened just a bit upon hearing Colbie laugh.

"No judgment, babe," Zayn said, leaning over the counter and waiting for a kiss. Colbie pretended to gag.

Poppy joined them a bit later, took two shots and shuffled Colbie off to start feeding on the drunkest humans present. Topher kept the drinks coming. In no time, the packed club cheered Poppy and Colbie on as they danced on top of the bar, shouting about relationships and chemistry exams despite Poppy claiming she'd done well on her test. Oliver joined them and even Topher laughed when Zayn started showering the three with the soda water. The cheering around the bar briefly cut off when his laughter and smile charmed all the humans gathered. Oliver even got caught in the sight and stumbled. Poppy nearly didn't catch him.

Colbie's shining eyes softened with pity just before Topher turned to restock some bottles from the back. The cheering picked up again behind him, the moment entirely forgotten. Well, almost. Oliver protested and sputtered when Zayn sprayed him right in the face for falling under Topher's charm.

Returning to the bar, Topher found his and Colbie's phones broken and soaked on the counter. Colbie stood above them, smile not at all sorry. He had to turn around to hide another grin of his own. Fixing his scowl in place, he served drinks from between Colbie and Poppy's legs, catching the witch's attention when she started to shine blue. She and Colbie climbed down from the bar, giggling and clutching each other for support.

Hours later, Zayn and Topher were closing up. Oliver slept with his face on the bar, Poppy spiking up his hair with the mess left by sticky drinks. Colbie sat and watched them, talking to Zayn about a recent soccer game they'd watched. It was a simple, easy moment.

Lana interrupted the calm. "Hello, darlings!" Her heeled boots clicked loud even on the alcohol-dampened floor. "Do I smell a dog in our midst?"

Topher shrugged. "Sometimes they come in."

"Like last night," Zayn said. "Sure you didn't just forget to wash your hair?"

"Hmm. Maybe. Miss West, nice to see you again."

Colbie rolled her eyes and turned back to the bar. Lana's lips pursed at the slight. "Christopher, Zayn, you're both off Monday night, right?"

They nodded reluctantly.

"Excellent. We have a big job. My position rides on my darlings making me look good. I'll need you at your best." She shot Topher a look. "That means no sweatshirts and you better be well fed."

They nodded again. Lana looked ready to breeze by but paused for a beat, eyes falling on Oliver.

"You mind?" she asked Zayn. Everyone along the bar stiffened. Zayn followed Lana's gesture toward his sleeping boyfriend. His jaw clenched, but he didn't protest when Lana bent and drank from Oliver's neck. He sighed and his eyes fluttered. Colbie let out a soft growl, cutting it off when Topher shot her a look. Zayn's hands balled into tight fists on the counter.

Lana came up and wrinkled her nose. "He's a little bland, don't you think?"

"He tastes fine to me," Zayn bit out. Topher knew he'd just fed off Oliver himself. The couple had likely developed a perfect balance of give and take in their relationship. Lana knew Oliver hadn't had the blood to spare.

"Well, then," Lana said, wiping her lip. "I'll leave you to it."

"She sucks," Colbie hissed once Lana left the building.

"Pick a different word," Topher and Poppy said in flat unison.

"She's just… the absolute worst," Colbie said. They all nodded. Oliver gave a feeble assent where he slumped on the bar, awake and unfocused. His face was ashen and covered in a thin layer of sweat.

"Go ahead. I'll finish up here," Topher said, pushing Zayn toward the exit. Poppy helped him get Oliver outside, offering a restorative potion she had in her car.

Colbie watched them leave, brows furrowed. "You're right, Toph. I can't bring her into this."

Topher could only nod, a familiar sensation emptying his chest.

Nora's phone rang and she shifted to get it from her back pocket. She checked it discreetly. Disappointment knifed when she saw the name on the screen. Not Colbie.

"Hello?" She tried to keep the misery from her voice when she answered. Sitting up, Nora pushed away from Matt where her head had been resting on his knee.

"Want to grab some lunch?" Annaliese asked.

Matt, insufferable about eavesdropping since he'd made the change, perked up. He leaned close and yelled into the phone. "Yes!"

"Hey, Matt. I don't think I was inviting you."

Matt pouted. "Do you always have to be so awful?"

Annaliese ignored him. "I'm outside, Nor." Annaliese hung up.

By this point, Nora had drawn the attention of the living room. Gabriel was on the couch behind where Matt and Nora sat on the floor. When Nora moved to get up, he put a hand on her shoulder.

"You should be thinking about spending less time with humans," he said gently.

Nora bristled. "We're here to protect the humans, remember? What's the point if we act like we're above them all the time?"

"Not above them. Just different. Even humans know better than to make friends with wolves."

Adriana leaned against the back of the couch as she came in from the kitchen. "Not all of them. Some like to keep wolves as pets. You a tame pet, Nor?"

Nora rolled her eyes and made to stand. Gabriel's grip forced her back down. She turned to look at him, exasperated. It was disorienting to make eye contact with him this close.

"I told your father I'd watch out for you. That's all I'm trying to do. And I like Annaliese. She's been a great friend to you through all this, but you need to start thinking about what's safest for her. You'll be out of control during the first months of the change. Is she going to stay away while I take care of you?"

"Not to mention…," Adriana began.

Gabriel shot her a glare over his shoulder and she slinked off. Nora felt a thrill watching him get his way with just a look. Gabriel turned back to her. Having Gabriel's undivided attention wasn't something she was used to. The power of the alpha rolled off of him. Intoxicating. Persuasive.

And it would only get worse once her wolf instincts solidified. "I'll handle it. Don't worry about me, Gabriel."

"You know I do," he said.

His thumb brushed up and down her shoulder before he let

go and leaned back into the cushions. Nora stood, ignored Matt's pleading look, and hurried out of the Den. She tripped over the rug on her way and ignored the pack's huffs of laughter behind her.

Annaliese's car was idling down the street in front of the house Matt deemed the Haunted Mansion. No one from the pack went near it without their hackles rising.

Nora got in and felt a rush of love for Annaliese when she pressed a piping hot chai latte into her hands.

"Why are you being so nice?" Nora asked, more out of surprise. They both knew why. Nora had waited the whole weekend for news from Colbie. She couldn't stop thinking about her. Memories that made her smile and float around all Saturday started hurting Sunday with each unanswered text. Annaliese listened to it all with surprising patience. Today, Monday, Nora hadn't even bothered to get out of bed until Matt insisted she come watch TV with the pack.

"You smell like a wet dog. There, better?"

"Hmm. Probably from Greg," Nora said. He struggled to shake his wolf characteristics, even in his human form. His smell was a running joke in the pack that Annaliese didn't laugh at now. She drummed her fingers on the steering wheel as she drove.

"Where do you want to eat?"

Nora just shrugged. She hadn't eaten breakfast but still didn't feel hungry.

"Let's just go to my place. My parents are out of town again."

It took twenty minutes to drive to Annaliese's suburb. Music filled the silence as they sipped their drinks. Usually, Nora insisted Annaliese play something other than her slow, sad, alternative songs, but they fit her mood today.

They pulled into Annaliese's circular drive and the six-car garage. Annaliese's mansion home had been a lot for Nora to take in the first few times she visited. Annaliese was very cavalier about it, but Nora felt like she was walking into a movie set every time she came over.

Nora couldn't imagine what it had been like for Annaliese and her mom to move out of their old middle-class neighborhood to this place with Annaliese's new fancy white stepdad. Annaliese sometimes mentioned the excitement of the early days, but it didn't take long for Annaliese's surly personality to put her on her new stepdad's bad side. When her mom got pregnant a couple years after the marriage, Annaliese was quiet, moody, and twelve. She'd been happy to slip into the background when the baby arrived.

Nora still didn't know the whole story behind the marriage or what happened to Annaliese's biological dad, but she knew better than to bring it up to Annaliese. Secretly, she thought it was sweet how happy Annaliese's mother was. Nora would never mention it, but she wasn't sure Annaliese was entirely fair in her opinion of the marriage.

Entering the mansion always smelled like lemon-based cleaner and a hint of incense from the yoga studio overlooking the yard. Annaliese slung her bag onto the marble kitchen counter and started rummaging through the fridge. She came up with leftover sushi. At Nora's nod, Annaliese set it on the counter and pulled out some chopsticks.

They tucked in. Nora could see something was on her friend's mind but didn't have the energy to pry. Annaliese would tell her when she was ready. The rolls had all been eaten before Annaliese pulled her bag toward her.

"I had class with Poppy this morning," she started.

Nora tried not to look too interested. She fiddled with her chopstick. "Oh?"

"She asked me to give you this. From Colbie." Nora couldn't help but wince at the name. "Apparently, there was a mishap with drunken bar dancing and her phone."

Nora tried not to look too eager as she took the folded letter Annaliese pulled from the front pocket of her bag.

Nora,

I want to start by saying you're incredible and I wouldn't be doing this if Topher thought there was another way. He knows what this means. But I have to trust him and he says this isn't safe for either of us. He's way more involved in supernatural politics due to reasons I don't want to get into right now, but don't hate him. So. It's over. I'm sorry.

I would never leave you with just that. I want to tell you I love how your eyes and nose are too big for your face. How it doesn't really come together unless you're smiling. It is my own supreme bad luck I've only been gifted that smile once.

If I could choose, I'd spend the rest of my days trying to see it again.

Yours,

Colbie

Nora read it four times, then waited for Annaliese to read it at her insistence.

"What does it mean?" she asked, voice cracking.

Annaliese frowned at the paper. "I don't know. That she's an ass?"

"Do you think she's in danger?"

Annaliese snorted. "I don't know. I wouldn't want to go against her. Too confident. And she seems like she was the kid that got returned after being kidnapped for talking too much, you know?"

Nora gave a feeble smile. "Then why did she give up?" Her voice broke on the last two words. She turned her head as tears filled her eyes. Nora reminded herself she'd only known Colbie a week. That Colbie was annoying. That she had her pack and her future in it to worry about.

It didn't help. Being with Colbie, even for so little time, had opened up an entirely new world for Nora. One she just realized she'd been excited to explore. It wasn't all about the cuddling and watching Colbie move and the kiss on the top of her head. That might be a big part of her disappointment, but it wasn't all of it. She'd finally met a witch. She was seeing the world her parents and Gabriel kept her too sheltered from.

They didn't blink at her friendship with Annaliese or her questions. They thought she should know more. That she deserved to. Until now, Nora hadn't realized how thirsty she was for knowledge.

"Looks like it's asshole bartender's fault," Annaliese said, shaking the letter in Nora's face.

Nora pressed the heels of her hands into her eyes. "What should I do?"

"What do you want to do?"

"I don't know. She's so confusing." Nora dropped her hands. "You know Colbie said she isn't part of the clubs? She doesn't even feel conflicted about drinking blood. She doesn't see anything wrong with us hanging out."

"And she's a lesbian and you're wondering if you might be one too?"

Nora groaned. Annaliese leaned closer, not touching but comforting in her proximity. "It's okay. But I wouldn't say Colbie is confusing. I'd say you're confused by what you feel for her. For what it's worth, there was something there. You could be bi, but…"

"But I've never felt anything like this for a guy."

Annaliese nodded. She'd noticed.

"But I can't be *either*. I know it's antiquated and I don't actually know how the pack would react, but Gabriel could potentially disown me. The pack puts so much value on tradition, pack hierarchy…."

"It's all crap, isn't it?" Annaliese said. Nora nodded. "You think you'll try to talk to Colbie again?"

"I don't know. Half of me wants to. The other half knows I'm going to have to find and kill one of her kind in a couple weeks and then, most likely, it won't matter either way."

"It'll always matter," Annaliese said.

Nora didn't contradict her but wasn't so sure. She'd seen pack member after pack member make the change. When they returned with Gabriel, their eyes were wild like an actual animal for weeks. Only his tight control kept them from running rampant. Even Matt almost killed the neighbor's dog. The scars marking Gabriel's body proved just how hard it was even for him to remind new wolves of their humanity.

It wouldn't matter. Soon. She'd forget Colbie and this new hurt. She just had to hold out that long.

CHAPTER 11

Monday night came too soon. Topher stared at the ceiling under his layers of blankets and wished he was warm. With a soft meow, Mouse pushed his way in the cracked-open door. His little feet made a puffing sound as they landed on top of the covers. Topher rolled and pulled the cat into his chest to pet him. When his alarm went off, Mouse jumped up, knowing full well what the sound meant and ready to be fed.

"Let's see if Soda Pop remembered to get your food," Topher said, throwing off his blankets.

Topher was watching the cat eat when Zayn and Oliver showed up at the door. Oliver shot him a cheery grin and continued to Topher's room, the sound of hangers sliding around the closet rod soon filling the apartment. Zayn stood in the doorway, shaking his head at the choices Oliver must be showing him.

He turned to Topher. "You sure Oliver's good here tonight?"

"He'll be fine. Poppy's set up so many wards sometimes *I* can't find the right door."

Zayn offered a small smile. "You fed yet?"

Topher shook his head.

"Quit putting it off. You need to be on your game if you're going to be covering my back."

"Please, you know you're just there to look pretty. I'm the one who needs watched."

Zayn winked. "I'm always watching you, boo."

Topher snorted through his smile. He slipped into the hall and took the stairs up a few flights. He hated doing this, but their neighbors were good in a pinch and Topher didn't have time to go to the Maker to find his regulars.

He picked a random door and interrupted a couple at dinner. Topher smiled at them and watched the confusion on their faces shift into hopeful smiles. He made quick work of opening their wrists, drinking, and healing them. He carried the couple to their bed.

"Sleep and forget my face."

Their eyes fluttered shut and Topher moved to the next apartment.

He returned to their apartment jittery from feeding. Colbie was perched on the island separating the kitchen and living space. She opened her arms to him and he let her hug him hard for just a beat before he pulled away.

"You pick something, Oliver?"

"Yep!" Oliver held up a navy button-up and black pants. Topher narrowed his eyes at the shirt.

"I won't apologize," Oliver said. "I'm a sucker for you in blue."

"Pick a different word," Colbie said while yawning.

Oliver lowered his voice. "I would, but my boyfriend is standing right there."

Zayn growled and reached for him. "I'll show you a sucker."

"Please do." Oliver laughed and tipped his head, stroking Zayn's hair as his boyfriend started to feed.

"Get a room," Colbie muttered.

Topher shook his head at them and took the clothes from Oliver before he dropped them. He went to his room to change. Once dressed, he frowned at his reflection. His cheeks were red from his recent feeding, eyes bright as the blue tones in the shirt made them pop. He fidgeted with the sleeves and rolled them up, knowing what Lana would prefer his tattoos exposed, her skull on his right arm and his thorny roses on his left. Topher bent and pulled on his gray sneakers before leaving his room.

Oliver kissed his fingertips. "Gorgeous." He giggled at himself, buzzing from Zayn's saliva. His smile was content and his eyes glossy as he looked from Topher to Zayn, who was striking in a pair of dark wash jeans and a deep purple sweater. Topher probably couldn't have pulled it off, but Zayn's dark skin had a way of challenging any color he wore.

"Lana's a bitch, but she knows how to pick 'em," Oliver said.

"So do you, babe." Zayn kissed Oliver and checked his watch. "We should go."

Oliver's smile dimmed and Colbie started to pout. "You sure I can't—"

"No." Topher kissed her forehead as he left and held the door for Zayn. They shared a long look once in the hall.

"Let's get this over with," Zayn said. Topher nodded and swallowed his dread. They continued on.

"Leaving already?" Poppy asked when they passed her in the parking lot. The sun was setting behind her, making the red in her hair shimmer. This soon after feeding, there weren't many details Topher missed.

"Yes. You'll watch him, right?" Zayn asked, nodding toward the apartment.

Poppy nodded and lowered her voice. "I tried, but I couldn't see anything about tonight. Just stay on your guard."

"We always do where Lana's concerned. Don't worry,

Popsicle," Topher said. He gave her the same forehead kiss he'd given Colbie and they climbed into Zayn's red Jeep.

They stopped at the Maker long enough to pick up Tamera and Brady. Then, they drove further down Fourth toward Happenstance, one of the most prominent vampire clubs. It was owned by Connor Grace, a member of the Big Three. He was Lana's maker and Topher's least favorite vampire in the city, though Lana was a close contender.

Lana was waiting for them out back when they pulled to a stop in the private lot. She wore a red dress and heels that looked too new to be standing near the trash bags stacked next to the dumpster. She was smoking a cigarette but passed it to Topher when they reached her side. He dutifully finished it off as she spoke, wishing for another once she finished.

"Connor's only given me leave to bring two of my darlings inside. Brady, you watch the outside, get a good number for how many underlings everyone else brought, especially the wolves." Lana's voice was drenched in charm, leaving Brady with no say in the matter. Not that he was one to argue either way.

"Wolves?" Tamera asked. She wore a short black skirt, bralette, and blazer open over it. Her crimson boots went up to her knees. It would seem she was trying to emulate their maker's style. Topher let himself appreciate the view. He caught her looking back and knew they were both remembering a night two months ago. Maybe it was time to revisit Tamera's room. She winked. Topher returned it, making her smirk. The distraction was enough to calm him momentarily.

"Yes. There's a new pack in town," Lana said, drawing back their attention. "We need to get numbers on them and figure out why they're here."

Nods all around. Brady slipped into the shadows when Lana waved him off. "Rest of you, with me."

Topher knew better than to comment they still had an extra. Lana always pushed boundaries. She craved any opportunity to assert her power. Grace had more seconds than any of the other Big Three. Lana longed for a special place in his ranking.

Lana lit two more cigarettes, passing one back to Topher, and led them into the pounding bass of the club. They crossed the dance floor, Lana's charm clearing a path through the crowd with ease. Happenstance was more open about the vampirism in the club. The bar was barely serving, but every few steps, someone was feeding. There wasn't a human with clear eyes in the place. The couches lining the room overflowed with slumped bodies recovering from too heavy feedings or intense highs.

Vampires watched Lana and her followers pass with barely concealed disgust, but they wouldn't dare cross her. Most vampires were content with their place here. They weren't strong enough to be makers, but they were claimed and provided for by Grace. Few understood Lana's desire to make her own followers and start a club. They called her the Big Fourth with derision.

The bouncers at the base of the stairs watched them approach and shared a look before letting Lana through. Topher greeted them by name and their expressions relaxed. Nick even whistled at Tamera as she slipped by. She cut the sound off with a glare and he cleared his throat, eyes returning to the dance floor.

At the top floor, another set of bouncers opened the double doors and let them into the meeting room. Topher took a drag off his cigarette, cringing internally when he saw he was mirroring Lana.

A long table took up the center of the grand room. Topher noted the other vampire seconds and city leaders had already taken their seats. The Big Three sat at the head of the table.

Lana had ensured they were late. The wall was lined with underlings and vacant-eyed humans. There was barely room left for two of them to take their place comfortably, let alone all three. The single seat left at the table was waiting for Lana.

"Always with your unnecessary entrances," Grace said from the head of the table. His tone wasn't quite disproving and wasn't quite fond. Topher always struggled to read his head maker's emotions.

Topher did a quick count. The Big Three: Grace, Solas, and Patter. Two alpha wolves, one of them Nora's alpha with mismatched eyes. Three human gang lords clinging to power. The chief of police. A few more wealthy humans with pull. City politicians, including the current human mayor and the witch running for mayor Poppy called Mother Kallow. The dean of the university was even in attendance. Topher could smell her nervous sweat from here. The rest of the table had seats for the higher-ranking vampire seconds. All the makers in the city in one room. No wonder the humans were struggling to focus. Unintentional charm filled the air. Maybe intentional.

Topher dropped his eyes when he saw Bryce Hunter in attendance next to Remi Umbras. If anyone could be blamed for his current state aside from Lana and Grace, it was those two. Neither of them bothered to acknowledge Topher, but he had seen the stiffening in Hunter's shoulders.

"I apologize, of course. My darlings had the wrong time," Lana purred, running her hand down Zayn's arm. He kept his face perfectly blank, Topher and Tamera matching the well-practiced look.

"You were only to bring two of your *darlings*."

"Oh, we can make this work." Lana's pulled out her chair. "Christopher, sit."

Her voice was full of charm. It was one of her more reasonable requests, so Topher didn't waste energy fighting her. He sat down and let Lana drape herself on him. He didn't let his expression slip.

"Again, unnecessary," Grace said, sounding bored.

"I didn't like the way Liz was looking at him," Lana said, shooting a look down the table to another second and taking another drag from her cigarette.

"You get *two*," Sarah Patter said from Grace's left. As one of the Big Three, her word carried as much weight as Grace's, though her charm was wasted on Lana.

At Grace's impatient nod, Lana flicked the ash of her cigarette and turned in Topher's lap to eye Zayn and Tamera, still standing by the door. "Zayn, dear, go have some fun downstairs."

Zayn gave a stiff nod and left the room. Tamera took her place against the wall as the doors shut behind him. Topher longed to join her, but Lana made no move to let him up. He set his cigarette between his lips and kept it there, letting it burn in Lana's face. Whatever tiny act of rebellion he could get. He made eye contact with the alpha wolf across the table. His blue and brown eyes were wide.

Topher winked at him.

"Can we begin?" Patter asked.

"Yes. Let's," Lana readily agreed. She shifted in Topher's lap to face the table, straddling one of his thighs.

"We called this meeting to, ah, welcome the newest members of our city and discuss a rising issue of abandoned vampire changelings," Solas began. The look she sent the new alpha was one of distrust.

He was unbothered by the less-than-friendly welcome. And not in a stoic, practiced way. In an understanding manner that said he knew what he was walking into and wouldn't let it deter him. He smiled and the two lines of a gagged scar down the left side of his face crinkled. It was so genuine Topher caught himself staring.

"Yes, thank you. My name is Henry Gould. Our pack has moved into the abandoned fabric mill south of the river for the time being. We understand this area is largely unclaimed and hope we aren't stepping on any toes making our home there.

At this point, we have made no alliances." The look he exchanged with the chief of police and Mother Kallow said otherwise.

"But surely you side with the humans," the alpha from Nora's pack said.

"We all side with the humans, Mr. Riesling," Grace said with a dismissive wave.

"I think we have a different idea of what that entails," the alpha responded, glaring at the humans against the wall. Lana edged forward on Topher's leg, excited by the tension building in the air.

"Do you see anyone complaining?" Grace asked.

"I don't think they remember how to."

"Sounds like a beautiful way to live, doesn't it, Gabriel?" Lana nearly purred.

Gabriel narrowed his eyes at her.

"I do sympathize with humans to answer your question," Henry pressed on. "But we strive to live among them, not as protectors or superheroes unless called upon. We just want to exist as they do and run under the full moon when it moves us."

Eyes widened at the new alpha's words. Topher looked to his underlings for any sign their alpha was lying. Their expressions were clear. Guileless. Topher's gaze lingered on the brown-eyed boy standing there. He was completely calm as he took in the room, a peace Topher hadn't seen on any other werewolves in the city.

Still, the alpha had specified unless called upon. Topher looked to the chief of police again and wondered if that was precisely what had happened.

Lana let out a laugh. Grace shot her a look and she settled back into Topher's chest, hair bunching up and itching his neck. Her cigarette had burned to the filter, so she extinguished it on Topher's arm. The heat of the burn was sudden and sharp and gone just as quickly as it came. Gabriel gasped across the table. Topher didn't have to see to know Lana was giving the alpha her wicked smile as she dropped the extinguished butt onto the floor. She ran a thumb over the faint burn mark on Topher's arm. At least it was the arm with *her* tattoo.

Grace, Patter, and Solas shared a look before Grace nodded and changed the topic of conversation. The Big Three had deemed the new pack not to be a problem. For now.

"Now, what's this about the rogue vampires?" Mother Kallow asked.

Mia Solas frowned, the black lipstick she wore exaggerating the expression. "We've found two this month. The one who survived capture didn't answer to my charm. They aren't mine or my second's."

"What does charm have to do with it?" Gabriel asked.

Topher almost rolled his eyes. The wolves could at least try to research other supernaturals before they showed up here.

Solas turned to explain. "Vampires can resist each other's charm in the way wolves resist us. However, a vampire's maker retains control over them. All the seconds here can be charmed by one of the Big Three, and all the second's underlings can, in turn, be charmed by their maker and us. For instance, if Grace wanted Lana and Christopher to stop their little show, he could tell either one of them to get up and they'd have to obey his charm." She shot Grace a look, obviously hoping the jab would spur him to do just that. Grace pretended not to notice.

"But someone with powerful enough charm can still potentially compel another vampire," Lana put in, wiggling in Topher's lap. He clenched his fists.

"Which is the main reason Lana is here today," Grace said. Lana stiffened at the slight, but only for a second before she relaxed against Topher again. "The effort it takes a vampire to force their charm on our kind is painful for both parties, but luckily we have someone who can handle it."

Everyone around sat straighter, glancing up and down the

table. Topher felt whatever color he had left from feeding drain from his face. Lana looked over her shoulder to smirk at him, running her fingers up his arm. Scratching too hard for the strokes to be meant as comforting.

Grace stood and gestured for those gathered to follow him into the next room. "Just the leaders, I'm afraid. We don't have the room for the extras."

Topher watched as the leaders filed out of the room through the back door. Gabriel looked back and watched Lana and Topher follow.

"Just you," he reminded Lana. "No underlings."

Lana gave Gabriel a sweet smile and ran a hand over his chest as she passed. The wolf flinched.

"You sure about that, handsome?"

Gabriel followed Topher into the room without another word, his anger warming the air between them. One of Grace's people shut them all in. The room they entered was cold and sparse. A wild-eyed vampire was chained to the floor. Even less present than the last unclaimed Topher had questioned. She was snarling and twisting, trying to break her bonds. Topher's stomach rolled painfully. The girl couldn't be older than fourteen. Her clothing was shredded, though the skin underneath had healed into thin scars already.

"You can't be serious," Topher hissed in Lana's ear.

His maker ignored him.

"Are you ready, Lana?" Grace asked.

"Of course, Connor."

"We need to know who changed her *and* who attacked her before we got there."

"We don't think the two were the same?" Kallow asked sharply.

"No. We don't. The other changelings were unharmed. We have no reason to think whoever this maker is means the turned any harm," Patter said softly. Even she looked moved by the youth of the new vampire.

Grace continued. "Whoever attacked ran off when they heard us coming. We only caught a glimpse before we gave her our attention. She was in bad shape for a minute there. We would *like* to give credit to whoever is helping us with this recent problem, but it would seem none of us are behind it."

Accusing looks were shot Henry's way, but he paid no attention, still frowning at the girl chained to the floor. If the new pack was taking out the unregistered and untamed new vampires, he wasn't admitting to it now.

Lana nodded and turned to Topher. "Go ahead, my darling."

Topher stood frozen, the force of Lana's charm hitting him hard. He clenched his fists, aware of every pair of eyes on him as he fought.

"She's just a child. And the last one—"

"She's dangerous. Ask her who did this to her, Christopher."

The girl started sobbing, tearless and panicked. Topher swallowed and resisted Lana as long as he could. With a snarl, Lana lashed out, nails dragging across his cheek and making him stumble back. The pain was real and distracting. The gashes she left wouldn't bleed, but they would ache even after the skin closed.

"You know what's at stake here," Lana hissed.

Colbie.

"Christopher," Grace said. Under the combined force of their charm, Topher stumbled forward.

"Fine." The urging stopped and his head began to clear. His will back in his own control, Topher pulled in a breath and knelt in front of the girl.

"Who changed you?" he asked without charm, hoping she was upset enough just to answer. The girl shook her head violently.

Topher hesitated only a second longer before he forced his

lips into a smile. The humans around the room relaxed their stances when his charm filled the air.

The thrill from the power came from every instinct Topher hated and battled constantly.

"What's your name?" he asked the girl. Her crying subsided, confusion lighting her dark eyes as the charm hit her in slow, calculated waves.

"Mary." Behind her, Grace began to smile and Topher knew he'd already gotten further than anyone else.

"Mary." She straightened when Topher laced her name with charm. Names had power. "Mary, who changed you?"

She shook her head.

"Mary." She winced when Topher increased his charm. Pain throbbed behind his eyes. His vision blurred, but he kept hold of his charm.

Mary's eyebrows gathered. "Stop," she whispered, her charm a pathetic wisp compared to Topher's. He shook it off with ease.

"Mary, who changed you?"

She whimpered and dropped to the floor so she could cover her head with her hands.

Topher switched tactics. "Mary, who attacked you?"

"A demon," she gasped. She moaned at the pain.

Topher's brows knotted. He glanced up and saw Grace's frown. Mother Kallow's eyes widened. "A demon?" the witch asked.

"Yes! It came out of the shadows!" Mary was relieved she could give these answers with ease. The pain lifted a bit as she willingly succumbed to Topher's charm.

"Enough nonsense. We have no demons here," Grace said. "Ask who changed her again."

"Mary, who changed you?"

She shook her head. Grace made an impatient gesture.

Topher took a deep breath and pressed harder with his charm. "Mary, who changed you?"

She started to scream. Topher's head was pounding, but he knew his pain was nothing compared to hers.

He tried again when the screams faded back to ragged breaths. "Mary, it won't hurt near so bad if you answer. Who changed you?"

She let out a wail and Topher could tell the exact second his charm overpowered her will. "She was white. Tall. Brown hair."

"More, Mary."

She spoke between gasps, her eyes sightless from the pain. "Southern accent. Wore a blue coat."

"What was her name?"

Mary shook her head and Topher gathered his charm in the air between them. He was breathing hard from the effort. His stomach was twisting. Mary began to scream again, writhing on the floor. "Answer me, Mary," Topher didn't even have to raise his voice for the effect to hit her.

"Please! Please! Make it stop!"

"Her name?"

"I don't know!"

Topher spared another glance at Grace. She was too close.

"Keep going," the maker ordered.

Topher's hands were shaking. The light in the room dimmed around the edges of his vision. He should have fed more. The humans along the wall smelled like life and energy. His mouth watered for a taste.

"Mary, tell me everything you can," he tried, but he knew it was too late. She broke. Mary was reduced to screams, straining against the metal chains until they groaned under the force of her efforts.

Topher barely heard Grace's sigh as they lost her. "Shut her up," he said.

Wincing, Topher lunged and clamped his fangs on the girl's neck. She instantly stilled, her incoherent screams shifting into moans of relief as his potent saliva filled her system. He didn't drink; her lifeless blood tasted rotten. He just let his fangs push their numbing effect until she went limp beneath him.

He backed off. "Relax." He could feel how welcome the charm was now. Mary accepted this order easily.

Topher lurched to his feet, head pounding so severely he worried he might collapse. Lana came up to him, crooning and wrapping her arms around his waist.

"Isn't he fantastic?" she asked the room. She held Topher upright when he swayed. The humans were still beyond responding.

"What's wrong with her?" Gabriel asked, voice strained enough that Topher noticed despite the agony in his head.

"She's snapped. Happens when the charm is too strong. Of course, we didn't know a charm could be strong enough to do that until Christopher. I repeat, isn't he fantastic?"

Gabriel looked sick. Topher felt like *he* would be sick. But he hadn't vomited since the change. He wished he could. It would taste better than Mary's rotten blood still in his mouth. Mother Kallow's gaze was intent and she glowed a haze of orange. The vampires who hadn't seen his charm before eyed Topher, unsure if he was a blessing or a curse.

He was a curse. The worst one to plague the city.

Lana led him from the room, supporting his weight until Tamera stepped forward to grab him. Lana took out her phone and called Zayn, ignoring the muttering city leaders behind her.

"Come collect him."

Lana froze. She turned to Grace. Eyes narrowed into slits, she removed the phone from her ear and put it on speaker. "Repeat that," she said, voice low with rage.

"Brady's been killed. I found his body in the alley."

CHAPTER 12

"You look like crap," Annaliese said. She took a seat at the desk next to Poppy's.

Poppy shrugged, in no mood to comment. It had taken three vials of sleeping draught to calm Topher down last night. The aftermath of the meeting made sleep difficult for everyone.

"What? Nora and Colbie can't be together, so we can't be friends?" Annaliese threw up her hands. "Fuck Topher."

Poppy's anger came in a hot rush. A stiff breeze swept through the room, blowing papers and hair. Poppy regained control and cut it off in a panic, snapping to open the door at the base of the lecture hall and hoping the humans would accept that was the cause of the sudden wind.

Annaliese's eyebrows shot up. She'd had her hair done. It fell in slim braids, fading from black at her roots to navy to ice blue at the tips. The braids were so long they brushed Annaliese's hips. Even sitting, the new look made her look taller.

"You have no idea what's happening," Poppy hissed. Not that Topher or Zayn had told her and Colbie what was going on. "You're are better off staying out of it."

"I disagree. Nora's miserable and I bet my dad's retirement Colbie isn't any better. Here. Give this to her." Annaliese held up a folded piece of paper.

Poppy took it, tempted to try sending it up in flames right then and there. But that would attract too much attention and Colbie *was* miserable. She needed a distraction after watching her brother get carried into the apartment last night. Zayn had barely restrained Topher from attacking Oliver. Colbie had to go down the hall and collect neighbors to slake Topher's thirst. It was a miracle Zayn had even got him to the apartment without Topher attacking anyone. Though neither would say what happened at the meeting, it was clear Topher used all his life energy.

After the near attack, Topher stared at the wall, guilt etched deep into his features. He sat shaking and wouldn't listen to anyone. The only relief to give him was sleep. Colbie had held his head in her lap and covered his eyes until he finally drifted off. Only for the nightmares to start.

A letter from Nora really couldn't make things much worse. Could it?

Oliver was waiting outside the building when their class let out. Annaliese stubbornly stayed by her side and Poppy could practically feel the girl's questions. Oliver offered Poppy the second coffee cup in his hands. It smelled more alcohol than coffee. She accepted the cup gratefully.

Oliver was on a pre-med track. They both had many classes on this side of campus and knew each other's schedules well. Before Annaliese, he'd been Poppy's only friend who didn't sleep the day away.

"He ever settle down?" Oliver asked. Zayn had gotten them out of the apartment when Topher started feeding. He'd had to drag Oliver from the room as Topher's charm worked its way into his victims.

Oliver was either the bravest or stupidest human Poppy knew. That wasn't the first time Topher and Zayn had ended a night in such a manner. Yet Oliver kept coming back, always with a smile. It would seem nothing could keep him from Zayn's side. Good thing Zayn was strong enough to subdue Topher even when he was victim to his basest instincts.

"Yeah. He's sleeping."

"Good."

"Who? Topher?" Annaliese asked. She was breathless as she matched their pace, her short legs working hard to keep up.

"Yeah." Poppy took a sip of the spiked coffee. It burned perfectly going down.

Oliver turned to Annaliese. "How's Nora?" He and Colbie spent the majority of last night talking about her while Poppy finished her homework.

"Not great," Annaliese said. Oliver winced in sympathy.

"Hope you don't have class later," Oliver said, watching Poppy take another deep pull.

She just raised her eyebrows at him over the cup. He was the one who gave it to her.

"If you need a ride, I'll spot you one, but you have to answer at least one of my questions," Annaliese said. They were crossing the quad now. Poppy ignored her.

"How was Zayn?"

"He's doing okay. Beat himself up for a minute, but I took his mind off it." Oliver winked.

"Who's Zayn again?" Annaliese asked, determined not to be left out.

"My boyfriend," Oliver said.

At the same time, Poppy answered, "The bartender who got you drunk at the club."

Annaliese grimaced at the memory and Oliver laughed.

"Did Zayn say what happened at the meeting?" Poppy asked.

"Well, Lana called, so I mostly got his story from listening to that, but I was half asleep at that point. I guess they have no idea who's changing them and there was something about demons. It sounds like no one actually knows what's happening. And Lana said something about Brady, but Zayn took his phone off speaker at that point. He doesn't work tonight so he promised to catch me up on everything later. We'll probably come by the club afterward. Zayn's pretty worried about Topher." Oliver sounded only slightly wary of the prospect of seeing Topher again.

Poppy squeezed his arm. "He'll be fine when he wakes up, same as usual. Miserable and moping."

"What happened?" Annaliese asked. She sounded more concerned than Poppy would have expected for "asshole bartender." Oliver pursed his lips.

"Probably better you don't know the details," he decided. "Just, if you see Topher, know the shitty mood he hits you with isn't personal."

"Yeah, I'm not sure you can call it a mood at this point. More so a personality."

"Salty, salty. Are we still on for tomorrow night, P?"

"Yes. We'll meet you at Patty's."

"Sounds perfect. Call me later. I got class." Oliver took the next turn in the path and joined a group of fellow pre-med students. They laughed and cajoled him when one caught a whiff of his coffee. Oliver pretended to stumble off the path drunkenly, inciting another round of laughter. Poppy was struck again by the simplicity of humans.

"He's goddamn cheerful," Annaliese muttered.

"He really is."

They walked toward the library in silence, Poppy nursing her drink against the bite in the wind.

"Can I ask a question?"

Poppy sighed. "When you give me a ride home. My lab gets out at 5:30."

"I think you'll be sobered up by then."

"Yeah, but I took the bus."

"Alright. I'll be there with bells on."

"Are you secretly an eighty-year-old man?"

"Yes."

Poppy hated how much she liked Annaliese. Nora too. It just made everything that much harder.

Annaliese was waiting in her car outside the Physical Science building right on time and snacking on some salt and vinegar chips. Poppy looked at the bag and let the disgust show on her face.

"Oh, you're one of *those* people," Annaliese said, clapping the salt off her hands before pulling onto the street.

"I just don't understand how people can eat those."

"Please, salty and bitter? These are my spirit chips."

Poppy snorted, the tension easing in her shoulders. Annaliese, for all her rough edges, was fun to be around.

"Can I ask my questions now?"

"I thought I agreed to one."

"What the hell even is a vampire?"

"You're not messing around," Poppy said, stalling. How to even answer that? Did she trust Annaliese enough to get into the theories that connected the supernaturals?

"Just explain what Nora is up against. I don't think she knows."

"Alright. I'll tell you the basics as I understand them. But I don't know much. Vampires have historically kept very quiet, letting the stories, which I think are mostly exaggerated, speak for them." Poppy adjusted her visor against the glare of the sunset. "Vampires aren't born like witches and werewolves. They're humans who have been changed by a powerful vampire, called a maker. I guess only a few of them are strong enough to do it and that's why a handful run the city."

Annaliese accepted that with a nod. "Are they immortal?"

"No, but they age more gracefully than humans. Fewer

wrinkles, hardly any health concerns. It's hard to tell how old they are, Topher doesn't even know how old Lana is, but they only live about ten or twenty years extra. But really, they don't get along well enough to survive that long. A lot of them are killed early."

"And they're strong?"

Poppy shrugged. "They're each so different, just like humans. It's not a catch-all thing. Some vampires are barely stronger than humans. Some are stronger than werewolves. Some have charm that makes them seem a little bit extra persuasive; some have charm that can make a human forget their name. Some have saliva that feels like taking a tiny hit on a joint; some have saliva like heroin. Some are powerful in all those ways, some in just one or not at all. They're pretty varied."

"Does it depend on who changes them?"

"No. There are theories it matters how a person is changed or that it's determined by human characteristics that carry over. But hell if anyone actually knows."

"And Colbie and Topher?"

"Colbie is honestly below average in most of her abilities. She could probably get you to do what she wanted but couldn't hold the charm for long and you'd know it was happening. She's strong but doesn't practice at any of her abilities like other vampires tend to, so she's behind."

"And Topher?"

"Topher… well, no one knows quite what to make of him."

"That doesn't answer my question."

"I think I've said enough for today."

They still had a way to go before the apartment building.

"Can I ask a non-vampire question?"

Poppy sighed but didn't say no.

"What Oliver said about demons. Are *those* real?"

Poppy's hair rose on her arm and she studied Annaliese's

profile. The girl's jaw was set, eyes focused on the road. She'd put on her glasses for the drive, adding a layer of seriousness to her expression.

"Yes, demons are real. My mom studied them for a while. Like the vampires, they aren't exactly what the stories say. They don't come from Hell or follow the devil. Pentagons aren't nearly as strong as a proper summoning circle, even if they look fancier. There haven't been any in New Brecken for years. They're attracted to witches, but usually, the ones that show up are alone and easily dealt with. They're very rare."

"What are they?"

"The most recent theory is that they're ghosts who linger on this side of the veil, longing for flesh and clinging to what little life energy they have for far too long. Ghosts stick around in different stages and, over time, corrupt their remnants of life enough to gain strength if they don't pass on. Some can make a breeze or knock over a glass or mess with electricity. Others can take form imprints of a physical shape in brief spurts, usually if they have someone connected to their past to draw from. A lot of witches try to hang onto their loved ones and attract spirits because we have a stronger life force. But if a ghost stays too long, their desire can warp until they are able to become and remain corporal. In other words, their longing manifests into a physical form. But they lose sense of everything at this point and haunt the shadows, doing nothing except hunt for more life energy and bring more death. Only when a witch uses her life energy to call them near do they find direction. A human can do it too, but I don't know that process."

"Do you think demons are in the city now?"

Poppy glanced out her window at the lengthening shadows. "It's possible."

Matt entered Nora's room without bothering to shut the door behind him. She looked up from her phone with two unanswered texts to Annaliese waiting on the screen.

"What's with this funk you're in?" he asked.

"There's no funk."

"You're all funk. Nothing but funk."

"Stop saying funk, Matt."

He smiled and flopped onto her bed. Nora forced a slight grin, guilty she'd been taking her mood out on him.

"There she is. Now, what's up? We've known each other our whole lives. I know when you're down."

Not that he'd consistently done much about it. Matt didn't handle tears or hard truths well. When her father died, he'd been the one to shut down for weeks. Nora went to Annaliese for comfort, solidifying their friendship as her and Matt's crumbled. He'd been trying more in the last year, especially when she was barely there for him during his change two months ago. Nora couldn't help but feel his attempts to rekindle their old easiness were coming far too late.

He hadn't been there when she needed him most. Trust took too much effort after that.

"I'm just struggling with all this." Nora made a helpless gesture.

"Use your words," he said, gentle and unsure. He was cautiously throwing her mother's words back at her. Nora hadn't spoken much as a child. Her mother had constantly directed her to speak up and voice her feelings. Nora tried not to react too negatively to Matt doing so now.

"I just… want to make an impact. With the vampire I kill."

Matt frowned. "Killing any of those monsters makes an impact, Nor."

"I want it to *mean* something."

Matt's eyes cleared with understanding. "Gabriel already killed Reelings, Nora. We've gotten revenge. That murderer is in the ground."

Yes, they'd avenged her father. Without telling her a word of it until the deed had already been done.

"I don't know if I mean revenge."

"Nor. It doesn't matter if you take out a Big Three or a straggler on the streets. Honestly, taking out a nonaffiliated one is better for humans— no one checks them. There have been way too many of them popping up and draining humans. We need help as it is cleaning them up."

Nora frowned. "I want it to mean something, Matt," she repeated.

"If it gets you into the pack, it'll mean the world." Matt took her hand and squeezed. "I can't wait to run with you. Take you to the national park on the full moon. Your mom will probably even show up. And I've already talked to my boss and he said he'd hire you. We can work together and…" he stopped, but Nora read the hope still lingering in his eyes. She didn't respond, overwhelmed by the future Matt had already imagined for them. Was it really so different from what she'd been hoping for?

Yes. But the future she always imagined was likely out of her reach. She squirmed with embarrassment even thinking about it. She should lower her sights. She was already forcing herself to forget about Colbie. A life partnered with Matt wouldn't be the worst thing.

The hope in his expression faded when she didn't respond. Matt cleared his throat. "If you need help, all you need to do is ask. If you're set on hitting a club, I can go with you back to the Maker—"

"*What?*" Gabriel was standing in the doorway, eyes flashing with anger. He was so quiet; Nora had no idea how long he'd been standing there. What all had they said for him to overhear? "You went to the Maker?"

Nora opened her mouth to respond, but words weren't coming to her. Matt shifted on the bed, the set of his shoulders making it clear he didn't like Gabriel sneaking up on them any more than she did.

"Well, I told her to go there. It's a new club. The vampire who owns it isn't even big—"

Gabriel crossed the room in two steps. His punch sent Matt sliding off the bed. Nora yelped and scrambled to help him. Matt waved her off and stood. Glaring, he wiped the blood from his split lip. He didn't dare say anything.

Gabriel pointed at them both, hand trembling, "You are *never* to set foot in that club."

"I don't get it!" Matt threw up his hands. "Lana was just posturing, she has a couple of lackeys, but Grace barely even acknowledged her. What the hell happened in that room?"

Gabriel drew a shaky breath, his fury just under the surface. His skin shivered as he held off the change. Nora silently begged Matt to keep quiet.

"What happened in that room is I learned even vampires fear certain vampires. They can destroy each other with their fucking *words*. The worst of them is caught up in the Maker and none, absolutely none, of my pack is going near them without me. Understood?" Alpha command laced his words, settling all the way down Nora's spine. It hit Matt harder. He sat down and his head bowed. The faintest whimper left his lips.

Who at the Maker could possibly have Gabriel so terrified? He rarely pulled his rank like this. She could count the number of times he'd made them submit on her hands, putting his alpha power this potently behind his commands.

Gabriel calmed a bit at Nora's nod and Matt's submission. He sat on Nora's other side. She couldn't remember Gabriel ever coming up to her room before, let alone sitting on her bed.

He took a deep breath. "But the Maker aside, Matt is right, Nor. We're here to help you if you need it. Above everything else, we're family here. Even if some of us are a bit overprotective." He sent Matt an apologetic look. Matt smiled. His lip was so healed it didn't even re-split. Balance was restored. Gabriel was a good alpha like that.

Gabriel nudged her with his shoulder and Nora nudged him back. He gave her one of his rare smiles. She blushed because she knew that smile had always been reserved for her. It was the smile he'd given her every time she kept up with him throughout their childhood, determined even when Matt fell behind.

Nora knew he meant what he said. They were family. Their pasts and future were so linked she could feel their bond wrapping her spine, sinking into her core. Gabriel had nothing before he found the pack. Her father took him under his wing and groomed him into the alpha he was today. She knew Gabriel had planned to leave and gather his own pack, make his way in the world as her father had. But then her father was killed. Gabriel stepped up to keep the pack from crumbling. He'd shouldered a lot when he did that. More than any other nineteen-year-old she knew. Since that moment, the two years between them had felt like miles.

"Nora, if I brought in a vampire making trouble, could you kill them?" Gabriel asked. He watched her intently, giving her the usual unsettled sensation when she met his blue and brown eyes.

Determined to look steady, Nora nodded.

"Great. C'mon, Matt. It'll take the whole pack to get the vamp here. We're meeting in the basement." Nora made to follow, but Gabriel stilled her with a hand on her shoulder. "It's too risky, Nor. Once you make the change, you can come to these things. Until then, enjoy your time left with Annaliese or something."

"But this is my kill! You can't just take that from me and leave me out of everything!"

"It will be your kill, but the statement will be the pack's. I need you to trust me on this. I can't have you getting hurt before your change."

"I'm a wolf, same as you! I might not be able to change, but I'm part of this pack."

"You are," Gabriel squeezed her shoulder for emphasis. "Let us do this for you. Packs build each other up. We work as a team. Everyone has a place and yours is staying safe for now. Your time will come."

Nora watched them leave, meeting Matt's apologetic glance with a glare. She threw her pillow at the door when it shut behind them. All she could hope was Gabriel was right and once she joined their ranks this feeling of exclusion plaguing her since her father's death would go away.

CHAPTER 13

Alone in her room an hour later, Nora texted Annaliese because she would have anyway, not because Gabriel suggested it. This time, Annaliese answered and came right away.

"It's late, Nora. I know I've been a pushover with your dating and hunting the creatures of the night, but this is getting extreme."

"It's 8:30. Stop whining."

Annaliese grunted and checked over her shoulder before flipping the car to the other direction, toward the bridge to go northside.

"Where are we going?"

"I've been craving a burger from that diner Poppy likes."

"Ouch." Nora mimed twisting a knife in her heart. "I don't need the reminder. Colbie didn't even write me back."

"What did you say? I would never have pictured you writing love notes. Words aren't really your thing, you know?"

"I know." Nora blushed as she remembered her insufficient note: *I miss you. I shouldn't, but I do. P.S. My nose isn't that big.*

Annaliese shook her head and Nora turned to look out the

window. The city was dark tonight, streetlights struggling to shine through the fog.

Nora's mind replayed her conversation with Matt, the hope in his gaze and Gabriel's strange reaction to the Maker. It seemed no matter who she was talking to, she was missing a large chunk of information. She was tired of guessing at motives and hidden meanings. She remembered her mother describing the silent communication the pack shared in wolf form. It sounded much easier than this world of misleading words and unspoken secrets.

Minutes later, they reached the diner. Annaliese burst through the door to the chorus of jangling bells like she owned the place. Few heads bothered to turn in their direction, but Nora quickly spotted Poppy's shocked expression. Oliver was in the booth across from her. He turned and waved them over with a welcoming smile.

Nora's eyes went back to Poppy. The witch flicked a panicked look to the bathroom. Nora didn't think after that.

Her heart pounding, Nora turned on her heel and went in that direction. She would never get used to following someone who lacked a scent.

Nora burst into the bathroom. Colbie stood behind a girl at the sink. The vampire looked up slowly to meet Nora's gaze in the mirror as she finished drinking from the girl's neck. She unclamped her fangs and licked the holes left in the skin. Nora stared as they instantly closed back up, leaving only two faint white marks.

"Go finish your meal, honey. You need it," Colbie bid the girl, her voice husky with charm. The girl straightened. Her expression was blissed as she rode the high from Colbie's saliva. Nora moved out of her way. She and Colbie were alone in the bathroom.

Nora was speechless for all the time it took Colbie to wipe her mouth and cross her arms. She leaned against the metal, off-pink side of the stall. Her eyes held Nora's and the buzz of nerves crowding Nora's mind hushed. She drew a deep breath.

"You didn't write me back," Nora said. Colbie's expression shifted slightly, but she was clearly working to keep her thoughts from her face. Nora loved that it took Colbie effort to hide her feelings. She loved that Colbie didn't keep secrets.

Nora stalked forward. "You ruined everything and you couldn't even write me back."

"What did I ruin, Nora?"

"Don't!" Nora heard her father's anger in her voice and her heart squeezed at the sudden memory of him. She let it strengthen her words even as she went against everything he'd ever taught her. "Don't say my name. I was supposed to kill you—"

"That sounds like a—"

"Stop! I'm talking now."

Colbie pressed her lips together, but they wobbled as she fought a smile. But Nora knew Colbie wasn't laughing at her. She looked... proud? Nora's breath caught. It took effort to look up from Colbie's lips. "I was supposed to kill you. You were supposed to be a monster. I was supposed to pick a mate in my pack and rise in the ranks. Make my father's memory proud. Be what my mother was. The pack has always been my family. Every time I think of you, I let them down."

Nora's hands were shaking. Colbie was still.

"How do you think of me?" the vampire asked.

Nora rolled her eyes. "You only care about yourself." Shaking her head, Nora backed up a step, realizing how close she'd come.

Colbie's hand snaked out faster than Nora's eyes could track. She grabbed Nora's wrist and pulled her near again.

"No. I care about Topher. I care about Poppy. I care about you. I care about how you think of me. I care that this is hard for you and you don't like it. If you hadn't been so reluctant, I never would have done what Topher asked of me. I thought I was doing you both a favor. Tell me, Nora. Tell me I was wrong. Tell me how you think of me."

"It hurts to think of you," Nora whispered. Colbie's eyes slid shut. It was easier to speak the truth when Colbie wasn't staring at her. "It hurts not to be with you. I wonder who you are all the time. I wonder why you make my heart skip around, even when I'm just remembering your smile. I've never thought about anyone the way I think of you. It wasn't an option to think about anyone but the pack. Now I don't have a choice but to think of you."

Colbie kept her eyes shut, but her hands were sure when they reached up and tangled in Nora's hair. Colbie pulled gently, guiding Nora's face closer, stopping when their lips were an inch apart. "Tell me you think about kissing me."

"I *dream* about kissing you."

Colbie's breath hitched. She closed the distance between them. Nora jumped when Colbie's saliva touched her lips and spread tingling warmth through her lips and cheeks. Her head went light.

"Sorry, I'm sorry," Colbie started to push away, eyes snapping open in horror.

"No." Nora wouldn't let her put distance between them again. "I wasn't expecting it, but I like it." Nora licked the saliva off her lips to prove the point. If she was going to defy her pack, she might as well do it right. The gentle, warm buzz eased the clenched anxiety in her stomach.

Colbie studied her. "I didn't think it would affect you. Like my charm doesn't."

Nora shrugged. "Maybe it's just kissing you."

Colbie laughed and started to respond, but Nora was done with talking. This time she was expecting the sweet taste of Colbie, the unexpected warmth so at odds with her cool skin. The buzz of Colbie's saliva danced pleasantly on her tongue and she wanted more. But Nora made herself experience the rest of this kiss. How Colbie was wrapping her hands tighter in her hair and pressing against her body. Nora stepped closer, one of her legs slipping between Colbie's as she backed her up into the wall of the stalls. Her hands pulled at Colbie's hips. She felt bold. She felt strong. Colbie welcomed it, matched it, encouraged it with breathless murmurs. They fit together. They fit so well.

Nora bit at Colbie's bottom lip. Colbie moaned and Nora's mind flickered. She was lost to Colbie. Colbie who sucked every rational thought from her head. Colbie who smiled like it was easy. Colbie and her wicked red lips that formed Nora's name with breathless perfection.

Nora tried to jump away when the bathroom door opened, but Colbie didn't let her move. She just looked at the woman who came in. Her charm thickened the air. "You don't see anything," she said.

The woman went into a stall, seemingly unaware of their presence. Colbie turned back to Nora, eyes possessive, the blue startling under the fluorescent lights. She tugged on Nora's hair and Nora let her head tip back, eyes landing on the water-stained ceiling tiles before she closed them. Colbie kissed the soft skin under Nora's jaw and stayed there, inhaling deeply as Nora's wild pulse pressed against her lips. Colbie came up with a smile, released her grip and dropped her head back onto the metal stall with a thunk that made Nora huff out a laugh. She wanted to keep kissing. She didn't want to leave Colbie's cool arms or the heat of her gaze. Colbie drew a finger down Nora's cheek, nail scratching lightly.

"We'll figure it out," she whispered.

Nora nodded and, on a whim, ducked her head to kiss Colbie's throat too. She nipped softly, claiming her place. She felt the vibration of Colbie's hummed approval.

The sound of the woman peeing interrupted the moment. She whispered into the soft skin, "I hate that our first kiss was in a public bathroom."

"We're nasty," Colbie agreed. "I love it."

"Is someone out there?" the woman asked, startled.

They stepped apart with a laugh. Colbie caught Nora's hand like it was the most natural thing in the world and led her from the bathroom. Nora clung to her slim fingers. They looked so delicate, but Colbie's grip was strong.

Poppy frowned from Colbie to Annaliese as Colbie slid back into her seat at the table, hand in Nora's.

"We kiss and make up?" Oliver asked with a cheeky grin. Poppy cut a look his way for encouraging them, but Oliver didn't appear bothered in the slightest.

"Yes," Colbie nuzzled Nora's neck. Nora glanced around the diner in a panic as if this and not the hand holding would give them away.

"Don't worry. They're LGBTQ friendly here," Oliver said.

Food came. Annaliese had ordered for Nora, but it didn't look like the girl would be eating much. She kept glancing at Colbie every few seconds. Colbie was always looking back.

"Adorable," Oliver said, his mouth full of fries. "If you need any vampire dating tips, I'm your man. Haven't quite figured out the sleep schedule, but it helps that I have to stay up all night studying half the time anyway. During the summer, I work nights and…" Oliver continued chattering away, filling whatever awkwardness the table might have held without him there.

Annaliese looked far too proud of herself every time she glanced across the table at the couple. Poppy couldn't decide if she should be angry or relieved. Colbie had been a wired mess between calling it off with Nora and Topher's drama. This was the first time she had really smiled since breaking it off. Poppy missed the sight desperately. And yet she couldn't help thinking about Topher.

Oliver finally took a break in his monologue to take a bite of his burger.

"Are you sure about this?" Poppy asked the couple. "Did you stop to think at all?"

"Poppyseed, when do I ever think things through?"

"But Topher—"

"Topher will understand."

Poppy felt her face heating. "You're so selfish, Colbie!" The words erupted. "He's killing himself trying to keep you safe and you're just making it harder on him! For a girl you *barely* even know."

Colbie carefully let go of Nora's hand and placed both her palms on the table. Taking a deep breath, Colbie met Poppy's eyes with an expression Poppy had never seen before.

Colbie spoke, voice low with just enough accidental charm to make Annaliese and Oliver lean closer. "Poppy. I love you dearly. I love living with you. I love being your friend. But you don't know Topher like I do. You don't know what I've given up for him, what he's given up for me. What I've done to him and what he's done to me. Our *entire lives* make up our history. You've only been part of the story since you signed the lease. He's my brother and I will always love him most. Our loyalty isn't something you're allowed to question. So I don't need you butting your head in where it doesn't belong just because you think you're in love with him."

Poppy went cold. The table started shaking, but Poppy couldn't stop the flow of magic.

Colbie continued, "He's my family. If I tell him I need Nora, he'll make it happen."

"I can't believe you said that," Poppy whispered. *Just because you think you're in love with him.* Colbie had seen right through Poppy yet still cast how she felt aside. Brushed it off like some whim. Like Poppy didn't know her own mind and heart. It was cruel. Dismissive. Humiliating. The bells jingled as the doors blew open. Annaliese was trying to hold the table still. Oliver's eyebrows were bunched with concern, looking from Poppy to Colbie like he wanted to step in.

Colbie rolled her eyes. She *rolled her eyes.* "You wouldn't be angry if it wasn't true. Calm down before you get yourself burned at the stake."

Poppy jumped to her feet. She snapped her fingers hard enough to create a blue spark. The water shot from her glass and sprayed Colbie in the face. The vampire barely reacted, but Nora let out a sudden, vicious snarl.

"Screw you, Colbie."

Poppy stormed out of the diner and straight for her car. She drove, no destination in mind. Her cheeks felt like they were on fire. She was embarrassed and frustrated and bewildered. The perfect storm to draw tears. How had Colbie been able to tell? Did that mean Topher knew how she felt? How long had they known and watched Poppy ache for him, too afraid to say anything herself? It didn't matter. The secret was out. If Topher didn't know now, he would soon enough. Too soon.

Poppy's tears left her cheeks and stayed suspended in the air around her. Her magic hissed and crackled. Rarely had she lost control like this. Separate from her humiliation and panic, she watched the tears float, fascinated. Like watching herself cry in a mirror. The car's interior was glowing from the blue cast off her skin.

Poppy drove in a twisting pattern through the streets of New Brecken. When she finally stopped, she was in front of a rusted, collapsing warehouse on the southside. Her mother would bring them here sometimes for practice. She stared at the dilapidated building for a long time, hands trembling on the steering wheel. The blue glow faded. She ignored her phone buzzing in her pocket.

Poppy got out of the car, her magic closing the door behind her. Walking inside was like slipping into a memory. Just herself and her sisters, her mother's disappointment a persistent pang in the background. She could so easily imagine her six sisters spread out around her, chanting as they practiced spells, filling the room with smoke and bangs. She walked carefully around a faded summoning circle left over from her mother's experiments. Experiments betraying an obsession they all pretended didn't exist.

Poppy stopped in the middle of the room and centered herself, pulling at her raging emotions. They were so close to the surface that just whispering the word "fire" made a flame crackle to life in her palm. She stared at it as it danced and warmed her face.

Why had Colbie said that? *Because you* think *you love him.* Of course Poppy loved him. It wasn't a matter of thought. It was a matter of him having a girlfriend. It was a matter of him distancing himself whenever a human was nearby. Him turning his affection on and off like a tap and leaving Poppy dizzy. It was the fact that he touched and smiled at her the same way he did Colbie.

It was a matter of the unknowable pain that sometimes crept into his eyes, making him seem truly like the creatures of the night her mother told her to stay away from until the day she vanished.

Poppy let the flame flicker out and sat heavily on the grimy floor. The smell of her coven's magic lingered in this empty place. Poppy dipped the toe of her boot in the brown puddle in front of her and looked up at the hole in the ceiling. She held up her hand with her fingers pinched and spread them like she was zooming out on her phone. Metal creaked as the hole widened, giving Poppy a view of the stars. She wished it was raining.

Her phone rang. Annaliese's name ran across the screen but undoubtedly it was Colbie on the other side. Poppy had yet to get them new phones after the bar dancing. Her chest twinged with pain at the happy memory.

Poppy looked down at the dirty puddle and debated trying

to contact her sisters. It was moments like these when the memories were so close that she could nearly convince herself it was a good idea. That they would welcome hearing from her. Maybe she would just reach out to—

"Why does it smell like smoke in here?"

Poppy whirled around on her knees and faced the boy who spoke from the doorway. A quick flare of her magic confirmed he was a werewolf. One of Nora's pack? He wore a black T-shirt despite the cool night.

It had been a long time since anyone had caught her unawares. Poppy put her guard up, reinforcing her personal wards and hiding the magic tang to her scent.

"I had a fire going." Poppy winced, wishing she'd thought up a better lie.

"Okay…" He took in the scene, sniffing, but trying to be discreet about it. And failing. He was all wolf.

The silence grew oppressive. Poppy stood up and brushed off her leggings.

"So, I hate to ask, but is that your car outside?"

Poppy frowned. "What about it?"

"I just chased off some hooligans slashing the tires."

Poppy groaned and rubbed her temples. "Some *hooligans*?"

He blushed and rubbed a hand through his hair. Poppy didn't smile, but a part of her warmed slightly to the boy. He had simple, mellow features: tanned white skin, medium brown eyes, and sandy blond hair. None of the painful beauty Topher and Colbie possessed with their sharp contrasts and charm.

"I mean, you do know this isn't a particularly safe part of the city, right?"

Poppy had known and should have put up wards around the warehouse the minute she parked, but she hadn't been thinking straight. She could maybe fix her car with magic; some was still crackling under her skin from the emotions of the night and the werewolf's energy, so close and vibrant. But she couldn't in front of him and would have to wait until he left.

"I know," she said. "But I'm fine. I'll just call my friends for a ride."

He kicked at the dirt with his red converse sneakers. When his gaze dropped, Poppy mumbled, "Hide the circle," under her breath. The summoning circle to his left vanished. A throb of pain pulsed in her temples. Maybe she didn't have as much magic as she thought.

"What's your name?" he asked.

"Poppy."

"Poppy is a great name."

"Yeah, well." She waited. It wasn't often she came across supernatural creatures without Topher's presence to take up their attention. Or her mother's before him.

"I'm Josh," he offered. A perfectly mellow name for a mellow guy. Poppy nodded and he heaved a breath. "Listen, I don't want to make you uncomfortable or anything, but I can't just leave you here on your own."

"You actually can. I'm fine. For all I know, you were the *hooligan* and I'd be better off if you left."

He grimaced and started walking around the warehouse. Poppy glanced around for any other evidence of witchcraft she needed to disguise.

"Why'd you come here?" he asked.

Poppy had this lie ready. "My father used to own the building. Not anymore, but I came here a lot growing up. Why are you here?"

"My crazy uncle bought the warehouse down the street."

"Interesting investment."

"Yeah, he's trying to convert it into an apartment complex. It's going to take a lot of work, though."

"No one would buy an apartment over here. We all know what happened with the warehouse apartments on the northside." Overrun with crime. With vampires so near, the area was somewhat better now, but the movement to convert the abandoned warehouses had halted.

"We take security measures real seriously."

Poppy considered him. She knew Nora's pack claimed the block by her old home, so was this a new pack?

"Who do you expect to move in?" she asked.

"Anyone tired of being scared," he answered.

Poppy felt something squeeze in her chest. This pack better be big or they would be chewed up and spit out by her city.

"Well, I'm not scared. And I don't need help. My friends are on their way."

He was closer now. A breeze blew in from the door he'd left open. When it lifted Poppy's hair and blew his way, he froze.

"You smell…"

Poppy held her breath. Her wards were strong. He shouldn't be able to smell her magic. He stopped talking, shaking his head.

"I smell?"

"Familiar?" he hedged. Poppy raised an eyebrow. He huffed a breath. "Okay, I'm not supposed to advertise, but I'm a werewolf. You smell like you've been around a werewolf."

Poppy shrugged, heart pounding. "I was on Fourth Street earlier. There's supposedly a lot of supernaturals over there."

He nodded like he wasn't convinced. "You took that easily."

"I think most people in New Brecken would."

He smiled at that. "It's been a long time since I've lived in a city. I'm glad this one is so accepting."

"I wouldn't say that. More so opportunistic."

"Well, opportunity isn't always so bad."

"You're just here for the money?"

"No." His eyes lit with challenge when he failed to elaborate. Poppy refused to rise to the bait and swallowed her questions.

She checked her phone. "Oh, look, my friends are here."

"Liar. My car is just down the road. Please, just let me give you a ride home." He winced. "Actually, that probably sounds way creepy. Can I at least wait with you until someone comes?"

Poppy narrowed her eyes at him.

"I swear I'll leave you alone after."

"Fine."

The answer came to her as they left the warehouse, Poppy downwind from Josh. It was harder to work the spell she wanted without speaking, but she managed by the time they reached her car. She walked a lap around it to inspect the damage.

"Um, I thought you said they slashed my tires? Kind of sketchy for you to lie about that."

"What?" Josh ran around the car, his mouth dropping open when he saw the pristine tires. "Holy cow."

Poppy took out her keys. "Maybe you scared them off before they could do it?"

"Maybe. But I was sure…"

"Anyway, nice to meet you, Josh." Poppy got in.

He yelled through the window to be heard. "It was nice meeting you too, Poppy. I hope I run into you again."

"We'll just have to see, won't we?"

He winked and stepped back, waving as she pulled into the street. She rolled her eyes but smiled a bit into the dark interior of the car. It shifted to a frown when she saw the tears still hanging in the air. She really didn't want to go home.

CHAPTER 14

Annaliese took Topher's bed yet again at Colbie's insistence. Without waiting for an invitation, Oliver made himself comfortable in Colbie's room, leaving Nora and her alone. Colbie paced in front of the TV and worried her lip. The sight was mildly distracting for Nora. Now that she'd kissed those lips, her mind was muddled with longing to do it again.

After another back and forth, Colbie let out a breath and tried calling Poppy again. She was using Annaliese's phone. Nora had to keep reminding her what the passcode was.

Nora heard it go straight to voicemail.

"Shit!" Colbie stared at the screen. "I can't believe I said that to her." She turned, stepped over the coffee table, jumped to the couch, and into Nora's side. "Well, I can, but I'm still a horrible friend."

Nora hesitated only a second before she put her arm around Colbie, who twisted so her back was against Nora's side. Colbie had been squirming and agitated since Poppy stormed out of the diner.

"Do you really think she's in love with Topher?" Nora asked.

"Please."

"Does he think so too?"

Colbie nodded, her bun flopping on her head. Nora wanted to take the hair tie out and see what Colbie looked like with her hair down. She imagined the curls loose would make her look softer.

"He doesn't like her back?"

"He doesn't think he's in a place where he can like anyone back."

"But does he?"

Colbie twisted to look up into Nora's face. "Maybe not? At least in that way. I mean, he does have a girlfriend, last I heard."

"*What?*"

"Last I heard," Colbie repeated. "I think he's done, but Julia doesn't know that yet."

"Jerk. Why wouldn't he tell her it's over?"

"I won't pretend to know what's going on in that head of his." But Colbie's eyes turned sad. There was more to the story.

"I think you do. If he didn't have Julia, would he like Poppy? Would he date her?"

Colbie smiled a bit and elbowed Nora's side. "Stop making me think about this so hard!"

"Well, I'm curious."

Colbie sat forward and spun so she faced Nora on her knees. She squinted her eyes as she thought. "Well… Topher is slow to love—"

"Like you?"

Colbie's smile was pure when Nora teased her. She pecked a kiss on Nora's cheek. Nora couldn't stop her own smile, making Colbie's eyes soften. Nora reached to run her finger over the rim of Colbie's ear, curious how it would feel. Cold, stiff, and smooth. As soon as she did it, she was embarrassed to have gone for the ear, but Colbie's expression was practically blissful. She pressed her cheek into Nora's hand before she could pull it away.

"You were a special case. Can we stop talking about my brother now?" Colbie whispered, her mouth inches away.

"Just finish that thought, at least." Nora couldn't say why this was important to figure out. Maybe she was just enjoying learning the patterns of Colbie's voice.

"Fine. He's dated Julia off and on for years. Like starting in middle school. They met through soccer. We all played since we were kids. But he's also confused a lot of friends with how affectionate he is—"

Nora snorted hard enough to hurt. "Topher? Affectionate?"

Colbie gave her a rueful smile. "Well, if you didn't come with a human attached to your hip, you'd see it more."

"What does Annaliese have to do with this? I thought Topher didn't mind her?" Nora shot a worried look to his door.

Colbie ignored the question. "Anyway, since the vampire thing, I've had an even harder time getting him to open up. He's pretty messed up in the head right now. He needs time to heal after—" Colbie halted and cleared her throat. "Never mind. I don't know how many times I've asked him about Julia. I don't think he's in love with her anymore, but he hasn't ended it either. He's probably clinging to the last of his humanity by stringing her along. Which isn't fair, but…" Colbie shrugged.

"What was he like? Before?"

"I thought we were finished talking about Topher?"

Nora grinned and leaned in, amazed by how easy the motion was. The kiss in the bathroom hours ago had been their first, but her lips felt like they'd known Colbie's for years. And the humming sound Colbie made every time they kissed was just sinful. Nora let herself fall back into the arm of the couch and Colbie pitched forward to stay with her. They were a tangle of limbs and heavy breathing when the door opened.

Topher's face barely reacted as he took the two of them in. "I'm guessing you did your best?" he asked Colbie.

"I really did, Toph."

"You held out longer than I thought you would, honestly."

"So little faith." Nora saw the exact moment Colbie remembered the issue at hand. She pushed off the couch. "Poppy's missing."

Topher froze. "Missing?"

"I was a bitch to her and she left the diner and hasn't come back. She's never not come back."

Topher checked the time on the microwave and nodded. "Tell Zayn Oliver's here before we go."

"We don't have his number anymore, remember?"

"Well, wake Oliver up to call him! We can't just leave them here unprotected."

Topher opened the door to leave but stopped short. "Never mind. She's here. Go apologize."

Colbie flew out the door and down the stairs. Nora heard Poppy let out an *oof* from the force of Colbie's hug before Topher shut the door behind her.

He went to the window and jerked it open. Cool night air slipped in as he pulled a pack of cigarettes out of his jacket pocket. Nora knew she was staring as he cupped one in his hand and lit it, but it had been a while since she'd seen someone smoke. The sight threw her. Topher raised an eyebrow as he inhaled and caught the smoke in his lungs.

"Those things will kill you," she said the first thing that came to mind. Topher blew the smoke out the corner of his mouth, eyeing her.

"They actually won't."

"Vampires don't get cancer?"

He nodded, looking slightly bored as he pulled in another drag. His movements were so practiced Nora wondered how long he'd been smoking. In fact, she abruptly realized she didn't know how old he and Colbie even were.

"Do you still feel it?" she asked, moving to sit on the recliner so she didn't have to twist to look at him.

He sighed, smoking pouring out from between his lips as he looked down at the burning cigarette between his fingers. "No. If I feed on someone who smoked recently, I get a hint of the nicotine buzz. If I hadn't smoked as a human, I probably wouldn't even know what I was feeling. It's just a habit. It's... comforting."

"How long have you been a vampire?"

"Almost a year now."

"Colbie too?"

"Yes."

"How did it happen?"

"To me or her?"

Something in his face said he wouldn't answer either way, but he was curious. "Your own story."

He shrugged, confirming her suspicions. "Wrong crowd, wrong place, wrong time."

"Colbie said she was attacked."

He nodded, taking an extra-long draw and releasing the smoke out his nose. "What did Colbie say to Poppy?" he asked, nodding toward the door. Nora could hear the low tones of Colbie's voice but not her words as she likely apologized.

Nora shifted in her seat and avoided his piercing gaze. "Ahh, she said, well. Poppy wasn't happy Colbie was making this harder on you. Us being, I mean, because we—"

Topher waved a hand in the air, halting Nora's stuttering. "Colbie fired back by addressing the elephant in the room?"

Nora nodded, and Topher actually smiled just a fraction. It hinted at a totally different face. "She does that. But she's also incredibly hard to stay angry with. They'll be fine. Poppy will be embarrassed, but she'll be fine. Best of luck to you, though." He tipped his cigarette in her direction.

Nora grimaced. "I don't know what I'm doing." She looked

down at her hands and found a hangnail to pick. Topher was hard to look at sometimes.

"Nora, I need you to understand something." Topher ground out his cigarette on the windowsill and came to sit on the coffee table in front of her. He brought the stinging scent of smoke with him. "Colbie is the most important thing in the world to me. I'm the reason we're in this mess and I'll do anything to keep her happy."

Nora swallowed, and readied to cringe away from the looming threat.

"That means taking care of you too now. Please, let me know if you ever need anything. If you're ever worried about her. I'll do everything I can to make this work. I don't know if it'll be easy, but we can figure this out."

Nora's mouth popped open. The sudden kindness in his steady gaze made the bright blue less shocking, more natural. She felt herself nodding. "I'm scared."

"It's terrifying," he agreed. His eyes turned sad, but he smiled at her.

Colbie's smiles were practiced. Each one a significant message she knew just how to get across. Each one beautiful and interesting and alluring.

Topher's smile was complete and innocent and alive. He had dimples. And crinkly eyes. He looked sweet. Artless. It was a stunning transformation.

"See what I mean?" Colbie asked as she and Poppy came in. Colbie was gripping the witch's hand and Poppy was letting it happen. "If he smiled like that outside, he'd cause a ten car pile-up."

Topher rolled his eyes and stood, smile dying. Nora saw the effort it took for him to smile at all, an effort she could only identify because she was familiar with the feeling. Suddenly she saw something mirrored in Topher that was constantly twisting in herself. Grief.

What or who had he lost?

Colbie crinkled her nose. "Stop filling the apartment with smoke, Toph. Popcorn?"

Poppy waved her hand. "Clear the air." A breeze rushed through the room, taking any residual smoke out the window. The witch looked exhausted by the spell.

"Better?" Topher asked them, looking pointedly at their hands.

Colbie batted her eyes at Poppy, who let out a sigh. "We're better."

Colbie pressed a kiss to the witch's cheek with an exaggerated *"mu-wah"* and Topher crossed the room to engulf them both in a hug. "Good."

The expression on Poppy's face when Topher's arms wrapped around her was so raw that Nora had to look away.

When Annaliese dropped her off at the Den the next morning, Nora hesitated before stepping inside. Her mind was full of Colbie's lips and smiles. Her lips were tender and bruised. She already missed being at the apartment. Something in her was changing, making it harder to walk inside this old house full of werewolves. Harder to hold onto her old plans and hopes for her future here.

It wasn't comfortable anymore. It wasn't the home she had known for years. She mourned the fact that it was her that changed, not the Den. This way of thinking felt dangerous. Unknown. She felt guilty. She was betraying the pack that raised her.

But she was also angry because maybe, just maybe, they were the ones betraying her.

She stepped into the living room and stopped short. Gabriel fell silent. The entire pack was stuffed into the room and gathered before him. These days Nora only saw them all together before they left to run under the full moon.

"You good, Nor?" he asked.

She didn't know what expression was on her face, but she worked to clear it. "Yeah. I'm fine."

"Have a seat. I was just getting started."

The room was full of tense shoulders and furrowed brows. Nora picked her way over the huddle of stacked legs and heads resting in laps to Matt's side, grateful she made it without tripping.

There wasn't much room next to Matt, but he scooted closer into the couch where he sat on its arm and she perched on the very edge.

"I texted you," he whispered in her ear. Nora pulled her phone out and saw the multiple messages warning her of the pack meeting and that Gabriel had news. She grimaced back at him, trying to look apologetic. He ruffled her hair with a smile. It held none of the brightness his grins usually did. Matt looked exhausted and Nora felt a pang. She had no idea what he and Gabriel had been up to lately, but it was taking a toll.

Matt settled his cheek on her shoulder. She sighed and was grateful again that Colbie lacked a scent.

"Now that we're all here, I'll get right to it. There's another pack in town."

Nora started. Several wolves around the room began to growl, making the whole place feel like it was set on vibrate. Nora turned to see what Matt thought of this.

"What? You knew?"

Matt shrugged. "Gabriel's been taking me to city meetings. We heard rumors, but then we met their alpha on Monday."

"What does this mean?" Luis yelled. His quick temper ignited in the left corner of the room. Other calls rose to answer.

"Quiet!"

Nora's back straightened and she flashed with pride when she heard the alpha's command deep in her bones. The urge to respect and listen and follow sang in her veins. No matter how disjointed she felt lately, she was still one with the pack. She turned her eyes back to Gabriel, pulse racing.

"As of now, they seem to want nothing to do with us. We haven't seen them making any trouble, but our territories have yet to overlap. They claim they've taken up in the southside warehouse district."

"How many?" Hank grunted, struggling to get his words out in the aftermath of Gabriel's order.

"At least fifteen. I haven't wanted to get too close," Matt answered. Nora spun to look at him. Since when was he running scouting missions?

Matt just nuzzled her shoulder.

"Will they protect the humans?"

"Will they hunt the bloodsuckers?"

Excited murmuring followed that question. Their pack wasn't big enough to truly hunt vampires without being decimated. But, if they had help… if they could grow their force. Nora didn't want to imagine how much more complicated her situation would become.

"All I want from you, for now, is to stay on your toes. If you so much as catch a whiff of them where they shouldn't be, I want to know about it. But don't act. Not yet. I don't want to start anything before I've talked with their alpha. That means behave." A layer of command entered his words.

Reluctant nods around the room.

"Now, on to happier news…" Gabriel nodded toward Heather where she sat on Patrick's lap.

She blushed. "I'm pregnant!"

Nora joined in the squealing, laughing burst of rowdy excitement. She even let out a howl with the rest before Gabriel gave them a stern look.

It had been years since someone in the pack had gotten pregnant. The instability of their lives and need to claim territory in the city worked against their reproductive instincts. Nora and fourteen-year-old Maggie were the youngest of the pack. No one spoke of it; they were too afraid to voice their concern that their pack could die out. But if Heather was pregnant, it meant Gabriel was fulfilling his duty as alpha, bringing a sense of safety and promise of a future to his followers.

Somehow Nora caught Gabriel's eyes in the midst of the celebrating. His smile was full of wonder. Not even he could believe he'd done this. In that moment, he looked younger than he had in years. She nodded to him, hoping to convey across the jostling room she'd never lost faith.

She wished her father was here to see it, but Matt caught her in a tight embrace before the sadness could dim the moment. Lupe lunged from the couch cushions to join the hug, and the three of them fell back into Chase, who laughed and wiggled on top of them. Nora saw only flashes of smiling faces through the squirming arms and torsos.

In their arms and warmth, Nora smelled wolf and home and acceptance and family. She thought of Colbie, who would never fit with this scene. Nora felt torn in two. Her thoughts on vampires, her body surrounded by wolves. Matt held on to her like his arms alone could pull her back together, face pressed into her neck. Her heart broke for him. This one time, she clung to him and imagined his uncomplicated affection could be her future.

But the image was just a flicker, soon surpassed by thoughts of Colbie.

CHAPTER 15

Topher woke with a dull ache behind his eyes. His bed smelled like Annaliese. His throat was already taut with thirst. His mind washed in familiar self-loathing, a pit he slipped into before he was fully conscious. His heart squeezed painfully and shame lanced. Topher stilled and made himself inhale the delicious scent of human. Forced himself to remember lunging for Oliver's neck nights ago, the sweet pulse there skyrocketing and singing to him. He'd been past even his vampire instincts at that point, which urged him to calm and charm his victim so that adrenaline didn't put a sour edge to the taste of blood. All he'd known was hunger and emptiness.

All he knew was no matter how hard he resisted, the monster was always there. It was who he was now.

His new phone pinged, a warning to get up and ready for work. It was already eight, the sun fully set. Topher could hear Colbie talking to Poppy, eager kindness dripping in her words. She was trying hard to get back on the witch's good side. The smell of sugar cookies sweetened the air.

He got up and dressed in jeans and a sweatshirt. Running his fingers through his hair, he did little else to make it look like he hadn't just rolled out of bed. Lana wanted him to try more but working on his image was unnecessary. Accidental charm earned him enough tips to cover apartment rent. If he tried harder, it would feel like stealing.

"Morning, Topher!" Colbie spun with a ready smile when he left his room. He couldn't stop himself from returning it. They were asking for it with Nora, but it was worth Colbie's happiness.

His heart stuttered when he saw the flush of blood race to Poppy's cheeks.

"Hey," she said.

He internally cringed from the awkwardness but kissed her temple and Colbie's as he crossed the apartment. "Late for work," he said, looking down to slide his feet into his sneakers.

"Don't think I missed you sleeping late because you aren't eating. Just because our deal is off doesn't mean you get to stop. You can't weaken yourself like that, Topher. Feed tonight, okay?"

"Sure, Colbie. Bye!" He hurried out the door. The smell of his human neighbors, more potent now that he'd tasted their blood, had him holding his breath as he ran down the hall on silent feet.

Poppy was the only one with a car at the apartment, something that wasn't a problem since vampire endurance and lack of sweat had become a thing, but Topher could feel his body was growing weaker and ran slower than usual, arriving five minutes late to his eight-thirty shift. Sammy quirked an eyebrow at him but didn't bother to comment. He took his place behind the bar, watching humans condense in front of him.

Raven showed up for her shift, the only human on staff though he knew she was in the process of registering to make the change. Topher focused on the drinks, the smell of blood mixing with alcohol until it was no longer appetizing and he could relax into his role.

Halfway through his shift, he brought in a keg and felt a

change in the air. Raven was clueless, but Sammy's expression pinched. The smell of wolf hit Topher in the next second. He straightened to face Gabriel. The alpha had taken a seat in the middle of his section.

Not even the animosity rolling off the werewolf was enough to deter the humans who crowded Topher's side of the bar. The wolf's scowl deepened the more they tried to get Topher's attention. Topher kept his own glare in place. The humans kept coming and Topher kept ignoring Gabriel's empty glass.

That was when Lana decided to make her appearance. She smelled like Grace's club, where she still spent most of her time, trusting Zayn and Topher to keep the Maker running.

"Christopher, our guest's glass is empty!" Lana called, sitting next to the alpha. Gabriel leaned as far from her as the close stools would allow, his lip curling.

Lana raised a hand to her cheek, mockingly affronted. "Well, don't give me that look. You came to *my* club. I can only assume that means you want to deal with me."

"No," Gabriel said. He watched Topher grudgingly grab his glass and fill it with the cheapest beer on tap. "I was hoping to ask your man a few questions."

"My man? My man," Lana looked like she was enjoying the taste of those words in her mouth. She straightened. "Quiet!"

The humans of the bar stilled, charm blanking their features. Across the room, Tamera cut the music with a smirk. Gabriel started in his seat, spilling some of his beer. What had he expected?

"Christopher..." Lana spoke in a tone that never meant anything good. Topher turned to her, dread a cold and familiar coil behind his sternum. His maker pulled herself up to sit on the bar, facing Gabriel. She tilted her head and stroked her neck. Swallowing his revulsion, Topher moved forward. He placed his hands on her waist and kissed where she'd indicated, running his lips lightly over the curve of soft skin, lingering where her neck met her shoulder. She liked it when he kissed there.

She sighed and spoke, voice carrying in the room full of waiting, silent humans. "This isn't a man, Gabriel. This is mine. My pet. My darling. My creation." She made an impatient sound, and Topher pulled her closer, trialing his lips under her short hair and paying attention to the other side of her neck. From the corner of his eye, he caught Sammy shifting uncomfortably but used to Lana's demonstrations by now. He let his mind slip, only half aware of the conversation.

"But..."

"I don't need to charm him, alpha. He belongs to me. Anything you have to tell him doesn't matter. If you have business with my darlings, you only have business with me. I've been feeling especially protective ever since my other darling was killed. It looked like an animal attack. I don't want to start pointing fingers, but your being here doesn't look good. Now, do you have business with me?"

"Let the humans go."

Stupid wolf. Lana laughed and Topher felt it rumbling where his lips stilled on her throat. Lana twisted under his hands, looking back to cup his cheek. "Christopher, take the humans."

He hid his grimace and sent out his charm just as Lana released hers. The human faces turned to eager smiles rather than blank, empty stares. Heads tilted in unison. Lana pressed her lips to his and he tasted blood from her recent victim. His stomach rumbled.

"They don't need to remember the last few minutes, do they?" she asked him, looking up from under her lashes. She toyed with the hair behind his ear.

"Forget this," he said, the intention behind his charm making the meaning clear. Most vampires had to be more specific. Topher hated this further evidence of his power.

Gabriel clutched his glass, knuckles white. Lana leaned in and pressed a kiss to Topher's throat. He obediently tilted his head, baring it for her. "There's a good pet," she whispered to his skin, breath cold. She nipped, just enough to break skin.

Topher felt nothing. Not the bliss. Not the shame. Not the anger. Just Lana's darling. He was far away.

"Your business?" Lana finally turned back to Gabriel.

He shook his head in disgust and stood fast enough to knock over his stool. "You can't live like this. You are not gods. You are not too powerful to fall. You can't just flaunt your control like this and not expect consequences."

"Are you threatening me, wolf?"

"Not yet." With quick steps, Gabriel pushed his way out of the club.

Lana smirked and slinked down from the bar. Topher released the humans, who carried on as if nothing had interrupted their night. Tamera turned the music back up.

Topher let out the breath he'd been holding as Lana let the crowd envelop her, pulling the most beautiful humans forward to clamp onto their necks. He lost so much inflection in his voice and expression that his charm barely touched the humans he served. Sammy kept shooting him looks and texting under the bar, probably Zayn, but Topher ignored her. Even when the club cleared out and they set to closing, he stayed silent.

"What do you think the wolf wants with you?" Sammy asked as they left. Topher lit a cigarette and shrugged.

"You think he knows about Colbie?"

Topher filled his lungs and shook his head.

Sammy put a hand on his arm. "You okay?"

Topher blew out the smoke. "See you tomorrow, Sammy."

He felt Sammy watching him as he walked away. No matter how much smoke Topher inhaled, he could still taste Lana on his tongue. He should probably be grateful she'd never wanted more than the kissing, biting, and cuddling, but she was just a nudge away from demanding more. Topher didn't feel he had more to give her but knew that wasn't true. Lana could keep taking long past what he imagined.

Topher passed Patty's. His roommates' scents lingered in the air. Annaliese and Nora too. They had long since gone, but Topher wondered how close their paths might have come to Gabriel's. The alpha had been blocks away from discovering Nora's secret. Topher hoped Lana's actions tonight would be enough of a deterrent for the wolves to leave him alone.

It was strange to hope Lana's presence in his life could lead to anything positive.

Colbie was reading with Mouse in the living room when he walked in. Poppy snored softly in her room; the door cracked. Topher kicked off his shoes and sat down next to his sister, resting his cheek on her shoulder. His shoulders slowly began to relax as he returned to himself.

"What's wrong?" Colbie asked, tossing aside her book.

"Nora's alpha came by the club again. Lana got… territorial."

"With you?" Topher didn't answer, but Colbie stiffened, guessing the situation correctly.

"Topher, you can't just put up with that."

"I'll figure it out."

"You didn't eat either."

"No."

"Are you ever going to call Julia?"

Oh Julia. "I don't think so."

"Why not?"

Topher shrugged and Colbie leaned away from him, forcing him to sit up or fall into her. He met her concerned gaze and licked his thumb before pressing it into the furrow collected between her brows. She smacked his hand away, but the old trick brought a smile to her lips.

"Talk to me. Please."

Topher sighed and looked at his hands. "I can't call her. She loves me so much more now that I'm a vampire."

"She's loyal, Topher. She loves you. Why is that wrong? You need the support."

Topher sighed and ran a hand through his hair. He caught the smell of cigarette smoke coming off his jacket.

"She loves me more now *because* I'm a vampire. Not because I need the support. All the things about this that I hate so much, she's drawn to. Just like all the other humans. When her mom decided she wanted family time the night before Julia left for college, she asked me to charm her mom into letting me stay. She was *always* joking about me charming people for her. And there was the saliva thing; she couldn't get enough of it. Every time we kissed, she'd just turn her head, wanting me to bite her neck. Every time, Colbie. I couldn't kiss my girlfriend without her wanting me to feed on her. Do you know how messed up that feels?"

"So why didn't you end it? When she started acting like this. Why did you even get back together after you got turned?"

Topher still couldn't meet his sister's eyes. His empty stomach twisted. He scratched Mouse behind his ears. "Because I needed to feed. I saw Zayn and Oliver and it felt better to feed from someone who knew what was happening than a stranger I grabbed at the club."

Colbie put a hand on his cheek, forcing him to look up. "Poppy says we have to avoid cliches, Topher. This conflicted vampire shit is old news. Break up with your girlfriend and keep feeding off the addicts at the club. They all talk about how much you're helping them stay sober. Get your head right because this isn't going away. You have to learn to control not only your thirst and your charm, but how you move in this world. You've made mistakes, but you've always been so good. That's all still there. You have every right to be here, Topher. Every right to be happy."

Topher smiled at his sister. "You all make me happy. I said I'll figure this out, and I will. You just have to let me be a cliche for now."

Colbie nodded, letting it go for the night. "I love you, Toph."

"Love you too, Colbs."

Topher got up to shower away the smell of smoke and went to bed, his thoughts heavy and swirling. He took a vial from his stash of sleeping draughts and swallowed it in one gulp. Only after he'd begun to relax into the pillows did he realize he should have asked Colbie how things were going with her and Nora. He promised himself he'd make up for it tomorrow night and let the potion take hold.

CHAPTER 16

"Thanks, Caleb!" Oliver turned from the counter. Nora stifled a smile at the horrified look Annaliese shot him. Her friend took issue with people who referred to strangers by the names on their nametags. She wasn't given time to comment before it was their turn to order their drinks at the café down the street from campus.

Once Annaliese paid, they waited at the pick-up end of the counter with Oliver.

"I should have gotten a cookie. Zayn says I've been stress eating and I taste— I mean, he can tell and is worried. Way too much sugar." When Oliver talked about his boyfriend, he reached up and placed his fingers on the two small scars on the left side of his neck. Nora couldn't stop her revulsion at the sight but tried to temper it. "But don't those look amazing?"

Annaliese rolled her eyes and went to find a table.

"They do look good," Nora agreed, just as a barista pulled the one she ordered from the case to hand it to her.

Oliver's eyes widened. "You know you have to share now, right?"

"Maybe a bite or two."

Oliver did a dance in place. Nora laughed again when

Poppy entered the cafe, came up behind Oliver and poked the sides of his waist, stopping his dance and making him jump with a whirl.

"I don't think you need any more caffeine there, Oliver," Poppy said as she sailed past to order.

"Devil woman!" he called cheerfully after her. "Oh, thank you, Tiffany!" He accepted his green Frappuccino stacked high with whip cream, wiggled his eyebrows at Nora, and went to sit with Annaliese.

Poppy joined Nora, holding the lid of her personal mug. "You coming out tonight?" she asked.

"I don't know. My alpha forbid me from going back to the Maker."

Poppy pulled a face. "I have so many issues with that."

"Well, I mean, his commands don't hold me like they do other pack members yet, so it's still my choice. But if he finds out, I'll be in deep shit. Especially if they find out about Colbie."

"You're just going to keep her a secret forever?"

Nora was relieved when the barista passed her Annaliese's tea and her latte. She avoided answering as she poured honey into Annaliese's mug. Poppy got her cup back, full of her bitter-smelling tea.

They found Oliver and Annaliese with their books already opened. Oliver had a whip cream mustache that made it difficult to believe he was comprehending the complex diagram of the heart he studied. He looked up when Poppy and Nora joined the table.

"Annaliese says she's going out tomorrow night, Popcorn."

"Tomorrow? I thought the plan was tonight," Poppy said.

"I made this plan with Alex and Molly," Annaliese said. "Thanks for that, by the way. Molly can't stop gushing about how you got him to ask her out."

"Love potion?" Oliver asked. Poppy shrugged and he raised his hand for a high-five. "Nice."

Annaliese choked on her tea. "You gave him a *love potion*?"

"I needed her help studying!"

Oliver laughed. "You're so badass, Poppy."

Nora was as stunned as Annaliese. It was one thing to watch Poppy brew potions for Topher or snap her fingers to summon the remote. It was another to realize she had no qualms against enchanting humans for her own gain. Nora remembered the wind blowing and the table trembling when Poppy was angry at Colbie the other night. That had been the first real hint at the depths of Poppy's power. It made Nora question the long-held belief in her pack that vampires were the biggest threat in the city. Nora liked Poppy, but how many other witches moved through New Brecken with that kind of magic?

The door of the cafe opened. Nora's instincts instantly came alert, rising like hackles. The newcomers smelled like wolves, but not her pack. She listened carefully as they ordered behind her.

"Are you okay, Nora?" Annaliese asked.

Nora made to answer, but one of the wolves approached. She swallowed the growl building in the back of her throat.

"Well, if it isn't Miss Poppy of the not-actually-slashed tires!" the wolf exclaimed. "I'm thinking now you might have lied to me about why you smelled a bit like wolf."

Poppy shot Nora a warning glance before they turned to the boy. Nora let out a quiet growl. He raised his hands.

"Hey, now!" He smiled reassuringly. Knowingly. "It gets easier after the first couple of shifts. Just take a breath, okay?"

The two other werewolves watched intently from the pick-up counter. They were blond and looked too much alike to be anything other than twins. Neither girl looked happy watching their pack member talk with them.

"This is Josh," Poppy said, not exactly pleased. "I met him the other night after, well, after that fight with Colbie."

Nora stiffened when Josh pulled up a chair between her

and Poppy and straddled it backward. He offered his hand. "You're part of the Morales pack, right?"

Nora reluctantly shook his hand, softening just a bit when he referred to it by her family name and not Gabriel's. "Yeah."

"How close are you?"

Nora shrugged. "Soon. Gabriel says this moon or next." If she ever found a vampire to kill.

Josh smiled. "We'll have to run together. My uncle's been trying to get ahold of your alpha, but he isn't the most open fellow."

"No, he's not. I'm really not supposed to be talking with you." Nora ignored the face Poppy pulled.

"Oh, the joys of being able to ignore a command." Josh winked. "So listen, our pack's been moving around for years—different parks and towns and cities. We're good at territory lines and sharing, so if you get a chance, tell your alpha we don't want trouble. New Brecken is the friendliest place for supernaturals right now, so we came here, but we don't want to step on any toes. My uncle was pretty intimidated by that mobster meeting y'all had."

"Mobster meeting?"

"You didn't hear about it? Oh well, my uncle didn't stay long anyway. I'm sure your alpha didn't say anything for a reason." He turned back to Poppy. "Anyway, I've been kicking myself since you left for not asking for your number."

"*Ahhh.*" Oliver beamed and drew the wolf's attention. Josh's eyes immediately fell to the fang scars on Oliver's neck. His entire body recoiled.

"Are you asking for it now?" Poppy asked, the words coming out in a rush as she tried to distract Josh. He pulled his eyes away from Oliver, rubbing at his own neck. Oliver blushed, but his gaze never faltered and he tipped his chin up.

"I suppose I am," Josh said.

Poppy stole one of Oliver's blank index cards. She hastily jotted down her number and pressed it into the werewolf's hand. "Looks like your friends are waiting for you," she said with a pointed look.

Josh hesitated, glancing around the table for a prolonged beat, but he nodded and rose. "See you around, Poppy. Nice to meet y'all."

"Bye!" Oliver waved, the moment already behind him.

Josh crossed the cafe and Nora tried to relax, especially when Annaliese leaned forward. "Seriously, Nora? You look ready to hulk out."

Nora growled softly, making Annaliese smirk. She forced herself to sink back into her chair. "I feel like he might be a problem," she said.

"I agree," Poppy said, picking up her phone and showing Nora the message Josh had already sent her.

"Are you going to text him back?" Oliver asked.

"I don't know."

Another question hung in the air. One they all knew to wonder since Colbie had exposed the witch. *What about Topher?*

No one dared to voice it as Poppy stared at the screen.

"I think you should," Annaliese declared, surprising everyone. "He seems nice. And I think it would be good for us to know what's going on with the other pack."

"You're probably right," Poppy muttered. "And the tea leaves did say we'd meet another wolf."

They sipped their coffee and Oliver turned back to his flashcards, hand drifting again to the scars on his neck.

As the sky reluctantly darkened outside the apartment, Nora's frowns toward Colbie's closed door grew more frequent. Her impatience was nearly comical. Annaliese pestered Poppy for updates on her conversation with Josh. The texts hadn't moved past careful small talk. Poppy avoided any mention of her family, roommates, or supernatural hobbies. This left only her life at the university open to discussion and an occasional mention of her cat. Josh's efforts to keep the conversation going were finally faltering. His responses grew more sporadic and each message shorter than the last. Poppy had high hopes of the talk just fizzling out.

Until Josh asked her to dinner the next night.

"He can't be serious!" Poppy exclaimed. Hadn't she done enough to deter the guy?

Annaliese quickly read the message and clapped. "Oh, you got him! He must like you to still be trying after all your dry-ass texts."

Poppy groaned and let her head fall back in the recliner.

A clatter came from Colbie's room as she woke and mumbled Nora's name from within. Nora perked up like a puppy. Colbie stumbled into the living room and collapsed on top of Nora and Annaliese on the couch. Annaliese immediately squirmed out from under her, looking distinctly uncomfortable. Nora wore a small, pleased smile as Colbie wrapped her arms around Nora's waist and nestled her face into Nora's stomach.

"I missed you," Colbie said, voice muffled. Annaliese snorted. She walked over to the plate of cookies on the counter and grabbed one as she settled on a stool.

"I saw you last night!" Nora laughed a bit. Poppy noted she had a nice laugh.

Colbie's arms tightened around Nora. "Only for a couple of hours."

Nora let out a breath. "My pack has been asking questions."

Colbie mumbled something else, but it was unintelligible. She went quiet, falling back to sleep in Nora's lap. It was just after five, still early for her and Topher to be up.

"They sleep hard," Annaliese said.

It had taken Poppy months to get used to how eerily still her roommates were when sleeping. She once held a mirror under Colbie's nose to see if she was still breathing, but her breath blew out too cold to fog the glass.

"They do," she said. "That's why the stories say they die during the day. Sometimes I can get Colbie up when the sun's out if I need one of them. Forget Topher, though."

"Why does he take sleeping draughts then?"

Poppy hesitated. "Nightmares. They help with that."

Annaliese frowned. Poppy knew she still bought into the persona Topher wore around humans to keep his charm at bay. A large part of Poppy hoped the girl never saw more of the boy who often stumbled out of his room like Colbie just did, hair wild and goal only to get closer to warmth, snuggling up with Poppy on the couch or standing close, chin resting on her shoulder as she brewed at the stove.

In those moments, Poppy had to cast a ward around her heart to muffle its sporadic beating. Apparently, she hadn't been careful enough. Of course they knew. And he hadn't done anything about it.

Poppy's phone pinged.

Josh: *It doesn't have to be dinner.*

Annaliese came near to lean on the back of the armchair and read over Poppy's shoulder. A satisfied gleam entered her eyes. "Say something sexy back. Like… what else do you have in mind? Oh wait, that was horrible. Nora, help!"

Nora looked startled by the concept that she would have any ideas. She lifted her shoulders in a shrug, jostling Colbie's limp form.

Poppy was glad the vampire was asleep. Colbie would be all too happy and capable of generating some ridiculous response.

Her phone gave a staccato buzz.

Josh: *We could go to the movies.*

Josh: *Or maybe you're into more supernatural things, judging from the company you keep.*

Josh: *We could prowl the dark streets of New Brecken.*

Josh: *We could make sacrifices to the moon goddess.*
Josh: *We could practice our howling.*
Josh: *...I'm really good at fetch.*

Annaliese snorted behind her. "I like him. Put him out of his misery already. Say you'll toss a few frisbees."

"You don't like *anyone*," Nora said from the couch. She was glaring at Annaliese, her protective instincts from the café reappearing.

Annaliese scowled right back at her. "I'm pushing this for you and the pack. I'm friends with them too, you know. Matt has been texting me nonstop, worried about you and the new wolves. If we can get information without risking anyone—"

"We shouldn't risk Poppy!"

Poppy bristled. "I can handle myself."

Nora glared between Annaliese and her, unhappy with them but at a loss for words. Poppy typed up a quick message, her pride smarting. She told Josh she'd go to lunch with him.

Annaliese's smirk was pleased. "Tell him kibble better not be on the menu."

Nora's scowl darkened, her mood turning foul enough that Colbie tensed and woke up, glancing around the room for threats. She sat and searched Nora's face. Nora's dark look relaxed instantly under her attention.

"What's going on?" Colbie asked.

"Poppy has a date!" Annaliese announced. Colbie's eyes were much too concerned when she looked at Poppy, making Poppy raise her chin.

"I met a werewolf the other night."

"Pop Rocks! You can't go out with a werewolf too! Topher will die from the anxiety of it all!"

Poppy's face flushed. "I can take care of myself."

Colbie looked ready to argue her point, but Poppy could see her struggling not to sound hypocritical. The healing wounds of their last fight held Colbie back. She opted not to speak for once, settling an arm around Nora and pressing her lips into a minor pout.

An hour later, pizza was delivered and eaten. Colbie was ready to go feed. She glanced at Topher's door. "Go wake him up," she said to Poppy.

"Why don't you?"

Colbie nuzzled Nora's neck in response.

Poppy pulled a face; she was determined to prove nothing had changed since the fight. She gathered herself and went to Topher's room like she had a hundred times before. She knocked briefly and pushed the door open.

He lifted his head, knocking the pillow covering it to the floor. He slowly blinked the sleep from his eyes. "Morning, Poprocks."

"Hey," Poppy cleared her throat after her greeting came out breathy.

She sat next to him on the bed, casting spells to keep her body's reactions to the proximity undetectable. He instantly curled up against her warmth. He was wearing a t-shirt and Poppy could see his elbow looked more knobby than usual. Even the roses of his forearm tattoo looked smaller than they had a few days ago. He was losing weight he didn't have to spare. "Colbie's ready to head to the club."

"I don't work tonight."

"You need to go feed."

"I need more sleep." He closed his eyes and pressed his face into his pillow. Poppy frowned at the number of empty vials on his nightstand. How many had he taken?

"You're tired because you haven't fed."

"I know. I'm going to sleep."

"Christopher…"

"Penelope…"

She had to fight a smile at that. "Please, go feed. I'm worried about you." He didn't respond. She shook his shoul-

171

der. "Topher! You can't just starve yourself. Colbie needs you. She won't give up Nora and—"

"Then tell her not to go to the club. She can feed on the street. You can go with her and keep her out of trouble as well as I could."

"But—"

"I won't tonight, Poppy. I'm fine for another day."

"You're being ridiculous, Topher. You have to get over this!"

"Now you sound like Lana. Just get out, Poppy." He rolled away from her.

Poppy left the room and paused, leaning against his closed door and looking down at the bracelets and rings she wore. It must be time to recast the wards around her mind and refresh the charms. Because Topher had effectively charmed her for the first time. The realization made tears prick the back of her eyes.

It was a struggle to keep her voice steady. "He doesn't want to get up. I'll go with you to feed, Colbie."

Colbie frowned but sensed something was off. She turned to Nora. "Will you stay and make sure nothing happens to him? We'll be right back."

Nora gave a curt nod and Poppy shook her head at the sight. Only Colbie could convince a werewolf to stand guard over a vampire.

CHAPTER 17

Topher woke to his door opening a second time, but he didn't bother to lift his head. Annaliese's scent proceeded her into the room. Crisp, warm, and intoxicating. It reminded him of his mother's favorite candles. His brain was too slow to name the scent—something floral but also like something baking in the oven.

"I'm stealing your bed," she said, standing over him, hands on hips.

He gave himself a beat, testing if this would be okay. His mouth watered enough for him to question himself, but he was in control. He rolled over to make room for her, flopping a pillow down next to him to separate the halves of the bed like last time.

She hesitated. "Aren't you getting up?"

He pulled his comforter over his head in response. After a short pause, Annaliese climbed in.

"You better not—"

He stuck his feet under her legs. She huffed and he couldn't help but release a small laugh. When Annaliese stiffened, his heart sank. Could his charm travel through a comforter with just a laugh?

"Are you *laughing*? Do you even know how to smile?" she asked.

Topher relaxed and did let himself smile. "Shut up. Go to sleep."

Annaliese huffed again but got situated under the blankets. Topher's feet slowly began to warm under her calves, a thin sheet between them.

"Topher?"

"Hmm?"

"What happened Monday night that has everyone so worried about you?"

He shifted, acutely aware of how close she was. How human. "I did a job for my maker. It... messed me up. I tried to attack Oliver after."

"Is it as bad as all that? The jobs? Are you in danger?"

"I'm protecting Colbie."

"That's not what I asked."

He sighed.

"Me being here, am I in danger?"

"Probably." His stomach clenched in another wave of hunger as if to prove it.

"Would you protect me too?"

It was impressive how casual she kept her tone when he could hear her heart pounding. Smell the adrenaline spike in her blood. She jumped when his hand found hers under the pillow separating them, but she didn't pull away. "I would."

"And Nora?"

"Yeah, her too."

"And Poppy?"

"Poppy doesn't need protecting."

"So why did you want to stop us from hanging out?"

"Because I haven't figured it out yet."

"Figured what out?" Annaliese's frustration hung in the air between them.

"One: how to control my charm. More specifically, if it's

even possible for me. Two: if I have any power in this or if my participation is only enough to keep Colbie safe. Three: why members of Nora's pack are involved and meeting with Lana at the Maker. Four: if this new pack was lying or not. Five: what Lana wants from me. Six: what Gabriel wants from me. Seven: if Colbie—"

"Okay, you've got a lot on your plate." She sounded annoyed, but her hand squeezed his just the tiniest amount.

"What do you know about Nora's pack?" he asked.

"I've hung out there a lot. They aren't a threat to humans."

"Just vampires."

"Yeah. There's bad blood there."

Topher smiled again. "Pick a better expression."

"History. There's history there."

They fell quiet. Topher focused on Annaliese's warm hand and keeping his hold gentle around her fingers. He waited for her to pull away. His mind played with the concept of just how easy it would be to drag it to his mouth and drink from her wrist. It was almost enough for him to let go.

She didn't pull away but didn't seem much aware of the point of contact either. Not squeezing. Not possessive. Not even comforting. Just there.

"She trusts them?" he asked.

"I think so. Matt has been weird lately, but I think he wants them to be mates."

Topher's hand twitched. "The plot thickens," he mumbled. Annaliese let out a short laugh.

"Are you laughing over there? You know how to smile?" Topher asked, matching Annaliese's incredulous tone from earlier.

Annaliese used her free hand to reach over the pillow and punch his shoulder. She laughed again when she saw he was still completely hidden by the blanket. "Shut up. Go to sleep."

Hand warm in hers, feet still beneath her, Topher did as he was told.

Topher slept poorly, his stomach often waking him with a painful clenching. Each time he let the sound of Annaliese's even breathing lull him back into a doze. Topher could hear his sister and Poppy when they came back. The sickly-sweet fumes of a potion floated under his door. He briefly debated digging out another sleeping draught but opted not to risk waking Annaliese.

It was early still when he woke to Annaliese leaving the room, using the bathroom, and stumbling back into bed. She hadn't closed the door all the way and moments later, Mouse nudged his way in. Annaliese started when he jumped onto the end of the bed.

"Oh my god. What the hell is that?"

"Mouse."

Annaliese kicked out and sat up. "A mouse?"

Undeterred, Mouse padded up the layers of blankets to Topher's waiting hand. "This is Mouse." He struggled to hold in a laugh as Annaliese slowly laid back down.

"Who names a cat Mouse?"

"Colbie, who else?"

Annaliese snorted. Mouse settled down on the pillow between their faces. Now that it was weighed down, Topher could see Annaliese on the other side. He worked to reign in any charm. It was easier than usual, his hunger dampening its strength.

Annaliese met his gaze, lips pursing and concern darkening her eyes. "Topher?"

"Hmm?"

"How long has it been since you ate?"

"Since I tried to kill Oliver."

"That was days ago!"

Topher shrugged and pulled a blanket up to his chin. Then higher, over his nose as if it would help mask her smell. He could feel the proximity of the sunrise, the promise of more sleep.

"You didn't do it on purpose," she said softly.

"Why do you care?" he asked, letting some of the edge he used around humans enter his tone.

She rolled her eyes. "Why shouldn't I care?"

"Because I'm a vampire. Because you don't really seem like the caring type? Because it was Oliver. *Oliver!* Because—"

"Topher, shut up."

He closed his eyes. He was so weak and tired. The bed rocked gently as Annaliese rolled fully onto her side to face him. Her breath, her delicious smell, broke over his face.

"Topher?"

He opened his eyes. "Yes?"

Annaliese bit her lip. Topher raised his eyebrows, inviting her to continue. If he hadn't been starving, her face would have gone slack and her thoughts would have spilled out of her. "I have some friends at school who want to go out. One said they were going to check out the Maker. I told them I could get in."

"How *have* you been getting in?"

"A fake. But, if you're working, will you serve me? I don't want a repeat of the last couple of times I was there." She shot him a look.

"Anything you want." Topher instantly regretted his words and the warm tone. He couldn't read Annaliese's face and worried he'd charmed her. But her eyes were intent, not unfocused and happily submissive.

"Um. Thanks. I know it shouldn't matter, but it'd be embarrassing to be turned away in front of them. Or puking my guts up."

"Why are you so worried?"

Annaliese scratched Mouse, snorting with amusement when he rolled onto his back and shamelessly exposed his belly for her. The sound of his purring filled the space between them. Topher didn't think Annaliese would answer, but when she did, her voice was soft. Sad. "Because I think Nora's going to leave me behind. The wolves are so private. Some of them date humans, but Gabriel doesn't like us around the Den. And she always tries so hard to keep Gabriel happy. She has Colbie now, so maybe she won't lose herself to them. To him. But I think that I need to play it safe and try to make new friends. Human friends. Just in case she cuts me out after the change."

"Regardless, friends are usually a good idea."

"Just don't get me too drunk, okay?"

"Don't order from Zayn and you'll be fine. I got you."

"You're not really an asshole, are you?"

"I have to be. We can only have this conversation without me charming you because I'm so damn hungry."

"You won't lose control and eat me, will you?"

Topher repressed a smile. "Oh, I'm at the end of my leash. But the sun's about to rise and that'll drop me. You should be safe."

Annaliese studied him. "You look like shit."

"You really are an asshole, aren't you?"

She smiled. The sight of it stayed with him.

Colbie bounced along beside Topher, having declared she would walk him to work. He laughed as she told him about last night, the smile on her face clearing his dark mood and distracting him from his hunger.

Colbie wondered when she should move past kissing if she was the first girl Nora had been with or if that mattered.

She groaned. "What if she decides the boobs aren't actually for her?"

"Then it's a good thing you barely—"

"Don't you finish that sentence Christopher James West."

"I don't think I have to, Colbie Fay West."

She smiled, but concern made it look strained. He knew his own smile didn't reach his eyes.

"You need to—" she began.

"I know."

They fell quiet, nearly to the alley Topher used as a shortcut to get to Fourth. Topher froze when he caught Gabriel's scent on the breeze. Colbie hadn't picked it up yet. She glanced up at him in confusion.

"Colbie," Topher laced his voice with all the charm he still possessed. It was enough, though the effort made him dizzy. Her eyes widened as she waited for his command. "Go to Poppy. Quickly. Don't worry about me."

Colbie turned and ran. Topher continued, turning into the alley to meet the wolves. Alone. His sister safe.

Gabriel stepped out of the shadows. The red-haired wolf, Matt, just steps behind him.

"Well, look who it is," Topher drawled, working to keep the tension from showing in his shoulders.

"Where's your master?" Gabriel asked. Wolves circled Topher, coming from both ends of the alley. Topher couldn't smell Nora among them.

"Lana? Oh, she's probably around here somewhere." Topher gestured vaguely with his hand and noticed it was shaking. He tucked it into his sweatshirt pocket.

"We're still two blocks from the club. I wouldn't say that's *around*."

Topher shrugged. "What's your endgame here, Gabriel?"

"You're the strongest vampire I've seen."

"Okay…"

"Too strong for someone like Lana to have in her pocket." Topher fought off a shiver. "Too strong for someone like Connor Grace to have in his pocket. We have to keep a balance around here."

Topher let them draw near, knowing he didn't have the strength to fight the wolves off successfully. His stomach twisted at the thought of simply giving up. Colbie would never forgive him if he didn't at least try. He snapped a fist forward and felt the satisfying crunch as it connected with Gabriel's nose. The alpha stumbled back. The smell of his blood, hot, fresh, and wild, saturated the alley.

Topher ducked a reaching arm and spun to the left, hitting the wolf's stomach so hard she wheezed. Matt came next, quick on his feet and quieter than his bulky companions. Topher barely got his elbow up in time and it wasn't a hard enough hit to the jaw to deter the young wolf. Matt caught him in a hold and two more wolves jumped forward to grab Topher's arms.

Topher straightened and faced Gabriel, his head spinning from his effort and hunger. The alpha was swearing and bleeding from both nostrils. His skin quivered as he fought the change. Breathing hard and visibly straining to collect himself, Gabriel stepped forward and tried to give Topher an injury to match his own with a lightning-fast punch. Gabriel followed up with a hit to the stomach that would have knocked the wind out of a human. Topher barely winced.

Topher managed to gesture to his face, where he knew there was no evidence of the blow. "Hey Gabriel, your nose is bleeding."

Gabriel snarled. His wolves jerked Topher away. When he stumbled, they didn't wait for him to get his feet back underneath him but dragged him to the alley entrance as a car came to a screeching halt before them. The wolves maneuvered Topher into the back and got in on either side of him. Their blood reeked, making Topher's head swim. He swallowed the excess saliva filling his mouth. Never in his life had he been hungry enough to find werewolf blood appealing, but right now, he could imagine settling.

Gabriel replaced the wolf driving and Matt got in the passenger seat. The young wolf kept looking back to make sure

Topher didn't try anything. At one point, Topher smiled at him.

"I never noticed the green in your eyes before," Topher said, dropping his voice. "It's nice."

Matt shot a worried look at Gabriel, but his alpha didn't glance away from the road. When Matt turned back, Topher held his pretty eyes and lifted his knuckles smeared with Gabriel's blood to his lips, licking them clean. The boy's face paled with disgust and he turned quickly to face forward again.

Topher sighed and let his head fall back against the seat.

At least he wouldn't have to work tonight. He could now confirm wolf blood didn't taste half as appealing as even the drunkest human at the club.

CHAPTER 18

Nora sniffed warily as they entered the Maker. Annaliese rolled her eyes but didn't say anything. Assured her pack hadn't been here tonight, Nora followed Annaliese, Molly, and Alex to the bar. Oliver was already there. The place wasn't busy yet and Zayn was holding up flashcards, testing him.

"Come on, O. You got this one last night." Zayn flapped the card in Oliver's face.

"Okay, babe, that really doesn't help." Oliver laughed and snatched Zayn's wrist, stilling his hand.

Nora's chest warmed from the sight. She hated the puncture scars on Oliver's neck, but the two of them were so obviously in love it was hard to remember why.

Nora felt a pang, wishing Colbie were already here. She checked her phone, but only a few minutes had passed since Poppy said they were on their way. Nora was still anxious about spending time with Colbie in public, but she told herself as long as Gabriel and Matt didn't show, it would be fine. Especially with Topher behind the bar. He wouldn't let anything happen.

"Where's Topher?" Annaliese asked as they shouldered their way next to Oliver.

Zayn shrugged, his smile fading into tight lips. "He's never this late." He handed Oliver back his flashcards and checked his phone, frowning either at the time or lack of messages from Topher.

Although Molly initially perked up when she saw Oliver at the bar, she was currently staring at Zayn like she'd never seen a man before. Annaliese rolled her eyes when she saw the look. Even Alex noticed. Nora couldn't blame the girl. Next to Topher's striking looks and compelling charm, Zayn didn't catch the same amount of attention behind the bar. But standing alone, smiling at Oliver's comment in his easy way with his perfect fade, earrings, and tattoos, Zayn was handsome and confident.

Alex cleared his throat loudly and Annaliese made quick introductions. Zayn poured them a round of shots and Alex's expression relaxed slightly when Zayn declared the first round was on him.

"You aren't drinking?" Nora asked Oliver after she'd finished wincing past the burn of the alcohol.

"No. I overdid it last time. Zayn wants me more alert in case Lana tries something again." Oliver shot an apologetic look at his boyfriend, who moved down the bar to help some men in suits. Zayn kept glancing back at them, shoulders tense. Oliver lowered his voice. "He doesn't like me coming here, especially when Topher isn't around for backup."

"I don't blame him. Is Lana really as bad as everyone says?" Annaliese asked.

Nora noted again how different her friend was around this group. Annaliese in school was always quiet and distant unless she and Nora were alone. What was it about Oliver, Poppy, and even Topher that made her care so much?

"Honestly? I think she's worse. Zayn won't tell me what exactly they do when she takes them on jobs, especially whatever she does to Topher, but I've seen the way she looks at him, you know? I think I hate her."

Hate was a strong sentiment for a boy like Oliver.

He turned to look around the club again, probably checking for Topher like Zayn had been doing. The angle of his head made his two fang scars come into relief.

"Does it bother you?" Nora asked without thinking.

"What?"

"The…" She touched her own neck.

Oliver smiled and placed his fingers on the marks lovingly. "No." His eyes warmed as he looked at Zayn. "I met Zayn when Lana and him were still at Happenstance. I discovered in high school that vampire saliva worked better than any medication for my anxiety. I probably could have gotten into a lot of trouble hanging around the clubs like I was, but I met Zayn instead. We figured out a balance and since we started dating, I haven't had a single panic attack."

"It helps your anxiety?" Annaliese asked. Nora didn't like the interest in her voice.

Oliver nodded. "According to Lana and Grace, it helps a lot of human diseases and problems with things like brain chemistry. I hope to study the effects of saliva more someday. It's never gotten any serious testing."

"What does Topher do?" Annaliese asked. Oliver tilted his head with confusion. "To, to eat. If he's so conflicted?" she clarified.

Nora watched Annaliese closer. It wasn't like her to stumble over her words. Nora did that enough for the two of them.

"Well, when Julia is in town, I think they have a similar setup to Zayn and me. But since she left, he feeds from an NA group. Helps them stay sober. That's Rebecca down there." He pointed down the bar where an older woman sat, looking uncomfortable and fiddling with a coaster. "Colbie will probably feed from her if Topher doesn't show, but they all prefer to get blissed from Toph when they can get it."

"How does he know an NA group?" Annaliese asked.

Oliver frowned as if realizing he might have said too much.

"Doesn't matter," he said, waving his hand. "He tries and does good when he can."

Nora accepted the second round of shots Alex bought to compete with Zayn. She could already feel a buzz behind her eyes. The slight numbing in her cheeks. Zayn lingered in their section, still watching the room.

"Hey babe, it's starting to get busy and Topher hasn't shown."

"You want me to go?"

Zayn pulled a face. "I don't, but I'm worried. I can't pay as much attention if I'm covering the bar by myself."

Oliver looked like he was trying to pout, but he was obviously basking in the loving concern in Zayn's dark eyes. "Oh. Okay. I guess I have to study anyway."

Zayn ducked under the bar hatch long enough to give Oliver a hard kiss, erasing the pout from his face entirely.

Oliver left soon after. Alex, looking much happier now with Molly's full attention, guided her to the dance floor.

Annaliese craned her neck, looking down the bar. "Where do you think Topher is?"

Nora shrugged. "What? Are you worried about him? I thought you hated him."

"Well, no. He said he'd be here tonight."

"When?"

"This morning."

Nora frowned. "He was with you this morning?"

Annaliese fidgeted with one of her braids. In the club's black light, the ice blue at the tips glowed. Nora took a second to really look at her friend. Annaliese wore a crop top and her favorite black, ripped, high-waisted jeans. She had a neat line of black eyeliner on, making her round eyes look practically twice as big. "You dressed up tonight."

Annaliese shrugged. She did a good job keeping her features mild, but a frown started to build on her lips. She was nervous.

"Oh my god. Not you, too."

"*What?*" Annaliese snapped.

"You like Topher?"

"Hell no!" But Annaliese was looking down at her hand as she spoke.

"Did you two spend all night together?"

Annaliese closed her hand into a fist and crossed her arms. "I like his bed. I'm just trying to figure him out. If you're going to be over there a lot, I think we should find out if they can be trusted."

"You can't even be friends with him. He can barely control his charm. In fact, you definitely *don't* like him; you're just under his charm."

Annaliese scoffed and rested an elbow on the bar. She picked it up quickly, frown deepening at the wet spot now on her sleeve.

"I'm just curious. Like I've always been curious about the pack. Supernatural stuff is fascinating."

Nora nodded, unconvinced. She wondered briefly if Annaliese would like Topher as she had seen him the other night, smiling with full dimples and promises to help. The hard exterior he wore around humans to keep from accidentally charming them was exactly the kind of guy Annaliese liked. Not that softened version. But if she'd only seen him scowling..., "Oh my god."

"Seriously, Nor, knock it off. I don't—"

She cut off when Colbie and Poppy arrived. Colbie wrapped her arms around Nora's waist and buried her nose in Nora's neck. It was so cold she shivered. At the first slide of Colbie's lips on her skin, Nora promptly forgot what they were talking about.

Zayn stopped by, looking harried, and poured a round of tequila shots for them. Poppy frowned. "Where's Topher?"

"Hell if I know!" Zayn whipped away to help the next

group shouting for his attention. For once, his easy smile was gone.

"Colbie?"

"What, Popsicle?"

"Where's Topher?"

"Don't worry." Colbie nipped playfully at Nora's earlobe.

"Why not?" Annaliese asked.

Colbie opened her mouth to respond, but her eyebrows drew together as if she had forgotten what she was about to say. The expression cleared quickly. She shrugged. "Just don't worry."

She grabbed Nora's hand and pulled her onto the dance floor. Colbie was refreshingly cool in the humid club. She wore a white crop top, ripped jeans, and Nora's navy cardigan. The blue color brought out Colbie's eyes and made Nora's heart flutter. Nora happily slipped her hands inside the flaps and placed them on the bare skin of Colbie's waist, warmth pooling in her lower stomach. This was all so much easier than she ever imagined it could be.

Unable to help herself, she pulled Colbie close, loving the wicked smile spreading on Colbie's red lips. Colbie fit their bodies together, pressed at every other point possible as they moved to the music. Nora felt like she just took three extra shots and pressed her burning face into Colbie's neck. Instinct made her try to smell the girl, but she only found her own scent left over there. Nora smiled into the crook of Colbie's neck.

She looked up. "You're just so…" Nora couldn't think of a word to describe what she was feeling.

She opted to kiss Colbie instead of struggling to finish the sentence.

Colbie dipped back, pulling Nora with her and deepening the kiss, turning it sinful and heavy. Nora felt a noise build in the back of her throat and Colbie pulled back just slightly and nodded. She hooked her hands behind Nora's neck and tugged her in for another delicious, consuming kiss as her fingers twisted into Nora's hair.

Nora lost track of time. The songs shifted around them and the crowd steadily grew, pressing Colbie ever closer. Colbie was breathing faster now, eyes burning as her hands explored places they'd never ventured. Nora nearly stopped dancing when Colbie's thumbs brushed the underside of her breasts through her shirt. She'd never been happier not to be wearing a bra. Colbie didn't reach further, separated for a breath. Colbie searched Nora's eyes for a reaction. Nora wanted more.

Colbie suddenly twisted her head, a quick, unnatural movement. A glare fixed her features. A tall, pale woman met Colbie's scowl with a smirk as she passed. It was the first time Nora was able to identify a vampire on sight. She felt her lips, still tingling from Colbie's saliva, pull back in a snarl.

The woman went to the bar and started yelling at Zayn, who was doing all he could to keep up with incoming orders. He threw his hands up in frustration.

"Lana," Colbie explained, voice low. They watched Lana pull out her phone and make a call, glare deepening when no one answered.

Nora was surprised to see Annaliese had moved down the bar and was talking with the recovering addict Oliver had pointed out. She was forced to look away when Colbie pushed Nora behind her. Lana was stalking back their way.

"Where the hell is your brother? Zayn and Sam are drowning!"

"Don't know," Colbie said.

"When did you last see him?" Was that actual concern in Lana's voice?

"On Sixth, walking here."

"And then?"

"And then..." The same puzzled expression from before crossed Colbie's face. "And then..."

"For Christ's sake. He charmed you!" Lana spun around,

her movements abrupt and agitated. She lifted her phone again. This time her call was answered and she barked at someone named Tamera to get down here. Lana continued to the club entrance, the crowd flinching away from her anger to let her pass.

"You okay?" Nora asked Colbie. The confused look hadn't faded.

"He didn't charm me. Why would he charm me?"

Nora shrugged. She couldn't begin to guess at what went on in Topher's head. "I thought vampires couldn't charm each other?"

"Yeah. Well. Topher's special." Colbie shook her head and her expression cleared. "He can take care of himself. Don't worry." The way Colbie said the last two words, repeating them from earlier in a tone that wasn't hers, made the hair stand up on Nora's arms. She let Colbie pull her close again.

Oliver was right. It was impossible to give in to anxiety when a vampire was kissing you.

Poppy stared at her phone on the coffee table with her eyebrows pulled together. Nora couldn't tell if she was more worried about Topher's lack of replies or Josh's rapid-fire responses.

Annaliese was curled up on the couch, a blanket from Topher's bed wrapped around her shoulders. "Nothing from Topher?"

"No."

"What did Josh say?" Annaliese asked.

Poppy snapped her fingers, setting her phone spinning and making Annaliese jump. The witch rarely used magic in front of them unless she was brewing potions on the stove. "I agreed to lunch tomorrow. I don't think I should go, though. Not if Topher is still missing."

They glanced at Colbie. This was harder for Nora as Colbie had made room for herself, half on Nora's lap in the armchair. Colbie looked up from her phone and raised her eyebrows. If she told them not to worry one more time, Nora was pretty sure Poppy would hit her.

As if to avoid the room's attention, Colbie pressed her face into Nora's arm and the back of the armchair. Nora was struck with a protective instinct and reached to cup the back of Colbie's head, hiding her more completely from Poppy and Annaliese's eyes. Colbie kissed Nora's arm. She shivered, keenly aware the tattoo claiming her alliance to Gabriel's pack was directly under her sleeve where Colbie's lips were pressed.

Nora's phone buzzed again. Matt had been calling for hours.

"Don't go." Colbie wrapped an arm around Nora's waist. For the first time since Lana accused Colbie of being charmed, Nora seriously considered there might actually be something wrong.

Her next words were heavy on her tongue. "I don't want to, but I should. Something might be going on with the pack. Matt doesn't usually call so much."

Annaliese jumped up to return Topher's blanket to his bed. She'd been ready to leave the club long before they were and made it clear she just wanted to be home. Nora kissed Colbie's pout, letting it linger. She pulled back. Looking at Colbie this close made it hard to breathe.

"You okay?" Colbie whispered.

"Yeah, you're just so…" Nora failed to find the words yet again.

Colbie smiled, the exceptionally soft smile Nora liked to think was reserved for her alone. She couldn't resist leaning in for another kiss. Annaliese cleared her throat by the door. Nora pulled Colbie in for a quick hug. It was so hard to leave her. But her phone started vibrating again. With a sigh, she got up and followed Annaliese out.

Annaliese was quiet in the car until they were nearly to the Den.

"Do you think we should be worried about Topher?" she asked.

"Colbie wasn't."

"Yeah, but obviously this is out of character for him."

"Are you worried about him or disappointed you didn't see him tonight?"

"I *don't* have a crush on him!" Nora flinched from Annaliese's suddenly harsh tone.

"Jeez. Okay. I believe you."

Annaliese hit the brakes a little too hard in front of the Den. All the lights were on though the clock said it was nearly one in the morning. Nora swallowed hard.

"Bye," Annaliese said with a pointed glare.

"He's probably fine. Maybe just skipping work to sleep more."

Annaliese turned up her music.

"Okay, bye!" Rolling her eyes, Nora got out of the car.

The hair on Nora's neck rose upon entering the Den. Only Maggie was in there, sitting stiffly in front of the TV. Her eyes shifted from Nora to the basement door and back to the screen.

Nora could smell the tension in the air. She stumbled to a halt, caught in the memory of coming home a week after her father's death. The Den felt like this then too. Right before she learned her mother had left her. Gabriel had told her, his voice shaking. She had left a note that said staying was too hard; she was leaving. Matt hadn't been around. Gabriel held her together until Annaliese arrived to take her back to the simplicity of the human world.

The pack had since spotted her mother a couple times in the national park, but in all these years, she hadn't shifted back from her wolf form. As she said in her note, she had no plans to become a human again. For Nora, it was almost as hard as her father's death. Some days she thought it might even be harder knowing her mother had willingly left her.

Nora's thoughts flew to Matt and his scouting missions. Gabriel dealing with the Big Three. Impulsive Adriana. Wise Tío Marcus. Pregnant Heather. She pictured each of them bloody and limp like her father's body had been. Gone. She almost crumbled with relief when Matt stepped through the basement door. His wide smile threw her off balance. She stood stiff as he engulfed her in a hug without noticing.

"We have something for you!"

"What?"

"Come on." Matt took her hand. It was strange how quickly she'd gotten used to Colbie. The warmth of Matt's grip felt foreign. His hand too big and rough.

He led her to the basement stairs, a place for storage she had rarely visited. She knew her parent's things were down there and felt herself tensing with each step.

Their storage had been moved, clearing the space within. Nora froze at the sight of her surprise.

Topher sat tied to a chair. His face gave nothing away when he saw her, save for the tiniest shake of his head. Her attention was arrested by the cut on his cheek, a deep, strangely pink, dry gash.

"Unnatural," she heard Gabriel say. The skin sealed rapidly over the pink and faded into a scar so slim it nearly vanished.

"No arguments here," Topher muttered. At that tone, Nora's heart caught. She rushed up to the chair.

"Gabriel! What the hell is this?"

"Nor, this is your vampire. Welcome to the pack." Nora had never seen Gabriel's smile so big.

CHAPTER 19

Josh sat in a booth fiddling with his silverware roll when Poppy entered Patty's. He looked up with a ready smile as the door jingled closed behind her.

Poppy slid into the seat across from him, doing her best to return the smile. Why was she here? She could have canceled. *Should* have canceled. She'd spent all morning trying to track Topher, but the magic was unresponsive. Her temples ached from the effort.

"So, how's Poppy?"

Josh was still fidgeting. Poppy realized with a dull jolt of surprise he was nervous. She knew she should be too; this was her first date, after all, but she couldn't dispel the worry she felt. Despite Colbie's assurances, Poppy knew something was wrong.

"I'm fine. How are you?"

"Great. Pretty busy, actually. New Brecken has a lot going on." Josh paused. Poppy nodded and looked at her menu.

"What's good here?" he asked.

"I like the veggie burgers."

"Ah, a vegetarian." Josh smiled.

"Yep."

Josh gave her a funny look but turned to the menu without another word. Poppy resisted the urge to rub her aching temples and took a drink of water. She just didn't have the energy to try and make conversation. She was exhausted. Spell spent, as her mother would have called it.

"So... What's new?" Josh tried next.

Poppy fought back a cringe. She'd told Josh everything she could about her life over text. She didn't have much else to add. "Um, I have a lab on Monday."

Josh quirked an eyebrow. "Interesting."

An uncomfortable moment passed. Poppy's phone buzzed with a text from Annaliese. It was a few fire emojis in the group chat they had with Oliver initially made to set up study times. It quickly deteriorated into madness, with Oliver sending an astounding number of memes and Annaliese doing a valiant job of keeping up. Poppy sent a laughing face back and put her phone away.

She realized then she probably should have returned Josh's question. The moment had passed. Josh slumped into the seat across from her, watching the waiter behind the bar with a dejected air. His hands now still on the table. She noticed a tattoo wrapped around his forearm. Pine trees rising from his wrist and the moon above in black ink. It ended below his elbow where he'd rolled his red flannel shirt sleeves. She wondered if it was his pack's tattoo or a personal choice.

Poppy thanked the Mother when Oliver came running into the diner. He looked as though he had gotten maybe ten minutes of sleep last night, but his smile was bright as always when he saw her.

"Hey, P! Hey, Josh!"

Josh started at being remembered, but that was just like Oliver.

Poppy jumped at the break in the awkwardness. "Hi, Oliver. How'd studying go?"

"Complete trash until Zayn got home. That boy can work

a deck of flash cards. But he said Topher never showed. Any word?" Oliver's face pinched with worry. Poppy was relieved to see it, instantly feeling less alone in her concern.

"Nothing. Zayn's worried too?"

"Yeah. Topher's never done anything to piss off Lana. Something has to be up. Have you tried…" Oliver twirled a finger in the air.

Poppy was going to assume that meant magic. "No luck."

"Damn." Oliver looked over his shoulder when the waiter called his name. "Well, keep me updated. Zayn doesn't work tonight, well, he might if Topher is still a no-show, but we can all look if he doesn't."

"Thanks, Oliver. Enjoy your lunch."

He smiled a bit and waved. He grabbed his food, thanked the waiter by name, and left just as quickly as he came in.

"So nothing new but one of your friends is missing?" Josh asked, not unkindly. "If this isn't a good time, you just had to say so, Poppy."

Poppy's eyes fell to the table. She felt a sudden, horribly unexpected rush of tears.

"Hey, hey, hey," Josh's voice turned soft.

"It's fine. I'm just so tired."

Josh got up and slid into the booth next to Poppy. He smelled like grass after rain. Fresh and full of life energy. It made Poppy's head swim. She momentarily forgot her headache.

"Talk to me. What's happened?" he pressed.

"I can't."

"You can. I know Lana is one of the makers and a bitch. Is Topher the lower she was hanging all over at the meeting last Monday?"

"What?" Poppy's voice cracked as she turned to look at him. He raised an eyebrow and held her gaze, steady and concerned. Poppy sighed and sagged against the back of the booth. She rubbed her temples.

"I mean, probably. I didn't know Lana hung over him, but she is his maker."

"Oh yeah, she was practically—never mind, doesn't matter. What happened?"

"He just disappeared last night. No one's heard from him."

Josh frowned. "That's not normal, right? Things are pretty peaceful between the supernatural groups here?"

"Usually."

Josh nodded. "How can I help?"

"You can't." Poppy's voice cracked. Her face was burning, embarrassment taking over now with a fresh rush of tears.

"Can I hug you?" Josh's voice was strained. Poppy found herself nodding and then Josh's arms were around her. Bigger and softer than the bony vampires she lived with, his chest was easy to fall into.

"I could help. Or my pack could. No one should just break the peace like that."

Poppy shook her head. "We don't know someone broke the peace. We shouldn't involve them."

"Why else would a vampire suddenly disappear? My pack has experience with these kinds of situations."

"We don't even know what the situation is!" Poppy threw up her hands and straightened out of Josh's embrace, barely keeping hold of her magic.

"Alright, alright. No one can think like this."

Their food came. Poppy tried to hide her red face from the waiter. Josh asked for boxes and shifted on the booth to get out his wallet.

"I can—" she started, reaching for her bag.

"Next time." He waved her off, going so far as to smack away her hand when she thrust her card forward. Somehow, even with everything, that made her smile.

They boxed up the meals and Josh took up Poppy's hand. They both drove there, but Josh led her to the sidewalk. She felt the tension in her shoulders ease as the slight heat wave

New Brecken was experiencing worked its way on her mood. The air was musty with the smell of dirty, melting snow, but it held the promise of warmer days to come.

Josh took them to a park nearby and dropped their bag of food on a damp wooden picnic table. He winked and laid down on one of the benches. "We just need to relax for a second and breathe. Then we'll think of something."

Poppy hesitated before she took the other, laying in the opposite direction so her head was aligned with his bent knees. She closed her eyes and let the sound of children running nearby distract her. The sun overhead turned her vision red behind her eyelids.

"So..." Josh began after a moment of deep breathing, "Let's start from the top."

Poppy sighed. "I just can't tell you much. We don't know you."

"That's fair. I was thinking more when did your friend go missing?"

"Oh. Last night. Maybe around 6:00." Colbie had unexpectedly returned from walking Topher to work, strolling into the apartment as though nothing were amiss at 6:10.

"No one was with him?"

"His sister."

"Vampires have sisters?"

Poppy shrugged. Even she didn't know the story there. "Topher does."

"Okay, focus, Josh," he said. Poppy smiled a bit at the use of the third person. "No one's heard from him since? Nothing?"

"Nothing."

"Has he ever done this before?"

"Only if Lana takes him somewhere, but even she was looking for him last night. She seemed pissed." And worried. Poppy didn't want to examine that after what Josh said about the maker hanging on Topher.

"I wouldn't want to see that. So, who are our suspects?"

"Suspects?"

"I think we already established he wouldn't disappear voluntarily. Do you think he would?"

An idea struck and Poppy sat up. She took out her phone. "He hasn't eaten in days. I doubt he's thinking like himself."

She pressed the number and held her phone to her ear.

"Not eating?"

Poppy waved off Josh's question. She definitely didn't want to get into *that*. Josh turned his face to the sun and muttered to himself, "A vampire with a sister who doesn't like feeding on humans…"

Julia answered on the fifth ring. "Poppy? Is Topher there?"

Poppy nearly hung up after hearing that. "No. Actually, I was hoping he was with you."

A pause. "No. I haven't heard from him in forever. Can you please ask him to call me?"

"Sure, Julia. I'm sorry I…" Poppy didn't know what she was apologizing for. It didn't seem to matter; Julia was already sniffling on the other end of the line.

"I stopped calling… I thought he might need space… I should never have come here. He needed me and I…I…" Sobbing. Poppy cringed and held the phone away from her ear. Josh looked horrified, staring at the phone in her hand.

"Make her stop!" he hissed.

"Julia! Hey, relax, okay?"

"I just, I just," More gasping breaths. Julia slowly got a grip. Poppy and Josh waited in distinctly uncomfortable silence. "I'm sorry. I miss him. You said he was missing?"

"We just haven't seen him today."

"Lana probably took him last night. I hate that, that…" Julia failed to think of a word to describe Lana. Angry was better than sobbing, though.

"I'm sure that's all."

"Okay," Julia sniffed loudly. "Hey, Poppy?"

"Yeah?"

"I miss you too. I know we didn't know each other very long before I left for school, but I think we would have been friends. I hope Toph and I figure things out and we can hang out more this summer. Maybe even sooner, my spring break is…"

Poppy pressed her phone into her chest so Julia wouldn't hear her sigh. Her heart squeezed for the girl and the hope in her voice. For the first time, she was genuinely angry at Topher.

"Yeah, maybe, Julia."

"Maybe. Anyway, please let me know if he's okay. I worry."

"I will."

They said their goodbyes and hung up, Poppy feeling even more exhausted than before.

"So we're ruling out his girlfriend?" Josh said.

"Do you start every sentence with the word so?"

Josh let out a laugh. "Not all of them!" He gently kicked Poppy's shin. "S— Ignore that, starting over." He cleared his throat. "I'm thinking you should be worried."

"I think so too."

"What can we do?"

"I don't know." Poppy laid back down on the bench seat, so frustrated tears tightened her throat. She fought them. Too many tears had already been shed on this disaster of a date.

"There are witches in this city, right? Maybe we could hire one to help us?"

Poppy made a noncommittal noise.

"Are they expensive?"

"Very."

"Hmm. Well, it could be worth a shot. I bet my uncle would cover it."

"I don't want to explain to him what's happening. I think right now, the fewer people who know about this, the better."

"Okay."

"I just don't want your pack butting heads with Lana or even Connor Grace if she gets him involved."

Josh sighed. He sat up and started ruffling through the food on the table. They ate in silence. When they finished and were no closer to answers, it became an acceptable time to separate. They walked back toward their cars slowly. Poppy was startled to find she didn't want the date to end.

"Josh?"

"Yes?"

"We'll probably go looking for Topher tonight. Would you want to come?"

"Sure, Poppy. I'll help you."

"You'll be helping vampires too."

"When and where?"

Poppy studied him, considering just how easily this could be a trap. Maybe he was leading them off the trail of his pack. But his face seemed so open. As much as she hated the cliche, his brown puppy-dog eyes were melting away her unease.

"Meet us back here at the diner. Around six."

Poppy let herself into Colbie's room right at five. She sat down heavily on the bed to wake her up. Colbie grumbled and Poppy got under the covers. It was still strange to get into a cold bed knowing its occupant had been sleeping for hours. Colbie yawned, so perfect even after sleep that she didn't have morning breath. Did vampires get morning breath?

Colbie rolled into Poppy's warmth. "What's up, Popsicle?"

"I'm worried about Topher."

"He never came back?" Colbie sounded confused, like sleep still clouded her mind.

"No," Poppy whispered. "What did he say when you left him at work."

"I don't remember taking him to work."

Poppy stiffened. It wasn't like Colbie to sound so unsure. "What do you remember?"

"It's... hazy. I think we got to that alley on Sixth."

"And then?"

"Then I just remember coming back because I had to get to you." Colbie sat up, rubbing her forehead. "*Shit*. I think Lana was right. Damn, Topher's charm is so strong. It's fading, I think, but she was right. He charmed me."

"I thought vampires couldn't charm each other."

Colbie dropped her hand, staring unfocused at the door. "He can charm me. He never has before, though."

"Because you're siblings? Or because he's so strong?"

Colbie shrugged. She was frowning, a look that didn't quite fit on her face.

"I went out with that werewolf. He said he'd help us. Maybe if Zayn isn't working, we should all look. We might be able to find him together."

Colbie nodded and got out her phone. "I'll call him. Should I invite Lana?"

"I don't want her to know I'm a witch." Poppy had no interest in seeing Lana.

"Does Josh know you're a witch?"

"No. And I'd like to keep it that way, but I trust him more than Lana."

Colbie snorted. "I trust the foreign prince in my DMs more than I trust Lana."

Poppy was so tired she nearly fell asleep as Colbie changed and made calls. "Nora isn't answering. Zayn said he'd come, but he's covering Topher's shift first. Oliver said he'd help, but I told him to just come with Zayn. Annaliese is texting me, but I don't think she could help and she's not with Nora."

"Where do you want to start then?"

"Retracing our steps? See where I lose memory and if we can find anything there?"

"Good plan. Should I invite Josh?"

Colbie did a quick shrug. "He probably won't smell anything more than I do, but maybe his pack is responsible." Colbie lifted a hand when Poppy opened her mouth to argue. "I'm not taking any chances. If Josh knows something, keeping him close means we can watch him."

Poppy had to agree. "But what if it's a trap for you too?"

"I'm not part of anything. It would be a waste of their time. Plus, you'll keep me safe." Colbie winked, but her expression didn't match her light tone.

In minutes they were out the door. Colbie pressed the first human she saw into an alley to feed. When she stepped out of the shadows, Colbie's blue eyes were clear. Her expression focused.

They met Josh at the diner. He eyed Colbie suspiciously, but the look quickly gave way to bewilderment. "You smell like that werewolf at the cafe."

"You mean my sexy, spicy-smelling girlfriend?" Colbie shimmied.

"Yes?"

"Thank you. You smell like a wet dog."

"It's raining."

"I didn't ask for your excuses."

Colbie flounced away. Poppy smiled at Josh, but it didn't feel right on her face. Colbie's lightness was heartbreakingly forced. Nora had yet to call back. Night had fallen an hour ago and there was still no word from Topher. Yet another day had passed during which he probably hadn't fed. Poppy didn't remember him ever going so long; even if he did, he'd sustained himself off the blood Julia had left him.

Colbie led them toward the alley on Sixth. She and Josh stuck their noses in the air. Poppy was tempted to cast a few spells, but something told her she wouldn't see anything of Topher in the memories of the alley. There wasn't a hint of an impression thus far.

"This is where I stopped," Colbie said. They hadn't turned down the alley yet.

"What did Topher say when he charmed you? Do you remember now?"

"Yeah. He told me to go to you and not to worry."

The hair on Poppy's arms rose. Colbie had sounded nearly robotic yesterday night, repeating don't worry. Repeating Topher's charm. Mother, he must be strong. "He must have known something was coming. Is it possible he smelled it before you?"

She nodded. "His senses are stronger."

Colbie turned into the alley, trailing her fingers over the bricks. Poppy followed, looking for hints of a struggle. Anything to tell the story of what had happened here.

"What the hell?" Josh's nose was crinkled. He and Colbie shared a look as they caught the same scent. A few steps later and even Poppy could smell it despite the rain.

"Is that bleach?"

"That is not healthy for the environment," Colbie tried to stay light, but she sounded strangled. Both she and Josh were struggling to breathe past the chemical smell. Panic was stark in Colbie's eyes. Someone had doused the entire section of the alley in an obscene amount of bleach, erasing any evidence or scent they might have followed to Topher.

"Someone actually took him," Colbie whispered. She clung to Poppy's arm, a bit too tight. "Where is he?"

Poppy pulled Colbie in for a hug until the vampire took a breath. She met Josh's serious gaze over Colbie's shoulder. Stepping away but keeping hold of Colbie's hand, she knelt in the dirty alley. Or maybe the clean dirt of the alley, as it was doused in chemicals. Josh was silent as Poppy began to mumble under her breath.

"Show me who poured this." Nothing was forthcoming from her magic. Poppy could feel how much weaker it was in the night. Josh's energy was a tempting draw, but she resisted pulling strength from him. She tried tracing the origin of the bleach, hoping to see a glimpse of who had handled it. Still nothing. Maybe the bleach bottles had been touched by too many people. Maybe Poppy wasn't a strong enough witch for the complex spell. The dirt and walls of the alley didn't hold answers either. Not even a flicker of a memory from the night Topher was taken.

Poppy frowned as she crouched back on her heels. At this point, she couldn't blame her less than powerful casting. She should have brought some brews, but she suspected something else was happening here.

She cut a look at Josh but didn't voice her suspicions. Her mother always complained that werewolves masked magic. Spells had to be cast on them indirectly and even then, most didn't work. They'd never moved away from the Den because it kept other witches from sensing their magic and finding their coven.

But if a wolf was involved in Topher's kidnapping, there was almost a fifty percent chance said wolf was in Josh's pack.

Poppy stood with a shake of her head. Colbie sighed and they continued down the alley. Whatever evidence, blood or otherwise, hadn't been tracked any further. The street on the other side told them nothing. Colbie hugged herself tightly, unblinking as the rain drenched her face.

With one more glance at Josh, Poppy cast a quick spell to block the rain from their little group. Colbie didn't notice, but Josh stepped closer and squeezed her hand.

"That explains a lot. But I won't tell. Promise."

Poppy searched his face. She was too tired to know if she should believe him.

Josh gave her a small smile. "What's next?"

Colbie turned to face them. "Let's keep walking a bit, see if anything comes up."

Poppy agreed, mainly because that seemed a better plan than waiting around at home. Colbie kept checking her phone.

She grew quiet as the hours passed, betraying her anxiety. They ended up back at the apartment twenty minutes before Zayn was supposed to be off. Oliver and Annaliese were waiting in the hall outside the door, talking in low voices.

Poppy unlocked the door with a snap and shifted the wards to allow Josh inside. Her head was truly pounding now.

"Where's Nora?" Colbie asked Annaliese.

"I went by to pick her up, but I guess something came up with the pack. She seemed worried." Annaliese shot a look at Josh and didn't elaborate. Her alliance was clear.

Colbie nodded and curled up on the armchair. Poppy sat on the arm and began picking the hair tie out of Colbie's hair, a process that could take up to ten minutes but always made Colbie's shoulders relax. Once the hair tie was free, she started finger combing the rain-damp curls of her hair. Colbie still looked tense, but she leaned over until her head rested on Poppy's thigh.

"I take it we're worried now?" Annaliese asked.

"Very," Oliver said. He paced the kitchen.

"What should we do?"

No response. Josh and Annaliese sat on the couch as a horrible, empty silence fell. Zayn arrived and Oliver hurried to him. They greeted each other with a kiss, but Zayn broke it quickly to glare at Josh.

"You're one of the new pack," he said.

"Sure am. I'm Josh."

Zayn studied Josh a beat longer, who met his eyes unflinchingly. Zayn glanced at Colbie, but when she only shrugged, he nodded. He took Oliver's hand and they sat down on the floor in front of the TV.

"You okay? Anything happen?" Oliver asked.

"I'm fine, babe. Lana's furious. I'm pretty sure she thinks —" he cut off with a glance at Colbie. "She looked for him all night and called Grace. He's gathering the other vampire leaders tomorrow night. Tensions are high. I'll have to go to the meeting. Seems like we can't go a week without having one these days."

"No! Don't go. Not after Brady."

Zayn pulled Oliver closer and pressed a wet kiss on his cheek, calming him with his saliva. "I'll be fine, Oliver. Lana won't send us off by ourselves anymore. We'll be in Grace's club, tats on display. No one will bother us." Zayn's gaze found Poppy's. "You didn't find anything?"

"Someone bleached the place he was taken."

He turned to Josh. "And your pack has nothing to do with it? The timing is a little suspicious, you have to admit."

Josh shook his head. "My un— our alpha doesn't know anything about gang dynamics in this city yet. It would be a stupid first move to pull. You're welcome to come to our place and check around."

Zayn raised a skeptical eyebrow but turned to Poppy. "What else?"

Colbie made a helpless sound. They knew nothing else. Silence fell over the room again.

Annaliese broke it. "No one can think what someone would want with Topher?"

"I can think of a lot of people who'd want Topher in their pocket and not Lana's," Zayn said.

"Can you get specific? People to ask? Places to check?"

"Not before Lana meets with the vampires. Trespassing is a good way to start a war."

Annaliese considered that. "I can check places. Poppy too, right?"

Poppy shrugged. "Some places. I can't risk getting recognized, though."

"Then I go in. Where should I look? Other clubs on Fourth?"

"You can't just stroll into the clubs." Zayn shot Annaliese a look of disbelief. His arm tightened around Oliver. "They aren't safe for humans."

"Well, we have to do something!"

"Topher's the one who does something!" Colbie burst out. "If any of us were missing, he'd know exactly where to go. I shouldn't have let him keep me out of all this!" She turned her head into Poppy's leg.

Poppy ran her fingers through her hair with more intensity. "This isn't your fault."

"It isn't, Colbs," Zayn's voice softened, "I've been to almost as many meetings as Topher and I don't know where to start either. *Lana* doesn't know. We might just have to wait until the vampire meeting. Hopefully, Lana gets something out of them. The other vampire leaders don't like how strong Topher is. They're my primary suspects."

Oliver snorted. "You need to stop watching crime show reruns at night."

Zayn rubbed his cheek against Oliver's hair. "I'll tell you everything that happens, Colbie."

"I should go with you," she muttered.

"Not happening. Topher will kill me if I let you come."

Colbie huffed, her breath cold through Poppy's jeans.

"We're just going to wait then?" Annaliese asked incredulously.

Poppy could feel in the air how much everyone hated it, but no one had any better options. Colbie checked her phone again. Still nothing from Topher or Nora.

CHAPTER 20

Nora barely slept. Her nerves felt stripped and bare. Her bed too comfortable, especially with Matt sleeping soundly next to her, one leg slung over hers. He'd sensed she was upset but thought it was nerves. Gabriel too.

She couldn't stop thinking about Topher downstairs, tied to a chair and slumped with hunger. She slipped out from under Matt, freezing when he turned and mumbled. He fell still again and she ventured to the basement. Her hands were slicked with sweat. She was relieved to find Tío Marcus on guard duty at the top of the stairs, the only entrance to their new prison.

"Can I get a moment alone?"

"Are you sure that's a good idea, Nora?" Marcus was her father's younger brother and was beta for years before her mother claimed the position. Members of the pack had been hopeful he'd step up as alpha, but Gabriel was the only one with the command.

Her uncle looked too much like her father for Nora to spend much time with him, but at moments like this, when her strength was wavering, she let herself take comfort from the familiar features.

"Yeah, I'll be fine. If I'm going to kill him, I just want to judge for myself."

"Well, from what Gabriel's told me, he needs to die either way. You'll do the right thing."

Nora nodded and her tío let her pass. With the door closed between them, she descended the steps slowly. She crouched in front of Topher. He met her eyes but squinted against the beginnings of sunshine creeping in the window. Nora didn't know what to think. Panic made her mind raw.

"Colbie won't forgive you," Topher whispered. His voice was just a rasp. "But I do."

"*What?*"

"I hate what I've become, Nora. I don't blame your pack."

"You really think I could kill you?"

With no humans around, Topher gave her a sad smile, dimples more pronounced than ever in his sunken cheeks. His lips were pale and would probably have been chapped if he were human. His eyes looked like bruises surrounded them. He was hard to look at. Still hauntingly beautiful. Even in this weakened state, Nora could feel in her bones she should hate the power he possessed. He looked unnatural.

He looked undead.

"We'll see what you decide. Considering you haven't told Colbie where I am, I find I'm not that hopeful." Topher's eyes lifted to the window set ground level in the wall in front of him. "The sun is coming."

"Topher, I'm not, I couldn't just—"

"You were going to kill one of us anyway. It could have been Colbie. But I'd take her place here in a heartbeat."

"Why wasn't she worried last night?"

Topher's blue eyes grew sad and his lips pulled up slightly in a humorless smile. "I charmed her."

"I thought vampires couldn't charm each other."

"It's difficult."

"Then how'd you do it so weak?" Nora's voice dropped to a whisper.

Topher looked at her. The mask he kept in place slipped. She saw all his misery. The self-loathing. "You should kill me."

"Topher…"

"It's easy for a vampire to charm another vampire if they're the one that turned them to begin with. If they're that vampire's maker."

Nora froze as Topher's words slowly assembled themselves in her head.

"You—" Fury shook her voice. Nora's skin was taut, begging to be released to the change. "Colbie said she was attacked."

"I'm a monster. I've been saying it all along."

Nora could think of nothing to say. Topher's squinted eyes closed reluctantly. The sun claimed him and he was dragged into sleep, head slumping forward. Nora watched him. It sounded like even drawing in air was difficult for him.

The door at the top of the stairs opened and brought Gabriel's scent. He stopped next to her, looking at her rather than the prisoner. He was well rested and already healed from the blow to the nose Topher had given him.

Nora couldn't meet his eyes. She was reeling from Topher's confession, but she couldn't let Gabriel see how shaken she was by all of this.

"He seems so weak," she said.

"He isn't."

"Why him?" What did Gabriel know?

Gabriel spared Topher a glance. The hatred on his face was staggering. "That meeting we went to ended with the vampires trying to find out who was turning the humans in the city. There have been more and more unclaimed vampires turning up and no one sticking around to tame them. Humans are dying. They took the leaders into a side room at the meeting. They had one of the unclaimed vampires there. They used this one to torture information out of her."

Gabriel pulled in a shaky breath. "Nor, his charm was so strong, *I* could feel it. He broke the unclaimed's mind with it. Imagine what he's capable of. What his makers are capable of with him under their command. I'd never even heard of a vampire who could charm other vampires without being their maker."

"So you kidnapped him?"

"Yeah. We're lucky he's so weak right now. Whatever his powers are, they must take a lot out of him. We just have to keep him hungry. You shouldn't have any problems killing him. Whenever you're ready."

"I don't have to wait for the full moon?"

"You won't make the change before then, but it'll carry through. I'll accept you into the pack once he's dead."

"And it has to be him?"

Gabriel almost looked amused. "Who else would you want to kill? He's the strongest vampire in the city, Nor. Much more important than killing a leader who will just be replaced by their second as soon as you're done."

Nora nodded. She felt gutted.

Gabriel set a hand on her shoulder. "Your father would be so proud. Do it when you're ready, but soon."

"I should spend some time with Annaliese first. If what everyone says is true, things won't be the same between us after."

"That's a good idea. Invite her over. I know we'll all miss having her around."

Gabriel smiled and Nora did her best to return it. Topher's skin was turning red where the sunlight reached him.

Colbie won't forgive you... but I do.

If she did this, could she forgive herself?

Could she forgive herself if she didn't?

The sun rose and Colbie finally fell into an unwilling sleep under a pile of blankets. Poppy gently pulled her friend's phone out of her hand and set it on Topher's nightstand. She settled down across the foot of the bed, resting her arm on her forehead. Poppy stared up at the ceiling and focused on breathing. She would just rest her eyes for a moment, then she'd go back to looking. Mouse joined them on Topher's bed, curling up against Poppy's stomach and rumbling with his purr.

Poppy woke with a gasp hours later than she intended to sleep, yet feeling as exhausted as she had when she closed her eyes. She spared Colbie a guilty look, remembering her promise to keep searching through the day.

Poppy slipped into her room and changed quickly. Her hair was beginning to string with grease at the top, but she'd already wasted enough time. She pulled it into two quick, messy braids and tied a bandana over the top. She donned her charms: three necklaces, jangling bracelets, and a ring for almost every finger. Crystals and spells woven in each piece. Poppy loaded her canvas messenger bag with vials of potions, pulled on her scuffed black boots, and left the apartment. Her stomach was a knot of nerves knowing where she had to go today. It was a last-ditch idea, but she didn't know what else she could do.

Poppy ran down the steps to the apartment building, avoiding a man lounging on the steps with his head tipped back into the sun. She yelped and jumped to the side when he stood with a sudden, "Hey!"

She pressed a hand to her racing heart when she realized it was Josh. "What are you doing here?"

"I was just going to come see if you wanted help today. I knocked, but no one answered. I brought you this." He bent and picked up the coffee cup that had been waiting next to him on the stairs. He eyed it before she took it. "Might be cold by now."

It was the same tea she'd gotten when she saw him at the cafe. "How'd you know?"

He tapped his nose. She thought he was being coy for a second, then realized he was indicating he'd smelled which drink it was. Poppy warmed the tea with a whispered spell and took a sip.

Josh stood a step lower than her, hands jammed in his pockets. He looked tired, his sandy blonde hair so rumpled on one side that Poppy wanted to reach out and flatten it. "So what's the plan for today?" he asked.

"I was going to go to my sister's."

His eyebrows lowered in confusion. The expression took three years off his face. "You aren't looking for your friend?"

"I am. She might be able to help."

Understanding cleared Josh's eyes and he cocked his head, an equally adorable gesture. Unable to help herself, Poppy compared him again to Topher. Even a year younger than Poppy, he rarely looked anything close to cute and only when his dimples were out. It was hard to look at Topher half the time. His face was too sharp with guarded expressions. Every movement he made was considered and deliberate. Josh's manner was instinctual and simple.

Poppy bit her lip. "You want to come?"

"Of course, let's go!" he turned on the steps, bouncing down them lightly. One of his red high tops was untied, but his feet were too nimble for Poppy to worry about him falling. With a small smile, she snapped her fingers and tied the lace. He didn't even notice.

"My car or yours?"

"Mine."

Josh climbed into her passenger seat. Poppy started the car and pulled out of the lot as Josh fiddled with the heater.

"You fixed your tires. Back at the warehouse."

"Yeah."

"I've met another witch before, you know. My uncle's ex was one. She made magic look a lot harder."

Poppy looked at Josh quickly. Nora made werewolves sound more conservative than that. She couldn't imagine anyone from Gabriel's pack dating a witch.

"It depends on the witch. My mom thinks the life energy of the father determines how strong the witch is."

"Life energy? Sounds kind of freaky. So your dad had a lot of that?"

Poppy shrugged. "My mother never talked about him, but I don't think so. My sisters are a lot stronger than me."

"Where is she?"

"In the city. We had a falling out." Easier to explain than the sudden disappearance and damning evidence her mother had left behind.

"Are you hiding from her?"

"Sort of."

"So seeing your sister is a risk?"

Poppy nodded. "I've always been closer with Margot than the others, but…"

"But you'll risk it for your friend." Josh gave her a sweet smile and rolled down his window. He closed his eyes and leaned into the breeze. When he started sniffing, Poppy had to laugh.

"Are you going to stick your head out?"

"Just might." He winked but stayed in the seat. "This part of the city smells amazing. I feel like everything north of the river is slightly rotten."

Poppy turned and took them behind a shopping mall and a group of apartment complexes. In time they reached an old suburb with tall, narrow houses. It was similar to the street she grew up on but better kept. A market sat on the corner and a vegan restaurant Poppy had been meaning to try had outdoor seating across the street.

"Nice," Josh said, looking at the pastel-colored homes with shingled roofs, small balconies, and rocking chair porches.

"I love this neighborhood. This is her place."

Poppy pulled to a stop in front of a mint green home. In front was a large white sign painted with matching green calligraphy.

Josh read it out loud, "Majestic Margot's Reading and Brews." He turned to Poppy with that confused look. "I thought witches preferred to stay in hiding."

"Most people think she's a human psychic. Honestly, she doesn't read the future very well. Her Sight is nearly as bad as mine. Mostly she's a tourist trap."

"Hiding in plain sight?"

"You could say that. Do you mind waiting in here?"

"Not at all." Josh settled back into the seat. By the time Poppy closed her door behind her, he already looked to be on the verge of sleep. This search was taking it out of all of them.

Poppy took a breath and walked up the path lined with winter-dead bushes. She rang the doorbell and waited. And waited.

When no footsteps approached, Poppy put her hand on the knob and concentrated. "Let me in," she muttered. The lock turned, the wards around the building weak in a way that made her stomach drop. Poppy pushed open the door.

All the lights were off. The table to the side of the door held a rose in a clear, slim vase, wilted and dusty. Poppy paused to revive it, feeling the house was already too cold and lifeless. She spread her hands in front of her, pulling from the magic in the air. A woman's vague outline shifted into view. Poppy guessed it was Margot's warded impression. Two weeks ago, she left in a hurry. She hadn't passed through this hall since.

Josh jumped when she slammed the car door behind her. She rested her forehead against the wheel and closed her eyes.

"She wasn't there. She hasn't been there for weeks. I don't know what to do."

"We'll just have to see what Zayn says after the meeting, right?"

"I hate feeling so useless." Poppy debated looking for another one of her sisters, but the thought made her stomach twist. It was too risky. It was probably too dangerous for her even to be here.

"You want to try talking with my pack?"

"No."

"Okay."

"I'm sorry. I just don't know who to trust. I don't know what to do!"

They fell silent. Poppy started the car and pulled into the street. They drove for a while, windows down and the air smelling like spring too early. Poppy drove the thirty minutes it took to get to the forested national park outside the city.

"Wolves come here a lot," Josh said, nose in the air.

Poppy nodded and stopped the car. She got out and walked into the trees. The surge of life in the forest brought on by the sunlight made her head spin. She turned to look back for Josh but only saw a pile of his clothes.

She yelped when something wet pressed into her hand. A wolf stood next to her, tan with familiar brown eyes. She could feel Josh's aura around him as a wolf much more than she could when he was human. Like the plants around her and Mouse's energy. She'd never been good at human readings. Animals and plants were easier. She could always tell just what they needed.

Poppy was surprised by the layer of sadness surrounding Josh in wolf form. She'd never even caught a hint of it when he was human.

He bent his head again and nudged her hand with his nose. Assuring, questioning. Poppy nodded. Josh turned and ran into the trees, his energy loosening into pleasure.

Poppy walked along the dancing shadows. She let the life infect her, pulled from it and let it replenish the magic she'd spent looking for Topher. The constant headache vanished, making her sigh. She was glowing. Josh stayed close, following scents and running in circles. Howling softly if he got too far.

Poppy worked to gather her strength. She didn't know what would happen tonight or in the days to come, but she owed it to Topher to be ready. The pure energy from the forest, from Josh's wolf form, would help her more than anything. When the time came, she wouldn't be useless.

CHAPTER 21

Nora took a deep breath. She opened her mouth, but dread stopped the words from forming.

"You're being weird," Annaliese said. She took another bite of the ice cream they had stolen from Matt's stash in the kitchen. He had hung out with them almost all day, just like they used to. Gabriel eventually came to collect him for patrols. Annaliese had raised an eyebrow when Matt kissed Nora's cheek on the way out.

Nora had never been so confused. Why did she find comfort in these little attentions from Matt? She longed to go to Colbie, but she couldn't. She couldn't even get up the courage to call Colbie back. She'd texted once she was sure Colbie would be asleep. Just a vague apology and noncommittal response to Colbie's invite to meet at Patty's tonight to talk about finding Topher.

"I know. I have to tell you something."

"Does it have to do with you avoiding Colbie? She was completely miserable last night."

"You went without me?" Unease flared. It was too dangerous for her friend around the vampires. They weren't nearly as innocent as Nora had let herself believe. Topher had turned his own sister. He'd tried to attack Oliver.

"Yeah. I tried to cover for you, so you're welcome. What's happening, though? Everyone here is so tense." Annaliese's eyes were already brimming with suspicion, her question purposefully leading.

"Okay. Come on," Nora said. She couldn't carry this alone. Only Annaliese would keep her secret. She knew what the pack meant to Nora. She knew what Colbie was to Nora.

With Topher slumped under the sunlight, no one bothered to guard the top of the stairs. Nora didn't want to know what her pack had done to test how deep Topher's sleep was.

Annaliese gasped, stumbling when she saw Topher. "*What the hell, Nora!*"

"It was Gabriel. He wants me to kill him to join the pack. Annaliese, Topher's dangerous. Gabriel told me—"

"I don't give a damn what Gabriel told you! That's Topher. We know him, Nora! You've made out with his sister!"

"Shhh!" Nora glanced up the stairs, but no one was coming. Annaliese ran to Topher's chair. She reached as though to touch him. Nora lunged forward and grabbed her arm. "Annaliese! He hasn't eaten in days! He'll try to feed off you like he did Oliver!"

"Let me go." Annaliese's voice was cold, her dark eyes narrowed far enough that Nora knew she'd crossed a line. She released Annaliese's arm and took a slow step back.

Annaliese took off her jacket and settled it carefully over Topher's shoulders.

"What are you doing?" Nora hissed.

"He's always cold. It's cold down here." Annaliese wouldn't even look at Nora. She bent to examine Topher's sunburnt face. Nora couldn't read her expression.

"Annaliese, let me explain."

"Fine." Her friend didn't move away from Topher, but Nora knew she was listening. She quickly summarized what

Gabriel told her and Topher's confession. Annaliese at least leaned away from him then.

"So tonight, we're going to ask him about the vampires. Like how they turn humans, what the Big Three are planning, who Lana is to them, and why there are so many unclaimed popping up. Annaliese, the vampires are dangerous. We've always known that. I have another day to decide what I want to do, but you know I have to join the pack. Topher said, well, I don't think he's even going to…" Telling her friend how Topher had already forgiven her, the tired, finished look in his eyes, was too hard. He'd given up. That made everything about what Gabriel wanted her to do so much worse.

"Nora, you can't. What about Colbie?"

"She texted me. They're meeting after Zayn's done at the vampire meeting. Gabriel is hoping tension will rise between the Big Three enough over this that they start picking each other off. The city has been run by the vampires long enough. I'll meet up with all of you at the diner. After we question him, I'll have a better idea of what I should do."

"You can face her after this?" Annaliese gestured to Topher. She was pacing the room now, trailing her fingers along the wall. Every movement agitated as she processed what Nora told her. Annaliese paused under the window, tilting her head to look outside.

Nora shook her head. "This is my whole life. This is my pack. I only just met Colbie. You don't understand…"

"You're right. I don't." Annaliese pushed past Nora, heading to the stairs.

"Don't say anything," Nora said, catching her friend's arm again. She remembered herself and let go quickly. Tears were closing her throat. Annaliese had *always* taken Nora's side. "You were willing to help me kill a vampire two weeks ago. You know what this means."

"I don't think I did. I know what it means to you now, though."

Nora watched Annaliese run up the stairs. For a moment, Nora let her go. It was going to happen anyway. Their friendship wouldn't survive the change. Gabriel always said as much. And she had to learn to trust him. Her alpha. Her family. She couldn't doubt him now.

But she did. She would put off killing Topher as long as she could. As long as it took to think of a way to get him out of this. Explaining to Annaliese what her pack had done only solidified how little prepared Nora was to face this. She couldn't possibly kill the vampire.

With one last glance at his limp body, Nora hurried after her friend.

Annaliese was pacing in the front yard. She saw Nora, huffed, and walked around the house, stopping in front of Topher's window. "I can't believe this."

"I won't…" But despite her internal resolve, Nora couldn't voice any promises.

"Don't let them hurt him, Nora. It's so wrong. And Colbie will never forgive you. You didn't see her last night."

"I know. It's just so complicated."

Annaliese lingered at the window. She bent down and rested her head against the glass. Nora wanted to ask her to back away. This was a strange reaction for her friend on a good day. Nora stayed quiet, though, not wanting to push Annaliese's fury any further.

"You swear you won't tell?" Nora finally had to ask.

"God, you sound like my little sister when she's scared of getting in trouble. Stop them from questioning him and I won't tell."

"I can't stop that."

"I have to go. I can't be around you right now."

"Annaliese!"

Nora watched her friend walk away. She wondered if this would be the last time she saw her. The full moon was close. There wouldn't be enough time to make up.

Nora was shaken. Despite his weakened state, Topher had resisted all their attempts to draw answers from him. Even Gabriel was looking at the vampire with new eyes.

"Come on, man. End this. You just have to tell us about the Big Three. Tell us how your abilities work. What can that hurt?"

"I tell you all that, then you have her kill me?" Topher asked, eyes darting to Nora. She flinched under his gaze. Her stomach was still roiling from watching Gabriel use the knife on Topher's back and chest. Without blood, it was hard to know how much damage Gabriel was actually inflicting, but Topher was panting and his whole body trembled.

Gabriel made a frustrated noise and stabbed the knife into Topher's pectoral muscle. Topher's eyes rolled. Nora wasn't aware she'd moved forward until Matt hauled her back. Gabriel ripped the blade out and Topher slumped forward, drawing ragged breaths. Gabriel watched, lips pressed with disgust as the wound, red with the edges of muscles showing, faded to a white gash of a scar.

When Gabriel first removed Topher's shirt, they had all been shocked by the scars already there. Topher wouldn't explain them, but they were different from the marks the wolves had been giving him. They looked like human scars, not the fine white lines that appeared moments after the injuries they inflicted.

"Which tattoo is Lana's?" Gabriel asked. Topher's arms were bound behind the high back of the heavy chair, but she had seen the roses wrapping one forearm and the smoking skull on the other. A sketch of a wooden coffin marked the top of Topher's spine. She didn't even know at which point in the last couple weeks she'd learned the skull was Lana's and the coffin was Grace's. Topher clamped his mouth shut and struggled to breathe through his nose.

The door at the top of the stairs opened. Wolves had been coming in and out all night, some with food and drinks, others with suggestions for the line of questioning. All of them stared at Topher with freezing hatred.

It was Heather this time, hand pressed on her still flat stomach. She frowned at Topher like the rest, but her eyes went wide with shock when he met her gaze.

A strange half-smile spread on Topher's face. "Heather. I wondered if this was your pack."

The room stilled. Heather approached, her face going pale. Growls and snarls ripped through the air, every pack member hyper-protective of their pregnant member.

Topher sniffed and raised his eyebrows. "Congratulations."

Another round of snarls. They didn't like that he could tell.

"Chris! What the hell?" Heather asked. Gabriel moved to stand between them.

"How do you know the vampire?"

"He isn't, wasn't...," Heather dragged her eyes away from Topher's face. "He was always at Hunter's parties."

"Don't make it sound so innocent," Topher said. He rolled his arm to show the inside of his elbow and the scars still dotting it. "Vampirism didn't heal my human scars."

Nora stared at the marks, her heart pounding. She remembered with a painful squeeze Oliver explaining how Topher helped certain humans maintain their sobriety. Had he met them when he was human? He was so young. So young to be around and trying such hard drugs. To go to rehab and NA. To be tied to a chair in this basement.

The sentiment was mirrored in Heather's horrified expression.

"Hunter paid us to watch his parties and... his drugs," Heather said. Nora frowned. She hadn't envisioned that when her pack talked about their jobs protecting humans.

"You were supposed to protect us," Topher whispered. Nora had never heard this voice from him.

"What?" Heather's voice shook.

Topher glared at her. "You weren't there."

Understanding lit Heather's eyes. She took a step closer to Topher and might have gone all the way to him, but Gabriel lifted a hand.

"You were attacked?" she asked, taking in the mangled scars lining Topher's chest and arms. The bite mark on his shoulder Nora had been staring at all night.

"You were supposed to protect us." Topher sounded years younger using that accusing tone. Heather's eyes filled, shocking Nora.

"Chris. Tell me what happened."

Topher glared. He was shaking again.

"Julia?" Heather asked.

Topher scoffed. Nora saw him blinking fast as he looked away. "She's fine. At school."

Heather gave a wobbly smile. "She got in?"

"Of course. She's a genius."

"Then, by *us*, you mean—"

Topher started to cringe, curling in as if to protect himself from whoever Heather was about to name. Gabriel interrupted.

"What's happening right now?" he demanded, voice rising to a bark that made Heather cower back a step.

"He was friends with Bryce Hunter's son. Always at the warehouse after school. Partying mostly. Hunter paid me to watch the warehouse when they were there. Chris was always one of my favorites." Topher flinched at her words more than he had from the knife wounds. "Chris, what happened? You disappeared."

"I went to rehab for a bit. Didn't quite stick, but I was trying. Then Hunter—" Topher caught himself. "Never mind."

Then Topher settled back in his chair and pressed his lips together. It was the same stubborn look he'd been wearing the past three hours as he refused to answer Gabriel's questions.

"How long ago?" Gabriel asked.

Heather waited for Topher to respond. When he didn't, she said, "Last time I worked for Hunter was about a year ago."

"You've only been a vampire for a year? How the hell are you so strong?"

Silence.

Heather left soon after, unable to stomach the sight of Gabriel beating Topher. Nora followed her up the stairs.

Heather turned and spoke quietly. "God, that's *horrible*." She shook her head. "He was a happy kid, just mixed in the wrong crowd. Such a good smile. Hunter used to bring him to deals. No one could doubt that grin. Sucked the tension right out of a room. He was just a kid."

"That's pretty messed up."

"This is all messed up." Heather cast a sad look down the stairs and pressed her hand to her stomach again. "He could smell I was pregnant."

"He's strong. Stronger than the other vampires, I guess."

"I have to find out what happened to him."

"Heather, Gabriel wants him to be my kill. To join the pack."

Heather's eyes slid shut. "I don't care how strong he is. If you knew him as a human, you wouldn't ever be able to see him as a monster. Something happened to that boy and I can tell you now, he didn't choose it. He made some bad choices, but he was good. Such a good kid."

Heather left Nora halfway up the steps, feeling absolutely hollow.

Annalise still hadn't called Nora back. Topher refused to give up any information, even when Gabriel taunted him with a bag of blood. Nora didn't want to know where her alpha had gotten it. They'd left Topher slumped in the chair, panting and slipping in and out of consciousness. Annaliese's jacket pooled on the floor at his feet. That was the image stuck in Nora's mind when she got out of the Uber in front of Patty's.

The group was sitting at the far table with the longest booths. Nora sat down across from Colbie and gave her a small smile, nudging Colbie with her foot under the table. It felt so good to see her, even with the guilt squeezing Nora's chest.

Colbie looked at her blankly and Nora's stomach turned. She thought she was stronger than this but seeing that look on Colbie's face nearly had her blurting out the truth. But she couldn't trust Colbie to think this through. She had to figure out how to save Topher without putting her at risk. Nora nudged her foot again under the table. Colbie's expression didn't change.

"Hey, Nora. Zayn's almost here," Poppy said. She looked exhausted. The wolf from the other pack was here, making Nora's lip tremble as she held in a snarl. She didn't trust him. She wanted him far away from Colbie. "But I was just trying to think of a way we could—"

"Hold that thought, Poppy." Colbie's voice was low. She was staring at the table, but when she met Nora's eyes, the abrupt fury in her gaze was staggering. "I understand you don't know much about vampires. I thought it was cute how ignorant you were. But I will tell you this one for free, Nora. Vampires don't have a scent... to others. We do between ourselves. Topher smells like caramel and our parent's house." Colbie's voice was shaking, her stare unflinching. She planted her hands and leaned forward over the table. "Where the fuck is my little brother?"

CHAPTER 22

Zayn burst into the apartment, eyes first seeking out Oliver in a way that made Poppy feel a little more hopeful about everything. Nora, sitting in the armchair, stiffened. The look Zayn shot the wolf was quick and deadly.

After checking Oliver over, Zayn pushed Poppy from her seat on the coffee table and sat himself down in front of Nora. She didn't meet his eyes.

"Lana and I went to your den," he finally said. Colbie pushed off the wall by her bedroom door to come closer. It had been all Poppy and Oliver could do to keep Colbie from going there herself. Topher would never have wanted her mixed in with a vampire and werewolf confrontation.

Nora paled and swallowed, eyes on her hands clenched in her lap.

"She's pissed," Zayn continued. "This could mean war. And Grace is backing her, so maybe you should save your pack, forget about your stupid animal pride, and tell me *where Topher is.*"

Nora's eyes shot up, her mouth dropping open. Poppy's heart stopped.

"He wasn't there?" Nora asked.

"No, he wasn't there. We searched the whole place, with your alpha right there. We caught his scent, but no one was there. Just a chair and Annaliese's jacket."

"She left that there earlier," Nora whispered. "Will Lana track it?"

"Of *course* Annaliese knew, too," Colbie muttered. She took up pacing behind the couch, arms wrapped around her waist.

"Gabriel claimed not to know what we were talking about. Said he didn't smell anything."

"Well…" Nora paused long enough for everyone to know her following words couldn't be true. "Maybe I do just smell like Topher from earlier."

Colbie's steps faltered. Poppy watched her face screw up as the lie hit her. She was feeling the oncoming sunrise, Zayn too. It was evident in the slump of their shoulders and dark circles forming under their eyes.

"Just tell me where my brother is," Colbie whispered. "*Please.*"

Nora at least had the decency to look guilty. Her eyes slid shut. While she debated her answer, Poppy ignored yet another call from Annaliese, no doubt looking for her wolf friend. She'd been sending messages too, but Poppy closed each one when the new message notification popped up on her screen. After the third call from Annaliese, Colbie threw her phone in the parking lot of the diner. Poppy would have to get her another one.

"I don't know. Honest."

Colbie's face crumpled. Oliver dropped his face into his hands. Zayn shook his head at Nora.

"He was there. I could smell him. I could smell him on the knife and the chair. I could smell how weak he was. Maybe you don't care about him, but if you assholes let him loose, if you don't watch him close, he'll lose control and those deaths are on you. Lana and Grace will make sure your pack is the one punished for keeping a vampire starved. That's the risk your little pack is taking. I can hold Topher back. Lana can keep him calm. Can your alpha promise the same?"

Nora stayed quiet, but Zayn's nostrils flared. "You're scared. You know where he is."

"I don't," Nora whispered.

The room went still save for Zayn flexing his hands open and closed. The world outside was beginning to lighten. Josh shuffled on his feet where he stood by the TV.

"Just let her go," Colbie said.

"What?" at least three people asked, Poppy included.

"Maybe she'll go find him. She can warn them."

"Or go kill him like she planned," Oliver said tightly.

"Maybe not. Just let her go. I can't take her being here when Topher isn't."

Nora had the nerve to flinch.

"Just get her out of here, Poppy!" Colbie crossed the room and slammed her bedroom door behind her.

Poppy sighed and went to the front door, opening it with a significant look. No one spoke as Nora slowly stood and searched the faces around the room, all closed off to her. She lingered, looking at Colbie's door until Zayn hissed.

"Just get out," Poppy said through her teeth.

Ducking her head, Nora hurried out. Poppy saw tears on the girl's cheeks as she passed. Poppy erased any trace of their scents from Nora and slammed the door behind her.

Zayn's shoulders sagged. He rubbed a hand on the back of his neck and Oliver went to him, wrapping his arms around him.

"We'll find him, babe. Nora, Josh, and I will keep looking."

"No, you won't. I don't want you anywhere near that pack. And you have class."

"I can skip one day." Oliver looked up, "Will anyone mind if we crash in Topher's bed? It's terribly difficult carrying Zayn once the sun knocks him out."

Poppy wanted to smile at the visual, but her face had

forgotten how. She nodded and soon, it was just her and Josh in the living room. He moved to flop down on the couch. She took the armchair. It was getting harder and harder to pretend keeping Josh around was harmless. Where Josh's easy manner had been calming before, it now filled her with guilt on top of everything else. He was so clearly interested in her and she was sick over this fear for Topher.

"So what's the move?" he asked.

Poppy could only shrug. She really thought Lana would find Topher at the Den. They were back to square one.

"Where *were* you going to look for him? If Colbie hadn't smelled him on Nora?"

Poppy rubbed her temples. "I was thinking I didn't trust Lana. Or any of Grace's vampires, for that matter. I thought if nothing came of the meeting, I could search her office for clues about who might use Topher to get back at her. I still don't get why they chose to attack him." Poppy looked up slowly. "Maybe it's still a good idea to check her out. It could help us find him wherever he is now. All I know is I can't just sit around and wait."

Josh considered, nodding slowly. "Sure. Better than sitting around. I was also thinking I should ask my uncle to check out Nora's den."

"Why?"

"He might find out something they kept from the vampires. He's been meaning to get over there anyway, to try and build a relationship. He was planning to invite them to run with us during the full moon next week."

"That might be a good idea. I wouldn't want to put them at risk, though. You don't even know Topher." It was getting difficult to even say his name.

"He can be discreet. We've been dealing with supernatural politics for years."

"And getting ran out of every city you try it in."

Josh spread his hands and gave her a wry smile. "Some of us haven't even unpacked yet. Won't be too big of a deal."

"Have you unpacked?"

Josh's eyes warmed as he nodded. "Color me an optimist," he said. He slapped his thighs and stood. "Let's go. I'll call the pack on the way to Lana's on the condition we can stop for coffee and something to eat first."

Poppy accepted the hand Josh offered. "Deal."

Topher knew sunrise was close. Maybe an hour away. Maybe two. He knew his body ached and his stomach was an empty, clenched knot. He couldn't think past those few awarenesses. He barely even processed the sound at the window. The thud of feet hitting the concrete.

Then all he knew was the smell. A human was nearby. He wanted every drop of blood in their body.

Topher had trained himself well enough to force the thought to quiet and the hunger to shrink. He shoved it to the background so hard it took a physical toll. He let out a groan as his stomach twisted painfully. If he were human still, he would be dry heaving.

"Topher?" the girl whispered.

He forced his head up. Annaliese. Stupid girl. "Get out." There was no strength in his voice.

"Are you going to attack me?"

He doubted he was strong enough to fight his bonds, but he clenched his fists anyway. "I'm trying not to. It hurts. Please go."

His mouth attempted to water, but he didn't have the moisture left. Topher was practically seeing in red, his mind so consumed with the smell of blood it overpowered his other senses.

"I'm going to give you some blood. Just a little. Just enough so you can get out."

"No. I won't stop. I can't…" Topher ended in a gasp. Sobbing without tears. He was going to kill her. Panic and hunger were dizzying. Desire staggering.

He felt his head tipped back, but he kept his eyes and mouth shut tight. He tried holding his breath. Now was a good time to find out how long a vampire could go without air.

He heard a metallic scrape and then Annaliese gasped and he couldn't stop himself. He thrashed against his metal bindings. He could smell it. Hear it. Blood. He couldn't break the bonds cutting into the flesh of his wrists, but something in the legs of the thick wood chair was giving. It would give. It took him a while to hear Annaliese over the roaring in his ears.

"Stop!" she was saying. Topher froze. He would do anything for it. "Tilt your head back and open your mouth."

He did. Trembling. Annaliese was breathing hard, listening for the sound of a wolf approaching. He forced his eyes open and saw her shaking arm hovering above him. She'd cut her palm and was squeezing a fist. His eyes locked on the drop of blood pooling pooling pooling. Gathering in painful slowness into a drip. He strained toward it. The chair creaked.

The drop was glorious. A rich coat that barely had time to wet his tongue before he swallowed it. The first drop was followed by another and another. Topher was desperate for more and more. But he forced his eyes to Annaliese's face. She tried to hide it, but her fear was almost as strong as the smell of blood. Adrenaline soured its taste. He forced himself to stop pulling against the metal bonds. As the drops fell, his mind started to clear. He wouldn't be a monster. Not to her. Not again.

Annaliese hadn't cut herself that deeply. Her shaking fist only produced so much, but it was enough for Topher to get his head. He wondered if vampires were like humans in that way. After days of starving, they could only eat so much food before they got full and then sick. Topher worked to convince himself he was full. That he didn't long for more. He still whimpered when she lowered her hand.

"Better?" she asked in a low voice.

"Better. I'm so sorry."

Annaliese rolled her eyes and started wrapping her cut palm. It was on the tip of Topher's tongue to offer to heal it, but if he licked her, he wouldn't be able to stop himself from biting. He made himself sit still.

"Thank you, Annaliese. You should go now."

She rolled her eyes again. She still had her knife out and walked around the chair.

"What are you doing?" he asked.

"I'm getting you out of here."

"If you free me, I might not be able to help myself." The admission made him nearly feel warm from shame. Annaliese walked back in front of him and crouched to his eye level. She was so short; she didn't have to bend far.

"Get it together, Topher. You'll be fine."

He desperately fought a smile. She was so serious, he nearly believed her. He didn't want to charm her now. Not when she'd given him her blood. Not when her palm was still bleeding gently into the cloth she'd wrapped around it, taunting him.

"They used handcuffs. Your feet are connected separately to the chair legs, but your hands are just cuffed together behind you. I think I can just tip you back and get the cuffs on your ankles off the chair legs."

"Probably keep them around my wrists," he said.

"I don't know how I'll get you out then."

"Please. Don't let me attack anyone. Or you."

"You won't. Just stay with me, Topher."

She went back behind him. The chair was thick and sturdy. Annaliese tilted it back, grunting as she tried to keep it from dropping. When Topher's weight became too much and it did fall, his hands and arms bound around the back muffled the sound. He winced when they were smashed into the concrete floor, shoulders wrenching.

"Sorry." Annaliese hurried to the other end of the chair and slid the two pairs of handcuffs connected to his ankles off the legs.

"You're a genius," he whispered.

"More so Gabriel's an idiot, but we can debate that later."

His legs free, Topher twisted and squirmed to get his arms out from underneath him. He rolled onto his knees and then to standing. But he stumbled and Annaliese scrambled to catch him. When she grabbed his waist, he closed his eyes and held his breath against the smell of her so close.

"Step back," he barely got the words out.

Annaliese hastily backed away, eyes wide. Topher waited until he regained control, counting her heartbeats and holding his breath. When they both calmed, he released it slowly, the initial urge to attack her dimmed. "Okay. What now?"

"My plan was to get you out the window."

Topher eyed it, still propped open from Annaliese's entrance. He had no idea how Annaliese made the drop without hurting herself. "Did this plan involve flight? How are you even getting out? Let alone me handcuffed."

Annaliese thought for a beat, then moved to lift the chair. She carried it over the concrete floor, set it with the back against the wall, and gestured Topher over. The empty ends of the handcuffs at his ankles clanked when he stepped. Annaliese hurried over and bent down. He almost smiled again when she solved the problem by closing the loose cuffs to their smallest circle and tucking them into his socks. The cold metal bit against his ankles.

"Okay, I'm going to try and help you out. I'll stand on the front of the chair and try to balance the weight while you step up on the back. If you need more height, I'll try and push you. Sit on the edge when you get up so I can use your legs to climb out."

"You're a genius," Topher repeated.

It took work. With grunting and clumsy shoving on Annaliese's part, Topher was able to press out of her palms and get his upper body out the window. He squirmed forward, rolled to his back, and sat up. When Annaliese had hold of his legs, he scooted backward. Only his remaining vampire strength made the motion feasible.

Annaliese's cut palm was bleeding with renewed vigor from the struggle, but if it hurt badly, she didn't show it. She got to her feet.

"Hurry. We don't have much time."

Topher stood, ignoring his head rush, he followed her to her car. She got the door open for him, waved frantically until he ducked inside, and slammed it shut.

When she got into the driver's seat, he pressed himself as close as he could to the window. Her scent was suffocating in the enclosed space. Her neck so close. "Roll it down!" he nearly shouted. His fangs sliced into his bottom lip.

Annaliese did as she hit the gas. Topher heard her pulse racing.

"I'm sorry about your hand. I'm sorry I can't control it."

"Shut up, Topher. You're doing great." The compliment stunned him enough to momentarily forget how delicious she was. "Just hold on a bit longer, okay?"

"Okay," he whispered. He didn't want her to notice how many times his hands had already strained against the cuffs to reach for her.

Annaliese drove to a rundown neighborhood closer to downtown. Topher's mouth dropped open when Rebecca and two other members of his old NA group came out of the nearest apartment building. They got into the back of the car.

"How did you—"

"Chris! What happened? She said you'd be hungry." Rebecca was all concern.

"You look like hell, man. Want me to get the cuffs off you?" Johnny asked. "I got my picks in my truck."

"Drink first," Annaliese said. Topher nodded.

Rebecca held her wrist up to him between the seats. It took all his willpower not to clamp down instantly. He couldn't say anything. He was clenching his jaw too hard.

Rebecca understood. "He doesn't like to bite. Anyone have a knife?"

Eyebrows drawn, Annaliese brought hers back out. Rebecca took it. "Will I get anything if I use a dirty knife?"

Nothing his saliva wouldn't instantly kill. Topher shook his head. Annaliese watched Rebecca cut her wrist and hold it up to him.

This time he drank. It was heaven. Relief like nothing he'd ever experienced. He probably took a mouthful too many, but Rebecca wasn't complaining when he licked her cut to heal it and moved to clamp his lips on Calla's waiting wrist, then Johnny's.

Still riding Topher's bliss, it took Johnny five tries to pick the handcuffs, but in relatively short order, the three humans were stumbling back up the steps to Rebecca's apartment and Annaliese was driving away.

"No one is answering," she ground out, lowering her phone again.

Topher was still experiencing a high from all the blood. He sighed. "I'm going to sleep soon anyway."

"Can you make it to the apartment?"

Topher shrugged.

"Alright. My place is closer." Annaliese swung the car to the left and got on the interstate. It was stunning how quickly the grungy apartments fell away to suburbia, yet Topher's eyelids were drooping by the time Annaliese pulled into her garage and out of the first rays of sunlight.

"Stay with me," she said, seeing his head give a sudden nod as he fought sleep.

"I'm trying."

"I know."

With blood thoroughly clearing his mind, Topher became aware of the state the wolves had left his body in. He winced when he got out of the car and breathed through gritted teeth down the steps to Annaliese's basement.

"You're really roughing it, huh?" he asked, taking in the entertainment system, the open door to her walk-in closet, and the welcoming king bed. Her back wall was covered in bookshelves. "Colbie would be in heaven."

"I don't want to be a bitch, but do you think you could handle showering before you get in my bed?"

"I guess I owe you that much." Topher braced himself and walked to her bathroom. He showered as quickly as he could manage and was wrapping himself in a plush towel when Annaliese called through the door that she had clothes. He changed without taking in any more than the sweats were soft and black.

The trip to the bed was also a blur. "You need more blankets," he said as he climbed under the two layers.

"Noted." Annaliese stood at the edge of the bed, hovering over him. The heat of the shower's water left him and Topher wished Annaliese would join him. She looked so soft and warm. The memory of the taste of her was still alive on his tongue. He rolled away, trying to dispel the thoughts.

He was stunned when the bed shifted behind him and she climbed in.

"Did I just charm you?" he asked, worried.

"I don't think so. You didn't say anything."

"Sometimes when I want humans to do something, I do it on accident."

"I'm tired too. Just shut up." She settled in close enough he could feel her warmth at his back. He bent his legs, cold feet seeking. She heaved a sigh and covered them with her legs.

"Topher, relax." He didn't realize until she spoke that he

was holding himself so tightly he was shaking. "Nothing will hurt you here."

"Colbie never answered?"

"No, but I'll go to the apartment when you're asleep and tell Poppy."

"I don't want you to leave." Topher was suddenly, painfully, distrustful of the sunlit world outside. Full of wolves and others who would be awake while he lay helpless in sleep.

Annaliese scooted closer. Topher stilled when she pressed up against his back. So warm. Her hand came up and ran through his wet hair. Her lips were mere inches from his neck when she spoke. "I can take care of myself, Topher. You're safe. I'm safe. Just sleep."

"Don't leave."

"I have to tell Poppy and Colbie."

"Don't leave."

"Shhh."

Topher worked to do as she said, knowing he was being irrational but unable to fully settle his mind as the past two days caught up with him. He let himself be comforted until the shaking stopped. Let Annaliese's familiar scent fill his head. Focused on her fingers in his hair, the rhythm of her breathing against his neck. The cold seeped out of his body. It had been so constant in that basement. The thought of his time there made him shudder. Annaliese hesitated a beat, then wrapped her arm around him tight. She pressed her face between his shoulder blades.

"It's okay, Topher. You're okay. Relax."

Slowly, slowly, he did as she said.

CHAPTER 23

"Stop with the calling, Annaliese! We have a—" Poppy started.

"Just let me talk! I have Topher."

Poppy almost dropped her phone. "*What?*"

Josh raised an eyebrow at her but didn't say anything when Poppy swerved the car into the nearest lot and jerked it into park. His pack was probably already at Nora's Den now. She put the phone on speaker.

"Nora showed me where they were keeping him. I broke into the Den last night and got him out."

"Annaliese! What were you thinking? He could have killed you!" Poppy hated that this was her first thought, but she'd seen Topher lunge for Oliver. The starved, wild look in his eyes. Pupils blown so that the blue of his irises were just thin, near glowing rings around the edge. His fangs bared.

"He wouldn't. He didn't. I got him out and fed. He's right here sleeping."

"The pack is going to smell you were there. They could track you," Josh said. Poppy was surprised by the force of his concern.

"I left my jacket there when I saw him with Nora. It's still there now. I walked to the window earlier too. They'll smell me and it might be too fresh, but I don't think they'll suspect me. They wouldn't think a human would do this. They'll probably think it was a vampire without a scent to leave."

Josh sat back in his seat, looking impressed. "Huh."

"Are you crazy, Annaliese? You should have called! Asked us for help."

"I didn't want to start something. I'm neutral. I hate this, but I didn't want it to hurt the whole pack. They've always been great to me."

"Shit. *Shit.*" Poppy groaned.

"What? Did something already start?"

"Lana was over there, but you must have just gotten Topher out. They had to leave when the sun started to rise. They didn't have time to do more than threaten the wolves," Poppy said.

"And my pack is over there, checking it out. I trust them to keep their cool. We should be fine. Poppy was just about to break into the Maker, though. We were going to see if Lana had anything to do with it. That could have been interesting."

"But Topher, he's okay?" Poppy couldn't keep the desperation out of her voice. Josh studied her closely.

"I wouldn't say that. Physically, he looks pretty stiff. I don't know what they did to him."

"And mentally?"

Annaliese hesitated. "I think he needs his sister. He didn't want me to leave him, though. We'll have to wait until he wakes up."

Poppy's thoughts were spinning so wildly that she briefly wondered where she was supposed to get chem notes if Annaliese had skipped today too.

"Shit. Nor is calling. What should I say?"

"You really want me to answer that?" Poppy asked.

"Did she show up last night?"

"Yes. Colbie smelled Topher on her right away."

"Oh. I thought vampires didn't have a scent."

"They do to each other."

"This is so messed up."

"You're telling me."

Annaliese went quiet. Poppy heard Topher's muffled muttering and Annaliese's shushing, calming noises. The gentle sounds were so incongruent with the Annaliese Poppy thought she knew.

Annaliese's voice was hushed when she spoke again. "I should let him sleep. I don't think Nora will come here, but as soon as he's awake, we'll go to the apartment."

"Okay. Call me when you're close. I'm going to put up new wards and I'll have to let you in."

"Sounds good." Annaliese hung up.

"That girl has nerve," Josh said.

Poppy shook her head at her phone, but she had to agree. "She barely even knows Topher. I honestly thought she hated him."

Josh shrugged. "Some people are just doers. They have their morals and they stick with them."

"People like Annaliese, though? Angry and guarded and…" Poppy didn't know what else. She kept hearing Annaliese comforting Topher, obviously in bed with him.

"What makes you think Annaliese pretends to be anything other than who she is? I don't know her well, but I don't think this goes against her character."

Poppy sighed. "You should probably call your uncle."

Josh grimaced and dug out his phone. "If he's talking to them now, the other wolves will hear what I say."

"So we just wait?"

Josh considered. "Might be best, yeah."

Poppy drummed her fingers on the steering wheel. "I still want to check the Maker," she decided. She put the car back in drive and continued down the street. The Maker was only a couple of blocks away.

"What? Why?"

"Because I want to know what Lana is up to. Zayn said something that has me worried."

"Worried how?"

"I don't know… just uneasy."

"Uneasy? Well, let me come with you at least."

"No way. She'll be able to smell you in a heartbeat."

She parked in front of the Maker. Josh reached to take her hand, shaking his head. "Poppy, you can't just—"

"I can, actually." Poppy pulled a vial out of her bag, hoping wolves weren't as resistant to brews as they were to uttered spells, she splashed Josh with her most potent sleeping draught. He slumped against his window, but his breathing remained light and easy. Not a deep sleep like Topher would have fallen into. She wouldn't have much time.

Leaving the car, Poppy could feel the Maker's daytime wards. It surprised her to feel the warmth of a witch's magic, but she shook off the feeling and focused on the wards. They were quite basic. Made to prevent those coming with harmful intent. She didn't want to hurt anyone or steal anything. She just wanted information. The wards accepted her easily. Poppy couldn't identify the imprint of the witch who made them, but it wasn't one from her coven. She couldn't tell if she was happy or disappointed about that.

A team of humans mopped and polished counters, all dazed and blissed from vampire saliva the night before. No one acknowledged her as she passed. Poppy swallowed her disgust.

She went to the back hall and crept up the stairs. Poppy had been to the roof, but Topher never mentioned what lay behind the doors of these upper levels. She discovered the second floor consisted of bedrooms. The first one belonged to Tamera, sleeping on a bare bed and cuddled up with a human man who just blinked when Poppy stuck her head in. Tamera was drooling on his chest. He absently played with the pool, spreading the bliss and swirling it in his chest hair. His eyes were so glossy Poppy wondered if a human could overdose on vampire.

The next door was locked. A snap and Poppy was inside. The room was in shambles. Clothing strewn about and the mattress flipped and settled against the wall. The window had been smashed and a cool breeze rolled in. A little more snooping and Poppy realized this was Brady's old room. Had someone's grief destroyed it? One of the lowers? Or was Lana capable of such feeling?

The next room was clearly Zayn's. Soccer posters covered the walls. A pile of books sat in the corner. It was a well-worn room, making Poppy wonder for the first time how long Zayn had been under Lana's wing. It felt abandoned now, probably since Zayn and Oliver bought their apartment downtown. A stack of flashcards was the only sign of Oliver within.

Poppy ducked her head in and out of the next room quickly. Sleeping on the bed was the huge vampire Topher referred to as Muscles. He usually worked the door as a bouncer along with the woman in the next room called Jaeger. The next bedroom brought Poppy up short.

She knew some days Topher stayed here when he worked late. But she hadn't imagined a space for him like this. A king bed took up the majority of the room. It was piled with more blankets and pillows than even his bed back home, with an overflowing basket of more blankets to the side. A cord snaked out from the bottom layer, revealing a heated blanket hidden in the mess. Poppy ran her hand over the clothes in his open closet, all high quality. Mostly suits. There were expensive sweatshirts and joggers folded and clean in the dresser. A faded soccer ball sat in the corner next to a pair of mud-spattered sneakers.

He had a desk. It was covered in notebooks, pages filled with bulky writing. A map of New Brecken dotted with two sets of handwriting marked where each of the lower vampires had been found and turned. In a flare of uncontrollable magic, spurred by unhelpful jealousy, Poppy conjured the imprint of Topher sitting at his desk. Lana was perched on the edge, smiling down at him. She reached and fixed his hair while Topher studied the map. Poppy waved a hand to dispel the image. She didn't want to think how often the two had sat like that for the imprint to be so vivid.

Poppy bent her head over a notebook, recognizing Topher's blocky scrawl.

July 13th. Lasted three questions. No information gained.

Lana's writing: *Learned lowers can resist all our charm. Important!*

Two on August 4th. First lasted five questions. Lived in warehouse district. Attacked at dawn, from shadows so no visual. They're getting stronger.

Lana: *You only lasted fifteen minutes. They could have gone longer. You need to keep practicing. This one is on you.*

Most jarring was the last note on the page.

December 19th. Third one dead. Bite marks look like

Whatever Topher had been writing, he'd been interrupted. Looked like what?

Poppy jumped when she heard someone out in the hall.

"Yeah, he's still missing."

"Are you helping Lana look?"

"Of course not. Not my problem if another one of her lowers got sick of her and left. She doesn't pay me enough to worry about that. I protect the Maker, that's it. Now help me find our intruder."

Poppy's breath caught. She hadn't felt anything in the wards signaling her arrival. She clenched her fists, wishing for the millionth time she possessed stronger magic.

"I'm sure it's just another human looking for a fix. Beth, wait. I need to ask, have you heard the rumors? Mother thinks you might know more than us."

"What rumors?"

"The shadows. Nadya was attacked last week." The woman's voice dropped. Poppy pressed close to Topher's door to listen. "By a demon. She barely got away. Do you know who would be summoning?"

"Are you trying to ask if I did this, sister?"

"Of course not. You're just involved with the vampires. We thought you may have heard something." The woman's tone was too stiff, though. The accusation remained in the air.

"I haven't. A demon probably just formed. No need to start thinking sorcerers. I think our guest is over here."

"Beth. I have to ask one last time. Do you know where the demon is coming from?"

"I swear on the Mother, Palla, I don't."

Poppy heard enough. The footsteps drew close. A snap and Poppy silently opened Topher's window. She climbed onto the ledge, staring down the drop.

"Winds carry me." Poppy jumped.

Poppy barely made it to the car. Going against gravity was a difficult spell. It was one of this world's most coveted laws and always fought back. Josh was awake by then and he leaped out of the car, catching her around the waist before she hit the ground too hard. Sensing her panic, his nostrils flared and he pushed Poppy into the seat he had just vacated. He circled the car and got behind the wheel.

Poppy noticed his nails elongating and pulling back in as he clenched the wheel. Poppy set a hand on his arm.

"I'm fine. Nothing happened. Another witch showed up, but they didn't catch me. I just didn't expect it. It's been a long time since I've seen another witch. And I'm tired from so many spells."

Josh didn't reply. He drove past city limits to the forest. He barely got to his boxers before he ripped into the change. Poppy hauled herself out of the car and followed him. She stumbled into the shade of the trees and settled flat on her back in the dirt with a groan. Josh circled her, growling softly until he calmed. He then sat at Poppy's feet. She squinted an eye open to watch him, unable to keep from smiling as his ears flicked around, listening for a threat. He caught her looking at him and snarled enough to make her jump and then laugh.

Josh huffed and lowered himself along her body. Heat radiated out of his tan fur. He didn't relax, continually sniffing the air and cocking his head to listen.

"Is it weird if I pet you?" Poppy asked. He just looked so soft.

He licked her cheek. She scratched the short fuzz under his chin, reaching around to get behind his ear and letting her fingers tangle in the tuft of fur. He *was* soft. As a wolf, he smelled even more like the rain. He laid his head down, trapping her bicep under his chin. He huffed another breath, rustling her hair.

Poppy closed her eyes and let the forest replenish her. She imagined the tension leaving her and seeping into the ground. The life around her rising to fill the void left. Josh was full to bursting with life energy. She barely needed to draw from the trees with him so close. If he noticed her borrowing his strength, he didn't react.

Poppy told herself Topher was fine. He could explain the notebook filled with his and Lana's handwriting. Explain his knowledge of the unclaimed and their mysterious, powerful maker. He could explain the hours he and Lana had spent at that desk, her looking down at him. Touching his hair. He probably even knew who the witch outside his room was.

Opening her eyes, Poppy turned her head to look at Josh. She thought about Annaliese pushing for her to text him. Annaliese murmuring to a sleeping Topher. All the nights the human had spent in Topher's room. How she'd been among the first to worry about him even with Colbie insisted everything was fine. Jealousy was unwelcome, but looking at Josh, the guilt was harder to bear.

"Josh," Poppy whispered. His ears twitched forward when she claimed his attention. Were his eyes this big and brown in human form? "Josh. I'm in love with Topher. It would be so much easier if this could work. I'm sorry."

Josh's ears flattened. He started to let out a keening whine but cut it off quickly. He stood, turned in a circle, looking lost even as a wolf. Then he exhaled loudly through his nose and disappeared into the forest, going back toward the car with his tail hanging low.

Poppy gave him a few minutes and followed. When she neared the break in the trees, she saw he was on his phone and wearing only his shorts. She didn't let herself admire the muscles along his stomach and chest.

"Shit. Okay…. Yeah… Okay. Tonight? Sure… No, thanks for trying… See you then." He hung up and turned his head to her, keeping his body angled away. Poppy realized then he'd always given her his undivided attention, full body alert to her every movement. The first stirrings of regret hit her, but she couldn't keep up what had felt like a lie.

"Can you get home?" he asked, nodding toward the car.

"Yes. Was that your uncle?"

"Yeah." He looked down at his phone. Nothing more.

"Josh?"

"Yes?" His eyes were briefly hopeful when he looked up.

"Please don't tell anyone. About my magic."

He sighed. His shoulders slumped forward and he looked away. "I won't. Keys are still in the car."

"You don't need a ride?"

Josh shook his head. He was wrapping his phone to his wrist with a hair tie.

"Your pack is okay, right?"

He made the change and left her standing in the shadows of the trees without an answer. Howling echoed from deep in the hills. Poppy didn't wait to hear if he answered. She ran for her car and slammed the door behind her, holding back her tears until she was on the highway.

"Hi. Hey, Colbie. I know you're sleeping. I just had to tell you, I mean, I need you to understand, I would never have killed your brother." Nora couldn't hold back a groan, rubbing her eyes with the hand not holding her phone. "Why couldn't we just have normal problems like how I haven't come out and my family is crazy traditional." Nora winced. Did she sound like she was taking this too lightly?

"I should have told you where he was. I'm sorry. I wanted to avoid a war. I wanted to avoid this— you hating me because I'm a werewolf. All I've ever wanted was to make the change and run with my pack. To see my mom again. To make my father's memory proud." Nora settled on her back to look at the clouds from the roof. A tear slipped over her temple and into her hair. She reached up and pinched the water out of the strand. She was swept suddenly by the memory of Colbie doing almost the same thing the first time they saw each other.

She took a deep breath. It shook, but she pressed on. "I can't even touch my hair now without thinking about you. I can't look at myself without wishing I saw my reflection the same way you used to see me. I feel you missing and it hurts, Colbie, it hurts so bad. I just need you to know I wouldn't have killed your brother. I need you to know I'm sorry because I watched them hurt him and I wasn't smart enough or strong enough or brave enough to help. I'm sorry, Colbie, I—" She dropped the phone away from her ear and hung up before she could say too much.

Nora sat and pulled on her hood. She crossed her forearms over her knees and hid her face there until she got her tears under control.

Nora heard the door of her room open below and quickly wiped off any remaining wetness on her cheeks. She waited with unease for Matt to join her on the roof.

He didn't, though, he only stuck his head over the edge, looking strained.

"Gabriel sent me to tell you to stay up here for a bit. We have company."

Nora frowned. "Why do I have to stay up here?"

"It's dangerous, Nor. Pack stuff."

"Am I not part of the pack?"

"Nora…"

"No. That's bullshit. You can't keep leaving me out of everything."

Matt blinked. "Look, I'm sorry, but you just can't defend yourself like we can yet—"

Nora snorted and pushed by him as she jumped into her room. She caught herself on her dresser when she tripped and hurried down the hall. Matt caught up, eyes nervous and one hand already rubbing the back of his neck. Nora smelled the other pack before she even got to the stairs.

Matt tried again, leaning close and speaking low in her ear. "Don't piss him off, Nor. Being in the pack means listening to your alpha. Gabriel said—"

Nora shot him a glare. Matt raised his hands in surrender, looking startled.

About half of her pack was in the living room. Standing inside the door were five members of Josh's pack. Their alpha, a man with blond hair beginning to gray at the temples, was making the introductions.

"So we have Cora and Rory," he pointed at the identical twins that had been at the cafe. They looked about Gabriel's age. The woman on the left seemed bored, eyes roving the room slowly. The other wore a scowl that might have rivaled Annaliese's. "This is my younger nephew, Daniel, and last but not least, Quinn is my beta. Oh, and I'm Henry."

Daniel looked just like Josh but didn't hold himself in the loose easiness Josh did. Even Nora could smell his nerves.

Quinn was a tall woman. She looked distinctly unimpressed as she took in the Den and the members of Nora's pack gathered. She positioned herself close to Henry's right and they moved in uncanny tandem.

Nora's mother had been her father's beta. It was practically unheard of for a woman to hold such status. Nora had always been fiercely proud of her parent's relationship, the balance of romance and leadership. She felt herself warming to Henry for allowing a woman to rise in his ranks like her father had. And that was without mateship bonding them.

The familiar desire to stand there, in a position of power, to hold herself tall and proud like that, struck Nora hard. When Daniel shuffled his feet, Quinn shot a look over her shoulder that immediately stilled him. Nora's heart skipped.

She looked at Gabriel, who still hadn't selected a beta or let them challenge each other for the position. They all thought he was testing Matt for the role. Matt, Nora's best friend now that Annaliese had gone as silent as Colbie.

"What is it you want?" Gabriel asked. His arms were crossed tightly over his chest. He must have been working on the van. He wore only a black muscle shirt, leaving the moon phases tattoo around his right bicep in plain view. His jeans were streaked with grease and dried paint.

"I wanted to extend an invitation. No reason our packs shouldn't get along. Alliances are key to survival in cities like this. So I wanted to ask if we could all run together next week. We would, of course, follow your lead. You could show us the park."

"Next week isn't good. We have a member making the change for the first time."

Henry's eyes landed on Nora as if he could smell her approaching shift. Gabriel stepped to the side, blocking her from view. Undeterred, Henry leaned to look around him with a smile, Quinn stepping back so he could.

"That's excellent news. You look just like your mother. You know, she was there for my first change."

The room stilled. It was suddenly hard for Nora to breathe.

"How do you know Helen?" Gabriel asked.

"We were part of the same pack growing up. We eventually crossed paths with Morales and they mated. We were chased out of our town up in Montana soon after, but I recently went back and found some messages she'd sent years ago telling us they'd settled here. I was hoping to see her." Henry's eyes were hesitant as they searched the room again.

Gabriel cleared his throat. The light seemed to dim as memories crowded Nora.

"My mom's been in wolf form since my dad was killed," Nora said, refusing to let her mother's fate diminish to an awkward silence. Matt squeezed her hand. Nora realized she'd reached for him.

"How long?"

"It's been two years since she's changed." Too long to hope she'd remember how to change back. Too long for her to remember her daughter.

Henry swallowed. His blue eyes filled with sadness. They didn't shine like Colbie's, the color wasn't quite right, but they reminded her of the vampire anyway. Nora's chest throbbed.

"I'm sorry to hear that. Hopefully, you'll see her again soon. Best of luck with the change," Henry said. "Maybe we'll run the next moon together."

Nora nodded, though the tension in Gabriel's shoulders gave her little hope of it happening.

Quinn spoke next. "Are you attending the meeting tonight?"

Gabriel crossed his arms impossibly tighter. "We were planning to."

"What do you think spurred the vampires to call another gathering?"

"I couldn't say. We generally keep our business separate."

Nora held back a snort.

"Lower vampires going unclaimed and killing humans seems like it would be everyone's business," the bored twin said.

"We're doing our part. Likely the vampires know more than they're letting on. We'll continue conducting *our own* investigation," Gabriel said.

"Excellent. Maybe we can join forces. We've found three of the bodies in the warehouse district. We helped Solas find one of the lowers, but she offered to take care of it from that point."

"You can't trust the vampires. Especially not the Big Three. They claim all the registered vampires in the city between them."

Henry nodded. He shared a look with Quinn over his shoulder.

The angry twin's phone went off. She glanced at the screen and, in response to Henry's questioning look, said, "It's Josh."

Henry nodded and the twin slipped outside to answer the call. Daniel followed her without waiting for permission, but Henry didn't appear bothered.

"So, any advice for the meeting tonight?" he asked, rocking forward on his feet.

"I already told you not to trust the vamps," Gabriel said stiffly. Henry raised an eyebrow and Gabriel blew out an irritated breath. "They might send out another message before the meeting specifying the number of underlings, but if they don't, you can be sure they're going to show up in full force. Each of the Big Three has at least three seconds that they keep close, and most of those seconds are also makers. They will each likely bring at least four of their favorite pets. They haven't sent the invite to the humans, but the witch, Kallow, is bringing her daughters. They'll probably cast barriers to keep the peace, but I'll be bringing my strongest and I suggest you do the same in case things go south."

"You think it'll go south?"

Gabriel shrugged.

"Okay. Thanks for the heads up." Henry offered a smile.

The twin came back in. She shook her head once and Henry's face cleared a bit. "Daniel?"

"Went to meet up with him."

"Alright. I suppose we should stop bothering you." He pulled out a business card and placed it on the table near the door. "Give me a call when you want to run or if you want help with the lowers. It was a pleasure."

Without waiting for Gabriel's response, Henry and his pack members made their exit. The tension in the room eased when the front door shut behind them. Gabriel walked over and picked up the business card. He tore it in half and then fourths before tossing it in the small trash under the table.

"I don't trust them. My command stands. Avoid interacting with them at all costs."

Nora frowned. She thought making allies was a good idea. Their pack had few members compared to the vampire clans. Joining forces with another pack could only strengthen their precarious position in the city, especially if Gabriel was pulling moves like what he did to Topher.

Not to mention Henry's connection with her mother. She opened her mouth to say something about it, but what came out was, "I want to go to the meeting. I want to know what's happening."

The tension fully eased as her packmates laughed. They *laughed*. Even Gabriel chuckled, the sound tired. "It's way too dangerous, Nor."

"You keep hiding things from me! I deserve to know what's happening."

"You will. Soon."

"I want to ask Henry about my mother."

The wolves stilled, pity staining their features. Gabriel walked to where Nora stood at the base of the steps. A step higher, she was just barely taller than him. Gabriel pulled her in for a hug. "You'll see her soon. Sometimes she runs with us. It'll be better then."

Nora doubted it, but she let him hug her. It felt like she could disappear from the world with his large arms and broad chest hiding her away.

Hours later, when everyone had gone to the meeting, work or sleep, Nora pulled the pieces of Henry's card from the bin. She taped it back together before hiding it under her mattress. As she waited for the meeting to end, she restlessly checked her phone for a response from Colbie and wondered what she would ask if she got up the nerve to call Henry.

CHAPTER 24

Topher swallowed a groan when sleep released him. His body ached, his fears resurfaced, and Annaliese was nearby, making his mouth water with the memory of those few drops of her blood he'd tasted. She had a crisp, vibrant flavor and he hated that he knew it.

Annaliese was working on the computer at her desk, sitting with one knee drawn up to her chest and her chin propped on it. Her braids were twisted into a bun on top of her head, the icy blue streaking against the darker shades closer to her roots. Topher remembered how far out of his reach his charm had been last night, how he'd talked to her without its influence. He'd felt nearly human.

He pushed himself up and winced, a hand going to the place Gabriel stabbed him with the knife. He shivered at the memory. Lana commented once, tone nearly bored, that people tended to lose their humanity when vampires were at their mercy. The lack of blood equated to a lack of pain in their minds. And the rapid healing. They didn't know the pain was still there, the drain of energy that hit each time the skin closed.

The horror of looking at a knife sticking out of you without blood to accompany it. Like a corpse.

"Morning," Annaliese said. She looked wary, even as she smiled a bit at the joke. Night had fallen outside.

"You let me sleep in," Topher played along. He didn't think before he warmed his expression.

Annaliese's smile turned dazed and she dropped the pen she'd been holding. Topher shuttered his gaze and looked away.

"S-sorry." She hastily bent to pick up the pen.

"It's on me, Annaliese," he said, letting frustration color his tone to reverse the charm. He got up and went to her bathroom.

She should have left him for the wolves.

By the time Topher left the bathroom, his cool mask was firmly in place. "Did you get ahold of Colbie?"

"Poppy. She said Colbie is still in bed."

Topher's chest squeezed. "Could you possibly give me a ride home?"

Her nod was on this side of mindless, but Topher told himself she would have agreed charmed or not. The car ride was a quiet affair. Annaliese kept glancing in his direction, worry coupled with flares of attraction brought on by his charm spiking her blood. He felt suffocated by his power and the lies it turned his world into.

They pulled into the apartment parking lot and Annaliese followed him up the steps. They passed the building's super wincing on his way down from the second floor. Topher knew he needed a clear head. He knew his body needed extra blood to heal. He knew his saliva made Mr. Smith's back stop hurting for days the last time he had to feed on him. And he knew Annaliese's stomach had turned last night watching him feed. Hopefully, watching him do it again would deter her from any insane heroics in the future.

Despite all this, releasing his charm made his chest tight.

He had to force the words out. "Mind if I?"

Mr. Smith nodded, forgetting Topher's preference and tipping his head to bare his throat.

Topher grabbed the man's hand and made quick work feeding while Annaliese shifted uncomfortably behind him. Mr. Smith moaned. Annaliese cleared her throat.

"Thank you," Mr. Smith whispered after Topher healed the cut on his wrist with a quick lick.

"No, thank you." Topher continued up the stairs, Annaliese at his heels.

"Why don't you drink from their necks?" she asked after a pause.

Topher shot her a look over his shoulder. The question hung in the air between them. He sped up as they neared the apartment wards, anxiety for Colbie clawing at his throat. He unlocked the door and rushed inside, barely returning Poppy's greeting before he ran to his room.

She was still sleeping in his bed. The covers were tucked over her head. Topher sat next to her and shook her shoulders. She woke and sat up so quickly that he laughed. It sounded slightly manic.

"Topher?"

"Hey, Colbs."

She threw her arms around him and he clung to her. In this familiar, steady place, Topher felt his shoulders begin to relax.

"Where were you?" she whispered.

"The Den."

"Lana went there looking for you. Zayn said you were gone."

"Annaliese broke me out."

"Really? I spent all night hating her along with Nora."

"Are you and Nora…"

"I can't look at her. She didn't tell us where you were. She lied."

Topher sat back. He licked his thumb and pressed it into

the furrow gathered between Colbie's brows. Her face cleared into a smile.

"We'll figure it out," he promised. "I saw her face when they brought her down; she didn't have anything to do with kidnapping me."

Colbie snorted at the wording. "I can't believe you let yourself get kidnapped."

Topher laughed. Everything was lighter with Colbie there. "With this face? It was bound to happen eventually." His smile fell. "What's happening with Lana then?"

Colbie shrugged. "The wolves played dumb when you weren't there."

Topher sighed and fell back into Colbie's pillows. "Let's just never leave the apartment again."

"Agreed." Colbie looked down at him intently. She put her hand on his forehead. "You okay?"

He closed his eyes. "I'll be fine. As long as the wolves didn't just drag me into a supernatural war."

"We'll see. Lana is capable of anything."

"I should go talk to her." They could hear Zayn's phone in the living room. There was a very good chance Lana was on the other end. Topher sighed and hauled himself back up. Poppy was waiting anxiously outside Colbie's door.

Topher halted. "Why do you smell like a wolf that isn't Nora?"

"Long story," Poppy said. She and Annaliese shared a look.

Topher frowned but leaned over the couch and plucked the phone from Zayn's hand. He set it to his ear and went to his room, heading straight for the box of cigarettes in his dresser. He shut the door behind him before he spoke.

"Lana."

"Christopher. Where the hell have you been?"

"I think you know the answer to that."

"How'd you get out?"

"With help."

"Why didn't you call me?"

Topher shook out a cigarette and yanked open his window before lighting it. "I was a little out of it."

"I need to see you."

"Why?"

"To charm you into never starving yourself again. This is getting ridiculous. You belong to me. I'm not going to let you die to get out of it. Especially now that this shit is going down."

"Define 'this shit.'"

Lana quickly explained what had happened at the meeting with the Big Three and herself. While none of them claimed to know anything about Topher's whereabouts, Patter and Solas weren't very upset at the idea of Topher going missing. They didn't like Lana and Grace having so much power. Then Solas brought up an attack on her club. Three of her vampires were found that day in a similar condition to Brady. Rico, a maker Topher knew and two of his lowers. Topher's heart dropped; hearing Rachel was the only one of Rico's line left. Poor girl.

"We're being hunted. When Colbie smelled you on one of the wolves, they became our top suspects."

Topher snuffed out his cigarette and lit another. "Do you think this has to do with the unclaimed?"

"Possibly. I'm going to Solas's club to look at the aftermath. The city leaders are meeting. You're coming."

"Okay. How long do I have?"

"Half an hour. Send Zayn to cover you at the bar."

"He's probably covered me all week."

"Then I guess you better make it up to him."

The line went dead. Topher let out a lungful of smoke. He was reluctant to put the cigarette out and leave the window. He kept it burning as he changed.

He was pulling on a black hoodie when the front door to the apartment burst open. The smell of the newcomer slipped under the door. Topher froze.

"Where is he?"

"Oh. Hello, Julia," Colbie's tone was casual.

"He doesn't answer my texts. He ignores my calls. He disconnects his damn phone. Then Poppy calls looking for him. He better have a damn good excuse or he better be dead."

"I think being dead would be an excellent excuse."

Topher didn't hear the rest. He'd already grabbed his box of cigarettes and climbed out the window.

"Lana, am I the only one you invited?"

"I don't need anyone else to protect me, do I?"

Topher didn't respond, understanding this show of force would be just as effective as the one Lana made at the last meeting. She grabbed his arm and pulled it over her shoulders, stepping in close to his side as they entered Blank Space. For once, they weren't the last ones there.

No humans had been invited to this meeting. Lana said they weren't happy about the effect Topher's charm had on them the last time they came. She sounded pleased when she told him. Topher hated pleasing her.

Mia Solas's club was at the end of Fourth Street, opposite the Maker. It was one level, but the rooftop space was the main draw. Full of fire pits and outdoor couches. Tonight, the entire club was closed. They stayed inside on the open dance floor, the square bar taking up the middle of the space. Vampire lowers milled around their makers. A group gathered in the back corner opposite the entrance where the bodies had been laid for observation. Even from here, Topher could see they looked disfigured. Mauled yet bloodless. He couldn't look long before his stomach turned.

The room was hushed, the atmosphere so tense Rachel Spears could be heard crying where she sat under the lip of the bar. Her boyfriend was among the bodies on display next to their maker. Supernaturals shot her looks as she sobbed tearlessly and ineffectually chugged from a bottle of vodka. It was cruel of Solas to make her attend.

They walked by Rachel on the way to the bodies, passing between her and Gabriel's pack. Gabriel's eyes widened for only an instant when he saw Topher. Matt failed to hold in a gasp but tried his best to disguise it as a cough.

"You know what, I'll go look. You get her to stop," Lana said, pointing at the sobbing vampire.

Gabriel's eyes narrowed. "She's grieving," he said. The wolves around their alpha went quiet. "You can't stop that with charm. That's just cruel."

"Is it?" Lana asked, raising an eyebrow at him. Lana continued to the bodies without waiting for his response.

Topher clenched his trembling hands into fists, seeing the knife sticking out of his shoulder and the hatred in the wolf's mismatched eyes as they both waited to see if Topher would bleed.

Topher ducked and sat down next to Rachel under the bar. She drew a shuddering breath and leaned her head on his shoulder. Topher ran a hand over her hair and used the other to pull out his cigarettes. She held the one he offered to her quivering lips while he lit it. He tried to think of something to say, but there weren't words for pain this fresh and sudden.

"Does it ever stop suffocating you?" Rachel asked.

Topher shrugged, making her head bob. "I think you just learn not to breathe."

He pulled out his phone and headphones. He started his most depressing playlist, the same one Rachel and Joe had teased him about a month ago. They had often hung out while Lana and Rico were in meetings with the Big Three and the other seconds.

Rachel huffed out a weak, smokey laugh and put in the headphones. She closed her eyes to the world. Topher sat with her until Lana returned, patting Rachel's leg before standing.

Topher took the stool next to Lana, close enough that Rachel would know he hadn't left yet. He felt Gabriel's eyes on his back and couldn't relax his shoulders.

The entrance of the new pack caused a bit of a stir. Every vampire watched as Henry went straight to Gabriel and said hello. At Henry's nod, three of his packmates went to examine the bodies. The whole pack was at ease surrounded by vampires, something Gabriel's pack could not begin to claim.

One of the wolves caught Topher's eye. The same one he'd noticed at the first meeting. He looked kind and tall and Topher couldn't stop himself from offering a small smile when their eyes met. Lana saw him do it and let out a laugh, attracting looks. No one else in this space was close to laughing. The wolf started, surprised to have drawn so much attention so abruptly.

"Oh, don't mind Christopher here. You're just his type," Lana told him, always ready to pounce on the opportunity to embarrass him. Topher narrowed his eyes at her and she innocently batted her lashes. "It's always the brown eyes with you."

Topher pulled a face while the new pack laughed. The boy was blushing as Lana continued.

"Don't worry, cutie. He has a girlfriend." Topher stiffened and Lana turned to him, amusement mounting, "What was that face?"

"Nothing, Lana."

"Christopher, tell me what that face meant," she purred with charm.

Topher reminded himself to pick his battles. Lana swore to stay away from Julia a year ago. "Julia showed up at our apartment," he muttered.

"No! What did she say?" Even Rachel pulled out one of the headphones to listen, although her eyes remained listless.

"I don't know. I left."

"You left?"

"Yes. I climbed out the window." Topher winced at the

confession.

Lana let her head fall back and laughed. "So spry for having just been kidnapped, isn't he, Gabriel?"

The wolves hushed. Gabriel's face paled. He struggled to keep his expression blank. "I don't know what you're talking about."

"Don't you?"

Silence descended.

Lana turned when Grace called her name from the bodies. "He better be in one piece when I come back, mutt," she said, pointing at Gabriel with a cigarette.

Lana breezed away, leaving Topher alone in the bubble of wolves and a dead-eyed Rachel. He busied his hands lighting a cigarette for himself.

Henry said something to Gabriel about the setup of the club and focus shifted off Topher. The wolf he'd noticed cautiously stepped away from his pack and took the stool Lana had vacated. Topher stiffened and dropped his voice, speaking around the cigarette between his lips. "Why do you and Poppy smell like each other?"

The boy ran a hand through his hair. "I was, ah, helping them look for you."

"Oh. Thanks."

"So." The boy looked around the club. In another situation, his discomfort might have been amusing.

Topher held up a hand. "Topher."

"Josh." They shook, his hand warm and rough under Topher's. He swallowed the flutter in his stomach, unable to push Julia from his mind. Why had she chosen now to come?

"You're gay?" Josh asked. Topher snorted at the bluntness of the question.

"Bi. My sister's the gay one," Topher said as light as he could. He cocked his head, trying to read the look on Josh's face. The wolf didn't smell like their apartment or Colbie. Poppy removed those scents.

Why had she let him walk away with her own still clinging to him?

"Oh…" Topher said when it clicked and smiled apologetically when Josh shot him a look. "Sorry, it's just, you like her?"

Josh sighed. "Yeah."

"And she was upset about my disappearing."

"Yeah." The moment stretched with Josh staring sullenly at the smoke trailing from Topher's cigarette.

Topher touched the boy's cheek with his free hand. He leaned close to whisper in Josh's ear. "But Poppy has green eyes."

Topher stood and winked at Josh's startled expression before turning to find Lana. He cut through the middle of Gabriel's pack. He wouldn't let them shake him. At least, he wouldn't let them see they'd shaken him.

He met Henry's gaze as he passed and the man smiled. Topher gave him a nod and blew out a puff of smoke from the cigarette, hiding behind it ineffectually. He pressed on through the crowd of vampires. Most parted for him. A few stared openly.

Topher was ready for this week to be over.

The witches burst through the doors. The roll of their magic passed over the room, feeling almost like charm as it calmed those in attendance. Only the wolves maintained their tense stances.

Solas stepped away from the dead bodies and murmured conversations halted as she crossed the room. Lana found Topher and wrapped his arms across her chest, leaning back against him as Solas jumped onto the bar and clapped to ensure the room's attention.

"Let's get started. Grace and Patter agreed to let me speak on the vampires' behalf for most of this meeting, seeing as it was my club that was attacked."

Lana bristled in Topher's arms, probably thinking about the lack of attention she'd received when Brady died.

"I will speak for the witches," Kallow said, stepping away from her daughters. They all had the same wavy brown hair and olive skin. Topher spotted Beth in their midst. Lana hired her to set the Maker's wards, but he rarely saw her these days. She'd come around at night less since Lana lost faith in Beth's visions of the future and went to another psychic for predictions.

Poppy rarely spoke about the other witches in the city. They lived shrouded in so much secret that Topher sometimes wondered if she even knew where her own mother and sisters were. For Kallow to reveal her seven daughters was unheard of. The first whole coven out in the open.

Topher was tall enough to see over the crowd as Henry and Gabriel shared a look. Gabriel nodded and stepped forward to speak for the wolves.

"What's new?" he asked.

Solas raised a thin eyebrow and gestured toward the bodies, now covered by a white sheet. "The murders are spreading. First, it was just humans being turned and killing more humans with no one to tame them. Then, something started killing these unclaimed and no one will take credit. Now legal vampires are dying. An unclaimed lower couldn't do all this. Something larger than a rogue maker is attacking our city."

Gabriel scoffed, drawing attention. He shrugged. "I disagree. Whatever is killing the unclaimed is helping the problem. A rogue maker remains the biggest threat. Potentially, a threat that's now been taken care of." He nodded to the body of the maker. Everyone heard the pained breath Rachel sucked in.

"That doesn't explain Brady's murder," Lana said tightly. "And if Rico was behind the attacks, Solas would have been able to charm the unclaimed."

"That is just part of the reason we have gathered," Kallow said before tensions could escalate too dramatically.

Topher stiffened. Would she bring up his kidnapping?

"We have found troubling evidence of sorcery on the east bank." The gathered crowd began to mutter, mostly in confusion. "For those who don't know, sorcery occurs when someone finds a way to siphon demonic power, usually through drinking the corrupted life energy in their blood. It produces unnatural, unstable, but powerful magic. And this magic takes a toll. Natural life energy is sacrificed in order to accept the demonic power. More and more demon blood is needed to stay alive, thus creating a spiral that leads to a quick death."

"Why are you telling us this now?" Grace asked. He, along with the majority of vampires in the room, wore a look of disgust at the thought of drinking a demon's blood. "We've been hearing whispers of demons for weeks."

"Because to summon the first demon takes a good deal of magic. Usually, a witch will turn to this path only in times of desperation. Our natural life energy is the most effective way to attract the dark magic."

"It sounds like you're saying witches are to blame then. Was it demons who killed my lowers?" Solas demanded. She and her people shifted, many of their bottom lips bulging as their fangs dropped. "Demons summoned by a witch?"

Kallow continued as if Solas hadn't spoken. "In my run, I have been attempting to meet with witches throughout the city, hoping to convince them to come out of secrecy for the good of New Brecken. I planned to make it part of my platform." Kallow took a deep breath. "It would appear, however, that my sisters were right to stay hidden. I have been unable to track most of them down. The three I have found, I found dead within their failed warding circles. Their blood drained and demons lifeless next to them. Someone is using natural witches to summon demons. They are taking the power without the sacrifice to their own magic. It's time to forget the unclaimed. This sorcerer is a curse on our city and they are only going to get stronger. They must be stopped at once."

CHAPTER 25

Colbie was on the opposite side of the island, watching Julia where she had fallen into an exhausted slumber on the couch. Poppy wasn't sure what Colbie had gone over there for, but she seemed stuck now. Just standing there and frowning at Topher's sleeping girlfriend. Poppy got up slowly and sat on a barstool opposite of her.

"What are you thinking?"

Colbie considered the question. "In the future, Pop Tart, you probably don't want to know what someone is thinking about when they just found out their girlfriend aided in kidnapping their brother and torturing him. They aren't happy thoughts."

"Oh. You were just staring at Julia, so I thought…."

Colbie quirked an eyebrow at Poppy. Poppy quirked hers back. Colbie leaned forward on the island and Poppy did the same, so their faces were inches apart.

"Do you think you could ever like Josh?"

Poppy jerked back from the question. She glanced over her shoulder, but Julia was still asleep. Colbie watched her, waiting.

"Why?"

"Because I don't know if, I mean, how does someone move on? What if I never feel like this for someone again?"

Poppy stared. "You've only known Nora a few weeks, Colbie. You can't possibly be in love with her."

Colbie shrugged, a stubborn look pulling at her features. "I don't know about love, but I've still never *liked* someone like this."

"Why? I mean, why her?" Poppy knew she probably sounded mean, but it had been a long few days and she couldn't really care. "She's so quiet and obsessed with her pack and hardly even laughs or jokes around. You two are completely different. I just don't get it."

Colbie considered the question as if she'd never bothered to wonder the same. She flattened her hands on the counter and Poppy almost cringed away. Colbie usually only did that when she was about to say something regrettable. But Colbie just sighed. She seemed to deflate, stacking her hands in fists and resting her chin on them.

"You know I'm unregistered, right? Topher made some deal with Lana to keep me out of all their business, but she hasn't made it easy. She got him registered and citizenship as a vampire but not me. I dropped out of college. I could apply for jobs or night school with my human IDs, but if they found out I was a vampire…." Colbie shrugged. "I thought about online school, but it seems pointless. What would I do with a degree? Topher doesn't want me working at the Maker either and it *does* seem like a stupid risk to press for it. They've been getting too much attention."

Colbie sighed and dropped her forehead onto her fists. She spoke into the counter. "My life for the past year has been completely, utterly, depressingly directionless. I've tried to focus on my friendships, you and Oliver and Zayn, but I've had to share all of you with Topher too. Meeting almost everyone through Topher. And it wasn't horrible, but I think I kind of detached and went through the motions. I felt like I was drifting night to night. I miss the sun so much. I miss my family, even Topher, how he was as a human. How he was before all this. I miss shopping. I miss beaches and traveling. I miss planning ahead. I miss it all, but I wasn't miserable. I was just... drifting. Then I made eye contact with Nora and I was suddenly, completely anchored.

"She was so *focused*. And at that moment, even though she was thinking about how to kill me, she was focused on me. My world became centered, you know? It was crazy. I know that. I know I'm crazy." Colbie looked up. "Can you blame any of us for going a little insane? If she could just look at me like that every day, or if she could have before she did what she did. I got to know her more and I could just hear how she was hurting. How she was searching too. I've always been good at helping people who are hurting. I mean, I can even make Topher smile." Colbie's shoulders lifted with a deep breath. "And Nora was mine. It was dumb and fast and what everyone says not to do, but I thought I saw my purpose in her." Colbie whispered the last few words.

Poppy's heart twisted. She reached over the counter to pat Colbie's head. Colbie frowned at her.

"I'm sorry," Colbie continued, "if that's how you feel about Topher. After you lost your family and all, I'm sure you were drifting too. I'm sorry I threw it in your face."

"It's okay." Poppy wasn't sure if that was how she felt about Topher exactly. He wasn't her direction. At first, she'd been determined to find out what happened with her coven. But then her life was consumed just worrying about the West siblings. Yet, she didn't think it was because of her feelings for Topher.

Colbie tilted her head, listening. "Speak of the devil."

Poppy's wards gave a tug and Topher came into the apartment. Julia woke from the noise and they caught eyes, but Julia's attention shifted when Josh followed Topher in. The girl instantly sized Josh up. Poppy tried to focus on that strange reaction and not the squirming in her gut that came with seeing Josh and Topher together. A blush crept up all the way from her collarbones.

Josh shuffled uncomfortably, but Topher acted as if he were immune to the tension crowding the apartment.

"Is Zayn off yet?" he asked.

"What the hell?" Julia burst out. Topher winced. Not immune. "Maybe a hi for the girlfriend you haven't talked to in weeks is in order?"

Topher raised his hands. "If someone doesn't talk to a girl for weeks, is she still his girlfriend?"

Julia's eyes narrowed at the same time Colbie's grew comically round. She said something that sounded like "*ope!*" before pressing her lips together and looking away.

Julia stood and put a finger in Topher's face. "Topher, I've known you too long to fall for that attitude. What the hell is going on?"

Topher took a steadying breath and pushed the finger to the side. The movements of their fight seemed oddly rehearsed. Poppy held her breath. Was Topher about to become single? Hope fluttered. Poppy felt Josh's eyes and tried to keep her face blank.

"Julia. This isn't normal. You called me three times a night when you left. Each time you asked me if I'd fed on the blood that you left yet. I didn't want to talk about blood with you."

"Do you know how much trouble I went through getting that? I just hated the thought of you feeding off anyone else."

"Why?"

"Because I'm your girlfriend."

"You were never jealous before I turned," Topher said.

Julia's eyebrows knitted. "This isn't—"

"Julia. I was the biggest flirt—a flirt and worse. You even caught me a few times and you laughed it off. You remember what you used to say?"

"You just had expansive tastes," she quoted flatly.

Topher pulled a face at those words. "You said as long as I didn't have sex with them, you didn't care. When I couldn't even do that, you still said you didn't care as much as you thought you would."

Poppy's stomach turned at those words. Maybe she shouldn't be surprised, but she didn't like this new image of Topher as a cheater.

"What's your point, Topher?"

"Why do you care who I drink from if you didn't care who I hooked up with?"

Julia's mouth opened and closed multiple times before she got out, "It's more intimate!"

"No. You just want the bliss to yourself." Julia's face drained. Topher held up his arm, slapping the inside of his elbow. "I know an addict when I see one, Julia. I was cutting you off. I'm still cutting you off. Poppy," Poppy jumped when he turned to her suddenly, "Josh and I need to talk to you."

Topher went to Poppy's room, grabbing Josh's arm and pulling him along. The poor werewolf looked completely bewildered.

"No way I'm missing this," Colbie said, scurrying around the island to follow them. Poppy shared a look with Julia. The human's eyes, a striking hazel color, were pooled with tears.

"This was a mistake," Julia whispered. "He really did change. That's not my Topher."

"If he acted like your human Topher, you wouldn't be able to form words right now; you'd be so gone for his charm," Poppy said as gently as she could while her heart pounded. "Whether you leave or stay is your choice, but I think you should go."

A tear fell. Julia wiped it brusquely with her sleeve and squared her shoulders. "You didn't even know him before, don't pretend you're some expert. I've known him since I was ten. The boy I knew... yeah, he was spoiled. He partied way too much and cheated on me and lied and got caught up with the wrong people. But he always came back. He would pick up all the blankets from the couches on his way to my room and we'd lose ourselves under them. He made forts and told me we couldn't leave until his hands were steady and the dry heaves stopped. When he couldn't stay inside any longer, we'd go to the soccer field and play for hours. Everyone he called would show up to join the game. He made us all laugh, him and Colbie saying the most ridiculous shit to distract the other team. He was so beautiful when he smiled like that."

Julia pulled on her jacket slowly, eyes distant. "He'd drop everything if I called, drunk or high or in the middle of whatever he got himself caught up in. If he didn't answer, I knew he was in trouble. Those stupid gangs, the drug deals. But he'd call as soon as he could, scared out of his mind. He said he'd get out of it for me. He went to rehab for me. I should have known that would mean none of it would take, but he tried so hard." Julia was openly crying now, all her words shaking. "He was going to travel the world and make every place he visited better. Topher West was the brightest part of my life. Then he broke up with me and got himself attacked."

Julia looked to Poppy's room. Topher stood leaning against the doorway, his face unreadable. Julia pointed at him again. "Topher West died that night with Dylan." Topher sucked in a sharp breath. "I just wish I saw that sooner."

Julia picked up her bag. She unzipped it, pulled out a soccer ball, and hurled it at Topher. He caught it easily in his stomach. Julia waited, breathing hard.

Topher's expression was hollow. His eyes reminded Poppy of Lana in a way that made her skin crawl. Empty, uncaring. Ready to cut.

"Bye, Jules."

Topher turned, set the ball down next to the door, and went back in. Poppy heard her bedsprings and Mouse meowing. Julia let out a sob and struggled to zip her bag again. She'd packed for a much longer stay.

"You're a monster!" she screamed at his back.

The apartment felt too small as Poppy went to her room and paused before shutting the door behind her, catching one last glimpse of Julia's ashen face. Holy Mother, even crying and furious, she was gorgeous.

Poppy gently clicked her door shut. They stayed quiet until the front door slammed. Topher sagged into Poppy's pillows, not even petting Mouse on his lap. Colbie tugged at Topher's sleeve until he leaned into her, resting his head against her shoulder. He looked almost as exhausted as he did after starving himself for days.

Colbie idly scratched the cat's neck. "I'm beginning to think Josh is a conduit for drama," she said.

Topher huffed out what might pass for a laugh. "Please tell me all about it."

Colbie caught Topher up on the search for him, the meeting they'd had at the dinner, and confronting Nora. When she finished, Topher shifted and put his arm around Colbie's shoulders.

"We've always done better being single."

"Maybe *we* should just date. Does incest count between vampires?"

Josh made a choking noise.

"If only you liked men." Topher sighed.

"If only."

Josh fell to laughing at that. Unable to resist the excuse to lighten the mood, Poppy let out a chuckle of her own. Josh's smile slipped when they locked eyes, but he nodded at her. She felt mildly forgiven, at least enough that she let herself relax. She went and sat at the foot of her bed, rolling her eyes when Topher and Colbie instantly stuck their icicle vampire toes under her. Josh sat on Poppy's desk with the soccer ball. He bounced it from hand to hand.

"We were at the meeting tonight," Topher said, explaining

Josh's presence at least a bit. "Poppy, do you know anything about a sorcerer in the city?"

"What? The witch at the Maker mentioned demons, but I don't know anything about that."

Mouse nudged at Topher's hand when he went still. "You went to the Maker? Was it Beth?"

"I guess it must have been her." Poppy narrowed her eyes at him. "I went today to check for clues about what happened to you."

Colbie shifted under Topher's arm to study his face. "What do you know?"

He sighed. "I don't know anything. Beth is one of Kallow's daughters and she works for Lana."

"Could Lana be involved with everything happening?"

Topher shrugged but looked doubtful. "Maybe she's capable? Demons bring power and Lana wants to rise in the ranks more than anything. She thinks finding the rogue maker will help her status. She's been going deeper and deeper into the black market, looking for clues. Maybe she hired them? The sorcerer, I mean."

"Yeah, apparently you and Lana spend a lot of time looking for unclaimed together." Poppy couldn't keep the bite from her tone. "You have a room there. Her impression is all over it. Why would you work with her? Why would you let her get so close?"

Poppy regretted the words immediately after they left her mouth. She'd meant to sound accusing for him buddying up with the enemy. How many times had they talked shit on Lana? But when Josh stopped bouncing the soccer ball, she knew she just sounded jealous.

Topher's expression turned sad. He pulled his arm away from Colbie. "Maybe I should just go ask if she knows anything."

"Topher. I'm just asking why?"

Topher pressed his lips together. He wasn't going to answer her.

"They're killing witches, Poppy," Josh cut in.

The hair on Poppy's arms rose. "Killing witches?"

"Yeah, sacrificing the natural witches so the sorcerer can use demon power without consequences."

"That's not possible," Poppy whispered.

Head spinning, she stood and went to her shelves. She grabbed a potion for Sight. She hated using this brew, but the pounding migraine would have to be worth checking. She swallowed the whole vial, the heavy dose of lavender burning her throat.

She sat and pressed her finger to the middle of her forehead, closing her eyes tight and whispering. "Show me Jane."

The blackness behind her eyelids didn't shift. Her heart stuttered and she swallowed hard.

"Show me Amelia."

The blackness shifted to hazy, muddled shapes like looking through murky water. Her second oldest sister and the next two, Margot and Rayna, still had their wards up, disrupting the Sight. Natalie's name brought only blackness like Jane's, filling Poppy with dread. She'd never seen that before tonight. She refused to consider what it meant. She pushed on.

"Show me Ru."

The blackness lifted and a clear image formed. It was almost as concerning to see as the darkness. Why didn't Ru have her wards up? Her youngest sister stood in the middle of a park field in the light of a streetlamp, the grass at her feet a burnt circle. Her sister, only sixteen, raised her hands as a black shape charged. The vision was without sound, but Poppy could hear in her heart when Ru opened her mouth and screamed, a white light bursting from her chest. The creature vanished and the dead grass circle grew as a wall of light separated Ru from the oncoming hoard of black beasts. Ru dropped to one knee. Alone in the park, her sister wouldn't last long.

Poppy came out of her vision, gasping. "We have to get to Pressing Park. We have to go now!"

Josh and Topher moved so quickly that Poppy almost cried in relief. She and Colbie followed, bursting out of the apartment and down to the parking lot. Colbie skid to a halt. Nora was standing there, hands jammed in her sweatshirt, no, Colbie's sweatshirt pocket. Poppy groaned. Now was *not* the time.

With barely a glance back, Josh shifted. Topher easily kept pace with his wolf form. They disappeared into the night. Poppy had no idea Topher could run so fast.

"Not now," Colbie hissed. She ran to the car and waited for Poppy to unlock the doors.

Nora's wide eyes pulled away from Topher and Josh. "What's happening?"

"You were followed," was all Colbie said before she ducked in behind the wheel. Poppy was in no shape to drive.

Neither said anything when Nora jumped into the backseat. Colbie peeled out of the lot.

Poppy twisted her head and saw a red-haired boy step out of the shadows. Following Nora, like Colbie said.

CHAPTER 26

What was she thinking? Nora twisted in the backseat and watched Matt shift. He followed Poppy's car on four paws, body sloped forward and intent. Nora swallowed hard. How would she explain this?

Poppy sat silently in the front seat, her face pinched, hands glowing blue where she braced herself on the dash. Colbie flung the car around corners and wove through the light traffic of the night. She hadn't turned on the headlights. She muttered a string of curses with every light. Poppy snapped to turn them green and they narrowly avoided multiple collisions.

"They won't make it," Poppy groaned. Her eyes weren't looking at the road.

"They will. Or Topher will. You haven't seen him really run. I don't know how fast Josh is, but Topher's got this."

"Should you be running?"

"I'm probably only as fast as the car."

Poppy nodded. The witch looked exhausted. She dug around in her canvas messenger bag and the clink of glass bottles filled the car. Poppy selected a softly glowing one and swallowed its contents with a wince.

They entered a neighborhood and narrowly avoided hitting

a black cat. The sight of it crossing their path set Poppy swearing even more colorfully than Colbie had been.

"It had a white nose!" Colbie shouted as she righted the car.

They screeched to a stop at Pressing Park. The scene that greeted them was unlike anything Nora had ever seen before.

A young girl stood behind a cylinder of shimmering white light. Grotesque, scuttling, humanoid forms, gray-black and rotted, surrounded her. Nora's nose crinkled at their potent smell. They threw themselves at the wall of light.

Nora had never seen a demon before. Had never even heard of them attacking New Brecken. But these creatures couldn't be anything else.

Topher and Josh battled their way to the glowing wall. As Nora stared, they managed to maneuver between the girl and the mass of creatures. Side by side, they fought. Topher's fangs flashed when he hissed. He moved so fast that Nora's insides chilled. How had Gabriel captured him? Topher hurled demons away, clawed out their eyes, and ripped out their throats. Never slowing or showing pain as the demons gave as good as they got.

Josh inflicted his own significant amount of damage. Fully shifted and snarling, he pounced from demon to the next with calculated bites and deep scratches. He seemed to make his way through the rotten bodies with a level of experience Nora hadn't seen from her own pack when they moved to fight.

Still more demons streamed across the park, scurrying over the play equipment. The creaking of swings left swaying accompanied the sound of rasping snarls. Demons attacked as quickly as Josh and Topher felled them. The girl's wall flickered and she sank to the ground behind it, clutching her head.

"Ru!" Poppy screamed. Several demons turned to the sound of her call; their focus riveted on Poppy now. Poppy began to mutter and her skin flushed in a haze of blue as they approached. Nora dropped into a crouch, eyes flicking to check where Colbie stood. She was moving toward the demons. Nora's heart crawled into her throat and she took a step to follow.

The wall of light blinked out.

The demons hissed in celebration, attacking with renewed energy. Nora barely had time to worry about Topher and Josh as they were swarmed. The nearest demons had almost reached Poppy, where she dug frantically through her bag.

Nora darted forward and tackled one before it could reach her. Rolling with her hands around the demon's throat, Nora tried to watch what was happening as it struggled beneath her.

Josh was overcome for only a second before he shook the demons off. But he was slowing. His tan fur was clumped with black demon blood and streaked with red. He healed nearly as quickly as the injuries formed. It still wasn't enough.

Colbie reached the outskirts of the demon mob, leaving Nora and Poppy to deal with the demons who'd gone for the car. Poppy finally came up with a vial as Nora succeeded in stilling the monster beneath her and lunged to protect Poppy from the next one. Nora could have sworn she heard the witch whisper, "Please work."

Poppy threw her bottle into the grass hard enough for it to shatter. It exploded in a brief burst of light. The demons nearest turned to ash, including the one Nora had grabbed.

"No! It wasn't strong enough!" Poppy cried in dismay.

"It seemed pretty strong to me!" Nora shouted. "Do another one!"

Poppy no longer in danger, Nora lurched to her feet. Coughing up ash, she ran toward the chaos, eyes on Colbie, but her clumsy legs chose the moment not to cooperate. Nora went down swearing and burning with frustrated humiliation. Never before had she wanted to make the change so desperately.

Colbie worked her way toward Topher and the young witch. The girl had collapsed, face deathly pale beneath her straight black hair. A demon slipped between Topher and Josh. The monster clamped onto the girl's throat with a vicious lung that stunned Nora into stillness on the ground.

Topher spun and grabbed the creature by its neck, hurling it to the side and into Josh's path. The wolf quickly took care of it. Nora scrambled back to her feet, buzzing and disoriented by adrenaline, both human and wolf instincts screaming. Her body wanted to run on all fours, but she was still unable. She forced herself forward when Topher froze, staring down at the blood flowing openly from the girl's throat. For half a second, Nora was hopeful he would overcome his instinct, that his hesitation was his humanity, calling out for him to deny the monster inside.

Then he flung himself down on the girl and clamped his mouth down on her throat. Unnatural. Sick. He was *feeding* on her.

Nora had to stop him. Focus narrowed, she took off, leaving Poppy muttering between her panting breaths, hands glowing feebly as she reached for another potion.

A red streak of fur came out of nowhere, flying over the writhing demons and hitting Topher's side, sending them both into the mess of demons Josh fought viciously to hold off. Colbie shouted and fought to reach the middle, but she struggled to press forward with more demons attacking her from behind. Nora's stomach rolled when a demon raked its claws down Colbie's back, but the skin knitted together quickly and Colbie didn't pause.

Topher and Matt rolled and tumbled, snarling. Nora hadn't seen Matt shifted more than a few times. She was amazed at his size. Topher fought to return to his meal, throwing off demons and wrestling with Nora's packmate.

Poppy threw up her hands and a blue wall flared to life between Topher and Matt just as Matt lunged. Matt yelped when he connected and fell hard against it. He soon regained his feet though shaking his head to clear it. The demons shuttered, cringing away from Poppy's light.

Topher turned back to his meal. Nora stumbled, halting when she saw Colbie stop at his side, standing guard so Topher wouldn't be interrupted as he fed. Matt had been forced to give his attention to the demons. For the moment, Nora was spared from watching him and Colbie fight.

A demon came at Nora when she paused, hitting her from the side. They tumbled across the ground and Nora growled with frustration. She grabbed the thing's throat, gagging at the give in the strangely soft skin there. She dug her fingers in and ripped the flimsy esophagus out. The demon fell on top of her. Nora couldn't breathe through its smell as she squirmed out from underneath it.

Nora regained her feet just as Poppy's wall fell and Matt lunged for Colbie. Her back was turned as she threw a fist at a demon leaping toward her. Nora screamed a warning and Colbie reacted just fast enough that Matt clamped his jaws only on the back of her jacket. He used the material to fling her away from the bleeding girl and Topher. Colbie hit the ground outside the clustered demons and rolled into a tree. Nora turned to go to her, unable to breathe until she saw Colbie get back to her feet, only to stagger. Her hair came loose as she shook her head and fell to her knees.

Poppy began to yell for bullets. The charge in the air told Nora she was summoning magic apart from her potions. A beam of blue light formed between the witch's hands. She hurled it at one of the demons. It yelped and went still, the light burning where it hit and slowly spreading, turning the creature to ash like the others.

Nora had nearly reached Colbie. The vampire had righted herself and was making her way back to the center, Poppy's beams helping to clear a path.

She grabbed Colbie's arm. "Stop! You're hurt!"

"Nora! Stop! Get off me!" Colbie's words were guttural

lisps around her fangs. She was stronger than Nora and easily yanked out of Nora's grip. Nora had no choice but to follow her back into the fray.

Josh was smaller than Matt, a light-colored blur of constant motion against the night. Nora watched in horror as two demons jumped Matt from behind. He spun to fight them. Josh ripped a demon off Matt's back, freeing his focus for the eerily little one crawling up to his neck. The demon swiped and Matt shifted faster than anyone Nora had seen before. The change startled the demon and its claws missed Matt's human head. Matt slipped from its loosened hold and shifted again. He lunged and clamped his jaws on the demon's stomach. Nora didn't know werewolves could fight like Matt was now. It was so risky yet finessed. She could see now why Gabriel kept Matt by his side.

Poppy's light beams were coming less frequently, each dimmer than the last. Some landed harmlessly in the grass, making it spring to life, a circle of stiff, green stems.

Nora fought by Colbie's side against the never-ending mass of demons. There had to be less now than when they started, but Nora couldn't think as she moved from one to the next. At some point, she'd bit her tongue. She spat blood.

Josh was nearest, covered in the foul-smelling bodies. Nora rushed to help him and grabbed a demon. She yanked it away and grabbed the next one, wishing she had some sort of weapon. Anything to help her kill them. Her fingers flexed, imagining claws.

A flash of light told her Poppy had taken care of the demon she threw. Nora grabbed the next one, grunting as she pulled it off Josh and into Poppy's aim. Even with her halting, uncertain movements, she was stronger than she'd ever been. Her body was already preparing, drawing power and occasional reflexes from the animal she would become. It made her smile as demon blood coated her face.

She could feel it now. The pull of the moon in the sky. The

snarling. The instincts her human brain barely knew how to interpret. The pack bond with Matt. She knew exactly where he was. Her fear settled into memory as her strength surged. She was so close to the shift. She would be someone and make a difference in the next fight. This was just the beginning.

Her time was coming. She would be the power in the night. Like her father had been. The thought made her heart pound harder. She lunged at the next demon with renewed force, snapping its neck with ease.

Nora freed Josh, breathing through her mouth to avoid the worst of the rotten smell. The claw marks raked down Josh's sides and cheeks were already healing. He sprang to his feet, bopped her thigh in thanks, and refocused his efforts on making his way to Topher. The vampire was exposed, still hunched over the witch, only halting his feeding when he had to defend himself. His nose crinkled as he snarled at any demon who got close. Blood was smeared up to his sharp cheekbones.

Just when Nora thought the rush of demons was finally slowing, she was swarmed by three of them and looked away from Topher to fight them off. Josh would get there and save the girl. She nearly screamed in frustration when she realized Josh had reached the vampire and turned away, defending Topher against the demons still trying to reach the fallen witch and letting Topher feed uninterrupted.

Nora's scream of frustration quickly slipped into a shriek when a demon hit her from the side with blinding speed. The air was knocked from her lungs, blacking her vision. She barely caught the demon's throat in time to keep it from biting her. It snapped at her face, strings of thick saliva flying. She let out a choked sob, fear crowding back in a rush, obliterating every fantasy she'd just had of power. Panic blacked the edge of her vision. This demon was more determined. One clawed hand raked down her bicep, almost loosening her grip on its throat. Another demon could attack while it took everything she had to hold this one back. Its teeth were sharpened and elongated. Nora's head went light. She couldn't breathe properly. Every breath she did manage was so tainted by the demon's foul presence it seemed to do more harm than good.

Gabriel was right. She couldn't fight. She wasn't strong enough.

Her hand slipped on the demon's strange, soft skin, allowing it to rush forward and break her grip. Nora knew then she'd never make it to the change. She thought of her father as she only saw teeth.

Then a rush of hissing and the weight lifted. Nora rolled onto her side, coughing as Colbie, hair loose and wild, ripped the demon's throat out with her teeth. It shuttered and stilled. Colbie spat black blood and gagged. Matt was just a few feet away, halted in his own efforts to get to her. Nora tried to rise and cried out in pain. Matt shifted into human form and dropped to his knees at her side.

"I'm fine," she gasped. Definitely at least one broken rib screamed in protest as she forced herself to her feet. "Save the girl!"

Matt nodded and shifted again, but Colbie was there, blocking his path to her brother, demon blood sliding down her chin.

Josh howled in triumph and chased the last of the demons from the park. Poppy ran, stumbling in her exhaustion, to Topher's side. She was probably too late to save the girl. Nora felt hollow as she watched. Topher had been there too long. She had already lost so much blood before he'd started feeding. Matt and Colbie were frozen in a standoff, Matt's ears flat and Colbie's head cocked in Topher's direction.

Poppy reached Topher's side. "It's working! Save her, please, Topher!"

"Matt, wait!"

He kept walking, aimed for the front door of the Den. He hadn't spoken to Nora after the park. Just ran to the apartment ahead of them and waited on his motorcycle for Nora to get on. The ride home had been fast and chilly. Matt's back stiff in front of her.

Nora darted forward and grabbed his sleeve. He yanked out of her grip and she gasped as the motion jostled her broken rib. Slowly, Matt turned to look down at her, his face pained. It was the look he'd given her for months after her father died. Nora cringed from it.

"How do you know them, Nor?"

"The Maker," she whispered. Her eyes fell to her dirty boots. "I met them at the Maker. Annaliese befriended them. We've seen them at the club since. She hangs out with the witch and another wolf sometimes at school."

Matt's hands clenched at his side. "Were you the one that let him go?"

"No! Matt, I didn't want to kill him, but I wouldn't risk the pack like that. This pack is everything to me, you know that!"

"Do I? Someone loyal wouldn't dream of hanging out with those monsters. Nora, what the hell?"

"You don't get to question my loyalty, Matt. My entire family is this pack. It's all I have left of my parents. My father made it to give me a safe place to grow up. To give me a purpose. This pack is everything! But we won't survive in this city if we don't make alliances. You saw tonight what's coming."

"We can handle a few lowers and demons, Nora. You can't get sympathetic. You just can't. If you don't kill one, Gabriel won't claim you when you make the change!"

Nora froze. Matt froze. "*When* I make the change?" she whispered. "When I make the change even *without killing one*?"

Matt looked guilty only for a split second before his mouth twisted. "Yes. Okay? *Yes!* You'll make the change either way.

But Gabriel's law, *your father's* law, was that a wolf had to kill a vampire to join the pack."

"But…why lie? Why tell me I won't change unless I kill one?"

"We couldn't risk you backing out."

Nora's world felt like it was tipping. "But. How could you—"

"How could I? Nora! How could you let them near Annaliese? What the hell were you thinking?"

He turned and started back toward the front door. "Matt!"

He whipped around, startling Nora back a step. "I'll forgive you," he said. "I have to because you're family. I believe you'll figure this out and join us. But I want you to know something. I have to tell you something. After you change, Gabriel said—" he hesitated and shuffled his feet.

Nora swallowed, thoughts swirling with the future. She blurted the first thing that came to mind. "Does Gabriel want me for his mate?"

Nora had never in her life wanted those words— that path to strength she only considered in the dead of night, that secret hope— to come out. She had been thinking about it more and more lately with everything happening with Colbie. Since her father began training Gabriel for leadership, Nora had fantasized about joining him at the forefront of a pack. She'd dreamed of him choosing her and rising as high as a female werewolf could go. Rising as high as her mother had. As Gabriel's mate, she would hold power only answerable to his own. And Gabriel wasn't the worse person to be stuck with in that way. He'd always had her back.

But this was a secret dream. A sacrifice she thought about making when no one was around. The one thing she'd never dared admit out loud. Especially after meeting Colbie, who made her consider for the first time that maybe the mating system in her pack was wrong.

Especially not to Matt's face.

Her words, the hope in her voice, cut him deep. He let out a strangled noise and clutched his hand back to his stomach. He'd been reaching for her. "You want Gabriel?"

Nora struggled for words. She wanted to deny what he said, but she was unable to say she didn't long for the position.

"You want *Gabriel?*" Matt nearly shouted the words. Any louder and the whole Den would hear.

"I want what my parents had," she whispered.

Matt stared at some point above her head, blinking fast. The muscles in his jaw were bunched. "Do you love him?" He pushed the question out.

She had thought she did. But then she met Colbie. "No."

Matt barely processed her response. His face slowly slackened with surprise. When he looked down, it was with new eyes. Betrayal etched deep. "He was waiting for you…." Matt's voice lowered as the realization hit him. "I wondered why he hadn't taken a mate. Why he didn't ask anyone to be his beta."

"I thought he might be," Nora admitted.

"You *hoped*." Anger came then. The shifting of Matt's emotions left Nora breathless. "And what? You just led me on? Let me keep thinking you and I—" Matt growled and looked away.

Nora stood mute. Matt took a deep breath and gained control of his features. He settled into the respectful, submitting aspect he presented to Gabriel. The look of a wolf speaking to his alpha. Nora hated the pride that rose when he looked at her like that, even knowing it was forced and masked real pain. In that moment, it was too easy to imagine a future of the pack looking at her like that.

"You won't last as his mate," Matt said. The pride died swiftly in her chest. "He might pick you, but you don't have the drive to hold the position against anyone who challenges you. You aren't like your father. We couldn't even tell you the truth about your first kill. You drop your eyes and you cower like a good pack member. You don't ask questions. You protest, but you never actually *do* anything. You even submit to a human, letting Annaliese make plans and make you play friends with vampires and witches. And when she isn't in your ear, you let the pack make every decision for you. Going to human school when you didn't belong, taking the room furthest from the door so we can protect you to the last man. Letting your mother change and leave without question. You didn't even fight for her when she left you. Nora. Oh, Nor. You don't have what it takes. You never will. I was going to offer myself as a mate. I thought you'd recognize the offer for what it was, the chance to be a beta's partner. The highest someone with your personality could hope to rise. Maybe Gabriel's waiting. Maybe he doesn't see it yet. Maybe he feels bad enough for you to offer himself. But once you bow to him, once you hesitate to make your kill, he'll see. They'll all see it."

Matt gave her a pitying smile. Nora didn't know the boy who stood before her. The one who said the exact words to cut her down. She couldn't think past the roaring in her ears.

Matt raised an eyebrow when she didn't contradict him. When she accepted his words without argument.

"See? You know your place. Time to grow up, Nora. You'll be a wolf in less than a week."

Matt left her standing on the sidewalk.

Nora was emptied. Gutted and hung to dry. She couldn't even cry. She couldn't deny anything he'd said. All she wanted was Colbie's arms around her. Just more proof Matt was entirely, utterly correct about her. He didn't even know she'd had her heart broken by a vampire. How much worse would his words have been if he did?

Nora started walking. She heard Annaliese's voice in her ear and must have responded, but she put her phone away before her brain processed the conversation. Eventually, Annaliese's car was there. Nora got in and let her human friend drive. Yet more proof. Nora hugged her stomach, welcoming the pain that flared in her rib. She let her head fall to rest on the window.

"Matt called," Annaliese was saying, words muffled by Nora's misery. "He asked me to tell you he didn't mean it. What did he do now?" Annaliese looked at her with concern, her tight grip on the wheel giving away her anger toward Matt. It was comforting.

Nora closed her eyes. It didn't matter. His words were and always would be the truth.

She hadn't even made the change, but she had already failed her pack. Nora found herself grateful her parents weren't around to see it.

CHAPTER 27

Poppy was unsettled by the silence of the apartment after such an eventful night. Julia was long gone. Josh left soon after they got Ru settled to tell his alpha what happened. On his way out, he'd promised to call later if his pack learned anything. Topher and Colbie hadn't been able to fight sleep any longer and crashed on Topher's bed.

Poppy went to check on them. Cracking open the door, she swore and rushed inside to take the smoking cigarette from Topher's limp fingers. She ground it in the ashtray by his window and turned when he whimpered. He curled up on his side, repeating the word "no" in a wavering voice.

His skin still looked gray. The demon and witch blood in his system had made him so nauseated he'd dry-heaved the entire way home.

Poppy's mind scrambled for some way to offer comfort, but Colbie shifted in her sleep and draped a hand over her brother's eyes. It calmed him enough to release the tension in his forehead. Poppy blinked, her heart breaking as it always did from these unexpected glimpses of the West siblings' childhood.

Poppy left Topher's room. She checked on her sister next.

Ru slept in Poppy's bed, sighing occasionally, but never fully waking. She hadn't woken since Topher healed her. For a second, Poppy was tempted to get into bed next to her. The thought tightened her chest with memories of climbing into her other sisters' beds. She had gone to each one for a specific comfort but never to Ru. Poppy perched on the edge of her mattress and watched her sister sleep. Memories she had pushed aside for months assailed her.

Poppy would go to Jane to ask questions about the day's lessons, determined that with enough extra help, she'd be able to keep up in front of their mother.

Amelia had been the one who snuck out regularly to see humans. Poppy was fascinated by every story her second eldest sister brought home. To keep the humans from checking on them and maintain their cover, their mother had also homeschooled them with the human curriculum. Amelia was the only one to show actual interest in these lessons. Under Amelia's covers, they studied human textbooks and whispered about college. They even applied. Amelia was talented enough to magic the funds into the system. But when Poppy showed up to class that first day, her sister hadn't been there.

Poppy went to Margot most often. She could lessen the sting of their mother's cruel words. She would sing and braid Poppy's hair while Poppy cried. Margot was the only sister who remembered which of their mother's callers was Poppy's dad. Margot was the reason Poppy knew her auburn hair was hereditary. That her father was a master's student studying chemistry. Their mother probably thought him full of potential and life energy. But he must have been lacking something. Before Poppy was old enough to cast, Margot had been the least gifted. She knew what it was to feel the chill of their mother's disappointment, to dream of someone who cared outside their coven. She had paid attention to her younger sisters' fathers because she wanted so badly to know her own.

Rayna was too quiet and cold to approach often, but Poppy

went to her to borrow strength when their mother yelled. And if their mother ever went through on her threats to lock Poppy in the chilly, rat-infested basement as punishment, someone had drawn a warding circle under the threadbare rug. If Poppy waited out the time inside it, one of her sisters upstairs kept up a constant spell to ensure it was warm and block the rodents out. Rayna was best at controlling environments.

Natalie was closest in age, a year younger than Poppy. She couldn't remember how many times she fell asleep while Natalie told her stories from the top bunk. When Colbie passed hours curled up reading on the couch, Poppy couldn't help but think of Natalie. Her sister always had a book hidden under her pillow.

Margot said their mother hadn't intended to get pregnant by Ru's father. She hadn't thought his potential substantial enough to be a sire to the seventh daughter, thus completing their coven. He worked at a restaurant a few blocks away, a small place their mother went to often for takeout. He'd just immigrated to New Brecken from Hong Kong. Poppy had dim memories of him at the house. He had the brightest smile, an infectious laugh. He was the only suitor that could make their mother laugh too. The only one to pay more than one visit. And apparently, his life was the most potent in potential, his energy unmatched by any of the other girls' fathers. His daughter was the most gifted witch in the Jennings coven.

Surrounded by their mother's pride, Ru didn't have to go to her sisters when she was starved for affection. She and Poppy never could relate well because of this. If Poppy was honest with herself, she'd always been jealous of her youngest sister. The seventh. The one with the Sight. The one Jane took and protected when their mother ruined them. Not even Natalie had stuck with Poppy when the wards around their home crumbled, opting to make her own way rather than let Poppy slow her down.

Poppy had been careful when she found herself alone. She

took brews to strengthen her personal wards until she'd practiced the spells enough to hold them without aid. She carried her bag with every ingredient and potion book her mother had abandoned to the attic at all times. With her little funds, she bought a hot plate and a pot. The first brew she made was a healing salve. She sold it on the black market. Those ten vials had been worth enough for her to buy her car and all the plants she needed to keep brewing. She made a sleeping draught that sold well enough to feed herself for a month after. Then she carefully crafted a memory charm. This one she sold for enough money to answer Colbie and Topher's ad looking for a roommate, down payment in hand.

Caught up in memories, Poppy paced to the kitchen and checked the four potions she'd started simmering on the stove. Her mind kept going to the blackness that appeared when she tried to see Jane and Natalie. Each time, she pushed the thoughts away. They were okay. They had to be. Her Sight wasn't strong enough for her to worry about anything she did or didn't see.

Still, the image of Ru falling, her wall of protection blinking out, replayed and brought back thoughts of blackness.

Poppy looked to the stove. She couldn't risk another night like the last. Natural magic worked best during the day when the world was full of sunlight giving life. She'd been weak. Ru had been weak. They wouldn't survive another attack. Especially since demons themselves fed off the death energy of the night.

Poppy opened the window to let in the rays of the sunrise and muttered to reinforce her wards. When she was sure they were safe and the potions were bottled, Poppy couldn't fight her exhaustion any longer. She sat down on the couch, vials close by and eyes on the front door. Mouse curled up on her lap. His soft purring and the gentle tug and catch of his claws on her hoodie pocket lulled her to sleep.

Poppy woke to her phone buzzing on the kitchen island. She snapped and it flew into her hand. Annaliese was calling.

"Hello?"

"What happened last night?"

"We aren't entirely sure. I'm still waiting for my sister to wake up and tell me." Poppy checked the time. She'd slept five hours. Hopefully, Ru hadn't needed anything in that time.

"Your sister?"

"What did Nora tell you?"

"Umm, not much past a mental breakdown about Matt. But she's covered in this disgusting black stuff. I couldn't even get her to shower before she fell asleep."

"Demon blood."

The line went so silent Poppy was sure the call had dropped. Finally, Annaliese said, "Demon blood? Where did you find demons?"

"They attacked Ru. She must have let down her wards." Poppy worried her lip.

"Your sister?"

"Yeah."

"And she's okay?"

"I think so."

"But Matt was there? Does he know about Colbie now? And why did demons attack your sister? I thought you said there weren't demons here."

"I don't know what Matt knows, but I think witches are being hunted. Humans were already getting attacked by the lowers and maybe even the demons. Vampires are being killed outside their own clubs. I don't know what's going on, but I'm guessing there will be another meeting now that Topher can confirm demons are in the picture. I'm sure they'll be taken care of."

"Damn."

"Annaliese?"

"Hm?"

"I know you and Nora are close, but I think it's time you backed out of all of this. It's too dangerous for a human."

"Nora's my best friend.

Annaliese hung up. Poppy scrolled through her other messages. Josh's pack had found a summoning circle five blocks from the park but couldn't trace any scents. Poppy groaned and dropped her head back into the cushions. When she opened her eyes, Ru was watching her from the doorway of her room.

"What's going on, Poppy?" Ru sounded years younger than sixteen.

"Ru, where's Jane?"

Ru looked down. "We were hiding out in the cabin. In the forest, you know? They, they left her corpse on the front steps three days ago. I was trying to find someone else. I even dropped my wards to let one of you see me, but you're all hidden too well."

Poppy wondered briefly what was wrong with them that neither cried. The most she felt was a dull roaring in her ears and a sweep of fear. Ru came forward and perched next to Poppy on the couch, hesitantly reaching to stroke Mouse's back. "What's happening, Poppy?"

"I wish people would stop asking me for answers."

Ru sighed and rubbed her throat. It was matted with light scares, the two holes from Topher's fangs the most prominent of the mess. Poppy still couldn't believe he'd managed to heal her. "I think Natalie is dead too."

Poppy nodded slowly. She didn't trust herself to speak. Her eyes fell on the book Colbie had left on the coffee table. That was almost enough to trigger a rush of tears.

Ru nodded toward Topher's door. "You trust them?"

"Yes."

"Okay." Ru nodded. She still looked terrified but resigned.

Probably just like Poppy looked when she'd had to move in with vampires. "You have anything to eat?"

Poppy smiled a little. She hesitated, just like Ru had, but committed and reached to stroke her little sister's hair. Ru leaned into the touch.

"Jane's dead," Ru whispered. "I burned her body and left the ashes in the forest. This wolf kept howling." She shivered.

"Shhh. You did the right thing. You were so brave." When Ru stopped shaking, Poppy said, "I'll make you something to eat and we'll figure this out. I'll keep you safe."

She looked at the vials on the coffee table and dared them not to be strong enough.

Poppy and Ru had nearly caught up on their lives in hiding when the sun set. Colbie was the first one out of bed and immediately began fawning over Ru. Poppy smiled when Colbie got Ru to laugh softly. They were going to be okay.

Topher came out of his room. He didn't look up in time to notice Poppy watching, so she caught a glimpse of the misery on his face just before his expression cleared. He joined Poppy where she stood at the stove.

"How's our Poppyseed?" He already had his cigarettes in hand, so Poppy knew this would be a quick check-in.

"I'm slightly overwhelmed. But I'm okay."

Topher nodded and perched an unlit cigarette in the corner of his mouth. It wiggled up and down as he spoke. Poppy ignored the squirm in her stomach. Was it weird to find smoking so attractive?

"You have any idea what's going on with the demons?"

"No more than you do."

Topher shrugged. He flicked his lighter on and off. He appeared to be recovered from the witch and demon blood. Two nights of keeping up with his feeding and he was a different person. The constant motion nearly matched Colbie's overflow of energy. "I'm going to talk to Lana before work.

The Big Three are reluctant to gather with the other city leaders. They think the meetings are making it worse, showing whoever is attacking who is strongest and targeting them."

"Do the Big Three think Nora's pack is behind the attacks now that Gabriel has made a move against you and Lana?"

Topher shook his head. "We told them I got caught up during a night out. I was with some human who was too slumped to wake me up. They don't know about the kidnapping."

"Really? Why would Lana lie for them?"

Topher's eyes slid away. "I told her not to let it distract from the issues at hand. She'll be certain to hold a grudge, but for now, she agreed to leave them alone." The lighter's small flame danced and died.

"I saw the notebook you two are working on."

"Yeah. We've been following the increase in lower vampires since I got turned."

"Why?"

Topher's eyes settled on Poppy's, arresting her in their startling blue.

"Because he thinks he was the first one. That it has something to do with whoever attacked him and Dylan," Colbie said.

"But I thought Lana—"

"Hunter sent me in to make a deal. I don't think he knew —" Topher cut off and hastily lit the cigarette. He pulled in a long drag without looking at them.

Topher's voice was muffled by the smoke in his lungs when he spoke again. "It doesn't matter. We just need to find whoever is behind the attacks."

He exhaled his lungful and Poppy waved a hand to disperse it, mumbling a spell for good measure.

Poppy was stunned. "So we're just letting go what Nora did?"

"I'm letting it go, yeah." Topher took another drag. He

raised a hand when Colbie started to protest. "But you do what you want. She lied."

Colbie nodded. "She lied."

"She might have been trying to protect you, but she lied," Topher added.

Colbie glared at him. "Oh, just go to work. Try not to get kidnapped this time."

Topher winked and pushed off the counter to do as she bid. "You coming by tonight?"

"Maybe near closing," Colbie said. "I could use a drunk feeding right now."

"Want to hit the field after?"

Colbie perked up. "Yeah!"

"Soda Pop?"

"Sure, Topher." Poppy thought about Julia as she agreed. What would the human girl think if she knew Topher still used soccer to get through the rough days?

CHAPTER 28

The trill ringing of Annaliese's phone woke them both. Nora rolled to press her face in the pillows. Annaliese groaned and slapped the nightstand twice before her hand landed on her phone.

"Topher?" she asked, voice thick with sleep. It had to be at least four in the morning. Nora pulled her head off the pillow to stare at Annaliese in bewilderment.

Nora strained her ears, but Topher's voice was the perfect pitch to be lost between Annaliese's ear and the low volume of her phone. Nora wondered if she'd be able to hear it next week, but the thought of the change didn't bring the thrill it usually did.

"Soccer? Now?" Annaliese asked. She frowned at whatever Topher responded, but Nora's heart sunk. Annaliese was considering his invitation.

"Where?" A pause. "See you soon."

Annaliese lowered the phone. "Want to go play a supernatural soccer game?"

"Was I invited?" Nora asked.

Annaliese sat up. "Topher knows we're a package deal."

"Since when does Topher call you?"

"Probably since I saved his ass." Annaliese got out of bed.

"*You what?*"

Annaliese's chin rose as she turned back to Nora. "I got him out of that basement. It wasn't right, Nora."

Nora stared, but Annaliese walked into her closet, flicking on the light. When she came out, she was dressed in a sweatshirt and joggers, her Nikes on and laced up. Annaliese was big on running. The light blue shoes, matching the tips of her braids, were probably her most worn-out possessions.

"You coming or not?" Annaliese gathered her hair into a low ponytail.

Nora fiddled with the blanket. "I don't think they'll want me there."

"So? Do you want to make up with Colbie? It won't happen unless you see each other."

Did Nora want to try again? Her chest ached with the thought. It couldn't work if she was joining the pack, but even that was suddenly an *if* for the first time in her life. Matt's words still had her feeling hollow. His doubt becoming a certainty for her. She couldn't kill a vampire, could she?

Nora swallowed. "I'll come, but I don't think I can play." Her rib had begun to heal, but it smarted when she moved to get out of bed. Her healing was faster than a human's but not as fast as it would be after the change.

Annaliese impatiently waited for Nora to get ready. She put on the spare clothes she left in Annaliese's room and wished she had something other than her ratty old jeans and paint-splattered sweatshirt from when she'd helped Annaliese's mom with the guest room upstairs. Her converse were still covered in dried demon blood, but there wasn't much she could do about that.

Topher sent Annaliese the name of the soccer field. It was an open field, like the one the B team practiced on at their high school and situated between two parking lots. The dry grass was lit by streetlamps, casting the field in a yellow haze. Poppy had placed some spell on the ball to keep it glowing blue while it was passed among the players.

Annaliese parked between Poppy's little car and Zayn's red Jeep. Oliver sat on a blanket in front of them, sipping a beer, the cooler open next to him. He smiled and waved at Annaliese and Nora as they approached.

"Hello! Welcome to the game! Losers who can't play worth shit and piss off their adorably competitive boyfriends, making Topher laugh and getting themselves helplessly charmed, sit here and DJ!" Oliver pointed his thumbs at himself and shimmied his shoulders to the beat of the song playing on the speaker beside him. He didn't look at all bothered to be sitting out.

"How much have you had to drink?" Annaliese asked as she stopped at the edge of the blanket. Oliver frowned at the empty cans scattered around him.

"Um, I think Poppy had a couple of these. Brown eyes had one for sure. And the twins took some…." Oliver shrugged like it didn't matter. "I'm more recovering from Zayn anyway," he said, fingers touching his neck and smiling.

As though summoned by the mention of his name, Zayn ran up to them, halting so quickly that Oliver leaned back on the blanket, swaying and grinning. Zayn threw a quick glare at Nora before he knelt in front of his boyfriend. Clearly, he hadn't forgiven her. Judging from the stiff shoulders on the field, Oliver would be the only one ready with a warm welcome.

Zayn's voice was surprisingly gentle after such a dark look. "Drink some water, love."

Oliver pouted and leaned forward to whisper something in Zayn's ear. Zayn stilled as he listened, one hand slowly curling into the front of Oliver's hoodie. Oliver ended by nipping Zayn's neck. The vampire smiled. He gave Oliver a quick kiss before he stood back up and kicked a water bottle closer to him.

"Deal," he said and went back onto the field. Though, not before shooting Nora another warning glare.

Oliver wiggled his eyebrows at Annaliese. "Scoring gets him frisky."

Annaliese snorted on a laugh. "What did you tell him?"

"You don't want to know."

Another set of footsteps approached. Nora dropped her eyes when she saw it was Topher.

"Perfect timing," he said, voice only mildly stiff. He wore the same blank look he usually sported around Annaliese, but it seemed more forced than usual. "We just finished a game. You two can get in on the next one."

No one else bothered coming off the field to greet them.

"I'm actually going to sit out. My rib still hurts," Nora said.

Topher nodded and gestured for Annaliese to follow him. Even from the edge of the field, Nora could feel the tension ease as the players realized she wouldn't be joining. Zayn watched her close, so she sat on the border of the blanket, away from Oliver.

They lined up to pick teams, Colbie and Zayn stepping forward as captains. It wasn't until then that Nora realized there were werewolves on the field. Josh was in line with the twins and his younger brother. Nora couldn't remember their names from when they showed up at the Den. She listened close as Colbie picked her player, fixing her bun and looking unconcerned compared to Zayn's intense energy as he considered his options.

Topher joined his sister's team and Zayn called for Poppy. Colbie didn't hesitate before picking Ru next, putting the witches on opposite teams. Zayn called Josh's name, Colbie picked his brother, Daniel, and the twins were separated next. Annaliese looked unbothered to be chosen last, especially when Topher and Zayn immediately fell into a burst of shit-talking, nose to nose. Whatever they said made even the twins laugh.

Annaliese was nearly bouncing, her competitive nature shining through.

"Topher's got his charm, but that doesn't help him against the other supernaturals," Oliver leaned toward Nora and explained. His breath stank like beer. "Zayn's stronger, but Topher might be faster. And he's better at soccer in general. Don't tell Zayn I said that. The witches are physically as good as humans, but every now and then, one will try to manipulate the ball with magic. Topher and the wolves can sniff out the spell and warn the witch on their team. The wolves are freaking fast and strong, but even Colbie can hold her own against them. She's good too. Really good. She and Topher were probably amazing players when they were humans. So far, they've been having a great time, though I can tell Topher's reeling it in for the most part to keep from charming me. He'll have to try even harder with Annaliese on the field. I doubt she's as used to it yet."

"What's it feel like? When he charms you?"

Oliver played with the tab on his beer can. "Sometimes it's just muddling, like losing your train of thought. If I'm looking at him, I can tell myself what's happening and usually shake it off, especially if he's just talking and doesn't mean for it to come out. When he laughs or smiles, it's just like… breathtaking in the extreme? I guess. I don't know, but it wipes my mind for a second. He'll catch himself and stop, but I can't usually tell how much time has passed. But, even then, if I'm ready for it and focus really hard, I can brush it off. Zayn can barely even charm me anymore unless I let myself submit to it. Colbie's charm is a little stronger than Zayn's, she got to me once, but she has better control over it and hardly lets it slip out unintentionally."

"What about Lana?"

Oliver's hand stilled. "Lana's charm can be like Topher's, and she means for it to be. I think she practices it a lot, and that's why it's strong. She doesn't even try to control it. I can't fight her off at all when she forces it on me. Although, if Topher ever intentionally used his charm on me, I doubt I could fight him either."

"Doesn't that scare you?"

Oliver pulled off the beer tab. "Sometimes. But I trust Topher and I know Zayn will take care of me. And Lana's a bitch, but she wants her lowers to stay loyal. And Zayn was her first lower, so she treats him, and therefore me, better than most." Oliver's eyes followed Zayn as he huddled his team. Zayn looked back and checked them, making Oliver smile. "But if the risk of getting charmed is the price I pay to be with him. It's all completely worth it."

Nora's chest squeezed. They fell quiet as the game began in earnest. Annaliese ran to cover the other team's goal, standing fearless even as Topher and Zayn charged at her from down the field. Zayn gave a lunge and kicked the ball her way. Annaliese reacted perfectly and shot a solid kick right past the twin in the goal. Her team cheered and Topher turned away from her to smile. Zayn tore into him about being too slow and getting his ass handed to him by a human. Annaliese smirked. Colbie took possession and the game moved back down the field.

Colbie shouted to Topher while she ran, feet expertly keeping the ball on track. With some complicated footwork, she sent it airborne. Topher spun and lost Zayn, bounced the ball off his chest and passed it on to Daniel. Josh yelled at Poppy, but his warning was too late. The ball sailed through the air from Daniel's kick and jerked suddenly, whipping around the twin guarding the net like a planet in orbit to make a perfect goal. Ru accepted Colbie's hug with a smile.

"Suck it, Z!" Colbie yelled.

"Pick a better word!" Oliver shouted from the blanket. Colbie shot him a finger gun, her eyes sliding past Nora as if she wasn't even there. Nora sighed, ignoring the twinge of pain from her rib.

Josh and Topher were closest. Josh punched Topher's arm. "You two play too well together. It isn't fair."

Topher dropped his voice and leaned into Josh's space to respond. Josh's cheeks flushed and he stuttered a response. Oliver let out a laugh. Josh looked over at the sound and rolled his eyes. He flipped Oliver off, but his smile was harmless.

Nora looked down the field in time to see Poppy turn from the scene, shoulders stiff.

"Um, is Topher flirting with Josh?"

Smile in place, Oliver glanced at Nora. "First of all, yes. Definitely. Secondly, forget whoever you think Topher is from the bar or watching him with humans around. I've barely gotten a glimpse of the real him myself, but at least I've seen him after hooking up with Rico. God, Lana was pissed." Oliver paused to laugh. "Third, I think Topher would flirt with a demon if it was his type, but I also don't think he does it with serious intent. More so because he's good at it? And he only can with wolves or vampires."

Nora accepted the beer he offered before she could think better of it.

"What about Julia?"

Oliver took a pull from his beer and swirled the contents idly. His grin fell away. "I feel bad for Julia, but she left and she falls under his charm as much as the rest of us. I see more of the fallout from Topher's issues than I think even Colbie does. Topher takes a lot to Zayn, especially his complaints about Lana, but Zayn won't even tell me everything that's going on there. Let's just say Topher isn't okay. I don't think he was okay before the change and he definitely hasn't been okay since it happened. And I think he considers cheating to be one of the least offensive things he's done since he turned. And you know what? Whatever that boy needs to feel happy now, he deserves it."

Nora's chest squirmed. She didn't know if it was guilt or discomfort at the thought that all these people seemed fine with the fact that Topher had turned his sister into a monster and was a cheater. None of them ever had a bad thing to say about Topher, yet Topher himself did. His friends just claimed she didn't know him. Did any of them know him, either?

Oliver was distracted by Zayn scoring. Nora watched Oliver cheer, basking under Zayn's attention when the vampire winked and kissed at him from across the field. Oliver made his love look so easy, his belonging so effortless. He knew what he wanted and took in his pleasure as readily as he breathed in air.

Nora longed for such simple happiness.

Her eyes were drawn again to Colbie, who hadn't come to this side of the field. She straightened quickly. Colbie was watching her back, frown in place, eyes shadowed. Nora's stomach fluttered with hope. Colbie shook her head and muttered something to Topher. Nora's skin crawled when he laughed at their secret joke, making Annaliese stumble as she walked to the ball. He was quick to shut down his expression.

It didn't matter how much Nora wanted this. How happy she'd felt with these people. She belonged to Gabriel and the pack. She belonged to the full moon and the trees of the forest. Her blood roared at just the thought. She couldn't stop her change. She couldn't risk going rogue when she did. Nora sighed and set aside her beer.

"Tell Annaliese I'm sorry," Nora said to Oliver. His smile died.

"Nora. It's not too late to make things better."

"Bye, Oliver."

Nora pushed herself off the blanket and started away. She's made it to the edge of the parking lot before someone grabbed her sleeve and spun her around. Nora winced from the sudden motion, hand going to her rib, but there was no sympathy on Colbie's face.

"You're just going to leave?"

"What do you want from me, Colbie?"

"I don't know. You could start with at least an apology."

"I'm sorry. I'm so sorry. I wouldn't have killed him. I don't think I could have. I didn't know what to do." Nora struggled to meet Colbie's eyes.

"What were you planning when you came to the diner?"

Nora pressed her lips together. Colbie backed up a step.

"I want to think the best of you, Nora. I've never wanted to give someone a second chance more, and you know now what I've forgiven Topher for."

"I don't deserve your forgiveness. It doesn't change anything. I have to join my pack. They'll keep me centered during the change and then you won't matter to me anymore. I have to let you go. This was stupid and I shouldn't have let myself get so caught up in you. It was never going to work out, Colbie. I tried to tell you from the start. We'll both be better off if you just keep hating me." Nora pulled in a heavy breath, amazed at herself for getting the words out.

Colbie swallowed twice, lips twitching downward. Finally, she looked away.

"Consider it done then," Colbie said. "Stay away from us."

Nora turned and forced herself to keep walking, refusing to wipe her tears until she knew the vampire at her back couldn't see her do it.

CHAPTER 29

In Poppy's dream, it felt almost as if her wards were being tested. The strange jolt woke her up. She rolled, squinting against the light coming in through the window. She whispered a few words into her pillow just to make sure the wards remained strong. Her protections remained unbothered, but sleep eluded her since that first jolt. Poppy carefully climbed out of her bed.

She looked down where Ru and Colbie still slept. Colbie had been sandwiched between the two sisters. Her cheeks still looked slightly flushed from the warmth. Poppy's brain lagged, trying to remember why the three of them had ended up in her bed, until she recalled everyone who'd been at the soccer field had come back to their apartment afterward.

Zayn and Oliver had taken Colbie's room. Annaliese, Cora, and Rory had claimed Topher's. It was hard to imagine those three snuggled under Topher's mountain of blankets and pillows.

Poppy smiled when she entered the living room and saw how the rest had situated themselves, more relieved than she cared to admit that Josh and Topher weren't cuddled up on the sofa. Josh and his brother were in wolf form, Daniel on the rug and Josh in a tight circle on the armchair. Topher slept on his stomach on the couch. One tattooed arm hung out from the blanket that covered him from head to toe.

Poppy rarely saw Topher without long sleeves on. She took a moment to look closer at the tattoo wrapping his forearm. She knew from his vague explanations it was from a human gang, but she wasn't involved with city politics enough to know which one. The pattern looked like a sketch of a rose bush, a faded red mixed into the black and gray of the petals. Above the sprawling tattoo, by tilting her head, Poppy could see two scars dotting his inner arm. She frowned at the sight and the mystery there. The Topher she knew kept such rigid control, rarely letting himself relax enough to enjoy anything. It was hard to imagine him falling into such a harmful habit. What had led him to that point when he was still so young?

He was entirely still as he slept covered—a corpse under a sheet. Poppy banished the thought and continued to the coffee maker.

The sound of nails clipping on the wood floor made her turn to the bathroom in time to see Josh's tail disappear inside. He came out a couple of minutes later in human form, fully dressed and stretching. Josh hoisted himself up to sit on the island, watching Poppy as she poured grounds into the coffee filter.

"Morning," he said.

Poppy couldn't stop herself from returning his grin. The soccer game had healed a lot of tension. She hit start on the coffee machine and leaned back on the counter across from him. "Good morning."

"Last night was fun. How often do you play?"

"Not as often as we'd like. I've slept through a few of them, too. But Topher's always up for a game when things get stressful." Poppy's eyes fell on his sleeping form. "He'd probably play every night if he could."

Josh nodded. "We have pack basketball games."

"That would be fun." They fell into a slightly awkward silence.

"So, no hard feelings, right?" Josh picked at the new grass-strained hole in his jeans.

"What? Why? Did you and Topher..." Poppy couldn't finish the thought.

"Well, no. I meant more *I* don't have hard feelings." His face said otherwise as he realized that, once again, Topher proved to be Poppy's primary concern. Josh dropped his voice. "Poppy, I have to tell you, I don't think he feels the same way."

Poppy wiped the expression from her face and turned to get a mug. Maybe there wasn't hope, but Josh wouldn't be the one to convince her. "You don't like boys too, do you?" She had to check. She hadn't even known Topher did before last night. How could she not have known that?

Josh sighed and shook his head. Poppy gave a curt nod and filled her mug. She went to the end of the couch, sitting carefully on Topher's feet to warm them. He didn't move. Josh settled into the armchair and Poppy snapped to summon the remote. The news came on and the scene nearly made her drop her coffee cup.

"—vampire lair. The club, called The Maker, continues to burn thirty minutes after the initial call was received," the news anchor stated. She stood at the end of Fourth, the Maker's windows billowing smoke behind her. "The fire started on the second floor, and although it has yet to be confirmed, it is believed it began at multiple points. It is with a heavy heart that I report the five vampires sleeping did not wake up to get out in time. No human lives have been lost, although several were injured trying to reach the sleeping vampires upstairs. The names of the deceased have yet to be released. It is rumored several were undocumented."

A sudden boom had the anchor ducking away from the building. The lower level, soaked through with alcohol, had caught, blowing the doors open. The firefighters began shouting, renewing their efforts, but Poppy had little hope for the building. She looked at Topher's still form, thinking about his burning room there. His fellow lowers.

"What the hell?" Josh was out of the armchair, nudging his brother awake with his foot and hurrying to Topher's room to wake the twins. He came out with his phone to his ear. Poppy was surprised at his urgency and action. Her mind was still struggling through the muddle of shock.

"We're on our way. No, Rory drove. *Don't* go to the Maker? But where… Yeah, okay. See you soon." He tucked the phone away. "You coming, Poppy?"

"No, I think I should keep watch over the wards here. Be careful. Let me know what you find out."

Poppy was aware her voice came out flat. She felt like the floor had dropped, leaving her emotions separate and high above. How could she tell Topher and Zayn? Were they the last of Lana's people? Was Lana finally out of the picture? Poppy shuddered. If she was, Topher was now completely in the hands of Connor Grace. A man who earned his position by killing his competition when his maker fell. Grace had only left two of his fellow seconds, Solas and Patter, alive. Her mother had suspected a deal had been struck between the three. It was the only reason Fourth Street hadn't collapsed into war.

Topher never said it out loud, but Poppy knew he preferred Lana to Grace by far.

"Where are we going?" Cora asked, coming out of Topher's room. Josh had explained last night that Cora parted her hair in the middle while Rory parted hers on the left. That was the easiest way for strangers to distinguish them.

She and her twin already looked alert and tense. Rory had her keys out and ready as they waited for Daniel to shift and get dressed.

"Should we tell them?" Rory asked, jerking her chin toward Topher.

Poppy shook her head. "We won't be able to wake them up."

"Do you think Lana is dead?" Annaliese asked, following the twins out of Topher's room.

"I don't know," Poppy got up and went to Colbie's room. She was relieved to find the couple within covered by the blanket. Oliver was pressed against Zayn's chest, Zayn's arms wrapped tightly around him even in sleep. Oliver could barely even lift his head to look at Poppy when the sound of the door woke him up. He was reluctant to do even that, blinking and frowning.

"Yes?"

"Does Lana usually sleep at the Maker?"

Unable to free his arm, Oliver rubbed his nose on Zayn's bicep. "No?"

"Is that a no? This is important, Oliver. The Maker is burning down. They're saying none of the vampires made it out."

Oliver's face went pale. He pressed himself even closer to Zayn. "No, Poppy. She usually sleeps at Happenstance. She only stays at the Maker when Topher does, as far as I know."

Poppy went cold hearing this, but she couldn't focus on that now. She nodded and backed out of the room. Oliver shifted before the door closed, freeing his arm and wrapping it around Zayn to lend his boyfriend comfort Zayn didn't even know he needed yet.

The wolves heard the conversation and left soon after. Poppy didn't know what they could do, but she prayed to the Mother they'd be successful.

As soon as Topher cracked his eyes open, he knew something was wrong. Poppy's scent was sharp with nerves, the apartment heavy with the smell. Annaliese was still there and Topher uncovered his head to find her asleep on the armchair, legs pulled up close and a line between her eyebrows. Colbie came out of Poppy's room, nose in the air. Together, they looked to the bathroom where Poppy was showering. Colbie sat down next to him and they waited.

Poppy came out in her robe, a towel in her hair. She froze when she realized she had their full attention.

"I have news," she said. Topher didn't need her to clarify to know it wasn't good. His phone rang, and he was quick to answer.

"Lana."

"I want your ass stuck to my side for the rest of the night. Zayn, too. *Now*."

She hung up and Topher jumped to his feet. He ran to his room to change, yelling over his shoulder. "Explain, please."

"The Maker burned down today."

Topher froze, reaching for the sweatshirt on the hook behind his door. He came out of his room shirtless to stare at Poppy. Zayn entered the living room at the same time and their eyes met in mirrored expressions of shock. Oliver was pressed to Zayn's side, chewing a thumbnail.

"Who?" Zayn asked. His eyes dropped to the new faint lines scarring Topher's chest since his time with Gabriel's pack and his expression tightened further. Topher quickly pulled on his sweatshirt.

"We don't know."

"Did you check with the wolves?" Zayn shot an accusing look at Annaliese, who was now awake. She met his stare without flinching.

"I think Josh's pack went to question them. They've been looking for answers all day. All they've discovered was the fire was started by a witch."

"Not a sorcerer?"

"No. They wouldn't be so strong in the daylight."

Topher rubbed a hand through his wild hair. "Lana wants us. Ready?"

Zayn nodded and turned to pull Oliver in for a quick feed and lingering kiss, ensuring his saliva had time to ease Oliver's racing heart. "Stay safe in Poppy's wards, got it?"

Oliver nodded and whispered, "You stay safe, too."

Zayn gave him another hard kiss. Topher stopped to hug Poppy and Zayn squeezed her arm, thanking her for keeping the apartment safe. Topher paused again to say goodbye to Annaliese but couldn't think of the words. When she held up a fist, he pressed his own to it. Her expression was guarded as she did the same with Zayn and watched them turn to leave.

But movement across the room made Topher freeze. His heart skipped when he saw Colbie reach for her jacket.

"You aren't coming."

"I am," she said. She pulled the hair tie off her wrist and yanked her hair into its bun, expression uncharacteristically serious. "I'm not leaving you two to handle this alone. I'm not useless. I'm a vampire and I should have gotten involved a long time ago. I should have been watching your back from the start."

"Colbie…" Topher thought about all he'd done. All he'd given Lana in exchange for his sister's safety. To keep her a secret and out of this life.

"Toph, we don't have time to argue. She deserves to know what's going on. It's her choice," Zayn said.

Colbie shot him a grateful smile.

Topher's heart squeezed as he nodded. "Keep up then."

"Just watch me, little brother."

The three of them hurried out of the silent apartment. They ran to Fourth Street and on to Grace's club. The street was hazy with smoke. It swirled thick under the streetlamps. There was an unsettling absence of people and thumping music. Reaching Happenstance, Topher caught the scent of Patter and Solas. Every inch of him revolted from the idea of bringing Colbie before the Big Three. He looked back at her, the words building in his throat. Colbie tipped her chin and brushed past him. They entered the club.

Lana waited just inside the door. She barely spared Colbie a glance.

"No one else made it," the maker said. Her voice was steady, but she smelled strongly of cigarettes and her hands were clasped tightly in front of her.

Tamera, Sammy, Muscles, Jaeger... Their faces flashed through Topher's mind. Smiling. Young. Powerful. Surprising in their gestures of kindness. Zayn made a distressed sound, but Topher was removed from the grief. Just as he had been when Brady died.

When would his life as a vampire become real? When would it stop feeling like a never-ending nightmare? A horrible dream that started with the events leading to his being turned. Maybe even before. He rubbed at the inside of his arm. Topher was ready to wake up.

Colbie's hand slipped into his, anchoring him against the spiraling thoughts. He drew in a deep breath. He was in this for the long haul. He'd brought his sister into this nightmare; he had to stick it through with her.

A huddle of humans clustered at the top of the stairs. Lana narrowed her eyes at Topher until he grabbed the nearest one. Once they were fed and at full strength, the humans lounging contentedly on the sofas, Lana led them into the meeting room.

It was full of vampires. Everyone Topher had met in the last year. Even a few unfamiliar faces, no doubt lowers who were so ungifted they weren't invited to the maker meetings. This was good, as it kept Colbie from garnering too much attention. It was strange to see vampires looking at Lana with something other than hatred, but pity burned their backs as they crossed the room to the secure chamber where Topher had broken the young girl, Mary.

The Big Three waited inside.

"This is all we have left of your lowers?" Grace checked with Lana. His eyes lingered on Colbie. Topher swallowed a snarl. He hated this.

Lana nodded stiffly.

"What happened to your wards?" Patter demanded.

Lana turned her cool gaze to the other woman. "They were breached."

"Impossible. Only the witch who cast them can let the wards down."

"Or a witch with said witch's blood could slip through," Grace said.

Solas ignored the other two as they began to bicker, her eyes fastened on Colbie, looking around Topher as he tried to block his sister from view with his body discretely.

"Bold of you to bring one of your unregistered here," she said to Lana.

"This lower isn't a concern. She is easily charmed and controlled. She isn't unclaimed. We have bigger problems right now."

"Hmm. You know, we've been thinking a good deal about where these other lowers are coming from. Who we've had questioning them."

Topher forced himself to stay relaxed as Solas and Patter looked to him.

"What? You think Christopher is behind the unclaimed?" Lana let out a laugh. Grace's typically controlled expression pinched. He wasn't comfortable with the turn the conversation had taken.

"Of course not. We think the only way his charm would fail to get answers from a lower, would be if they were under a charm his couldn't touch," Solas said.

"The only question is, are you or Lana creating them?" Patter continued, raising an eyebrow in Grace's direction.

"Let me get this right. You are accusing me or Lana of

these attacks?" If Grace was angry, his voice didn't betray it. Yet still, Patter shifted, growing wary. He wasn't a tall man, but in Topher's eyes, he filled the room.

"Well, the thing is," Solas stepped in, "it doesn't matter if it was you or Lana. It has always been your job to control your seconds. Lana should never have turned Christopher without going through the registration process. You should have ended her for breaking the law. More lowers have appeared ever since. The wolves have convinced us what is needed to discourage this trend from continuing."

Lana and Topher had made that connection with the timing. Topher's change and Dylan's murder seemed to kick off the emergence of other lowers. Topher longed for his notebook, either burnt to ash in the Maker or in the hands of the arson. The hours of writing he'd put into those pages were a part of him. His need for answers kept him sane as thirst and guilt crowded in. He'd been so close.

Patter regained her confidence. "We must have peace. The clubs are working. There is no vampire clan so powerful or free as us. We need the wolves and witches off our backs. We need to keep the humans happy. What we don't need, Grace, is *you*."

Patter turned to Topher. "Hunter told us what happened to his son. What was left of a demonic ritual. And out of it comes the strongest vampire in ages. Undocumented until Grace pulls the strings."

Topher's hands clenched.

"The gang has agreed not to go to the human police," Solas continued, "in exchange for the boy and those who changed him. Who have been attacking humans and turning them, leaving them and demons scattered throughout the city."

"By making the humans happy, we'll finally end the attacks. The city will have peace. Your reign is over, Grace. Your line through Lana ends here," Patter said.

The situation hit fully then. Topher bared his teeth,

summoned his charm, and crouched, ready to fight. He'd do anything to save Colbie. To save Zayn. He'd already done so much. What was another fight? What was his life? He couldn't watch his sister die. He couldn't watch anyone else he loved die. He knew how long it took a soul to recover from that. How ineffectually.

But a witch burst into the room before Solas or Patter made any move to attack.

"What are you doing, Beth?" Lana demanded. But there was hope in his maker's eyes. Topher put it together faster than she did. The wards weren't breached. Beth had crossed them effortlessly, the one who set them. She'd killed them all.

"Bring me the day!" the witch shouted. Light flared between her hands. Squinting, Topher glimpsed Gabriel standing behind the witch's shoulder. Smiling.

Topher made to attack, but his eyelids grew heavy and he stumbled. The pull of the sunlight conjured in Beth's palms dragged him into sleep.

CHAPTER 30

"I just don't understand why they attacked the Maker of all places," Oliver said.

He looked down at his phone again, two fingertips pressed into the scars on his neck. It was nearly sunrise and the vampires hadn't returned or sent word.

Poppy had the same sense of foreboding she experienced when Topher first went missing. She paced in front of the TV and tried to distract herself with the mystery of the Maker. Her mind scrambled through everything she knew. The enemies Lana had, the impact it would have on Grace, if it related to Topher's kidnapping, the surge in demons, the arrival of a sorcerer.

Poppy didn't get it, either. The problem felt too big. Too many pieces of New Brecken's supernatural classes were involved. Topher and Zayn had kept too much hidden.

Expelling a huff of air, Poppy turned to the wall. She flicked her fingers at the entertainment system and it moved out of the way. She swayed with the effort and ignored the concerned look Ru shot her.

"Something big is happening," Poppy said. "The attacks

are coming from too many angles. We need to figure this out. Get things straight."

Knowing she and Annaliese worked well off a whiteboard from numerous study sessions, Poppy snapped and glowing words appeared on the wall.

Gabriel's Den was the first section. "Do we think they did this?"

Annaliese looked away, lips pursed. Oliver was already nodding, eyes wide like it was obvious.

"They took Topher," he said. "Whatever they wanted from him, they didn't get. Why wouldn't they try again?"

"They took Topher for Nora to make the change. She wouldn't go through with it, though," Annaliese said. "Matt knows she's friends with Topher now and burning the Maker wouldn't do anything for Nora."

"But why did they take him in the first place?"

"To weaken Lana and Grace?" Annaliese suggested. "Topher's just a lower. Grace has all the real power, right?"

Poppy nodded and wrote that on the wall.

"But that's not entirely true. Topher is so strong. Maybe they just want him out of the picture," Oliver said, sounding like the words pained him.

"But as long as he's under Lana's control, he isn't a threat," Annaliese said.

Poppy wasn't sure, but she wrote Lana's name down. "That would explain why they went for the Maker next," she said.

"We think Gabriel burned the Maker down?" Oliver asked. "But how would he get past the wards?"

"They must have had help," Annaliese said, warming to the idea despite her reluctance to cast blame on Nora's pack. "Grace has to have more enemies than just the pack, right?"

Poppy fidgeted, unwilling to reveal to the room how a witch's magic wasn't as strong against werewolves.

"But who would help Gabriel?" Oliver asked. He and Annaliese were leading this conversation, and Poppy was grateful. "The pack is so distrustful. All the different supernatural groups are."

"Witches?" Annaliese asked.

"Doubtful," Ru cut in. "I know Kallow has been trying to expand her relationships with the wolves, but she also wants peace with the Big Three. They're so powerful. She wouldn't go against Grace."

Annaliese sat forward on the couch. "What exactly is the Big Three?"

Oliver fielded the question, looking pleased to have a concrete answer. "Before they even legalized vampires, many groups were fighting for territory here. The human gangs and black market were already thriving, so it was easy for the vampires to come in. One vampire beat out all the other clans. He and his seconds ran that section of the city. All of them were makers."

"Not all vampires are makers?" Annaliese cut in.

"No, it takes a very compelling charm from what I understand. Anyway, when they started floating the idea of coming forward and legalizing the supernatural, the vampire leader was against the move. He wasn't a huge fan of humans, Zayn says. Three of his seconds, Grace, Solas, and Patter, were in favor of the laws. Zayn says they stepped aside when one of the wolves, Nora's dad actually, attacked their maker. They were able to sign the laws and made peace after. When all was said and done, the vampires were registered as makers and lowers. That's when the wolves realized the three of them were responsible for every vampire registered in the city. They've been called the Big Three since then."

There was a knock on the door. Oliver was so focused on the task at hand that he started and nearly fell off his perch on the arm of the couch.

"Let him in," Poppy whispered, still looking at the wall. The door opened for Josh, the only person besides their vampire friends who could get through the wards. He took in the room and joined Ru and Annaliese on the couch.

"How many vampires are there in New Brecken?" Annaliese asked, still focused on the topic at hand.

"Nearly two hundred." Surprisingly, it was Josh who supplied the answer without missing a beat.

Annaliese nodded, eyes on the wall. "The vampires let Nora's dad kill their leader. They had an alliance. So, what happened to ruin the peace?"

"A vampire went rogue and killed Morales. All the Big Three deny it was them or their seconds, but Gabriel killed their suspect anyway. Zayn won't tell me more. Then, all the other packs started leaving town. The wolves lost their power. They were just too outnumbered and humans got in the way as they came to enjoy the clubs."

"None of this explains why they are only targeting Lana. None of Grace's other seconds have been attacked," Poppy said.

"But Solas's were," Josh said.

Poppy rubbed her temples.

"Well, it was Solas's lowers and a second. Their maker, Rico. From what I hear, he was close with Lana," Josh said.

Oliver looked surprised by the intel. "He and Topher knew each other. They didn't tell me he got murdered."

Josh took a deep breath. "Actually, I have more news. Rumors are spreading."

"And?" Annaliese prompted.

"And they're saying Lana's the one behind the unclaimed. That it started with Topher. He's too strong and the unclaimed keep getting harder to kill. Less and less humane. They're saying that Lana and Topher were placed in charge of the search for the culprit and that's why they haven't come up with any answers. Because it was them, well her, this whole time."

The room fell into a shocked silence. Josh pressed on.

"Word is she's being dealt with. Solas and Patter have told my alpha he's better off staying out this."

"What are you saying?" Poppy asked. Her hands had gone cold.

"When did Topher get changed?" Josh asked.

"Last April," Oliver supplied when Poppy stayed silent.

"Did he go through the application process?"

"I don't know," Poppy whispered.

"Lana claimed him and registered him," Oliver shifted uncomfortably, "But Zayn said Grace had to pull strings to make it happen. It didn't sound like he applied for the change and he doesn't act like it was something he wanted."

"And Colbie? She isn't registered, right?"

Annaliese's eyes widened. "Nora said Topher changed her. Lana kept it quiet."

"She also kept it quite that he's a maker. His registration only says he's a lower."

"How do you know?" Poppy asked. Josh stayed quiet. She stepped forward. "Does your pack think Topher is the one changing the unclaimed and letting them run wild?"

"*I* don't, but he's strong enough, isn't he?"

"But..." Poppy shook her head. "I found his notebooks in the Maker. Tracking the lowers—"

"Tracking them or keeping track?"

"But Zayn's been helping the hunt for them," Oliver burst out. "All the supernaturals are."

Josh put up his hands. "I hate this too. But, if Lana is behind this, Topher and Zayn don't have a say. She controls them with her charm. Maybe Grace is controlling her."

Oliver went for his phone. He called Zayn again. "So where are they now?" he asked, voice rising.

Josh spoke gently, but Poppy felt her panic curling in her gut. "All we've found out today is no one's angry the Maker burned, save for Lana. Solas and Patter say they haven't seen her tonight. I don't think they even have proof Lana's behind the unclaimed."

"And what if they find some? What happens to Topher?" Annaliese asked.

"I'm guessing they'll want to figure out his innocence too."

"So we need to prove he's innocent. That he's a victim, not the one changing people."

"My uncle would defend him if we can do that. Our pack would step up to keep the peace."

"Can we show that?" Oliver asked.

"If changing wasn't his choice," Josh said. "If he was changed against his will by Lana, we prove he was the first victim."

"Do we even know how he got changed?" Annaliese asked, looking between Poppy and Oliver.

Poppy shook her head. Oliver shrugged.

"Can we find out?"

Ru and Poppy shared a look. There were ways.

In Topher's room, Ru and Poppy murmured to the magic under their breath. Poppy went to Topher's closet first. She knew nearly all the clothes here were purchased in the last year. They were looking for an object with an impression of the night he'd been changed. If Topher had kept one, It would be older than the rest of his belongings.

Poppy regretted the instant her hands were guided to the item she'd need neatly folded and tucked into the back of the side shelf. It was a worn blue sweatshirt. Covered with dark smears, spatters, and pooling stains of blood. The shoulder had a ragged tear. Humanity clung to it.

Poppy had to clear her throat to speak. "I found something."

They gathered in a circle on Topher's floor. The more of his presence they felt, the stronger the spell. Ru lit the candles. Poppy could already feel her sister's power drawing the room's energies. She forgot what it felt like to be around such a strong witch. It made her head spin. They were both already glowing faintly.

Poppy cleared her voice. "Josh, do you mind if I borrow some of your energy?"

Josh didn't even blink. He knew so much about the other supernaturals that he just offered a hand without question.

"We'll need to borrow from everyone for a spell this complex," Ru said. She settled cross-legged on the floor and held up her hands.

Annaliese closed the door on Mouse when he tried to get in the middle of their circle of held hands for the second time. Poppy carefully placed the sweatshirt in the middle. They eyed it warily. Folded peacefully on the floor, Poppy could feel violence and misery clinging to the cloth. Why had Topher kept it?

Ru nodded for Poppy to take the lead. Poppy reached with her magic and let it mingle with the pull of Ru's life force and Josh's. The humans were a flicker of pure life energy, but it was enough to help.

"Eyes closed. The sweatshirt's history will play like a movie. I don't know how to prepare you, but this definitely won't be pleasant. There's a lot of grief here."

Annaliese's hand tightened convulsively on Poppy's. "Should we even look then?" she whispered.

"Only if we want answers," Ru said.

There was doubt around the circle. But no one protested further.

Poppy and Ru began to call on the magic. The vision bloomed behind her eyelids. Annaliese gasped and the world fell away to the memory.

The scene came to life in bits and pieces first. A sleek black car parked near the river. Warehouses across the water let beams of the setting sun filter through. Poppy knew nothing about cars, but this one screamed wealth. Whoever was wearing the sweatshirt was watching the figure leaning on the car. His breath quickened. They could all see why. Topher West, tanned and human, smoking as he stared out across the water, was stunning. He looked so young.

Poppy was dimly aware of Annaliese stiffening next to her. In the memory, the boy wearing the sweatshirt spoke. His image was becoming clear. He had black hair and wide-set eyes that soaked up Topher like he was the only thing made in color. The boy was short and slight. The sweatshirt was too large on him, but the way he tucked his hands up in the sleeves made the size look purposeful.

"You're late."

Topher's pensive expression eased. He turned to the boy and a smile lit his face. Dimples tucked, eyes crinkled, a peace settled over Topher as he took in the sweatshirt wearer.

"Hey, you. Time got away from me."

"I missed you." The words were practically blurted. Topher's smile grew.

"I missed you too," Topher said. He had a practiced way of speaking around his smile that drew the eye. Like Colbie did.

The boy in the sweatshirt was lost to the sight.

The wind picked up, ruffling Topher's hair. He threw away his cigarette and crossed his arms, goosebumps rising on his skin. The sweatshirt wearer's throat bobbed. Topher lacked the skull tattoo that currently marked his right forearm, but the roses were there. The boy's eyes dropped to Topher's elbow. Topher patiently bared his forearms.

"I smoked last night. Colbie's home, so we used a bit of her stuff, but I'm safe, Dylan."

Dylan nodded. He reached and pressed his thumb into one

of the tiny, faded needle marks. His eyes traveled down to Topher's forearm and the roses tattooed there. His hand trailed to brush over them and Topher's gaze softened. He reached and tugged at the bottom of the sweatshirt, one side of his mouth still lifted in a smile. "Your dad is waiting for me, babe."

"What did he call you for?"

Topher shrugged. "Another deal. That's all he said."

"I'm coming."

Topher lowered his head to rest it on Dylan's. Forehead to forehead, he closed his eyes and dropped his voice. "He told me solo mission."

"I'm coming."

Topher tugged Dylan closer. Topher's hands settled on Dylan's hips, both of their breathing turned unsteady. Topher's fingers slipped under the sweatshirt and skimmed Dylan's skin. When his hand found the gun tucked in the back of Dylan's jeans, Topher nodded reluctantly.

"I trust you."

"I trust you."

Topher tugged at the sweatshirt again and Dylan rolled his eyes.

"You know I'm always cold," Topher said.

"I know you're always needy." Dylan took off his sweatshirt and gave it to Topher, who pulled it on with a smile of thanks. The same rose tattoo marked Dylan's left forearm, though his looked older and faded. Dylan reached to flatten Topher's hair and Topher caught his hand to press a kiss to his wrist. Without a word, the boys walked down the street and into a side office building, stepping apart at the last moment before they entered.

A man looked up from the desk. "Chris. You're late."

"Not so late."

The man waved away his words. "I need you to take this to the Umbras. Should only see Mark there. We were going to

327

send a wolf to escort you, but they were all busy tonight. Can you handle Mark?"

"Yes."

"You going too, son?"

"Yeah," Dylan said softly. Something shifted in Hunter's eyes. Worry? Fear?

"I'm going to ask you not to. At least stay in the car. Mark's been missing a few payments. You know we trust Chris with the difficult cases. You don't need to get in the way."

"Sure, Dad," Dylan said, but his chin rose defiantly as soon as Hunter turned his attention back to the desk. Topher smirked and picked up the paper bag Hunter set out. They turned and left.

"I hate him," Topher said as soon as the door closed behind them.

Dylan waited until they'd rounded the corner before stepping close to Topher's side. They walked to the car, knuckles brushing often and purposefully.

Topher got in the driver's side and watched Dylan carefully lower himself so his gun rested comfortably.

"We could leave," Topher said. "This city is sucking the life out of everything."

Dylan sighed. Clearly, they'd had this conversation before. "We can't just leave. You've missed enough school as it is, Toph."

"I don't care about school."

"We don't have the money."

"That's what jobs are for."

"What would we do?"

"Sell insurance? Become plumbers? Bartend?"

"Topher. Be serious."

"I am."

"What about Julia?"

"What about her? We broke up. I thought I told you, Dylan."

"You didn't," Dylan straightened in his seat. His face brightened. "Did she find out about us?"

Topher shrugged. "She just wasn't good for me. We're good as friends, but that's it. She's too… intense. I know she wants the best for me and I'm grateful she's in my life, but I couldn't deal with her pressuring me so much after being gone. She doesn't trust me, but she wants to be with me enough to ignore all the bad or constantly try to fix it. I don't want to ignore the bad. I don't like feeling broken. When she looks at me, it's like she's seeing who she wants me to be and not who I am. It's just not easy with her." Topher gave Dylan a look. "Not like it is with you."

Dylan reached for Topher's hand. "She did do the right thing. Telling your parents. Getting you to rehab."

Topher sighed and turned to stare out the window. "It doesn't matter. It's only you. I know you aren't supposed to replace one addiction with another. And I don't want to put my semi-sobriety on you. But I really don't care about anything else."

"Yes, you do. You're so excited Colbie's home."

"She's only back a couple days."

"You have school."

"I hate school."

"Your parents?"

"They're great and all, but you know we aren't close. They want me and Colbie to do our own things."

"My dad?"

"I'll protect us from him. His reach doesn't go that far, babe. It barely crosses the river anymore. The vampires are stealing his business and that has him scared. We'll be fine."

"You can't promise that, Topher. He loves his power. He won't just let us leave."

"All I've ever wanted was to get out of this city," Topher whispered, turning back to Dylan. Dylan reached and touched the inside of Topher's elbow, thumb gently pressing the scars again. "Now, all I want is to get out of the city with you."

"I know, Topher. I know."

Topher pulled Dylan closer. Their kiss began slow and halting. Topher couldn't keep that pace long. He groaned and clutched at Dylan as though any air between them was unbearable. Dylan responded in kind. The kiss deepened, becoming wild and desperate. Topher bit at Dylan's lip, making Dylan moan. Topher drew in a ragged breath at the sound and rose in the seat to press closer still. He crumpled the paper bag between them. The sound broke the moment. Dylan pulled back and ran a finger over Topher's lips, drawing in a shaky breath. Topher's eyelids fluttered and he let his head rest on the seat.

"You really broke up with her?" Dylan whispered. "For me?"

"Jules has been my best friend for years. But I didn't know what it could be like. Not until you, Dylan. There's only you."

"There's only you," Dylan agreed.

Topher smiled, dimples out, content as he started the car and took Dylan's hand. Letting go only to shift gears, they drove out of Hunter's territory and over the bridge. Soon they were out of the car, Topher kissing Dylan one more time before they pushed into a dilapidated warehouse. Birds fluttered between the rafters high above.

"Chris! Hey, buddy! And little Hunt. I wasn't expecting you." A man stepped forward, hands twitching at his sides. Dylan shuffled closer to Topher, eyeing the agitated man with distrust. The man let out a high-pitched laugh that made Dylan cringe.

"Mark, you aren't using the product, are you? Dad's already mad at you for lowballing that last haul. You don't want him to take it up with Umbras."

Mark glared at Dylan, but Topher stepped into his line of

sight with a smile. "Not that it's any of our business. We're just here to make the drop."

"Always the diffuser, huh, Christopher? That's the charm we can count on." Mark raised his voice, "I told you the kid was brimming with potential."

Confusion crossed Topher and Dylan's faces. The warehouse door slammed behind them. Topher didn't turn, only narrowed his eyes at Mark as he let Dylan check their backs. No one was there.

"What the fuck is this?" Dylan demanded.

"Language, honey," a voice said from the shadows. "Mark, you said there'd only be one boy."

A witch stepped forward, form blurry and voice distorted by warding magic blocking the Sight.

"Well, listen," Mark began. Eyes shifting, he licked his lower lip. "Dylan won't be a problem. His daddy has always fought his battles. He'll just leave. Won't say anything, will you, little Hunt?"

"You should go, Dylan," Topher whispered. He kept his eyes on Mark but stepped back enough to nudge Dylan toward the door with his shoulder.

Dylan's face set and he pulled out his gun, hands steady. "I don't know what you think you're doing, Mark. Let us leave."

"This isn't personal, guys," Mark said, carelessly raising his hands at the sight of the gun. "It's all on Hunter, driving up prices when vampires offer a better high for free and legally. This city is falling to the supernaturals. Umbras is just trying to keep up where the money is good."

The blurred witch snapped her fingers and a duffle bag flew across the room, landing at Mark's feet. He bent and checked the contents. Stacks of money. He smiled and yanked the zipper shut.

Mark backed toward the rear exit, smirking at the boys. "Like I said, it's not personal. You should have left when you had the chance, Dylan."

"Dylan, go with him," Topher sounded fearful for the first time.

"Oh, I don't think so," the witch said. Even distorted, amusement tinged her voice. "I wanted a young life. One barely lived. Full of potential to fuel the magic. You brought me an addict, Mark. That future is already too soiled. But the other one... he's just waiting to make his push in this world. And love is driving it. It's very sweet. And also, a lot to lose. *That's* potential. That's *magic*." Sick excitement edged the witch's voice.

Mark looked at the two of them for a long moment. "I am sorry, boys. If Hunter hadn't screwed us, I never would have...." He shrugged, shook his head, and turned to leave.

"Kill him," the witch said, tone chillingly bored. A dark form leaped from the shadows. Mark didn't even have time to scream before he was set upon by the demon. There was a wet, ripping sound. Blood sprayed. Then Mark was lying on his back, a gaping, bloody hole in his stomach.

Topher turned slowly, finally dismissing Mark as a threat. Dylan held the gun pointed at the witch. Topher wrapped his arms around Dylan's waist and pressed his lips to the curve of his neck.

Dylan made a whimpering noise and pressed back into Topher. He was trembling now but held the gun firm. Topher propped his chin on Dylan's shoulder and studied the witch.

"What do I need to do for you to let him go?" he asked.

"Topher," Dylan's voice was full of warning.

"Oh, you are a sweet thing, aren't you? Beautiful. It's been a long time since I've seen eyes like yours. They practically glow. You know how to work them too. Have you ever not gotten your way?"

Topher shook his head and released his grip around Dylan's waist, stepping neatly to block most of Dylan's body from her view. "I'd prefer this not be the first time." He flashed dimple, but the smile was too forced.

Topher glanced around for the demon, but it had vanished back into the shadows.

"Topher," Dylan whispered. Fear strained the word. Topher looked over his shoulder at him, ice blue eyes meeting his warm, wide brown.

"Separate them," the witch said.

The demon reappeared. Topher reached, but Dylan was whipped back. The gun fired and the witch stumbled. Topher's only concern was Dylan as he was dragged across the floor and into a summoning circle. Topher ran, but a wall of gray light erupted from the circle on the floor and became a barrier between them.

"Hold him," the witch said, gesturing toward Topher. She was panting slightly. "He'll watch and his fear will add fuel to the summoning. Really, I couldn't have planned better circumstances."

The demon let go of Dylan, passed through the circle and plowed into Topher, knocking him to the ground. He struggled against its claws, grunting and spitting and swearing. Shouting Dylan's name.

Dylan got to his feet and staggered to the wall. He pounded with both fists, but no sound escaped. The witch stalked forward, stopping only when she was directly in front of him.

Topher's struggles doubled. "Get away from him. Dylan!" His voice cracked under the force of his screams.

Topher was already sobbing by the time he saw her pull a knife.

Dylan backed away a step, but by then, his eyes were on Topher. Whatever Topher saw in his expression made him still.

"There's only you." The words didn't carry, but the meaning was evident as his lips formed the words.

"There's only you," Topher agreed.

He watched the witch enter the circle and bury her knife in Dylan's chest. Topher made a broken sound. It was the only noise in the warehouse as the boy stumbled and fell.

The shadows in the room rioted. The demon grew excited. It squirmed and clamped its jaws on Topher's shoulder. His face drained with pain, but he didn't stop staring at Dylan as the gray wall dissipated.

Dylan fought for breath and reached for Topher. His whimper finally stirred Topher to movement.

"Dylan!" Topher's scream drew the witch's attention. He scrambled to push the demon off of him. The witch approached and knelt at his side. Her blurred form reached and ran a hand down the demon's spine.

"We can't have him telling what happened here. Make sure he can't run but leave him to die. His grief will fuel the summoning too. The longer we draw it out, the heavier the spell."

The demon scurried to Topher's legs. It ripped and gnawed but Topher seemed beyond the pain, glaring at the witch. He tried to rise but cried out from the weight he put on his shoulder. The witch huffed a laugh and Topher forced himself to still. He was gasping, eyes taking on a shining quality with the pain. The demon tore into him. Topher grunted past gritted teeth but refused to scream. The witch watched.

"You weren't long for this world either way. You just aren't the type to make things last. Two beautiful lives lost, one love story cut at the quick. It's lovely and dark and delicious. It's power." The witch inhaled it deeply.

Topher looked away, back to Dylan. Somehow the boy was still conscious and watching them, blood trailing from his mouth down his cheek. One of his hands was on the knife hilt sticking out of his chest, but he didn't pull it out.

The witch stood. "I suggest you don't fight it. The end. The demons will come soon enough. Not even I want to be here when they do."

A clang sounded at the other end of the warehouse. Swearing, the witch hurried from the sound and beckoned her demon to follow. Topher didn't watch them leave. Once she and the demon were out of his path, he grunted, rolled, and began clawing his way to Dylan, legs a useless bloody mess behind him. He ignored the circle of ash that remained of the gray wall and he pulled himself to Dylan's side. Dylan tried to talk but only coughed up blood, spattering Topher's cheeks. Topher shushed him and did his best to pull Dylan close, pressing his lips anywhere he could.

"I'm here. I'm here."

The doors rattled again. Topher lifted his head to squint at those invading on his grief, arms protective around Dylan's limp form. He was shaking. Hard.

"It would appear we're a bit late to the party, Lana."

"Damn." Lana and Connor Grace approached the circle. "Wait. They're still alive."

"Barely."

"Oh, look at him, Grace."

"Don't ask."

"But he's gorgeous. Look, they're Hunter's. No one will miss him."

Grace glared at her, but the eyes he turned back to Topher were calculating. He knelt and looked closer at the ash circle.

"Let me keep him, please," Lana pressed.

Topher struggled to keep his head up. "You're vampires. Can you save him? He, he's still warm. He's breathing."

Grace answered. "No. We can't save him."

Topher's eyes dimmed. He pressed into Dylan's neck and held him tighter. Dylan's breaths ended with a wheeze.

"What did you see? Who did this?" Grace asked.

Topher didn't bother to look back up. "Save him first."

Grace's eyebrow rose in a practiced move. "Tell me what happened, and we'll save you."

"I don't want that. Save him."

"It's too late for him. Tell us what happened," Grace repeated, voice melodic with charm.

Topher met his eyes, lips pressed tight. Grace cocked his head and pushed to his feet.

"Interesting." He turned, stopping to grab Lana's arm. "Keep him. You know the move, Lana. Get me answers after he's taken care of anyone left to look for him. We were close tonight. We need answers."

Lana nodded, fangs dropping as she knelt.

"We're going to have so much fun," she whispered to Topher, words lisping with her fangs.

Topher watched her come with dead eyes. Topher turned his head to stare at Dylan as she clamped onto his throat. Dylan, who blinked one last time, fingers twitching around Topher's.

Lana began to drink.

Dylan died in Topher's arms, body stilling as the blood pooled.

"Only you," Topher whispered.

The blue of his eyes lit with a glassy shine as the bliss came over him, but he didn't smile.

CHAPTER 31

It was actually warm out. The taste of winter still hung on the end of the breeze, but the smell of spring's approach made it easy to ignore. Nora ran until the scents swirled and her breath came out in pants. She ran so long that the agitated energy that seemed to tremble her bones, threatening cracks and fissures, finally eased. Nora was losing control of her body. The animal kept slipping out. She was cocking her head more often, swallowing growls at any and every potential threat. Her attention was short, unfocused until it centered on a hunt. But she couldn't hunt. Not in the city. Not yet.

Gabriel thought her distraction was funny. "You'll be a wolf, alright. Your instincts are already strong."

He promised to find her an unclaimed lower to kill when the time came. He promised it would be fine. It was natural. Her father would be proud. She would be part of the pack. Nora agreed, voice hollow even to her own ears. She needed his protection and she could feel just how much the world would need protection from her. The more her mind refused to stabilize, the more she craved Gabriel's steady presence. He was her alpha. Only he could calm her enough to stop moving.

It was terrifying to imagine herself after the change. The thought of losing even more control was enough to raise Nora's arm hair. She didn't like the price she would pay for Gabriel's support, but the unclaimed lessers were wreaking havoc. Growing stronger, faster, and more chaotic. She'd heard Adriana ask the other day if they were sure the creatures were vampires as Luis put stitches in her arm.

The unclaimed would be killed either way. She'd have to hunt them after the change to protect her city. Wolf or not, she could do this.

Except she wasn't confident she could. Her stomach rolled at the thought of killing. Every time.

She constantly pushed Colbie's smile from her mind.

Matt had been distant since their fight. Coming home exhausted at strange hours. He wasn't the only one. The pack had been busy since the night the Maker was attacked. Gabriel said they were on a job and she'd know all the details when she was strong enough to join them. Until then, she should worry about preparing herself for the change.

And Nora was worried. She had to put complete trust in Gabriel right after Matt had shaken it to the core. Matt must have told Gabriel about their fight, like the good puppy he was. Since then, every other pack member had pulled her aside to share the story of their first kills and the nights following. Most were old enough that her father was centered in their memories of that time.

She tried to reconcile this new image of her father standing aside as his pack members killed vampires before stepping forward to subdue them and lead them on their first runs with the man who sang to her at night. It didn't fit in her scattered mind. Nora was ready to stop thinking about it. She was ready to give in and leave it to Gabriel to find her humanity later. It was exhausting. She'd been worried and conflicted and torn for too long.

She'd think about everything when she possessed the clarity of a wolf.

For now, it was time to say her goodbyes. Goodbye. Singular. Nora finally stopped, panting in front of Annaliese's mansion. She was so close to the change that she could hear the clink of glassware inside. She circled the house to the floor-to-ceiling windows of the dining room. Annalise's mother and stepfather talked to each other from both ends of the table. Annaliese sat between them, dressed in black with her black-to-blue braids twisted into a bun on top of her head. Nora took in her friend's stormy expression, the dark circles under her eyes. Annaliese's mother offered her a bowl and Annaliese shook her head, bringing a frown to her mother's face. The giggling child on her mother's right quickly claimed her attention, though.

Nora's stomach dropped when Annaliese spotted her and her scowl deepened. She asked to be dismissed and rose from the table with her plate without waiting for a response.

Nora continued to the back of the house and waited outside the kitchen door. Annaliese joined her quickly. Her friend smelled overwhelmingly human after the days Nora had spent surrounded only by the pack. Nora followed her human friend as she stomped across the yard without a greeting. Annaliese stopped when she reached the edge of the river, deep in the cover of trees. Nora tracked the movement of a squirrel running up one of the trunks and turned her attention back to her friend with some effort.

"You came by the Den," Nora said.

Annaliese knelt at the water's edge, hugging her knees to her chest. She looked younger, even smaller, in that position. Nora crinkled her nose as she sat down beside her. Annaliese smelled a bit like Josh and his packmates. Territorial anger flared.

"You didn't return any of my calls. Do you even know what's been going on? Colbie—"

"Annaliese, I'm not here to talk about vampires."

"You know, Poppy found a way to look back? I saw the night Topher changed her. Lana changed him and told him to go home while he was starved and scared out his mind. He did. He couldn't stop himself from attacking Colbie, but he—"

"Annaliese, stop. I don't care about them."

"You can't live your life hunting vampires for the sake of hunting vampires, Nor. Topher, Zayn, and Colbie are mis—"

"Annaliese! My change is tomorrow night. I have to focus on that, not some vampire."

Annaliese rested her cheek on her knee as she looked at Nora. "The change already happened. You cut me out. You promised you wouldn't and you did."

Nora fiddled with her shoelaces, untying and retying the bow. "It's only natural. It had to happen. Humans aren't friends with wolves."

"Bullshit. Josh has no problem with it."

"Humans aren't friends with wolves," Nora repeated. She could hear the echo of Adriana in her voice. "But dogs are. Josh's pack isn't the same as mine. They don't know this city like we do. They aren't here to make the difference my father wanted."

"So, you don't care?"

"Of course I care about you, Annaliese. I will until the moment I change."

Annaliese's eyebrows drew together. "Do you even know?"

"Know what?"

"Where Colbie is?"

Nora forced herself not to freeze. She breathed through the effect those words had on her. It wasn't her business. But her hands remembered smooth, cold skin. Her lips remembered the tingling warmth of bliss-inducing kisses they shouldn't have played a role in. The dip of a waist under her palms. The rhythm of a scentless body pressed close, dancing against hers. Nora tipped her head back to look at the sky. She knew the moon was coming, but it felt as far away as a pair of blue eyes and a wicked smile that stilled every thought.

"I don't want to talk about the vampires."

"But Nora! They're—"

"I came to say goodbye."

Annaliese's mouth shut with a snap. Her lips pursed as she looked back across the water.

Finally, she spoke. "You're leaving me. You're leaving like everyone else. You're promises meant as little as theirs." Annaliese wouldn't look at her.

"Annaliese, it's for the best. We can all taste the war that's coming. You can't get caught up in it."

"I already am. And I know my side. I hope you enjoy yours."

Annaliese rose and left Nora sitting there. The stupid, foolish human with her weak body and stubborn mind. Nora would do what it took to keep her safe, to keep her separate from this, but her blood chilled knowing Annaliese almost certainly wouldn't accept the help. Maybe the vampires she loved so much now could keep her safe. Nora balled her fists.

Their friendship wouldn't survive this. Nora remembered the last words her mother had stated, completely detached, voice flat. She'd looked at Nora, her father's blood still streaked over her cheeks.

"Nothing lasts," Nora repeated the words to the river now. Her voice was lost to its muted roar and swept away. Nora let her thoughts go with it. Annaliese gone. Matt's trust, gone. The human life she'd clung to, gone.

Red lips. Bright eyes. Late-night phone calls. A smile that refused to dim. A laugh that stirred Nora's blood. Hands that moved, so sure and sweet and right and good. The sound of her name spoken in Colbie's voice. Curves and weight and jagged edges and the light that surrounded every moment together.

"Gone." Nora's voice broke on the word. She stood slowly

and followed the river until she couldn't pick out Annaliese's scent any longer.

Nora went home. She climbed the stairs slowly and showered off any trace of Annaliese. But she didn't continue to her attic bedroom. She went down the hall to the room she hadn't been able to approach since her parents died and left her. Gone.

She knocked. Gabriel answered. She was so close to the change she basked in the power rolling off him. Alpha. Protector. Leader. Her heart began to pound, remembering their last conversation. She would be his second. His unmatched eyes had been steady when he'd made the promise.

She would be so strong.

She made her own promises the night before. She would be his. It was her destiny. Who she was born to be. She would prove Matt wrong. Prove to herself she could have everything she'd dreamed. She would have the power her parents shared. She would take her mother's place in this pack her father built. She'd loved them all her life and now she would truly join them.

He smiled when he saw her, only one side of his mouth lifting. He leaned against the doorjamb and tilted his head to look at her, the full force of his eyes sweeping through her.

"We found another unclaimed lower. We captured it easily. Tomorrow night, when it's time, we'll shut you in a room with it, and that will be that. You likely won't even remember it. Then we'll run together, Nor."

Nora nodded and waited. Gabriel's smile broadened, the other half of his mouth gradually lifting. At the look in her eyes, his voice dropped. "We have all the time in the world for this after your change."

Nora didn't move. She held his gaze steady. Gabriel's eyes flicked up, glancing down the hall before he pushed off the doorway and stepped closer. His scent, burning like cinnamon bark, rose her hair. The energy in her bones gave a lurching throb. She closed the space between them. The taste of his power, his position, his familiarity, his promise, was just what she needed. Nora needed it to be what she needed. She made herself step closer still.

"I just have to be here. I can hardly think when I'm not here."

Gabriel nodded. He stepped to the side and she walked inside. He shut the bedroom door behind them.

"You know? Zayn and I hated him for weeks when he first showed up," Oliver said. "He always looked away when we kissed. Like it hurt him to see it. We thought he was homophobic. It wasn't until we saw him flirting with Brady that we decided he was worth befriending. I can't believe he never said anything."

Oliver shook his head and let it drop into his folded arms. He looked completely frayed.

Poppy nodded. It had been two days since they watched the impression on Topher's sweatshirt. Three nights and none of the vampires came home. Oliver hadn't left Colbie's bed more than a few times, the last place he'd been with Zayn. Poppy had stopped trying to make him eat. Instead, she brewed potions to sustain him. He'd already lost too much weight. The memory of Dylan's death haunted every conversation about the vampires' disappearance.

They'd received the one text from Colbie's phone.

Hey, we're looking into the fire. Might take a few nights. Don't worry.

Don't worry. The words she'd repeated over and over the night Topher was taken. It meant they should worry. Poppy tried everything to track them down, her and Ru combining their strength. Nothing came of it. Just like Topher's first disappearance.

Annaliese checked the Den but couldn't find anything.

They wouldn't let her in and Nora refused to come out and talk. Annaliese said the basement was empty this time, but Poppy knew the pack could be hiding the vampires anywhere.

Henry's pack was scouring the streets, but there wasn't a scent left to follow. Attempting to shadow members of Nora's pack hadn't turned up anything. They moved too cautiously and more than once caught the members of Henry's pack. The vampires questioned claimed Lana and her lowers never approached them after the Maker burned. None of them cared where she was either way. All that mattered was there hadn't been an unclaimed since she vanished. Even Grace was quiet. Henry hadn't even gotten a meeting with him.

Hoping it might connect with their disappearance, Poppy and Josh threw themselves into the search for unclaimed lowers and the demons. This led nowhere. The city was abruptly quieter than it had been in months. Not even the college students were around. Spring break had cleared them all away.

Three knocks sounded on the door. Annaliese and Josh had come in and out so often Poppy knew who it was just by the pattern of the quick rapping. With a snap, she opened the door and the wards welcomed Annaliese with ease.

"Nora came by my house last night. I don't think she knows about Colbie. She's just obsessed with her change."

"It's easy to get like that the first time," Josh said. He was halfway through a pint of ice cream. Poppy and Ru hadn't eaten nearly as much of their own flavors. The one he brought for Oliver was melting. Poppy sighed, snapped, and refroze it. The effort made her head light. Oliver didn't even notice.

"In other news." Annaliese put her phone on the island in front of Poppy. She stared at the screen, disbelieving.

Josh leaned and read upside down. He glanced quickly at Oliver and shoveled another bite of ice cream into his mouth.

"What is it?" Ru asked. Poppy shook her head, but Oliver finally looked up. His face paled, assuming the worst.

"It's not Zayn," she was quick to assure him.

"Then what?" Ru asked. She got off the couch and joined them at the kitchen island.

Annaliese answered. "Connor Grace's club has changed hands. A new vampire runs it now."

"Who?"

"One of his other seconds, probably," Poppy answered. "But not Lana."

Oliver's forehead furrowed. "Grace would never give up his club. And Lana would never let one of the others run it over her… Whoever has Zayn, Topher, and Colbie must have them too." Oliver swallowed and gripped the edge of the counter, breathing hard. "If they're strong enough to take down Grace—"

"We're not going to jump to conclusions until we know more." Josh's words fell on deaf ears. Oliver's horrified expression didn't falter.

"It's been three days," he gasped. "Three days they were asleep and vulnerable. Probably starving. Whoever did it burned down the Maker. They killed everyone there. If it's the wolves—"

Oliver's breathing turned so erratic Poppy ran to her room for a calming potion. The others watched in silence as Oliver tried to refuse it and Poppy coaxed him to take the bottle. Finally swallowing its contents, Oliver dropped his head. He drew ragged breaths and occasionally shuddered as the potion took hold.

"I don't understand why they'd attack Grace," Annaliese said, gently directing their focus off Oliver while he caught his breath.

"Maybe he *is* the one behind the lowers," Ru said.

"But they didn't know what had happened to Topher when they got to the warehouse. He didn't even want Lana to change him," Josh said. It was an argument they'd repeated often. The words were stale and tired.

"Maybe we should check the warehouse again."

"There was nothing to find. Whoever made the circle got rid of everything."

They'd found the warehouse number from a newspaper article yesterday. The warehouse floor was cleaned of everything but Mark and Dylan's bodies by the time the cops had shown up. Now nothing remained. Poppy and Ru could have used the remnants of the witch's circle to find out who lit it, but she'd carefully gotten rid of all the ash. Not even Dylan's spirit remained to give them answers. Ru had valiantly chanted inside her ring of candles for half an hour before they'd been forced to give up. Dylan had been too strong to let the violence of his death trap him on this side.

Poppy rubbed her temples. She stared sightlessly at the wall, watching the scene unfold in her mind again. Watching the horror that was the night Topher was turned. She could practically hear him dragging himself to Dylan's body, legs bleeding, mangled and useless behind him. Pulling himself to Dylan.

Poppy stood so quickly that she knocked her stool to the floor. She impatiently snapped to right it.

"What is it?" Annaliese asked.

"Topher pulled himself through the ash," Poppy practically yelled. Ru gasped, eyes widening with understanding.

Poppy ran into Topher's room. The sweatshirt was still on the floor. No one had touched it since it had given them all the information it could provide, ending with Topher attacking Colbie and Annaliese breaking the circle when she'd cringed away from the sight. Poppy carefully knelt next to it. She fingered the soft material, her heart squeezing. This was the only piece of Topher's past he'd brought into their apartment besides Colbie. Not even Julia had been allowed to stay.

The dark smudge of ash was so mixed in the blood stains that Poppy almost missed it. She concentrated, hovered her hand over the area, and separated the ash from the fabric.

She held the particles in the air between her hands as she walked back to the kitchen. Ru opened an empty vial for her and Poppy directed the cloud of ash inside. She started to brew.

By the time Poppy finished, Oliver was sleeping fitfully on the couch and the others watched TV with empty eyes. The potion was sludgy, gray like the wall in the memory. It glowed faintly as Poppy poured it into a mug.

Ru wrinkled her nose at the chunky consistency. "Are you really going to drink that?" she asked.

It was a complicated, disgusting brew, but Poppy had used her own blood. She was the only one it would work for.

If it worked at all.

"Yes. Wish me luck?" Her eyes went to Josh when she said the words. He nodded slowly, gaze more serious than ever. He still had chocolate from his ice cream on the corner of his lips. The sight made her want to smile. She'd assured them all the potion wasn't dangerous.

Josh had been the only one who could tell Poppy was lying.

Poppy closed her eyes, ignored the instinct to blow on the liquid in her mug (it only worked hot) and downed it in one burning gulp. She didn't even have time to gag at the taste before she left her own mind.

Her consciousnesses slammed into the witch's and if Poppy could hold her breath, she would have. She focused on trying to keep herself small. If the witch felt her presence, she could kill Poppy off effortlessly. Her consciousness was helpless in another person's skull. It was tricky, risky magic breaking through a witch's wards.

Slowly, she grew aware of her surroundings, taking in what the witch saw. Nothing attacked her mind, leaving her to hope she'd done at least this part of the brew right. Now she just had to wait for something to give the witch's identity away. A pass in front of a mirror. Someone saying her name. Anything. The sooner, the better.

But she didn't expect the answer to come so quickly. The witch was in a dark room, pacing, muttering.

"Would you sit down?" someone asked, their voice weak as if old age had sanded it down. The witch ignored them. "You're making me tired just watching you."

Poppy realized it was a man speaking. The witch cut a glare at him and he raised his hands in surrender. Disappointment knifed when Poppy didn't recognize him. But then his image flickered. Poppy realized she was looking at a ghost through the witch's eyes. She'd never been able to see a ghost before. Her gift of Sight was too weak.

"Oh, because you're helping so much?" the witch demanded.

"It's not my fault! They're all warded too well. We both know whose fault that is."

The witch snorted. Poppy's thoughts slowed as her brain rejected the answer she knew was coming. She refused to put it together. But the room was familiar. The witch's voice was familiar.

"What about Ru? She left Jane's wards. She's too young. She doesn't know how to make new ones and hold them."

"I told you. I found her, had my way blocked by those horrid demons, and now she's under someone else's wards."

"Who?"

The ghost shrugged.

"Someone needs to warn them. The ceremonies didn't work. We need to stop—"

"I know, I know," the ghost sounded bored. "Oh, don't look at me like that. We both want what's best for them."

"You don't know what you want," the witch scoffed. She approached the small bar to the side of the room, stretching out a hand toward the wine bottle and giving Poppy a clear view of the ring on the woman's middle finger. The Tree of Life was engraved there.

The same image was tattooed at the base of Poppy's neck when she turned fifteen. The Jennings family crest.

The vision cleared as Poppy returned abruptly to her own mind. Josh was holding her up, an arm around her waist. Ru was in front of her, crying. Poppy didn't have time to worry about what her body had done in her absence.

"It was Mom," Poppy whispered, just before the worst of the potion's side effects hit and she blacked out.

Poppy woke slowly. She was in her bed, hand fisted in the fur of the large form sleeping next to her. Josh. Mouse's small body pressed warmth into her other side. The little guy was slowly learning not to fear the wolves.

Poppy released her grip on Josh's scruff. His ears flicked as he woke up.

"It's too dangerous to keep involving them," Poppy whispered, voice hoarse from sleep and the potion. "Ru's only sixteen. Oliver and Annaliese are human." Josh pressed his nose into Poppy's arm. She took that as agreement. She hoped Josh couldn't hear her heart pounding, but it wasn't likely. "If we go somewhere, I can let down my wards. I can let her find me. We can capture her, make her tell us why she summoned the demons to New Brecken. Why she killed Dylan and if she knows where Topher and Colbie are. If any witch knows how to track a vampire, it would be my mother."

Josh blew out a huff of air. He studied Poppy's face intently, so much humanity in his stare. Finally, he gave her arm a quick, dry lick and got off the bed. Poppy closed her eyes when he shuffled his paws awkwardly. She heard a sound like joints popping when he shifted and rustling as he pulled on his clothes.

"I'm covered," he said, taking a seat on the edge of her bed. "Annaliese fell asleep on the couch. Oliver is awake in Colbie's room, but Ru is in there watching a show with him. If something happens, will they be okay here?"

Poppy nodded. "I've been teaching Ru to read and weave into my wards. If my magic dies, she should be able to hold them."

"Oh, that's not exactly... I mean, let's try not to let that happen."

"I'd appreciate that."

They slipped out of the apartment, Poppy masking the sound of their steps and the door with magic. It was twilight now, so her abilities were sluggish, but she drank a daylight brew to boost her magic. The magnesium she'd mixed in gave it an extra kick and she pulled up her hood to hide how she glowed. The bag at her hip tinkled with the potion vials she carried.

Josh called his alpha and told him the situation as Poppy drove. She cringed when he explained who Poppy was. It was hard letting go of her secret. But she pushed her mother's cautions from her mind. Hers was the last voice Poppy wanted inside her head.

"Josh?"

"Yeah, Poppy?"

"I just wanted to apologize. And say thank you for, you know, sticking around."

Josh silently watched the road so long that Poppy felt like squirming.

"I don't know how you, Colbie, and Topher managed to create your little bubble in that apartment. How you all came together or really why, but I hope you understand the bubble has popped."

"What do you mean?" Poppy was almost afraid to know where he was going with this.

"We'll do this and my pack will have your back. But they're my pack, Poppy. They're my family. It'd be really shitty if we did this for you and you dropped away into hiding again. We'll stick our necks out and hopefully, one day, you'll stick out yours. I'm not saying we wouldn't do this for free, but if supernaturals are going to figure out how to live together, that means the good ones need to have each other's backs."

"I don't know if I *am* a good one. My mom raised us to take care of ourselves. When she disappeared, the Jennings coven just crumbled. I was honestly surprised to learn Jane took Ru in." Poppy sighed. "It was just us. My sisters and mother were the only people I knew. We didn't go to school. I only dealt with humans who sold the materials I needed for my potions, most of which were on the black market. But our mother taught us that one day she wouldn't be there to lead us. We would have to create our own covens. We couldn't be loyal to each other forever."

"That sounds lonely."

Poppy shrugged.

Josh's next words came out in a rush. "It also sounds like Topher is the first good guy you've gotten to know."

Poppy's hands tightened on the wheel. "So?"

"So I don't think he's ready for you. Not after what we saw. And I don't think you're ready for him, which is why you haven't made a move. I think Topher and Colbie are your first friends and you've fallen in love with your life with them as much as you've fallen in love with them. Him." Josh pulled in a deep breath. "I think if you gave other people a chance, you might love them too."

Poppy went quiet. Her face heated with anger at his words. To suggest she only felt the way she did because Topher was the first boy she'd gotten to know… She couldn't even explain why it bothered her so much.

Josh waited for her response. When it didn't come, he sighed. "I'm just asking you to give me a chance, not even for *more*, but just, like, let me in your bubble." The defeat in his voice drained a portion of her rage.

"Why?" Poppy winced at the harsh question, but Josh didn't blink.

"Because Topher's hurting. That doesn't mean you have to suffer with him."

"He needs me."

"He needs a friend. That's all he's asked for. I've seen him flirt, Poppy. It's hollow and practiced compared to what we saw in the impression. Maybe it's convincing to the right people, but I think he just uses it for a release. For a taste of the familiar, just like his smoking and the soccer games. He isn't ready for more." Josh's voice gentled further, "And either way, he doesn't flirt with you."

Poppy wanted so badly to hold her anger. But when tears caught in her throat, she knew it was because Josh was telling the truth. All those times Colbie never encouraged her. All the forehead kisses Topher gave her and then Colbie. All of it was deeper than the flirting smiles Topher gave Josh, even the looks he'd sent to other vampires. She'd even seen Topher brush his fingers down Tamera's spine and dismissed it. What Topher gave her meant more.

So why did she so badly want the less? Why did she long for hollow, flirty smiles? Why did it feel like her chest was being crushed as she admitted to herself that Topher loved her? Why should it hurt to know he'd opened himself up to her after all the tragedy of his past? That he loved her but couldn't be in love with her?

Wasn't what she had better?

Josh was silent as Poppy sniffled and drove. Maybe it was so much harder now because he was in danger. Maybe it was harder now because she missed him and Colbie so badly.

But Poppy knew it was harder at this moment because she'd seen a glimpse of Topher in love. It wasn't the easy way he'd reached for Julia, the kisses he's pressed into her neck. Poppy had wanted that, longed for it when she thought that was the extent of Topher's love. When she thought that was what he was capable of as a partner.

Yet that was nothing compared to the way Topher had

watched Dylan. Dylan had been a single, burning torch lighting Topher's world. Anyone could see it in Topher's eyes. And that light had been extinguished.

Poppy wanted *that*. To be that to him. Now she had seen what he was capable of, the depth of his feeling, and she longed for it even more. She wanted him to brighten again because of her.

And she knew she'd never get it. Never even get a hint. Topher had already given her everything he was able to. He was too tired for more. Even Josh could see that.

Poppy felt foolish for ever even hoping, but Josh was quiet. The energy rolling off him wasn't even one of pity. When they reached the warehouse where he and his pack were living and Poppy turned the car off, they sat together until her breathing steadied.

Poppy finally nodded. "Okay."

"Okay?"

Poppy wiped her eyes one last time. "Okay. Let's go talk to my mom."

CHAPTER 32

Nora was sweating. The trickles of it itched her too smooth skin. She could feel her cheeks burning. Practically hear the blood that pulsed to them. Her nerve endings buzzed. Her muscles twitched. She kept compulsively rubbing her arms, expecting the tingling there to have given way to fur already.

She fought the urge to growl as Gabriel drove too slowly. He glanced her way and the compulsion in his unmatched eyes was nearly as strong a force as the moon at the brink of rising. She settled back into her seat. He would help her. He wouldn't let her succumb to the beast. She waited with breathless anticipation for him to tell her so. He looked back to the road, the corner of his mouth drawing up into a smile. She knew what he was feeling. Gabriel liked the power. She wanted it. It was so close for her. She let out a keening whine and Matt leaned forward in the backseat to press steadying hands on her shoulders. She was distantly surprised by the gesture.

"Soon, Nor," he whispered.

Nora remembered how he cringed when he smelled Gabriel on her and her on Gabriel. The image vanished when a smell from outside caught her attention. Nora turned her face into the breeze, panting a bit. Her lungs moved air too quickly. Her ribs felt strange. The pain in her broken one had been gone when she woke up this morning.

"Where are we going?" Her voice didn't sound right. She didn't sound human. Nora trembled slightly. Control was spinning away. She loved the power. Hated not being able to tame it. Matt's grip tightened. Everything she understood about herself and her body was crumbling. She wished Gabriel would look at her again.

"To the northside warehouses. There's a basement in one strong enough to hold a vampire. Hunter made it."

"Hunter?"

"A human. We've been working with him to find the unclaimed. They started showing up in his territory at the beginning. His son was killed by one."

Nora swallowed. It took her a second to realize what Gabriel was doing. Letting her in on a pack secret. Treating her like a member of the pack. "Tell me more."

"Hunter thinks Grace is behind the attacks. Christopher was with his son. They turned him but left his son to die. Christopher might have even been the one to kill him when he was turned. Hunter wants revenge. We're trying to help him get it. *You're* going to help him get it once you make the change."

Nora nodded under the force of the command. "Was that why you kidnapped him?"

"We needed answers, but if we wanted true revenge, we would have kidnapped Lana or Grace."

"I don't think Topher had anything to do with it."

Gabriel and Matt stiffened, Matt's hands tightening on her shoulders. Nora realized belatedly she'd used Topher's nickname. She'd let something vital slip. But another scent caught her attention and she lunged for the window, forgetting the conversation. Gabriel grabbed her arm before she could even stick her head out. Matt pressed her firmly back into the seat.

Nora's groan turned into a high keening. She hated the pathetic sound but couldn't stop it.

Gabriel took hold of her hand and Nora told herself she could trust him. Follow him. Maybe even love him. Her heart gave a pang at the thought. She wanted it to be right. It wasn't yet, but maybe, when the moon claimed her, when he claimed her as her alpha...

They parked behind a warehouse. The river's smell rolled at Nora, musting the air unpleasantly. The dense humidity caught at her hair. She could hear the strands rising into a frizz.

She followed Gabriel, her bones and joints protesting at being so confined. Her skin too tight. The moon was almost here. She was breathless with anticipation. She needed to run. Fear clawed at her throat when she stumbled. The clumsiness had been horrible today. She kept fighting the urge to lurch forward. Drop onto her hands too.

Gabriel opened a creaking door and she cringed from the high sound. Inside, the warehouse was empty save for humans standing around with guns. They nodded at Gabriel as they passed and entered the office. As Gabriel promised, there was a set of narrow stairs to a basement room. The lights slammed on to illuminate the metal steps and huge, windowless, barred shut door at the bottom.

"Hunter kept product here back in his prime. No one's breaking down that door, not even a vampire. Hopefully, not even you after you shift, but I'll be just outside if you need me."

"What product?"

Gabriel didn't answer. They stopped in front of the door. Nora already could hardly remember how they'd gotten here. She felt drunk. The moon's pull was tugging at her skin. It rippled like a wave. She shuddered at the sight, but Gabriel smiled down at her. He'd been smiling so much today.

The lower was just on the other side, as wild and uncontrolled as she would be without Gabriel's guidance. But unlike her, the lower thirsted only for human blood. The hair on the back of Nora's neck rose. Instinct urged her inside. She could do this. Protect the humans and keep the balance.

"We let you wait until the last possible minute. Now, you'll make your kill whether you truly want to or not. You won't be able to help yourself."

Nora dragged her eyes from the doorway, confusion blurring her thoughts at the shift in Gabriel's tone.

"Don't worry, you won't have any memory of it," Matt spoke more gently. "The first change you lose too much control. Hardly anyone remembers the details. Just know this will all be over quickly."

Someone started to growl. Nora cut off the sound when she realized it was her. It was no use, though. Something was off. Gabriel wasn't smiling anymore, but he was smug. The rumble in her chest built up again.

"You'll do this for us. Then I'll go in and calm you," Gabriel said, unconcerned by the sound rumbling in Nora's throat. "I'll get you to the forest. Just like I promised. For now, you need to give in to the wolf. They'll be weak and hungry, but they'll try to fight back. They're too strong for us to risk ourselves. The first change will give you the strength you need. Nothing compares to the power of a first change. Don't fight your instincts. You won't be able to hold back. And then you'll be one of us. Nora," her name jolted through her, "your father would be so proud."

Nora needed to trust her alpha, but the damning doubt she'd had for the last week filled her mind full force.

Gabriel pulled back the huge deadbolt. He opened the heavy metal door. It smelled dead inside, making Nora's nose crinkle. She had a memory of fighting demons. She didn't want to go in. The moon was bright outside. She could feel it. She longed to run beneath it. To leave the smell of humans behind and dive into the nearby forest. She wanted to howl at the sky, Gabriel at her side. Guiding her. She didn't want to be alone. She whined.

"Go in," the command in Gabriel's voice forced her forward. She swallowed her whine. It was almost over.

Her eyes adjusted to the dark room. She was facing Colbie. Horror washed over every other thought.

"Fuck," Topher gasped to her left.

Nora recoiled as the moon finally claimed her. "Colbie," she got the whisper out just before she lost her human mind.

Power finally came.

Josh's pack had all made the change by the time Poppy finished setting up her ceremony. She didn't have the ease of Sight like Ru, but she thought she could summon a ghost with the proper preparation and a full moon. Josh promised to hold off his shift as long as he could and sat shirtless just outside the circle Poppy drew on the floor. He twitched restlessly, but his gaze held her steady when she looked up.

"So what happens?" he asked.

Poppy wiped her sweaty palms on her leggings. The black material was dusty from the chalk.

"I drop my wards and the ghost my mother was talking to should find me. The demons will come too. They're drawn to the life of our magic. They can sniff it out from miles away without wards. When Ru left the wards, the demons attacked her before the ghost could reach her, so I'll call him here. Hopefully, he can beat the demons and we can talk so I can get my wards back up quickly."

"We can take care of a few demons."

"I don't know how many there are now. It could be a lot more than a few."

"Trust us, Poppy."

Poppy nodded, but her heart was racing. Josh's alpha,

Henry, sat nearby, tail thumping occasionally. She kept glancing at him for assurance and his gaze never wavered.

Since the day her mother taught her to hold them, Poppy had never purposefully dropped her personal wards. It was instinctual now to keep them in place no matter what, even in her sleep. Without wards, any witch could use the Sight to track her location. Anyone could use magic on her. She wiped her palms again.

"Let them find me," Poppy bid the magic. The air around her rippled with blue as her protection fell. Poppy felt vulnerable and naked, but she pressed on.

Kneeling, she lit the candle at the edge of her circle and sat opposite. "Bring the ghost I seek." Her magic would know the one she referred to; he was still so fresh in her memory. Nothing happened. "Bring the ghost I seek."

As Poppy chanted, her mind flexed like using a muscle rarely exercised. The effort started to strain at her temples. Poppy continued her chant. She heard a commotion as the first demon attacked but didn't look up from the candle flame before her, drawing from its warmth to appeal to the ghost.

A window shattered. Snarling. Ripping. A yelp. Poppy's voice shook, but she pressed on. From her periphery, she saw when Josh swiftly changed and lunged.

The temperature dropped.

"Well, I wasn't expecting you to call," the ghost said. He sat cross-legged in front of her, mirroring her posture only an inch from the ground with the candle lit between them. He was faded but looked to be in his forties. His hair dark, his form bulky. The flame had shrunk to a small sphere perched on the tip of the blackened wick.

"Where is my mother?"

"Give me your blood and she'll find you when your wards go back up."

"Why is she murdering people?" Poppy focused on holding the ghost in place. She couldn't look around, not even when a wolf to her right let out a howl that was cut off quickly. Please, don't be Josh.

"The longer you wait to agree, the longer this attack lasts."

"You could use my blood for your own gain." A witch's blood freely given was a powerful thing. Poppy didn't even know all the uses.

"I have no desire to become corporal. I would have done so by now if I did."

"Why should I trust you?"

He waited. Poppy glared at him. His blurry face shifted enough that she could tell he smiled. "Oh, Poppy. You look just like your grandmother. None of the others quite got the chin. That hair."

"How do you know my grandmother?"

"I fathered some of her daughters. In fact, I may have fathered your mother. Didn't realize at the time what I was being used for. Just a means to an end—a way to create a coven. But I tasted the magic and have stayed close ever since. My life force is too intertwined with your family's."

More thuds and crashes. The air was thick with the sulfuric smell of demon blood. The energy the wolves used to fight was making her dizzy.

Poppy's thoughts scrambled to keep up with the information. The ghost, her grandfather, was smiling now. "Just like your mother. You don't care who falls on your way to answers. The truth means power. I think she'll be happy you were the one to find us."

"Probably not." Poppy was running out of time, that much was obvious. Even the ghost was fading. She couldn't hold it. "I need aids for strong magic, always have, and she never appreciated brewing. But I will give you my blood if you give her this."

Poppy took out a knife and a vial filled with a milky blue liquid from her bag. The ghost was already nodding. With a quick breath and a murmured spell, Poppy sliced her palm.

She rolled the small container in the blood and held it over the candle. The ghost's hand looked nearly solid, like marble, when he grabbed it. Poppy blew out the tiny flame and he vanished.

Without pausing to examine the chaos of the room, Poppy pulled another potion from her pocket. The glass was warm, maintaining the heat from the brew. She'd altered the proportions and prayed to the Mother it was strong enough now. She closed her eyes, reset her personal wards, and threw the vial at the ceiling. Bottled sunlight flashed bright when the vial shattered against the rafters. A sudden, shocked silence filled the space as the demons ashed immediately.

Without pausing, Poppy scuffed and broke her chalk circle before running to the nearest entrance. The wolves parted for her as she slammed the door shut, a demon thudding against the outside. Those outside that her potion hadn't killed were still coming. Poppy slapped her bloodied palm to the door and extended her wards.

"Hold them back. Make it strong. The demons aren't welcome. Protect this place. Hold them back. Make it strong."

The walls of the warehouse drew from her power. Her blood was tugged out of her palm as the magic strengthened and took effect. Pain spread, acting as a dual sacrifice. Her wrist throbbed and the fire spread to her forearm. Her life energy sparked and glowed dully in the spreading blood. Josh came to her side. With a grateful look, Poppy wound her free hand in his fur and borrowed from his energy. The strength the moon gave him was an endless well of power.

A flood light in the ceiling shattered before her magic could reach the top of the building, but the wolves were quick to kill the invader. Her magic finished its seal. The walls glowed briefly and settled. Poppy gasped at the last throb of pain in her shoulder and cradled her arm to her stomach as she slid down the wall and sat heavily on the floor.

Josh nudged her with his wet nose. Poppy realized her eyes

had closed. She forced them open and met Josh's questioning gaze.

"She should come soon," she whispered. "Once she opens the vial."

Poppy looked to the second summoning circle she had created. Still undisturbed after the fight, it was made of the same blue brew as was in the vial, only in chalk form. With Poppy's blood, her mother could find her anywhere, even with her wards back in place. Poppy could only hope her mother's curiosity would be enough to make her open the potion first.

Poppy waited with bated breath among the wolves. A quick check showed none were too seriously injured. Daniel, distinguished by the white marking down his chest, was limping, but all the others licked only minor wounds.

Josh remained at Poppy's side while she stood and walked to the edge of the second circle. Henry was behind her, easy to spot by the jagged scar over his eye. His second occasionally growled at his right. Quinn hadn't liked this plan from the start. Poppy couldn't blame her. She had no idea what to expect from her mother.

Poppy sighed in relief when the ring flashed blue. Her potion had been opened. "Thank the Mother."

Light blue mist filled the circle, the same fog that had poured out of the vial when her mother broke its seal and the liquid touched air. The potion would transport her mother inside its chalk equivalent and trap her inside. It was an advanced brew. One she found in the attic of their old home in a dusty potions book her mother had probably never opened. Poppy allowed herself the tiniest smile. Any good brewer would have been suspicious of that particular shade of blue liquid in the vial.

Tiff Jennings appeared, coughing, and swatting the mist. When she saw Poppy, she looked at her empty hand. The glass vial didn't travel with her. Neither did the blood coating it that would have given her mother an advantage over Poppy's magic. Seeing that, Poppy's shoulders finally relaxed. Her small spell had worked.

"Mother."

"Penelope. What an interesting brew. I should have known it was you filling my head earlier." It was jarring to hear her full name in her mother's voice after all this time. Though, even hearing someone call her Poppy was dimly surprising after living with the West siblings for so long. She'd grown so accustomed to answering to the names of food products.

"Where are the demons coming from?" she asked.

"You know where demons come from, Penelope. How many times do I need to tell you the importance of not wasting words? Although, I suppose that never truly was a concern for you. You prefer the speechless magic forms." Tiff eyed the circle holding her with distaste.

"Why are you summoning demons?"

"To kill those bloodthirsty creatures. Someone has to protect this city and it won't be Kallow." Tiff spat out the other witch's name. She glared at the pack beyond Poppy. "Nor the dogs."

"That's your excuse for using sorcery?"

Poppy's mother curled her lip at the thought. "My magic changed when it brushed the demons, but I would never consume their essence. I am no sorcerer."

Poppy made a sound of disbelief. "What does this have to do with the unclaimed vampires?"

Tiff walked closer, testing the circle's boundary. It held.

"Sacrifices had to be made to stop them."

The image of Dylan with a knife in his chest filled Poppy's mind. Her hands clenched at her sides, shooting pain up from the slice in her palm. "I saw you murder a boy. I saw you kill him so you could summon demons. Why should I believe anything you say?"

Tiff sighed. As if Poppy was inconveniencing her. Poppy saw red. "Yes, I killed the boy. I misjudged how much he would be missed. He summoned even fewer demons than the old woman I killed before him. Don't give me that look. I summoned the demons because they are the only ones strong enough to kill those creatures. I set them on our city to keep it safe. I began with what sacrifices I could. I killed the boy. One life, one love, one future filled with potential was the cost I paid. But the creatures kept appearing. I needed more time. I have to find whoever is responsible."

"How many have you killed?" Poppy whispered.

"The question is how many of those creatures my demons have killed. Our magic is nothing without life. The question, Penelope, is how many I have saved?"

Zayn was the last one to wake. The days without feeding had been hardest on him. Tonight, even Grace woke with a brow furrowed in pain.

Colbie rubbed her throat. "How do you do this so often?"

Topher shrugged. Colbie groaned as she stood and stretched, swaying a bit with her arms above her head. Grace's frown deepened. He hadn't taken to Topher's outspoken sister and Topher was quick to step between them. He and Grace had butt heads more in the last couple of nights than ever before, but their snarls always fell off when laughter sounded outside the door. Especially after one of the wolves outside happily declared they were going to kill each other off and save them the effort.

Lana had been a surprisingly neutral force. The loss of the Maker had quieted her. She kept her focus on what was important. She was quick to redirect Grace's attention away from Colbie and worked more than anyone to think of a way out.

Topher didn't see the point of trying to make plans. He was just happy she'd gone three nights without goading him. Colbie probably wouldn't have stood for that. Topher vaguely wondered how much effort it would take to hold one of the makers under his charm. Boredom tempted him to try it, but he knew how important it was to conserve his energy.

Zayn rubbed a hand over his face as he sat up. Topher had been careful to keep him and Colbie near the back wall and behind him. He was painfully aware the door could open at any moment. They were only growing weaker.

Colbie stepped forward and sat beside him, resting her head on his shoulder. Grace rolled his eyes.

"You think they're just waiting for us to starve to death?"

"I think they would have killed us by now if they just wanted us to die."

"The waiting alone is killing me," Colbie said. "This is such bullshit."

Grace bristled. Colbie had noticed the older man didn't like her swearing within the first hour. Her language had never been fouler than the last three nights.

"This sucks," Zayn agreed.

"Pick a different word. I'm too hungry," Colbie said. Topher let himself smile and rested his cheek on his sister's head. Her hair tie had broken yesterday, provoking a truly impressive hour of cursing that had Grace looking ready to lunge for her throat and the guard outside the door shuffling their feet.

Clanging on the steps outside alerted them to the guards changing, but when more than one set of footsteps started down, Topher and Colbie got to their feet. Topher stepped forward, angling himself between Colbie and the door. Zayn came to his side, hand going to the small of Topher's back to let him know he was there.

"It's that alpha," Grace hissed. Topher was a bit worried that they'd picked up the scent at the same time. He thought he was stronger than Grace.

But the alpha's scent wasn't what made Colbie tense at his side. She took a step forward. It was Nora.

"It's the full moon," Topher said as he realized. Grace cut him a sharp glance.

The door opened. Nora walked in with bright eyes, jaw already fitting strangely in her human face. She froze when she saw Colbie.

Topher gasped. "Fuck."

Grace cut him a sharp glance.

Nora barely managed to get out his sister's name before the change ripped through her. She screamed, the sound giving way to a yelp and then labored breathing. Colbie tried to rush to Nora's side, but Topher caught her arm and held her back.

Topher caught sight of Gabriel's face over Nora's hunched back. The alpha was watching Nora with a puzzled look. He'd heard her say Colbie's name.

Before Topher could wonder what that might mean for them, Gabriel spoke.

"Kill them." His command felt like a heavy charm in the air. Nora was now a wolf, bowing under the weight of Gabriel's words and panting. The door slammed shut, locking them in.

Nora lunged. Topher moved quickly, grabbing Zayn and pulling him and Colbie behind him. He kicked at Nora in the same movement, catching her ribs and sending her skidding across the small space with a yelp. Grace snarled when the wolf landed in front of him.

"Christopher, defend me." The charm made Zayn and Colbie straighten, but it wasn't for them. Topher clenched his jaw. He'd waited to pick his battles. It was time.

Nora bared her teeth at the vampire leader. She lowered her head and began to circle.

"Fuck you, Grace." Words had never tasted so sweet on Topher's tongue. "You were too late. You saved the wrong one."

"Christopher! Get her away from me."

Grace's eyes widened as Topher shook off his charm for the second time. He'd always been able to resist the maker, but this time it was easy. Starving so long had made Grace weak. Topher watched with satisfaction as Nora struck. Grace lifted an arm and she caught it in her new, powerful jaws. She ripped it from his torso and threw the limb at the door. Colbie gagged. Grace barely had time to shout before Nora went for his face.

Topher felt himself smiling. His charm sang in response to shaking off Grace. It had been so long since he let it sweep through him. So long since he embraced its power.

"Chris…" Lana's voice was low. She tried to weave in her charm, but she was even weaker than Grace had been. Nora turned her attention at the sound of Lana's voice.

Lana changed tactics. "Zayn, defend me."

Zayn started forward.

"No!" Topher's shout brought the full force of Nora's wild eyes. Topher clutched Zayn's arms and pulled him back behind him so forcefully that his body smacked into the wall.

"We can fight her," Zayn protested. His arms were flexed, his fangs dropped. He'd always been strong enough to hold off Topher, but a freshly changed wolf was another matter entirely.

Nora's head cocked, but she'd focused on Topher. She'd recognized him as the biggest threat.

Topher didn't look away as he spoke to Zayn. "You are *not* going to die. We aren't doing that to Oliver. I— he won't recover from that."

Topher flexed his hands and crouched. He wasn't really seeing the room. He was diving deep into the unnatural side of himself. The vampire. The half he avoided as often as he could. His eyes briefly fell on Grace's still body. Topher let his smile build.

His charm danced as it filled him. As always, it brought an echo of the sensations that came with Dylan's death. Horror, disgust, self-loathing. Strength, trust, security. Heartbreak, grief, regret. Love and loss. This sensation, this power behind his charm, had filled Topher through their clasped hands as he was drained and Dylan died. It was witchcraft. That murderer had intended for Dylan's essence to be used for her benefit. Dylan had squeezed it into Topher's hand instead. It remained when Lana revived only him. One last gift.

Topher knew his strength came from Dylan. From that circle of ash and the violence and anguish. He loved it. He hated it. It tore him apart. But he needed to use it now. He couldn't lose anyone else.

Nora snarled. She was crouched and taking deliberate steps. Topher mirrored her. She eyed him. Her wolf instincts weren't sure what to do with him. Thick ropes of drool fell from either side of her mouth. Her coat was black like an oil slick. She was larger than Josh in wolf form. Topher braced himself, but when she jumped, her new hunches propelled her quicker than he anticipated. They both went down, Nora landing on top. Topher got his hands at the base of her throat. Her teeth snapped at his face but didn't reach past his straightened arms. Her weight lifted and Lana was there, pulling the wolf off and hissing. Nora barely even acknowledged her. She slammed Lana out of the way as she lunged again.

Topher might have caught her a second time if Zayn hadn't pushed off the wall. All Topher could see was Oliver, smiling at Zayn like knowing all the answers of the universe suddenly didn't matter. Smiling in a way that made Topher's heart shatter with memories of Dylan, the weight so heavy sometimes he checked his sternum to make sure nothing was actually pressing there.

Here in the basement where he and Dylan shared their first kiss, the memories and pain were unbearably close.

Topher rolled, grabbed Zayn's ankle, and yanked hard enough to send him into Colbie. Nora flew through the air and landed on Topher's awkwardly twisted body. Topher accepted the teeth she sank into his shoulder, the claws she raked over his chest. He could live through this.

And if he didn't, Dylan was right there.

Topher gathered his charm close. It built in his throat, choking as it eagerly awaited release. He wasn't sure what he'd use it for, but it was his only advantage. Maybe he could imbue Zayn with enough strength to break down the door. Maybe he could—

"Nora. If you kill my brother, I could never look at you again," Colbie's voice was breathless with unshed tears.

It was enough to make the wolf pause. Nora lifted her head, caught Colbie's eyes, then dropped her gaze to Topher. The hazel color was the same. Topher hoped the girl inside was the same too. That she was worth saving. For his sister, he would do everything in his power to make sure they all left this room.

He opened his mouth. Charm interlaced with his words. The most he'd ever used.

CHAPTER 33

"Where do we stand, Penelope?"

Poppy frowned. The wolves paced as they denied the moon's pull for her. Poppy could practically smell how badly they longed to let loose and run. She looked down at Josh, the only still wolf. He hadn't left her side.

"You can go," Poppy said to the room. "She won't get free. Run while the moon is still high."

Josh cocked his head, considering. His alpha huffed in relief. The wolves yipped and howled, streaming out of the warehouse. Josh told her earlier they planned to use the moon's extra strength to search for more unclaimed lowers and demons. Poppy hoped they were successful. A surprised yelp pulled her attention away from her mother and to the door. Annaliese, Ru, and Oliver were ushered inside by the wolves' prodding noses. Poppy's stomach dropped.

"You summoned Mom without me?" Ru asked.

"Oh, my baby," Tiff breathed the words from within her prison. Ru flinched. Before seeing the look on her mother's face at the sight of her youngest, Poppy would have thought herself past experiencing the familiar pang of jealousy.

"We thought you were dead. It was black when we tried to see you," Ru said.

"My magic is altered." Their mother shrugged.

Annaliese walked closer, undaunted by the magic circle and the witch it contained.

"You've been summoning the demons?"

Tiff laughed. "This is no place for a human."

Annaliese kept her expression flat. She crossed her arms as she waited for an answer. Nearly a full head shorter than Tiff, with no magic to speak of and a barrier separating them, Poppy's mother still shifted with discomfort as the silence stretched and Annaliese's stern gaze never faltered.

"Yes," Tiff finally said, exasperated. "I've been summoning demons. I've been protecting this city, as I said."

"You said you didn't summon enough demons to protect the city," Poppy said.

"I said the boy's death didn't summon enough."

"Who did you kill during your last summoning?" Poppy asked.

"No one. I sacrificed our coven."

Ru made a strangled noise. Poppy stepped back and let Ru press into her side. At this point, she was happy to let Annaliese take up the questioning.

"But why demons?"

"They are strong enough to hunt in the night when I could not."

"Are you a sorcerer?" Annaliese asked. Oliver and Josh watched the conversation, gazes bouncing back and forth between the two.

"No."

"What do you know about them?"

Tiff shrugged. "They took some of my demons. I believe they connected that my demons were hunting the lowers, used the lowers to bait a demon, drank its perverted life force and gained their abilities."

"Why are you hunting the lowers? Everyone else is already."

"Not enough."

"What do you mean?"

"I have seen what they will become. They must be stopped."

Annaliese mulled that over for a second. Tiff offered no more details. "And the dead witches?"

Poppy's mother stilled. She looked to Poppy. "Witches?"

"Natalie and Jane went black. And one of Kallow's daughters was murdered."

Poppy watched her mother's face crumple and realized how little she'd let herself grieve. She should be crying with Ru now, but all she could think was how easily they cast her out. And she held on to that familiar anger. It was easier than grief by far.

There would be time to cry later.

"Who would be killing them? Why would they be attacking vampires too?" Annaliese pressed.

Tiff moaned and grabbed at her gray-streaked hair. "I don't know. My daughters. I don't know…."

She looked ready to dissolve into sobs. Poppy gently freed herself from Ru. "It all has to be connected. And I think we can find who did it. But you have to tell me first, how do you track a vampire?"

It was a surprising enough question that her mother cut off a gasp. "W-what?"

"Is it possible to track a vampire?"

"It's a difficult, dark spell, Penelope. They pull their life energy from their victim intrusively. You cannot use magic against them without causing similar harm."

"So blood magic?" Poppy had been hiding her bleeding palm. Her mother would never forgive her for using her life energy to protect a werewolf den as she just had.

"Blood magic is victimless if you use your own. It must be

from a vampire's victim, given to you as they give their life force to the vampire."

Poppy's blood went cold. Oliver stepped forward as they all knew he would. "Do it. Do it, Poppy. We *have* to find them!"

Her mother's eyes went to the scars on Oliver's neck. "He'll do. The vampire leaves some of their essence behind. It is impossible not to with something so intimate as a bite and the blood magic they pull."

"Do it now!"

"Oliver, this won't be pleasant…." Poppy saw how useless the warning was. Oliver wasn't listening.

She sighed and nodded, pulling her knife back out of her waistband. It was a slim blade. The tree of life was etched into the base. The edge was still slicked red with her blood. Ru murmured a spell to clean it and Poppy took Oliver's hand. She glanced at her mother, who gave her a nod. Poppy cringed and sliced the blade over Oliver's palm. Then, only allowing herself a moment's hesitation, she spat into the wound, leaned in close, and put her teeth to his neck.

Oliver went rigid under her lips. With her hand pressed to the blood spilling from Oliver's palm, she didn't need to bite hard enough to break skin, but as her mother said, it was intimate and uncomfortable to mimic Zayn's magic. Poppy murmured against Oliver's neck and he shivered from the brush of her lips.

"Show me where he is." Oliver's breath caught, but Poppy focused on the remains of Zayn's essence as she drew it from the blood in Oliver's palm. The scars on his neck. Oliver swayed. Poppy felt the pulse in his neck slow. Her own picked up speed, Oliver's energy flowing fast into her.

Her thoughts snapped into focus, centered on the river just north of them. No, not the river. She stepped away and steadied Oliver as he staggered.

"They're in a warehouse. Just across the river."

"But those are human-owned…." Ru trailed off. They were

all thinking the same thing. That was Hunter's territory. Where they'd seen Topher and Dylan meet.

"No one ever suspects the humans," Annaliese said, already turned and walking to the car. Oliver held his bleeding hand and followed her, stumbling slightly until Annaliese took his arm.

"What about Mom?" Ru asked as they hurried to catch up to the humans. Poppy stooped to grab her bag of supplies.

"The spell should hold as long as no one breaks the circle. We'll deal with her later."

They didn't look back as they hurried out of the warehouse.

Annaliese drove quickly, barely giving anyone a chance to buckle themselves in before screeching into the street. Oliver looked about ready to be sick. Poppy pulled vials out of her bag until she found a salve to stop the bleeding of their palms.

"It'll itch like hell but should heal up in the next couple of hours. I put a bit of Topher's spit in it. That'll help with the sting."

Oliver watched her smear it on with wide eyes. Poppy remembered suddenly he had plans for med school. A doctor would give a good deal for the magic she specialized in. This was precisely the kind of information her mother urged her never to share with a human.

Hoping it wasn't a huge mistake, Poppy gave Oliver the entire container. He took it carefully and placed it in his pocket. He tried his best to smile in thanks before he looked back out the window across the river. Poppy grabbed his shoulder. "He's alive. The spell wouldn't have worked if he wasn't."

"Okay," Oliver said, voice a whisper.

Josh stayed in his wolf form and ran down the streets, the whole car tilting as Annaliese hurtled around turns and kept up with him. They crossed the bridge and Josh veered suddenly. Poppy figured he must have caught a scent. His gait grew longer and he let out a howl, bringing other members of his pack out of the shadows to join him. They swarmed the car. Annaliese's eyebrows drew together in concentration as she drove among the wolves.

"Please, please stay in the car Ru," Poppy turned in the seat to beg her sister.

Ru glared. "I have as much right to go as you do! You're barely four years older than me. I even found you when you left us!"

"Four years is a long time for magic to advance! And you only found me because I dropped my wards. Stay in the car or I'll ward you in."

Ru crossed her arms and turned to glare out the window, but Poppy caught the slight drop in her shoulders. She was relieved by Poppy's command but didn't want to show her fears. It was almost enough to make Poppy smile.

Poppy leaned forward between the seats and opened her mouth, but Annaliese cut her off.

"Don't even think about it. There's no way in hell I'm staying behind."

"You can't possibly think you stand a chance against a bunch of supernaturals!"

"Supernaturals? Pretty sure we're going into human territory."

"Humans with allies who helped them capture incredibly powerful vampires! Topher was weak and starved the last time the wolves got them or else they never would have stood a chance. I don't want to imagine what we're coming up against this time."

"Well, don't you have any fancy potions to help us?"

Poppy's hand went to her bag. She did have more vials, specifically to aid her when her magic faltered in the night.

"Please, Poppy. I have to find him," Oliver whispered, eyes on his cut palm. His hand was shaking.

Poppy frowned between the two of them and finally pulled out a clear plastic bag. The potion within dried into a fine, olive-green powder. Annaliese dragged her eyes from the road long enough to eye it suspiciously.

"What is that? Do I have to snort it?"

"It'll give you a sort of physical warding. Like a tougher, magic second skin." She didn't know how better to explain it. "It doesn't last super long, but it'll help you if something attacks. I just have to...." Poppy put a pinch on her palm and blew it on Annaliese, her breath activating the powder. She turned and did the same to Oliver, making the corner of his mouth quirk.

"Pixie dust," he said, almost sounding like his normal self.

"They'll need to feed, though," Annaliese said. Oliver found his puncture scars on his neck with his fingers.

"They'll be so hungry you'll need this protection from them, too. They can feed on the humans who kidnapped them."

Annaliese nodded. Oliver leaned to look closer at the powder, eyes traveling to her messenger bag, likely wondering what other potions it contained. Poppy dug out another sunlight brew and swallowed it. She was down to one more bottle. She prayed to the Mother that it would be enough. The glow off her skin lit the interior of the car. Her head spun. She was going to experience a hell of a crash tomorrow.

Annaliese swerved to follow the wolves between two buildings and hit the brakes. A red wolf was waiting in front of the side entrance of the warehouse.

"That shit better work," Annaliese said. She pushed open her door. "Matthew Garrison! You tell me where Nora is right now!"

Annaliese stomped past the wolves of Josh's pack as they gathered. She stopped in front of Matt. His head ducked a bit but didn't move.

"Fine. Where's Gabriel?"

Matt looked around him, but he was beyond speaking in wolf form. Yet some kind of communication occurred. More of Nora's pack turned the corner of the building until Annaliese was the only thing standing between the two packs in the city, nearly all with hackles raised. She planted her feet and crossed her arms, not even backing down when the huge wolf that had to be Gabriel approached. He made the shift as only alphas could during a full moon. Henry did so as well. Annaliese didn't bat an eye at the naked bodies.

"Where's Nora?" she asked again. Poppy and Oliver wove through Henry's wolves, stopping on either side of Annaliese. Josh nudged Poppy's hand with his snout.

"Earning her place in the pack."

"*Earning* her place?" Annaliese asked. Gabriel frowned as if he'd said too much. Annaliese turned to look at Henry, eyes growing wide. "Does a wolf have to kill a vampire to make the change?"

The horrified expression on Henry's face was answer enough. Annaliese turned back to Gabriel. "She didn't earn her place when the pack raised her? When she watched her mother leave her? When her father died?"

"He made the rules, Annaliese. Morales wanted packmates who proved their loyalty to our cause. Nora is currently doing so several times over and getting rid of a corrupt vampire line in the process. Grace and Lana's people won't be a problem for this city any longer. The two of their clubs account for one-third of the human draining in the city *and* the unclaimed lowers. We, Nora included, are doing our part to keep the city safe."

"Earn their place..." Henry was still caught up on the concept. "That's barbaric! What if the vampires kill her?"

"She's strong under her first moon and the vampires are weak. They haven't fed in days."

Henry shook his head. A chorus of growls rose in the wolves behind him. They edged closer, spurring Gabriel's pack to do the same. They were about to be in the middle of a bloodbath. Poppy couldn't let that happen. She began drawing on her magic. It would be weak when used against the werewolves directly. She scrambled to think of a way around that.

The door behind Matt opened and Hunter stepped into the night. Poppy wouldn't have known him if not for his role in the sweatshirt memory. The former drug lord appeared to have aged ten years since that night. Anger hardened his features. Poppy hated seeing the rose tattoo on his arm, wrapping up his bicep and disappearing into his shirt. He'd sent Topher to make the drop. Had he known what was going to happen?

"It's gone quiet down there," Hunter said, smiling. Oliver gasped and ran forward. Annaliese went to follow, trying to shove past Gabriel. He caught her with ease and she immediately began to struggle.

"Put me down! Fuck you! Fuck you, Gabriel! You *asshole!*"

Annaliese sank her teeth into his forearm, but Gabriel only hissed. A few kicks more and Annaliese went suddenly and utterly limp in his arms. The trick remarkably worked. She hit the ground when he let her drop and lunged around him and between the wolves. She caught up with Oliver, who knocked Hunter out of their way so hard the man stumbled back inside the warehouse.

"Wait!" Poppy had been rooted with indecision but now moved to go after them.

Gabriel made to grab her, but the sunlight running just below her skin made him stagger. Poppy almost smiled at her successful brew. But the wolves were truly snarling now. Still torn, Poppy looked back at Josh. His ears were tucked in close; teeth bared, hackles raised. He'd done so much for her tonight, hoping she would return the favor one day.

With one more look after her human friends, Poppy snapped and barred the door behind them, preventing any wolves from following them inside. She sent up a prayer to the Mother for their protection.

Poppy stepped forward and took Annaliese's place between the packs, startling the wolves into momentary stillness. She raised her arms. Blue light erupted in a wall between the packs just as Matt and Daniel lunged for each other. They smacked Poppy's barrier with twin yelps and she grunted under the weight, barely keeping the magic from crumbling. She had no plan as she stood there. Only hopes to keep the blood loss to a minimum.

Under the warehouse lights, she had never glowed so bright. The wolves prowled, waiting impatiently for her to burn out.

CHAPTER 34

Blue eyes. Intense. Burning through every instinct. Charm. Nora could feel it grinding against Gabriel's command. Against her natural defenses. She could feel the intention to free her. She couldn't look away, but she let the image of Colbie swarm her thoughts.

She let down her defenses. She let the charm in. It was staggering.

"Nora, don't follow your alpha's command."

The words themselves didn't mean anything. She barely heard them. All she knew was the swaying cadence of his speech and the burn of his gaze. She thought maybe she could have still fought it, but she didn't. The words took hold. She shouldn't live to serve Gabriel. Gabriel couldn't command her. Topher was right.

Nora started as the words finished swirling and changing her mind. Regret flooded in as they violently snapped something inside her. She ducked her head, breathing hard and staring at the floor. A whimper escaped her chest.

"What did you do?" Colbie asked. Then, seeing her brother had collapsed, "Topher!"

Nora could only focus on the shattering. The blood lust

induced by Gabriel's compulsion smoldered to ash inside her. Horror replaced it as she realized what had snapped, what had been lost. What Topher was strong enough to accomplish. What she'd allowed to happen. She scrambled away from Topher's still form.

In a way she couldn't process before, she became aware of her new strength, how easy and right it was to move on four legs, the way her tail responded to her every thought. She wanted more than anything to be able to enjoy this. She let out another keening whine.

Because now she could think. Now she felt the moon's call and only that. And she was alone. She couldn't sense the bond to her pack anymore. The assuring strength of Gabriel's pull was gone. She couldn't feel the warmth of their presence. Until this moment, she hadn't even known she'd carried this warmth in her mind her whole life. She hadn't known she belonged to them on such an innate level. The bond had formed when her father and mother claimed her and raised her among their people. Instinctual love and loyalty. Family.

It was gone. It was all gone. A hollow emptiness took its place. A black hole waiting to claim her. She lifted her head to the moon, the only draw still tethering her, and howled her loss. Howled because she was lost. Alone. The worst fate for a wolf. What had she done? What had Topher done?

Someone knelt in front of her. Nora cringed from the pair of bright blue eyes.

"Nora! Please, look at me." It was Colbie. It was Colbie. Safe from her. Safe from Gabriel's command. Nora whimpered again. Ripped in two.

"He isn't waking up." Zayn was bent over Topher. "He usually wakes up by now after he uses his charm like that."

Nora's stomach roiled at the sight of Topher's torn skin, not bleeding. Not healing. No, healing too slowly. She'd done that. Nora flinched at the memory of raking her claws over his chest. The ripping and taste of his shoulder. With a shudder,

381

she looked down at her hands and realized she was in human form again. Her eyes filled.

"What did he do?" Nora whispered. She curled sideways and wrapped arms around her knees at her chest, trying to hide her naked body. Colbie looked ready to reach for her but thought better of it.

"He charmed you," Colbie answered in a soft voice, the softest Nora had ever heard her. The vampire was stunned.

"Impossible," Lana whispered. Nora started, having forgotten the maker was there. Grace's body lay at her feet. His arm was across the room. Nora's hair rose and suddenly, the change ripped through her again, leaving her panting as a wolf but still in control. Colbie frowned. Her hands shook as she looked between Nora and Topher's unnaturally still form. It was clear she didn't know how to help either of them.

They all turned at the sound of shoes slapping down the stairs.

"Get your hands off me!" Nora's ears flipped towards the familiar voice. She started toward the door, snarling. Blood cold with the knowledge that her friend was in trouble. The sound of a gun being cocked echoed in the stairway.

Colbie stood, but it was Zayn who suddenly ran for the door, face a horrified mask. He turned as though guarding it, looking from Colbie to Lana and even Topher laying there with wild eyes.

"If any of you touch him—" he started. The door was pulled open and Zayn spun around without finishing his threat. He jumped forward, making Annaliese and Oliver grunt as he pushed them out of the way of the starving vampires and into the wall. The tendons in his neck strained. Lana and Colbie ran past them so fast Nora was amazed she could track their movements.

Someone managed to get off a shot and Zayn stumbled back into the room. Oliver rushed in after him. A strangled yell came from the stairs as Lana and Colbie attacked the humans, hissing their hunger. Oliver caught Zayn as he dropped to a knee.

"No, no, no," Oliver whispered. He wiped his hand off on his jeans and pressed it to Zayn's mouth.

His skin slowly closing around the hole in his shoulder, Zayn pushed away. He gasped as he turned, drawing fresh air.

"I'm too hungry," he said, clutching his arms around his middle. He didn't even lick at the blood already smeared on his lips.

"You won't hurt me," Oliver insisted. Zayn made a desperate noise and nodded, accepting Oliver's hand this time slowly. But all he did was lick to clean the blood and seal the wound.

"That tastes horrible." His voice was strained.

"The salve had Topher's spit in it," Oliver told him. Zayn let out a huff of a laugh and cupped Oliver's cheek, but his eyes went to Topher, still lying there. Oliver gasped and hurried over to check him.

"Don't!" Zayn pulled Oliver back. He kept swallowing. His fangs were out.

"It'll be okay. Go feed. Quickly, babe."

Zayn hesitated only a moment more. His hunger won out. "I'll be right back. Be careful with him. When he wakes up—"

"You'll hear and be stronger. Go."

Zayn reluctantly turned and joined the others on the stairs, pausing only to nod at Annaliese.

Nora didn't trust herself to move. She was terrified to face her pack again. To see Gabriel. He'd locked her in here, but the anger over the fact couldn't mask her sense of loss. So she sat and watched as Annaliese knelt at Topher's other side. There was the sound of a body, then another, slumping down the stairs. Nora cringed further into the wall. It felt unnatural to cower as a wolf.

Annaliese pulled out a knife. She tried three times to cut

her wrist, each time more aggressively until Nora moved to stop her.

"Damn pixie dust!"

"Annaliese, stop! He'll drain you!" Oliver said, catching Annaliese's wrist.

Annaliese shook her head and Nora growled. These humans were too trusting by far.

"I've got it!" Colbie shouted from the top of the stairs. Nora cringed again when she heard the charm enter Colbie's voice. "Oh, Hunter. I think you owe my brother an apology."

"He killed my son!" Despite the protest in his voice, he was following Colbie down the steps.

"I spent my life killing spiders for my brother. And I spent the three months before Dylan's death listening to Topher talk only about how incredible he was. You know as well as I do Topher had nothing to do with his murder."

Nora felt her head quirk in confusion. Annaliese and Oliver shared a look but didn't comment as Colbie came into the room, Hunter helplessly following her.

"He killed my son after the vampires changed him. I know he did. Then he went home and attacked you, right? But they changed you instead. Since then, he's been making all those lowers and they've been killing humans. My people. He's out to ruin me. You can't tell me he isn't a murderer."

Colbie rounded on Hunter. "He isn't a murderer. That wasn't Topher."

"How would you know? He and Lana get into all kinds of shit, I bet you. He's messed up in the head, your brother. I put up with him because he was good in a bind and Dylan loved him. Look where it left me! A funeral and all my business lost to vampires like him. Like you."

Hunter eyed Topher's limp form. He spat, but the glob missed. Colbie spoke again, anger and charm lacing her voice. "He has only ever made one vampire and claimed me right

384

away. The unclaimed aren't Topher's. And it wasn't Grace either. Now, let my brother drink."

Nora's hackles rose at Colbie's cold tone. Colbie didn't care if Hunter died from this. Nora stepped forward but halted when Annaliese cut a glare her way and held up her arm, getting between Nora and the vampires.

Why was she even here?

Hunter lowered himself, baring his neck.

"He doesn't like that," Annaliese said.

She took the knife in her hand and grabbed Hunter's arm, slitting his wrist before anyone could protest. She guided his arm to Topher's mouth and stayed close even when Topher abruptly woke, clamped the bleeding wrist to his mouth with both hands and drank deeply. Hunter sighed and relaxed, eyes glazing over. "That's good," he moaned.

After a few bobs of Topher's throat, Hunter's face turned gray. His sounds of pleasure made Nora growl and Colbie grimace. Hunter swayed on his knees and slumped to the floor. With visible effort, Topher let go and backed away.

He covered his face with both hands, muffling his voice. "Tell me he's not dead."

"He's not," Annaliese sounded mildly disappointed. She pocketed her knife and finally looked at Nora. "What's going on here?" she asked, waving a hand in Nora's direction.

"Topher charmed her somehow," Colbie answered.

Topher lowered his hands, looking at Nora from over his fingers. "Nora, I'm so sorry."

So he knew what he did. Nora's snout crinkled as she bared her teeth at him. Topher dropped his eyes.

Nora didn't care to hear the rest. She went to Annaliese and carefully took the back of her jacket between her teeth, dragging her away from the vampires.

"I'll come. Let go before you rip my jacket." Nora did and Annaliese followed her up the stairs. Nora ignored the bodies littering the steps in the starved vampires' wake. Most were still alive. Some weren't. Nora trembled but remained in control of the urge to return to the basement room and retaliate for the humans. She met Zayn's eyes as he hurried back downstairs, but his gaze slid past her in favor of Oliver.

"Is it over?" she heard Oliver ask.

"Yes, love, we're okay."

"Well, there's still the wolves," Oliver said. Nora realized they were following her and Annaliese upstairs. She bristled.

"Oh, relax," Annaliese murmured. "I'm their ride."

Nora glanced back and saw Zayn and Oliver awkwardly climbing the steps while trying to hold one another close. Colbie and Topher were talking under their breath. Lana was nowhere to be seen. She'd never returned to the basement.

Annaliese was the first one out, holding the door for Nora. Still in wolf form, Nora's eyes went to Gabriel, where he stood as a human. He's shoulders relaxed in relief at the sight of her, only to tense up again as he studied her more closely.

Then the vampires followed her outside.

A chorus of growls rose from her pack. Gabriel's pack. "What is this?" Gabriel demanded.

Only Matt knew to let out a whine.

"We're leaving, Gabriel," Annaliese said.

Gabriel was still staring at Nora. She'd grown up around wolves. It was easier to make the change in their presence. Easier to bear her naked human body. But it was the hardest thing in the world to meet Gabriel's eyes after having done so.

"You're..." he whispered the word before his face shut down entirely. He turned from her, facing Henry on the other side of a shining blue barrier. Poppy was shaking in the middle of it, sweating with the effort of holding it.

"We're done here," Gabriel said stiffly.

He slipped into wolf form. Nora watched her former pack, the only family she'd ever known, run into the night. They left her behind. Alone. Only Matt glanced over his shoulder. Nora felt so cold her shivering induced her body to make the change again. She pressed closer to Annaliese.

"Well. That's unexpected," Henry said, eyeing Nora and the vampires. "Feel free to come by any time if you have questions, Nora."

She hated him at that moment. His kind voice. The pity she saw on his face. He made the shift and led his pack in the opposite direction as Gabriel. She could hear in their howls how relieved they all were to finally run loose beneath the moonlight. She longed to do the same, but the thought of running alone was unbearable.

Only Josh stayed behind. He stuck by Nora's side as they ran behind Annaliese's car back to the apartment. She felt no connection to him, only an echo of Henry's alpha energy. It had no hold on her. Topher silently trailed them. Nora didn't know what else to do except stick with Annaliese. Looking in the back window, at no point during the ride to the apartment did Nora see Oliver and Zayn break apart where they sat in the backseat. Poppy's poor sister pointedly stared out the window.

Annaliese parked and went to follow the group inside, only halting when she saw Nora wasn't with her. Topher paused and looked back at the two of them.

"I think we're going to go," Annaliese told him.

Topher nodded. He looked at Nora. "I truly am sorry. I couldn't let you kill them."

"What about you?" Annaliese asked.

Topher blinked. "What?"

Annaliese didn't repeat herself, crossing her arms as he met her gaze. He couldn't hold her stare long. He rubbed the roses on his forearm and tilted his head back to look at the moon.

"I owe you twice now, Annaliese. Thank you. Will you text me when you get home safe?"

Annaliese nodded, but Topher still wasn't looking, so he didn't see it. "Yeah, I'll text you."

"Good," Topher lowered his eyes and gave Annaliese a

small smile. Nora bristled when her friend's eyes went dazed. The smile quickly died on Topher's lips. He turned without another word and went inside.

"Dammit." Annaliese yanked open her door and slammed it shut once she was seated. Without a word, she drove into the night, Nora following.

CHAPTER 35

Josh paced the small apartment, sniffing every nook and corner. Poppy couldn't help but wonder what it cost him not to be with his pack right now. And what he was smelling. They weren't the deepest of cleaners. Each time Josh crossed the room, he nudged his nose into Poppy's thigh.

Colbie checked the hall one last time, looking for Annaliese or Nora or both, and closed the door. Poppy's shoulders relaxed as her wards took hold. They would be safe for the night. Topher and Colbie finally back where they should be. If Poppy had her way, they wouldn't leave her wards again.

A moment of calm descended as they fully accepted the worst of the night was over. They had survived. Poppy hated that she felt this was only the beginning. Hated that it seemed they had more questions than ever, despite hunting answers for days.

Oliver broke the silence. "Is the kidnapping going to be a regular thing?" he asked Topher. "I don't think I like your influence on my boyfriend if he feels the need to participate now."

The tension of the night eased with the laughter that filled the room. Zayn bent and pressed more kisses into Oliver's neck. Oliver was more relaxed than he'd been in days. When Zayn gently urged him to eat something, Oliver was happy to comply. He went straight for his ice cream in the freezer, making Zayn roll his eyes to the ceiling, a smile playing on his lips.

Topher tugged at his ripped shirt and went to his room. He was quiet and Poppy was worried for him. He abruptly halted in the doorway and Poppy's stomach dropped. They had forgotten to put the sweatshirt back. Topher turned, face expressionless. He knew to look at Poppy.

"We were looking for information," she whispered, gesturing to the wall of dates. Topher's eyes flicked that way only for a second. "We thought your being turned might have something to do with the unclaimed. It fit the pattern...."

Topher nodded and went into his room. He knelt slowly and lifted the sweatshirt with heartbreakingly gentle fingers. Before placing it back in his closet, he pressed it to his nose. Poppy looked away to find Colbie's face set in a glare. She pointed a finger at Poppy.

"You don't get to touch Dylan. That had nothing to do with you."

The tension was very suddenly back in the room. Ru shifted guiltily on the couch, accidentally hitting the TV remote. The screen blinked as the news turned on.

"Rumors of these unclaimed vampires have been circulating for months. Last night they ran rampant through the city, doubling the number of murders in just a few hours. So far, there have been twelve deaths, two hospitalizations, and four missing persons. We have received reports their master, Connor Grace, was found murdered, explaining the sudden spike in their attacks. The attacks have occurred throughout the city, beginning—"

Topher came out of his room, cigarette box and lighter in hand. He shook his head at the screen. "I should find Lana," his voice was flat and something was missing in his expression.

"I'll come," Colbie said immediately. Poppy was shocked when Topher nodded reluctantly. Zayn gently untangled himself and Oliver. Hushing Oliver's slightly panicked protests, Zayn crossed the room and grabbed Topher's arm.

"Thank you, Toph. For what you did in there."

Oliver joined them by the door, watching Topher accept Zayn's hug. When Topher stepped back, Oliver frowned up at him. "You saved him?"

Topher shook his head, but Oliver saw through the lie and smiled. "You're a really great person, Topher."

Topher ducked his head and shook a cigarette out of his box.

"Ahh, that's the face he would make when he used to blush. You made him blush, Oliver." Colbie sounded delighted. Poppy suspected she was trying hard to cheer Topher up. Colbie wrapped an arm around Oliver and her brother's necks, an action that had her standing crooked with Topher being so much taller. She turned her head and spoke in a mock whisper to Oliver. "I'll sleep with Topher or Poppy today, but if my sheets aren't clean by tomorrow morning, I'll drain you."

Colbie pulled Oliver's head close and pressed a hard, sloppy kiss on his cheek, making him laugh and swat her away. Poppy drew a deep breath of air, basking in the happy energy that flushed the apartment. She had missed seeing smiles.

Zayn ducked and scooped Oliver up over his shoulder, making him yelp. Quickly crossing the apartment, Zayn kicked Colbie's door closed behind them. Poppy waited until Colbie was finished pretending to gag before she cast a sound muffling spell on the room.

The news continued playing. Colbie jerked her chin toward it. "At least now those bastards realize this means you didn't have anything to do with the unclaimed."

"Might be one of our less pressing worries. Not if word spreads that I can even charm wolves."

Josh, still in wolf form, made a huffing noise of agreement.

Topher turned to him. "I'll let you know if I find anything out. Think your pack is taking care of the new lowers?" Topher still sounded like he wasn't entirely present. He was too monotone. The words cost him too much effort. Poppy wanted to tell him to feed. Tell him to go to bed. Tell him never to talk to Lana again. Never to leave the apartment.

She wanted to go to him and wrap him in her arms and make him feel something good.

Josh repeated his noise of confirmation and Topher reached for the doorknob. Poppy remained frozen in place.

"We'll be back before sunrise," Colbie promised as she followed him. "A person can only get kidnapped so many times, right, Topher?"

"I sure hope so."

Poppy tried to laugh at their banter, but worry made her smile wobble. She didn't think she could take any more disappearances. The apartment went quiet when they left. Ru had fallen asleep on the couch. Josh's tail swished as he took up pacing again.

There were too many sunlight brews in Poppy's system. Without her friends there to protect, she needed to occupy herself. Find more answers and be useful. "I think I should go check on my mom. Want to come?"

Josh was at the door the next second, practically pawing at it in his desire to get outside again. Poppy smiled as he ran down the stairs. A couple of women who lived on the floor above screamed when they passed him on the steps, one falling against the wall and clutching at her roommate's leg. They smelled like vodka.

"Help them forget," she bid the magic. The warm energy from all the smiling upstairs eased out of her as the magic drained it. Poppy reached the bottom step to the sound of the drunk women laughing, having decided the one on the ground must have just tripped.

The night felt different now. The light of the full moon

nearly overwhelmed the glow cast by the streetlights. Poppy tipped her chin back to look at it, enjoying its gentle tug on the supernatural swirling within her. Josh nudged her hand and without thinking, Poppy passed it over his snout and through the short hair on his head, petting him like a dog. His tail thumped twice on the pavement, so she supposed he didn't mind.

It took them fifteen minutes to reach Josh's den. None of Josh's pack had returned yet, but someone howled nearby, prompting Josh to respond. His call was rich with a vibrato that pricked Poppy's arms with goosebumps.

Poppy continued inside, Josh prancing around her legs. She froze at the sight that greeted them. Her mother wasn't there. The circle had been broken; a footlong section wiped away.

"Shit," Poppy whispered. Josh let a warning growl fill the warehouse, but the space was empty. Poppy didn't need his keen sense of smell to know that. She walked to the circle and examined it closer, hand going to her bag as she scrambled to think of a potion that would help her figure out what happened.

"I changed my mind."

Poppy whirled. The ghost of her grandfather, now in faded colors and planted firmly on the ground, smiled back at her. "The vial with your lovely blood, left behind with no one to see me use it. I couldn't resist in the end. The draw of magic has always been too strong for me."

"You didn't—" Horror choked the rest of Poppy's words.

"I did. I really wasn't expecting this," he gestured to his semi-solid form, "You said your blood ran weak. I figured a taste of it would let me do a few tricks. Maybe sample something sweet for the first time in years. But it took hold rather firmly, I'm afraid. I went to your mother, hoping for some advice. Imagine our surprise when I got through your blood wards. I freed her. I admit it wasn't my best move, but I was quite panicked. Then things got strange. Her magic didn't affect me. I suppose you know what that means."

Josh was growling in earnest now, searching the warehouse for what had Poppy so terrified. He couldn't see the ghost. No, the poltergeist. Poppy's mind whirred. All she knew about magic forming an answer she didn't want to confirm. He was solidified, for her, by her blood. The bloodline they shared strengthening its force. The blood she'd fueled all night with a potent sunlight brew. He consumed it at the exact moment his master, her mother, had been locked away from her magic and any hold she had on him. The entire act backed by the strange qualities cast from the full moon's light, always a factor that weakened the veil. He was now likely trapped. Not a demon. Not a ghost. Stuck in between by the strength and life in her blood.

Her grandfather was watching her warily.

"You're mine," Poppy whispered.

"Your word is my command." He swept into a low, mocking bow.

Poppy thought she might be sick.

Topher followed Lana's scent in the hotel across the street from Happenstance with Colbie on his heels. Topher paused on the sidewalk out front, looking at Grace's club. It was packed. He didn't know if that was Fredrick, Jesse, or Trevor's doing. Trevor was Grace's first lower but wasn't a maker himself, so likely he wouldn't be in the running to fill Grace's shoes. Lana was.

"Tell me again why we're meeting with her? She ditched us back there."

"I have to make sure she doesn't think I'm a threat."

"What do you mean?"

Topher crossed his arms over his chest, frowning at the

lights flashing through the club's floor-to-ceiling windows. "She saw me resist Grace's charm. I can resist hers, too, meaning I'm in the running for leadership. I don't want it. She knows I don't. But that doesn't mean I'm worth the risk of keeping around. And we were close to figuring out who was making the unclaimed. Or it felt like we were. That's the most important thing. I think whoever is making them knew we were figuring out their patterns. Maybe that's why we were set up. Hunter wouldn't have come up with that on his own. He hates the vampires almost as much as Gabriel, so I don't think the two of them wouldn't have gone to Solas and Patter for help unless someone else placed the idea. A week ago, no one suspected Grace. It all flipped too quickly. We have to find whoever did it, and when we do, we need vampires to take them down and pick up the mess left behind."

"Why? Why do we have to get involved?"

"Because they all know about me and they know about you now too. These unclaimed keep getting stronger and stronger. I," Topher dropped his voice, stepping closer to his sister and admitting what he hadn't speculated out loud yet. "I don't think they're vampires. Not like us. I think they're something else and I think they're being made to frame the vampires. Only the people of the city who enjoy our clubs are fine with the power we've attained here. There are a lot of groups just waiting to knock us down. We were united under Reelings, legalized under the Big Three. Now, Grace is gone and his seconds will all want his place. Vampires work under a certain hierarchy. If they keep taking out our leaders, they'll keep weakening us."

"Vampires aren't the only ones getting attacked, though. The witches are being killed. Humans are being murdered more than anyone. Nora's dad was killed. The other werewolf packs fled the city... What if there is no big plan? What if the unclaimed, different from us or not, are making more of themselves? What if it's all just chaos we need to stop?"

Topher dropped his cigarette and ground out the ashes. Colbie shot him a look and he picked it up to throw it in the nearest trash. "Then, either way, we should do what we can to stop it. Are you sure you want to be involved?"

Topher desperately wanted Colbie to say no. The last year he sacrificed so many parts of himself following Lana's orders and desires so she wouldn't give Colbie up. He wanted Colbie safe and away from this and protected from the monster inside him.

But it was her choice. Colbie might not be the strongest vampire, but she was far too clever and full of life not to survive this life. It was her choice, no matter how much Topher hated it.

"Lana will help?" Colbie asked.

Half of his and Lana's searching had led to them healing the humans left in the wake of the unclaimed. As much as he hated his maker, she valued life. She knew what was at stake here and didn't want the humans she enjoyed taking advantage of to suffer. Everything she had went into her club. And these unclaimed lowers threatened the vampires' citizenship. Threatened the delicate laws Grace's generation worked so hard to get passed. Lana wanted this finished. She wanted a club and she wanted a position within the Big Three. That could lead to stability and that was what New Brecken needed now.

"Right now, our interests with Lana align," Topher said, "I just have to make sure she still trusts me."

Colbie nodded, but she didn't like it. As much as he hated that she was now involved, Topher was relieved he didn't have to face Lana alone. They crossed the hotel lobby, Topher following Lana's floral scent with ease. No one else's smell clung so heavily in the air for him. Because she was his maker. Topher pushed every floor on the elevator, making the woman who had gotten on with them scoff in disbelief. Colbie laughed.

"Oh, relax," Colbie said. Topher shot her a sharp look for

the charm in her voice, but Colbie's answering smile was all innocence. The woman settled back, shoulders drooping and a grin taking years off her face. For good measure, Colbie made quick work of feeding off her. She backed away with a content smile that only grew when the woman's glossy eyes took their time looking Colbie up and down.

"I love New Brecken," the woman said.

"Honey, me too."

Topher was relieved when the doors opened for the third time and Lana's scent flooded in. He grabbed Colbie's arm and pulled her outside.

"Come back soon!" Colbie called to the closing doors.

Topher led her down the hall, stopping at the right door.

"She's already found one of the unclaimed," he said, catching the familiar, slightly rotten smell.

Colbie's face likely mirrored his own when she looked at him, eyebrows drawn together. He licked his thumb and pressed it into the furrow. They exchanged shaky smiles as Colbie wiped off the space between her brows and Topher knocked.

"What took you so long?" Lana hissed, pulling them inside.

"You have an unclaimed here?"

"Yes, she attacked me on the way over. They were swarming Fourth Street. Most of them got slaughtered pretty quickly," Topher's stomach turned at the casual way Lana said that, "but I thought you might be interested in questioning this one."

Topher narrowed his eyes at her. Charming Nora had taken a lot out of him. He wasn't eager to push his limits again so soon. Lana smiled at the look.

"I'll tell you what, Christopher. Obviously, my priorities are shifted now that dear Connor is dead. Thank you for that, by the way." Topher nodded, suspicious. "As I'm sure you've guessed, I want his position. His position won't be there if the laws are gone, so yes, we still need to find who is making the lowers. Then, you're going to help me get to the top. We have to convince my fellow seconds to stand down."

Lana gave him a significant look, eyebrows arching. Topher swallowed, but he nodded again.

"Excellent. So, as a show of good faith, I'll help you take care of the unclaimed a*nd* I will get in touch with my contacts and legalize Callie here."

"Colbie."

Lana waved off Colbie's correction. "And I won't tell the world about your witch friend, so long as she helps pick up where Beth left off."

Colbie and Topher exchanged a look. Topher nodded, hoping Poppy was willing to pay the price for her secrets.

"Why would Topher want to take care of an unclaimed?" Colbie asked.

"Go look for yourself." Lana waved them toward the bathroom.

Topher moved cautiously. These strange, unclaimed lowers had a specific scent. It reminded him of demons and dark magic but still mixed with the remnants of human blood in their systems. Colbie pushed open the door.

She gasped. *"Fucking hell!"*

Tied securely, covered in dirt and blood, sat Julia. Eyes wild with bloodlust.

Topher's heart plummeted.

This was his fault. Another person punished for loving him. He couldn't find his balance. The world was shrinking around him. Narrowing on all the harm he did to it and those he loved. It wasn't enough to lose Dylan. To turn Colbie. To constantly put Poppy and their friends in danger for him. He would infect every piece of good offered to him.

Colbie was still letting off a stream of curses. She sounded miles away. Julia watched them with a dull gaze, realizing their blood wasn't what she craved. No hint of recognition in her expression. No sign of the intelligence that always drove her. She looked even less human than Mary had. Worse than every unclaimed Topher had questioned to the breaking point.

Topher's stomach twisted and flipped. If he were still able to, he would have been sick. With a trembling hand, he closed the bathroom door and leaned his forehead against it.

"We have a deal?" Lana asked.

"We have a deal."

Nora returned to human form with the sunrise and took a long shower in Annaliese's bathroom. She didn't care if Annaliese could hear her as she cried. No one from the pack had answered her calls. Her texts hadn't delivered. Only Matt's came up as read. Everyone else had blocked her.

She'd lost them.

When she finished, she changed into the sweatshirt and shorts Annaliese offered and climbed into bed. She ignored her wet hair as she settled into the pillows.

Annaliese got in next to her and spoke to the ceiling. "What happened?"

"Topher charmed me. He broke Gabriel's hold."

"So you're what? An unclaimed werewolf?"

Nora shrugged and covered her eyes with her arms. There wasn't a term for what she was.

"You're not that different, though? Like last time I saw you? We're still cool?" Hope laced Annaliese's words.

Nora considered the questions. She felt like herself. Not wild and untamed and animal. She couldn't even be a wolf properly in the capacity she had left, but she felt the shift under her skin. If she wanted to, she could change.

Nora had been terrified of losing herself to the wolf. She hadn't wanted to lose Annaliese. She hadn't wanted to lose her pack more, but at least at this moment, she wasn't alone. Nora resisted the urge to reach for her friend's hand. Annaliese didn't take comfort from touch like most people. Or if she did, she cringed away from the feeling. Nora's eyes filled again thinking of the easy physical affection within her pack. She'd gotten so much at home that it hadn't mattered that Annaliese pulled away all the time.

"We're cool. I feel different than I did right before the change. More myself."

"Maybe those instincts were tied up in the pack. Like Gabriel encouraged them."

Nora shrugged again. She didn't want any positives to come from this yet. "It's okay if I stay here, right?"

Annalise hesitated. "Yeah, that's okay."

Nora turned her head to look at her friend and wondered at the pause, but she was tired of talking. It didn't take long for sleep to claim them both.

They woke hours later, ordered a pizza and ate it in Annaliese's bed as they watched a mindless romantic comedy. The movie ended and Annaliese started browsing for another one. Nora's head cocked to the sound of a car pulling into Annaliese's drive.

"Someone's here."

Annaliese looked at her watch. "Maybe a dinner guest?" Her parents had "important people" over a lot.

The doorbell rang. Nora listened as Annaliese's stepdad answered. She could hear everything so well.

"Hello. How can I help you?"

"I'm just going to go talk to Nora and Annaliese."

"Of course, of course."

The hair on Nora's arms rose, hearing the charm in Colbie's voice. Colbie walked through the home and down the stairs to Annaliese's room like she owned the place. Nora was so shocked by the vampire's sudden appearance and use of charm that she never thought to run.

Colbie strolled into the room without knocking. "Hey."

"Did you just charm my stepdad?" Nora was surprised by the level of outrage in Annaliese's voice.

Colbie raised an eyebrow and moved to sit on the back of the couch, leaning back as she balanced there, feet off the ground. "I need to talk to Nora."

"You can't just—" Annaliese started.

"But I did. Can I talk to Nora, or do I have to charm you too?"

Annaliese scowled, her hands fisting at her sides.

"I don't want to talk to you." Nora fell back onto the bed to punctuate her words. She fixed her eyes on the ceiling and tried to calm her racing heart. It was all too much.

Nora didn't see whatever silent communication Annaliese and Colbie had, but she knew to be betrayed when Annaliese left the room. They heard her linger at the bottom of the stairs just outside the door. Ready to come back in for the rescue. Who would need rescuing had yet to be determined. Nora growled softly when she heard Colbie approach.

The bed dipped as Colbie settled on it, sitting with her back against the footboard. She nudged Nora's leg with her foot.

"How are you doing?"

"It doesn't matter to you. This is over. It's *been* over. Too much has happened and now your brother has taken everything from me. Don't you get it? Vampires and werewolves *don't* work."

"At least you're done pretending you don't like girls."

Nora lifted her head just enough to glare at Colbie. The vampire smiled, but it was forced and quick to fall away. Colbie looked exhausted. She curled into herself, hugging her knees to her chest. She closed her eyes.

"Have you ever gone three days without eating or drinking, Nora?" Colbie barely waited, knowing Nora wouldn't answer. "I've never gone hungry. But after the first night, I started to feel it. Like a constant, painful tug. All we could do was sit there, feel our hunger, and watch the walls get closer and closer." Colbie's voice was more hushed than Nora had ever heard it.

"It was… creepy. Topher always got this haunted look when he starved himself. I felt it. You feel like your body is already dead. You realize that it's not the human blood, it's the life the blood contains that keeps you alive. I felt like a walking corpse. Those nights were the first time I ever felt like a monster. I started to understand what went on in Topher's mind all the time. All the self-hatred."

"Why would I care? About any of this?"

"I guess you don't. I just, I couldn't think. When you came in. You were in even less control than I was, Nora. You were going to kill us. You did kill Grace. How can you look at me like you do when I've never come close to ending someone's life? Could you really have lived with killing Topher? With killing me?"

Nora pressed her lips together. She'd already been plagued by nightmares of killing Grace. She suppressed a shudder, remembering how it felt to crush the life out of him with her jaws.

"Nora. You wanted to *kill* me. I get to have my say."

"I don't want to talk to you, Colbie."

Colbie's voice was rough, like there were tears threatening. But Nora knew now that vampires couldn't even cry. "Well, you have to. You owe me that much. You *reeked* like him, you know that, Nora? So you're going to listen to me because you broke my heart and tried to murder me. Because you slept with someone else while I was locked away and *still* trying to think of how to forgive you for lying to me and hurting my brother. Because even after that, Topher wasn't mad at you, so I thought maybe I could come around. I imagined how to convince you we could still be together. And what were you doing?" Nora was silent. Words were hard to come by on a normal day. There was too much now to search for them.

"So yeah," Colbie said, ruthless. "Topher broke your damn bond with Gabriel. Is that so horrible compared to the alternative? To *killing* me? To being *mated* to him?"

Nora still couldn't find words. Colbie was looking at her with everything stark on her face. She was heartbroken. She was angry. She was confused. She was still here. Why was she still here after everything? What could she possibly want?

When Nora finally spoke, she wished she had a better argument. "What Topher did was wrong!"

Colbie got to her feet. "What your pack did was wrong! What that asshole did was wrong! Trying to force you to kill! Telling you who to be friends with! Who to mate with? And you…. I know they raised you, but goddamn—"

Nora sat up. "You don't know anything about it, Colbie!"

"I know I have friends and a family that would never have done that to me. They don't care who I love. They do everything they can to protect me. They care about my happiness. Because of that, they all cared about you. I *know* your pack was in the wrong. I wanted to believe you were better than them."

Nora was crying now. "Get out!"

"Nora! This is ridiculous. I'm here! Okay? I'm with you. Right now. After everything. Where are they? Where are you? Why is this," Colbie gestured between them, "so absolutely horrible for you?"

"You don't understand," Nora whispered.

Colbie took a deep breath, eyes to the ceiling. "You're right. I don't."

"I'm a wolf, Colbie. My whole life has only been about that. Watching my family sacrifice everything to keep the vampires in line. Helping the wolves and humans survive in this world that could so easily be run by monsters. Every childhood memory I have has Matt in it. Most of them have Gabriel too. My parents left me to be raised by the pack because they built it and trusted them. They were all I had left of my parents. They were my friends, my family. Every day I came home to multiple smiling faces. I went to Adriana for my hair cuts. Chancy if I wanted to go running. Heidi taught me how to make cookies and always let me lick the bowl. Those are people who can't be replaced. Who I never thought would ever leave me." Nora's voice shook and tears threatened, but she pressed on. "Now, what am I? Homeless. Jobless. Unclaimed. I have to find an alpha to watch over me before the next full moon or I will lose even my humanity."

Except now, that thought wasn't as terrible as it once was. Being human meant feeling too much. Nora wondered if she went to the forest before the change she could find her mom. If as a wolf, her mother might not reject her again. If they could run together as animals when Nora was unable to find herself again with no alpha to bring her back.

"Oh, honey."

"Get out, Colbie. Your brother took everything from me. I don't need you here reminding me of the fact."

"No. That wasn't an 'oh honey, I feel sorry for you.' That was an 'oh honey, don't you get it?'"

Nora blinked at the change in Colbie's tone. "What?"

"I didn't think so. It's why I'm here. Just to tell you this, so you aren't completely lost. Though I don't know why I bothered."

Colbie leaned closer, her blue eyes so vivid and beautiful and set in a face Nora loved so much she couldn't breathe. Every line and dip and edge sang to Nora. Her life had taken so many turns since those eyes had first captured her.

She was as helpless now as she was then. She didn't move as Colbie lifted her hands to Nora's cheeks. Colbie brushed her thumbs along Nora's cheekbones. She pushed her fingers back to tangle gently in Nora's hair. The ice in her gaze softened. Nora loved the way Colbie looked at her. Cautious, like Nora was capable of striking. Like Nora was strong enough to be feared.

No, it wasn't fear. It was respect. It was admiration. It was everything she'd wanted to see on the faces of her packmates.

Their faces were inches away and Nora wanted to hate how close Colbie was. Instead, she hated the distance remaining between them.

"You're thinking about this all wrong," Colbie said, cold breath brushing Nora's face.

Nora had enough presence of mind to scoff. Colbie rolled her eyes and dropped her hands, curling her fingers into fists. Nora realized that Colbie hadn't meant to reach for her. After everything, Colbie could still lose herself to Nora like Nora lost herself to Colbie.

What did that mean?

Colbie stepped away and went to the door, turning back to speak only when she was as far away from Nora as she could get. "Topher didn't just break the command Gabriel had on you. We could all feel it. Josh agrees and told me someone had to let you know what happened if you didn't realize it. It came down to him showing up here or me. Josh says it was just below the surface. Gabriel's hold just had to end. You just had to shake him off."

"What are you talking about?"

"Nora, you're not unclaimed. You're an alpha."

Colbie left. Nora's stomach dropped when the vampire didn't look back.

ACKNOWLEDGMENTS

So far in my writing journey, this book has been the most fun to create. I'm so grateful to Anna, Ben, and Allison for finding it just as exciting. They loved these characters and city so much that they convinced me to publish it ahead of schedule and haven't stopped asking for book two.

A special thanks to Anna. My little sister amazes me every day with her efforts toward self-discovery and the bravery she has shown in expressing all she finds out. She introduced me to books with found families that inspired the dynamics in the Maker. She wanted a book she saw herself in, and in trying to write her one, I went on my own journey of self-discovery. (These characters were just too easy to write if you know what I mean.) For that, I am always grateful to my role model, who happens to be ten years younger than me.

ABOUT THE AUTHOR

Kelly Cole graduated from the University of Wyoming where she studied English and Creative Writing. She is working on a self-publishing career and enjoying every step along the way. Kelly is most active on Instagram and enjoys sharing her latest and favorite reads. She lives in Wyoming with her two crested geckos and her dog, Maya. She spends most of her time writing and playing seemingly endless hours of fetch (not with the geckos).